# THE COMMITTEE

Justin A. Bailey

Copyright © 2015 Justin A. Bailey
All rights reserved
First Edition

PAGE PUBLISHING, INC.
New York, NY

First originally published by Page Publishing, Inc. 2015

ISBN 978-1-63417-281-3 (pbk)
ISBN 978-1-63417-282-0 (digital)

Printed in the United States of America

I would like to dedicate this book to all of those men and women who have served and fought from the time this nation was brought forth to the war on terror in Iraq and Afghanistan. They have sacrificed much to protect the freedoms we cherish. We should never forget those that have made the ultimate sacrifice. May God bless each and every one of you, Thank you.

In memory of

Ronald W. Bailey
United States Air force 1964 to 1968
September 21, 1946 to January 25, 2012
My big brother who never got to see this finished, Rest in peace.

Kenneth Lee Perry
Specialist Fourth Class United States Army
August 13, 1948 to September 19, 1969
Killed in action Long Khanh Province, Republic of Vietnam

Lester C. Martin
Sergeant, Fourth Marine Division
United States Marine Corps
Killed in action Iwo Jima, February 1945

This book is a work of fiction. I have used real people and events to create the story. They were in the right place and time in history; I have taken artistic license with many of those events. The author has no knowledge of any specific actions or conversations I attribute to them. Those have come from my imagination. No disrespect is intended to anyone living or dead. Any errors in this book are mine and mine alone.

There are many people I wish to thank for their patience in putting up with me during this project. First my wife Theresa, She has been there for thirty one years. Who would have thought we would be where we are. My Daughter Claire, my first editor and critic, her input made it better. Marcia, my big sister who I owe more than I can ever repay, she had to wait for two years to finish reading the book. Sorry you had to wait. The young marine who graciously took the time after the Braves game to speak with me about this project and provided valuable input. Marines are some of my favorite people.

To the Men of the Hickory Flat Fellowship men's breakfast and especially Pastor Scott, they know why. Last but certainly not least Richard Roma, Nick Hoffman and all of the people behind the scene at Page Publishing, Thank you for your encouragement and belief in this project and the work you have done correcting all my errors and leading me through the process.

# SYNOPSIS

The Founding Fathers risked everything in the Revolution. The new nation is struggling to survive. The Constitution emerges bringing a form of Government the world has never seen. It must be protected at all costs, even from its own citizens. The Founding Fathers form a secret Committee to preserve those freedoms they fought and died for. Or will it? The Committee, everything is destined to be under their control, Senators and Congressman even the newly elected President.

Dan Oliver is looking forward to retiring from the FBI, until his daughter comes home from college with a letter penned by James Madison. He has always suspected there were secret power brokers behind the Government, now he knows. Can he find them, can he stop them and will he even survive The Committee…

# PROLOUGE

Oval Office
January 21, 2013
3:13 AM

"I, Bennett Arthur Cain, do solemnly swear that I will faithfully execute the office of the president of the United States and will, to the best of my ability, preserve, protect, and defend the constitution of the United States. So help me God."

"Congratulations, Mr. President," the chief justice said to the new president as he extended his hand. Ben Cain had waited to repeat that oath for what seemed his whole life. All the time spent working toward this, the endless campaigns, all the little things he had to give up, now it's finally happened. The inaugural ball had finished hours earlier; the party afterward was finally over. Cain and his wife, Marilyn, walked out of the east room of the White House. The last of the guests had left only moments earlier. He turned to Marilyn and asked, "Care to step into the Oval Office and take a look?"

"No, you go on. I'm exhausted. Don't be too long. The job starts for real in the morning."

Cain leaned in and kissed her. "I'll be there in a few minutes. I want to take it all in." Leaving her in the elevator to the residence upstairs, he made his way down the corridor. As he walked toward the Oval Office, his thoughts wandered to the men who had shared this residence and walked these hallowed halls before him. He was now one of them, president of the United States.

He wanted just a few quiet minutes to himself to savor his hard-earned victory. He nodded to the ever-present Secret Service agent and slipped into the Oval Office. As he made his way to the Resolute desk, now his, that had served so many before him, the chair swiveled around and the nondescript man sitting in it smiled at him and said, "As I suspected, you couldn't wait."

Stunned, the only thing Cain managed to say was "Who in the hell are you?"

The man stood up and said, "Why don't you sit down, and let's have a talk. It's time you found out what is expected of you. Don't look so surprised. You wouldn't be here if it wasn't for us."

Badly shaken, Cain stepped backward. "The Secret Service is right outside and will be here in seconds."

The man merely laughed. Then he walked to Cain and pushed him gently into the chair behind the desk. Standing over him, he said, "You really don't understand, do you? You were selected long ago. The agent outside won't come in here until we are done." He then walked over to the bar, poured a drink of Cain's preferred Famous Grouse whiskey, and handed it to him.

"Sitting on that desk is the letter from your predecessor. There has been a letter like that for every president since George Washington. You will have plenty of time for that after I leave. Right now, all you need to know is that you belong to us. We put you in this office. As a matter of fact, the college you chose, the job offered to you after college, even your political career, all carefully selected for you. All that money for your campaign, it all came from us. Everyone who sits in that chair belongs to us. We own it all. Every nominee for any position is cleared by us, even your wife was approved by the Committee. It has all been in place since the beginning. Some things we won't interfere in. You will soon learn what those are. Read the letter."

With that, the man turned and walked out the door.

## THE COMMITTEE

Ben Cain sat in stunned silence. Suddenly it all made sense. Sometimes it had seemed destiny that he chose a political career. Now he realized it wasn't destiny at all. It had all been carefully planned, just not by him, as he had once believed. Every time he was discouraged and about to give up his dream, someone had always been there to change his mind and keep him focused. Even Marilyn, ever steady, always by his side, was that all planned for him as well? He reached for the letter on what was now his desk. Picking it up, he looked at it and realized it was addressed to 45. He was the forty-fifth president of the United States. Just then the door opened and the agent who had been outside stepped in and asked, "Everything okay, Mr. President? Is there anything I can do for you?"

The president looked up at the agent and slipped the letter in his jacket pocket and said, "No, everything is fine. I'm just about to head upstairs to bed. It's been a very long day."

The agent smiled and replied, "The first day on the job usually is. Have a good night, Mr. President."

The Constitutional Convention
Philadelphia, Pennsylvania
Monday, September 17, 1787

Benjamin Franklin slowly made his way to the chair set aside for him as he accepted the cordial nods of greeting from the gathered delegates. As he eased into the chair, his mind was going over the many conflicting thoughts he had over the proposed constitution. Clearly, the new country was struggling. Something had to be done or the new nation would fracture. He reached over to fellow Pennsylvanian James Wilson and handed him the speech he was too weak with age to deliver himself. Wilson took the speech and made his way to the lectern. Franklin quietly retreated into his own thoughts. He had put to words his greatest fears for the new republic about to be born. He felt in his soul that the men gathered in this room would protect the United States. What worried him were the future generations of Americans as yet unborn. Would they understand the sacrifice this generation had paid in blood? Could they be trusted to protect it, as had its founders?

Less than one-third of even this current generation had been willing to stand up for even the most basic of rights. Most had simply been willing to go along with the British crown. After all it was safer; there was no risk.

Once this document was signed and ratified by the states, the new government would be formed. For the foreseeable future it would be sufficient. What would happen when the people became corrupt? Should he even worry? All he and his fellow patriots could do was take care of the new nation in their lifetimes. Beyond that, no one could promise. He had shared these thoughts with only his dear friend General Washington. Now they were being put to words, hopefully as a warning. Would it be heeded? Or was he merely wishing it so? No matter, it was about to be done. He could do no more. His time on this earth was drawing toward its close. He had no options but to put his trust in future generations he would never know.

The vote was taken. It was now up to the states. Rhode Island had even refused to send delegates to the convention. It would take some time to even find out whether it would be ratified. The European countries were almost arrogant in their disdain for the United States. Britain considered her no more than a rogue colony. Even what was left of the Spanish empire was causing problems. It was only because of the French fleet that the surrender at Yorktown had even happened. Now finally the Americans were in control of their own destiny. It was with these thoughts that many of the delegates headed home to their own states. The ratification process for the new constitution would take almost two years. The founders had risked everything to bring this nation forth. If they had lost, all of them would have been at the end of a British rope. They would do what must be done to protect it. It was the beginning of what would become the conspiracy.

New York City
The Burr residence
June 12, 1799

The Founders committee had decided to send Alexander Hamilton to speak with Aaron Burr regarding the upcoming election.

# THE COMMITTEE

It had already been decided that John Adams had to go as president. They would need Burr's power in the New York legislature.

Alexander Hamilton stepped from the carriage in front of Aaron Burr's stately residence. The two men had been adversaries for years. It was humbling for Hamilton to offer Burr the vice presidency in exchange for his support of Thomas Jefferson as president. Hamilton knocked on the door and was greeted by Burr's valet, Charles.

"Good day, sir. I believe you are expected. If you'll step into the parlor, I will announce your arrival." With that, he turned and left Hamilton standing in the parlor. Humbling as it was for him to ask anything of Burr, the necessity of seeing Adams replaced warranted his humility. He stepped to the window and gazed at the quiet street in the exclusive neighborhood as he waited to see his political rival.

Charles stepped into the office Burr maintained in the back of his finely appointed residence. "Mr. Hamilton has arrived, sir."

"Thank you, Charles. I will see him in a moment."

Aaron Burr and Hamilton were not mutual admirers. All he knew was that Hamilton had requested an audience to discuss an important matter. As he stepped into the parlor, Hamilton turned from the window to face him. "Good day, sir."

"And to you as well. What is it you wish to discuss?"

"As you know, the election for president will be held in December. I have come to solicit your support in the endeavor to replace John Adams as president."

Surprised at the boldness of the statement, Burr paused to gather his thoughts. "If I choose to offer my good offices to anyone, why is it you are asking?"

"I believe you as well, sir, are of the opinion that the president has been much too vocal in his support of British interests, much to the detriment of the United States."

"Who would be to the benefit of my support, and what advantage would I be to gain?"

"If you were to see that Thomas Jefferson would receive the electoral votes of New York, your name will be placed on the ballot as vice president."

"Merely put on the ballot? Or do you have the support to guarantee that?"

Hamilton hesitated slightly before answering. "Are there any guarantees in this life? Yes, the support is there."

"I will promise nothing, but it is not out of the question. I will consider the offer. Are there any other matters before us?"

"This is the only matter I have come to discuss. I have no personal agenda in this. It is what is best for our nation. Thank you for agreeing to see me. I can see myself out." With that, Hamilton turned from his bitter rival and made his way to the door. As he walked to his carriage, he wondered what manner of trouble this deal would cause.

Aaron Burr had worked long and hard to become a political power. They were now coming to him. He could turn this to his advantage. The next steps would not be difficult to arrange.

Mount Vernon
December 1, 1799

Thomas Jefferson dismounted and handed the reins to Joshua, Washington's longtime stableman. He strode purposely across the lawn and walked up the steps toward the front door. The door opened and Ruth, the house servant, bowed in respect. "How is he doing?" Jefferson inquired.

"Not well. Miss Martha is with him now." Entering Washington's Mount Vernon residence, Jefferson moved quickly toward the general's bedchamber. As he slipped inside, Martha Washington stood and acknowledged his presence with a curtsy.

"I know you need to speak with him, but please keep it short. He hardly has any strength." With that, Martha Washington left Thomas Jefferson alone with her failing husband.

President Washington turned toward Jefferson and mumbled one word, "Well?"

Jefferson moved closer and knelt by the bedside of the first president of the United States and one of the most powerful members of the Founders Committee. "The replacement has been selected and voted on by the founders. All we need is your agreement."

Washington closed his eyes and nodded in agreement. "I pray we have made the right selection."

Jefferson nodded his acceptance. "We all know what is at stake. He will not even be told until after."

Washington's reply was barely audible. "It shall not be long…"

Thirteen days later, it became necessary for the first replacement founder to be seated on the Committee.

The State Capitols
The electoral college vote
December 3, 1800

In various state houses, the electors who would travel to the nation's capitol to cast the ballots for both president and vice president were selected. As required by the Constitution, each elector selected two of the four candidates for president. Whichever candidate received the most votes would be the president; the candidate with the second highest vote total would be vice president. What was so unexpected was the tie: seventy-three votes each for Aaron Burr and Thomas Jefferson. This would force a vote in the house to choose the next president.

The founders committee had to meet. They had already succeeded in replacing John Adams. Now Aaron Burr could possibly become president. Not only would this be far worse than Adams, the unforeseen oversight in the constitution would have to be dealt with. Burr could not be allowed to hold the office of the president.

The pressure was applied to the selected members of Congress. Three days and thirty-six ballots later, Jefferson would succeed Adams as president. The constitution would be corrected with the twelfth amendment. That left Aaron Burr to be dealt with. A deal had been made; Burr had been put on the ballot with Jefferson to deliver New York's electoral votes. He had agreed to be vice president. Breaking the deal, he had tried to become president. Burr would be an outsider for the rest of his term as vice president. The Committee decided to contain him. He may have become vice president, but he would be trusted with nothing, and they would see to it he did not get a second term.

# JUSTIN A. BAILEY

The Duel
Weehawken, New Jersey
July 11, 1804

    Alexander Hamilton had misgivings about agreeing to this duel. He had spent the previous evening writing his will and making sure his affairs were in order. Now the time had come for him to face his lifelong nemesis on the field of honor. Their disdain for one another had only grown after the election in which Burr had tried to become president. When he had broken the deal, the bad blood between them had only grown worse. When Burr had then run for governor of New York and Hamilton had actively opposed him, Burr had taken offense to many of the comments that Hamilton had made about Burr being an unfit candidate for governor. He had then issued the challenge to Hamilton. There was no way he could refuse; Burr would never accept an apology even if one were offered.

    Hamilton, along with his second, Nathaniel Pendleton and Dr. David Hosack, left the barge that had brought them from Manhattan and made their way to the bluff overlooking the Hudson River. It was on this same field Hamilton thought with foreboding that his eldest son had been killed in a duel three years previously. Would his fate be the same? Perhaps, he thought, the premonition of his own death was his own fears.

    Burr turned to his second, Elias Payne, and motioned to the approaching trio. "I am surprised he has chosen to face me."

    "He could hardly do otherwise, could he?" Payne responded.

    "Considering the options, I suppose he felt he had no choice."

    Hamilton and Pendleton walked to the table holding the dueling pistols, which separated them from Burr and Payne. Cordial greetings were exchanged by all the parties. This was the field of honor and the protocol dictated the greeting. "As the rules have already been agreed to, let us proceed with this business at hand." Hamilton directed to Burr.

# THE COMMITTEE

The practice of duels to demand satisfaction from a public insult was beginning to be on the edge of legal. It had started with the use of swords. The purpose was to procure an apology. It could be offered from either party up until the last moment. Seldom was the intent to kill. In its earlier forms using swords, two strikes to either party or the drawing of blood was usually enough to end the duel. With the use of pistols, the more severe the insult was considered the fewer the paces. Ten was the agreed number. The bad blood between these two along with Burr's wounded pride would not allow any apology. The duel would take place.

Hamilton selected his pistol and handed it to his second to load. If he managed to kill him, the problems he was causing the committee as well as the nation would be over; it was worth the risk. Burr picked up the remaining pistol and handed it to Payne. The field had already been marked off by Pendleton and Payne as the protocol demanded.

Hamilton retrieved his pistol from his second, turned toward Burr, and said, "All the rules will be observed I trust."

"Agreed. My honor demands it." The two stood back-to-back. Hamilton's second began to count the paces. When he reached ten, both men turned and faced the other. As Hamilton leveled his pistol to take aim, Burr fired. The bullet struck Hamilton in the chest. As Hamilton dropped to the ground, his last conscious thought was that he had failed to protect the nation from this madman. He had never even discharged the pistol. Pendleton and Dr. Hosack rushed in to the fallen Hamilton. The pair carried him to the barge and tended him as best they could. He was then taken to his home in New York with the bullet fired by Burr lodged near his spine. The next day Hamilton succumbed to the bullet fired by Burr.

Another member would have to be selected for the Committee. Samuel Adams had passed away the previous October of 1803. His replacement had been seated on the committee for only a little over six months. This selection would mean only seven of the original ten founders were still on the committee.

The Burr Residence
New York City
July 12, 1804

Aaron Burr nervously paced back and forth. Word had reached him that Alexander Hamilton had died. While he had taken some personal satisfaction from that result, it would force him to flee New York. He had never managed to put the feud with Hamilton behind him. The last four years he had spent as vice president he had been treated as an outsider, his name would not even be put on the ballot again. This would even cost him all the political influence and power he had amassed in the state of New York. Hearing a carriage on the cobblestones of the street, he quickly moved to the parlor and peered out the window. Elias Payne stepped from the carriage and quickly moved up the walk toward the stately residence of Aaron Burr.

Burr opened the front door and ushered Payne into the entrance foyer. "What have you managed to learn from your inquiries?"

"As soon as they can, it is planned to arrest you and try you for the murder of Hamilton."

"I must leave at once. There is too much at stake. There are several matters you will have to deal with in my absence." Burr turned and made his way toward the office in his residence, motioning Payne to follow. As he stepped into the office with Payne, his thoughts turned to what he must do.

"I am going to go to Philadelphia. I will send word when I arrive. You will have to see that I have the assets to stay for some time. I dare not risk going even to the banks."

Payne nodding his acceptance and replied, "I will do whatever must be done. I have as much riding on our next venture as you."

Burr moved behind the ornate desk, sat in the elegant chair behind it, and opened the lower drawer. Taking from it a leather-bound journal and a considerable stack of currency, he handed the journal to Payne. "In here you will find the list of all the accounts with the balances and to whom the next payments are to be made. The plan will have to be enacted faster than planned." With that, Burr left the office with the currency and began packing for his escape.

# THE COMMITTEE

Washington DC
The White House
July 25, 1804

Thomas Jefferson looked up from his desk in the Oval Office; the door opening had interrupted his thoughts. Standing in the doorway his manservant, Ezekiel, had waited to get his attention. "Mr. Dayton is here to see you, Mr. President."

"Thank you, Ezekiel. Please show him in."

Jonathan Dayton, one of the founding members of the Committee and the youngest signer of the Constitution, walked into the Oval Office and greeted the president. "Good morning, Mr. President. You are well I trust?"

Jefferson stood and made his way to Dayton, clasping his shoulder as he extended his hand in greeting. "I am doing as well as these trying circumstances will allow. It was good of you to see me so quickly."

"I could do no less considering. We must act decisively. This could escalate beyond our control."

"Word has reached us that Burr has gone to Philadelphia. Funds will be provided for you, and anything else you will need can be arranged. We have to know what he is up to."

"I will leave in the morning. It might take some time to contrive the circumstances to gain his confidence. He trusts no one at this point."

"The nation could be put at risk. We have all sacrificed too much to allow this madman to destroy it now. We must know what he is planning. Others have to be involved. It is of the utmost importance to learn who they are. Also, we must not risk any exposure of the founders. You will be alone in this undertaking. We will do what can be done to protect you afterward."

"I have decided to remove myself from the committee. If I fail, no connection can be made. There is too much risk otherwise. There is no one else we can enlist."

Moved, Jefferson embraced the younger man. "Jonathan, your dedication to this cause is noble. We have given so much to protect this young nation and the form of government our constitution has brought about. I could not bear to see what we brought forth with our sacrifice destroyed by the crazy delusions of that madman. Go with God."

With that, Dayton took his leave from the White House and the current president and became, in essence, the first covert operative of the Committee. By removing himself from the committee, only six of the original founders remained.

Newark, New Jersey
Westminster Academy
May 14, 1979

Edwin Bennett Cain's Lincoln limousine drove up the tree-lined drive and up to the main entrance to the Westminster Academy. His chauffeur, Trevor, put the limo in park and quickly opened the door, got out, and discreetly scanned the entrance to the school before opening the rear door of the limo. His employer paid him well to not only drive him wherever he needed to go, but also to make sure there were no surprises or anyone that might be a potential problem. Trevor took his duties seriously. "The Boss," as he thought of him, was not only chairman of the board of Atlantic Holdings, a privately held investment firm, he was becoming a power in state politics. There was even talk of him becoming either the next governor or possibly senator. When you started moving in those circles, Trevor thought, enemies could be anywhere.

Edwin Cain exited the limo, looked at Trevor, and told him, "Make sure we can get out of here quickly after the ceremonies are over."

"Certainly, Mr. Cain. Do you want me to stay with the car?"

"No, Trevor, you come in. I want you to be with the family. Ben is close to you as well. Marjorie and Catherine are already here."

"Yes, sir, I will be in as soon as I park the car."

Edwin turned and made his way into the private academy his son, Ben, was soon to graduate from. He was almost late. He hated being late for anything. The meeting had run longer than planned. Business had always seemed to take him away from his family more than he liked. This had caused more than one rift with his son. Ben was not only graduating today, he was the valedictorian. As he entered the auditorium, his wife, Marjorie, walked up to him, grabbed his arm, and quickly led him to their seats. His daughter, Catherine, was already seated.

She leaned in and whispered in his ear, "I was beginning to wonder if you were going to make it."

He quietly took the mild rebuke, smiled at her, and squeezed her hand. "Sorry I am late. The meeting ran long." With that, he turned his attention to the ceremony that had just begun.

The headmaster, Gordon Newell, moved to the podium and addressed the audience here to see their offspring take the first step into the rest of their lives. "Ladies and gentleman," he began, "these fine young men and women before us have completed the first step toward becoming the leaders of the future. We are proud to have taken a role in readying them to reach for greatness. I know you are extremely proud of them as well."

Edwin's thoughts began to wander as the headmaster continued with his remarks. That day, the sixteenth of January in 1961, when the doctor walked out and informed him he was now a father. All the sleepless nights, all the dreams for his son, everything he had missed. He had worked so hard to become successful and build his career. There was still so much to accomplish; his business was doing well, and he was even contemplating a move into the political arena. He had been making all the right friends and had been approached by the chairman of the state Republican party. This could open up a whole realm of possibilities, not just for him but for Bennett as well.

Edwin looked up and suddenly realized he had missed not only most of the ceremony, but his son's valedictorian speech as well. The diplomas were being handed out, and his son stepped forward to receive his from Gordon Newell, the headmaster. "Bennett Arthur Cain, Valedictorian" came over the speakers as Edwin watched his son shake Newell's hand and receive his diploma. So much yet to accomplish and so much potential, Edwin thought as he watched his son receive his high school diploma.

# JUSTIN A. BAILEY

The Committee
The World Trade Center
New York City
November 12, 1976

    One at a time the limousines began to arrive in the parking garage of the World Trade Center Tower One. It was not at all unusual to see. The office spaces in the complex were considered some of the most prestigious in the city. Powerful international businessmen, politicians, stockbrokers, bankers, lawyers, and many influential individuals and corporations all leased offices and even multiple floors. Limousines were commonly seen. These limousines, however, were passed to the private security-controlled floor in the parking garage. It was there the members of the Committee could unobtrusively exit their limousine. They make their way to the private elevator accessed only by private security codes and manned twenty-four hours a day by security personnel. They would then be whisked to the 101st floor. The 101st floor was not accessible by any of the regular elevators. If one were to push the button labeled 101, it would not light up and nothing would happen. At least nothing the elevator occupant would notice will happen. Button 101 would activate a camera concealed within the elevator. The image would then be viewed by the security officer in the small windowless office unknown even to normal building security.

    There, the officer would pay strict attention to the visitor until it was determined if the button had been pushed by mistake or by intention. Wherever in the building the visitor would depart the elevator, he or she would be quietly observed until such time as they exited the building. If the button had been accidentally pushed by one of the employees of the building's other tenants, their image was kept in a database to be verified by the security officer. Too many pushes of the button by the same individual would cause them to be quietly investigated by security.

    Floor 101 and the floors above and below were leased to Atlas International Trading. Floor 100 was where the normal day-to-day import-export business conducted by Atlas International was managed. Floor 101 was believed to be, by the employees of Atlas, the executive suite, conference rooms, and offices for the CEO and board members. Floor 102 was also staffed by Atlas employees. The business conducted on this floor was the main business of Atlas International. The employees on this floor were as carefully selected by the Committee as were the candidates themselves.

Atlas's main business had nothing to do with trading, international or otherwise. Atlas International was a privately owned shell corporation set up by the Committee. There was just enough import and export business handled by the 100th floor employees to actually turn a profit who had no idea they were nothing more than cover. The real work of Atlas was tracking the candidates, funneling money where it was needed, and taking care of the Committee's business interests. The employees who did this were not aware of the other employees who did this. Not one of them knew what their purpose really was. It was the perfect setup.

"Gentlemen," the chairman began, "let's bring the meeting to order. Since we meet as a full committee only once a year, and this time we have a new member"—as he motioned toward Gold—"let's do the background as we give our reports. As we all know, the current election is past. The mess created by Nixon will soon be forgotten by the voting public. With his resignation and Ford's ascension to the Oval Office, we did not control the office of the president. We will again control the office of the president in January. Let's start with the Congress. Jade, I believe that is your area. You have the floor."

The member of the Committee known as Jade replied, "As of this election, the count is 138. That is an increase of 10. We have been working only on the urban areas to this point. Concentrating on those who will be the chairmen of the various committees in the House of Representatives has been the priority. Most of the more important committees, such as ways and means, we already control. We will possibly get our man to head the foreign relations committee this time as well. Over the next two years, the focus will be placed more on the rural areas of the Midwestern states. Ohio, Michigan, and Indiana are going to be the targets. The unions can help us there. It will mean a sizeable investment to start the marketing campaign, but it should pay off nicely. The unions are mostly interested in getting control of pension funds and increasing their power base. It is actually quite easy to manipulate them into doing our work for us. They already publish a list of union-endorsed candidates in their newsletters. We have several very promising young candidates in the pipeline. We plan to get the PR campaigns moving faster this time."

The chairman, also known as Diamond, nodded his acknowledgement of the report. "Now moving to the Senate. Onyx, where do we stand with that esteemed institution?"

"We currently have twenty-six. As you know, the elections are held every two years. However there is only one-third up for reelection each cycle. Some of the incumbents have held their seats for several terms and are more difficult to unseat. There are fewer retirements expected for the next election cycle. I believe that four more seats are within reach. I plan to work with Jade, combining the marketing strategy within what is already happening. We are beginning to get enough power within the Senate to put several more of the committee chairs in play. We already have six. It also takes more money to fund the campaign contributions as those are statewide and not limited like congressional districts. The upside is each seat is only up every six years. The downside is it makes progress slower."

Obsidian motioned to the chairman. With his nod to take the floor, he looked at Onyx and asked, "Can that marketing plan be dovetailed with what we are preparing for the governors' races? I'm worried we might overload this time around. We do not want too many questions asked about the sudden increase in campaign contributions. If we see to it that it goes to the national committees of both party's coffers, it may be less obvious. Do we have the influence there to see it used as we want?"

The chairman motioned to Emerald. "The influence should be in place by the time it's needed. What I would suggest is starting the donation process of the funds earlier. Then it can be directed as necessary the closer we get to the elections. That leads me to the question of the candidates. Has it been decided who they will be? The earlier we have them in place, the sooner the funds could be directed."

The chairman looked to Coral, his nod giving him the floor. "Gentlemen, as we all know, the selection process takes anywhere from ten to twenty years to have a candidate at that level. We select them in high school or college. While there, the education is carefully administered. They must believe it is all their choice. We start with a number far above what will ultimately be successful. Fewer than one in four are selected for anything beyond local government. Taking into consideration the residency requirements to run for office, we cannot, at present, cover all of the states every single election. If you will all recall, that was why the regional strategy was implemented. That was twenty-five years ago. We currently have twelve in Ohio that we decided are viable, several of those reside within the same districts. The numbers in Michigan and Indiana are similar. We have to cover both political parties. That reduces the number further. Those that did not win in the primary can often be kept viable for the next election cycle for another office. That is two to four years. Gentlemen, let me remind you to be patient. We do not need to be in a hurry. If we continue at the current pace in another twenty years, we will have a majority in both houses. That brings us to the need to keep the pipeline well supplied with potential candidates."

"Let's go ahead with that. Give us the background." The chairman motioned to Granite.

"The plan has been to coordinate the selection process with the regional strategy. We have to stay ahead of the regions by ten to fifteen years. Right now, the Midwest is the current region. The South is running almost concurrently. The next president is from Georgia. So we are on track with both of those. As always, we will select the right candidate outside the target regions. In addition, we must maintain the pipeline in the regions we have previously targeted. We have only been working on the Senate for the last seventy-five years. We, of course, had to get the seventeenth amendment ratified first. Prior to that, the senators were appointed by the state governments. The first step was to get them elected by the people. Then the marketing could be implemented. Congress was started almost a hundred years ago. The state and local level was only used as a training ground to prepare the candidates for the national offices. We only began twenty or so years ago to realize the potential of controlling the state legislatures. The governors were used as stepping stones to the presidency. We only used the more populous states due to the larger number of electoral votes. Occasionally, a senator would be selected."

"Thank you," the chairman responded. "Now, gentlemen, it's time to move to the selection process. Everyone is constantly on the lookout for possible recruits. Remember, nothing written leaves this room. Who would like to begin?"

Malachite said, "I will start if no one minds." There were no objections. "There is a very interesting family in Newark, New Jersey. The Cains, the father is Edwin Cain, forty-six years old. He is CEO of the privately held investment firm Atlantic holdings. He is becoming a power on the political scene. He is considering a run for governor or possibly the Senate. He is not currently one of ours. His son, Bennett, fifteen, is enrolled in the private academy Westminster. We recruit from there regularly. The daughter, Catherine, is twelve. His wife, Marjorie, is active in the local community, church, and charities. They live in the upscale area of Forrest Hills. Good background. I would think the son is a good potential candidate."

The chairman nodded his acknowledgement. "Who would care to go next?"

Onyx stepped up next. "I have been keeping my eye on a young man in Nevada, William Parker. He is eighteen, preparing to go to UCLA. His father, Stephen, is employed by the state gaming commission. His mother, Veronica, is a secretary for the gaming commission as well. That is where she met Stephen. There are two other children. A brother, Phil, age sixteen. And a sister, Lisa, age nine. The family is close to the current junior senator who, by the way, is one of ours."

Ebony volunteered to go next. "I have been thinking. It is time to select more minority candidates. There is one in Hawaii. Barry Satero, sixteen. His mother, Anne Dunham, is white. The father, Barak Obama Sr., is a Kenyan native. The parents met at the University of Hawaii. His father then moved to Harvard and returned to Kenya. The mother then married an Indonesian, took the boy there for a time. He then returned to Hawaii to be raised by the grandparents. Very promising."

One by one the candidates were discussed. Selections made, plans implemented.

# THE COMMITTEE

Each and every one of the members of the Committee was a power in their own right—chairman of the board, CEO or chief financial officer of major corporations, bank presidents, and even one that owned several of the largest and most influential newspapers in the country. They were used to exercising their power.

The chairman looked at all ten of the members of the most powerful, exclusive, and secret committee ever conceived. He was the most powerful of them all. There had only been twenty-one men ever to hold the chairmanship. They were now on the thirty-ninth president of the United States; then again, they were not up for reelection every four years, as was every president the nation had elected.

Louisiana Territory
February 17, 1807

The rain started coming down harder; the wind seemed to be laughing at him. A cold, bedraggled, Aaron Burr placed one foot in front of the other, kept his head down, and continued walking down the muddy road. How had it all come to this? Practically run out of Washington at the end of his term as vice president. He could never return to New York. The duel with Hamilton had seen to that. A gust of wind threatened to lift the battered beaver hat from his head. He reached up and tugged it down tighter on his head. Drawing the ragged woolen coat tighter about him against the cold, Burr heard the hooves of the horses. Looking up, he saw the soldiers round the curve in the road before him.

Sergeant Joshua Stone reined in his horse, holding his hand up to signal to the soldiers with him to do the same. He peered at the figure on the road ahead. He then motioned to Corporal Hezekiah Wooten to come up next to him. Walking his horse, the corporal drew next to Stone.

"Corporal, take two men with you and see if that gentleman is who we have been looking for."

Complying with the order, Wooten pointed to two of the mounted soldiers. "Lets' go." Moving at a trot down the muddy road, the trio approached the man on foot.

Aaron Burr had nowhere left to run. He simply gave up. The mounted soldiers surrounded him and ordered him to continue walking toward the rest of the soldiers and Sergeant Stone.

Stone looked down at the scruffy, bedraggled figure of Aaron Burr. "Well, what have we here, a man who would be king?" Laughing, the soldiers then tied Burr's hands, tied a lead rope to that, and unceremoniously began to lead him toward the small hamlet of Wakefield.

Burr's fall from grace was complete and total. After the fateful duel with Hamilton and his escape to Philadelphia, he realized he would have no future in the United States. He had been working on an alternate plan to carve his own kingdom from the territory of Louisiana and the western states. Now that was never going to happen. Everyone had betrayed him—that bastard General Wilkinson, the commander in chief of the army, had even written a letter to President Jefferson detailing everything.

As the group of soldiers with their captive in tow reached Wakefield, Sergeant Stone was contemplating where they could keep him for the night. Turning to his men, Stone ordered, "Take him to the blacksmith's and put him in a stall for now." Stone then turned his horse and walked it over toward the small inn. Dismounting, Stone tied his horse to the hitching post and walked inside. The proprietor, Charles Larue, looked up from his seat behind the bar. Seeing that Stone was in uniform, he wondered what the soldier wanted. "What can I help you with, sir?"

Looking over at the scruffy barkeep, Stone replied, "I need accommodations for the night for my men. Also if you have it, a place I can keep a prisoner."

"Aye, there is a cellar in the back, and I can provide you room for the night." He then proceeded to negotiate the price with Stone.

With the negotiations completed, Stone then returned to his men in the blacksmith's barn. Motioning to Corporal Wooten to follow, he then stepped out of the barn. "Corporal, we can keep him in the cellar behind the inn. I have made arraignments for the men to stay there. Post a guard and see they are relieved regularly. We can then have some supper. When that's done, I'll buy you a pint."

# THE COMMITTEE

Surprised at Stone's sudden generosity, Wooten saluted and said, "Yes, Sergeant," and hurried to comply with his orders.

The next morning, Sergeant Stone walked past the soldier standing guard to the cellar door and unlatched it. Looking in, he saw Burr sleeping in the corner on an old blanket. Walking across the dirt floor, he took the toe of his boot and, none too gently, nudged Burr in the side. "Up with you, we've a date with the magistrate." From there, Stone led him outside and loaded him on the back of the provision wagon that was headed to Fort Stoddert.

As the wagon slowly rumbled down the rutted road to Fort Stoddert, Louisiana, Burr contemplated the collapse of his plan. Elias Payne had withdrawn the funds from the banks in New York. Making the specified payments, Burr had believed the plan would fall into place. Anthony Merry, the British minister to the United States, had led him to believe there would be money and ships to help with the conquest. Everyone he had recruited and paid had betrayed him. None of them had fallen as hard or lost as much as he had. His dream was shattered.

Elizabethtown, New Jersey
September 3, 1807

Jonathan Dayton looked up from the fireplace he was vacantly staring into. The loud knocking on his door had interrupted his thoughts. He heard the door being opened by his servant and stood up to make his way to the front parlor of his stately residence. He highly suspected he was going to be arrested. Earlier in the year, Aaron Burrs' plot to create his own empire had fallen apart. Unknown to anyone outside of the Committee, his own role in the affair was believed to be as a coconspirator. In reality, his mission working as a covert operative for the Committee had been to keep an eye on what the madman Burr was planning.

Stepping into the parlor, Dayton was confronted by the local constable, Henry Shelley, and several armed soldiers. "What pray tell is going on?" Dayton asked.

Shelley looked at Dayton and responded, "I think you know why we are here, Mr. Dayton."

Nodding in acknowledgement, Dayton replied, "So that is to be the way it is. I see. You believe I was party to treason?"

"I have no say in the matter, sir. That will be left for the courts to decide. If you would come with us, Mr. Dayton."

"At least grant me the courtesy of being properly attired. If I may, may I get my coat?"

"Certainly, sir. I will accompany you."

Dayton turned and walked away, the constable following closely on his heels. Retrieving his coat, he slipped it on his shoulders. Turning to Constable Shelley, Dayton inquired, "What, if I may ask, have you been instructed to charge me with?"

"That is for others to decide, sir. I was merely instructed to arrest you." Constable Shelley had known Jonathan Dayton for most of his life. He would never believe such a fine gentleman such as he could really have been a party to that of which he was being accused.

Dayton nodded his acceptance and allowed Shelley to lead him past the soldiers and out the door. He had sent his wife to visit family, fearing this outcome. He could only hope the Founders could somehow extricate him from this mess. The committee must be protected above all else. The cost of being a patriot, to protect this nation and its Constitution could be his downfall. If that was the price, it would be paid.

The White House
Washington DC
October 12, 1807

Thomas Jefferson stood, his hands clasped behind his back, staring absently out the window of the Oval Office. The lawn and the street beyond were not consciously registering; his thoughts were elsewhere. This nation had been through so much—the struggle for independence, the bloody Revolution, the chaos that almost tore the country apart before it truly began, the constitutional convention, and the form of government it brought forth. He and the other founders were making the commitment to protect this nation at all costs, even from its own citizens. He had his own private doubts that they were right to form the Committee. Every time he began to doubt the wisdom of the founders, he had to look no further than his own vice president from the first term. Aaron Burr had almost single-handedly destroyed the fledgling nation.

Just then his quiet reverie was interrupted as Ezekiel opened the door and patiently waited for his presence to be acknowledged. He turned from the window and motioned Ezekiel into the Oval Office. "Yes, Ezekiel?"

"Mr. President, Mr. Madison is here to see you, sir."

"Thank you, Ezekiel, you may show him in."

James Madison entered the Oval Office and walked to the window where his fellow patriot and founders' committee member still stood. Extending his hand, gripping Jefferson's hand in his own, the handshake quickly turned into an embrace. "I am glad to see you, Thomas. These times have been quite trying. The trial caused quite a stir. I am grateful that sorry episode is behind us."

"As am I, James. I pray there will be nothing else that we must put this nation through. I understand Burr was acquitted."

"Yes, he was. The chief justice so narrowly interpreted the definition of treason. The jury probably felt they had no option but to acquit. It may be for the best. Could the nation have withstood a vice president being convicted?"

"You may be right, James. Does he present any further danger?"

"His career is in shambles. The power he had in New York has evaporated. He is no longer a threat."

"Do we know who else was involved?"

"He is not saying. We do know General Wilkinson played a role, some of the others we know. The rest, I suspect will lay low. They should cause us no further problems."

"What of Jonathan? Can we protect him?"

"Jonathan knew what he was risking. If you will recall, it was his idea to get close to Burr. That is also why he removed himself from the Committee, to protect us as well."

"Can we protect him? We all owe him. The shame may very well be how history will portray him as a traitor. Future generations will never know the sacrifice he made."

"You cannot protect him. You are the president. The office must be kept above this sort of thing. We have to think of the nation, not just now, but the future. That is why the committee was formed in the beginning."

"There must be something. It is not right to just let him be thought a traitor. He may be tried as well."

"As I said before, you cannot protect him. That does not mean the committee is powerless to do so. We can see there will be no trial."

"Is that the best we can do?"

"Thomas, it is enough. Jonathan knew the risk. The nation, the Constitution, and the future are larger than any sacrifice any one of us can make. We have all given so much. Allow him to do what must be done. It is for the best. We are on this earth for a purpose. In God's eyes, we will all be judged. What man thinks is of no consequence."

"Perhaps you are right. James, what of us? Have we overstepped our bounds by forming the Committee? Perhaps old Ben was right, can we trust the future generations? We can hardly trust our own."

"Some things we will never know. Thomas, we do not do this for our own purpose. We can only trust it will always be so."

"James, sometimes I am troubled by our belief that we…I do not know how to say this, but we think we are above the corruption of power. Not one of us trusts our citizens to protect this republic we have brought forth. How can we be so arrogant?" Jefferson wearily walked to the window and brought his hands to his temples as if to massage away his own doubts.

James Madison moved next to Thomas Jefferson, and they both stared out the window of the Oval Office. It was as if they were looking into a future only they could see and understand.

"Thomas, we are committed to this path. We almost lost this nation to that madman Burr. If we had not done what we did, I shudder to think of the consequences. All we are doing is ensuring that this nation will always have a president who truly believes in the oath of office they have sworn to uphold. That is why we insisted the oath be put in the Constitution."

"James, there were ten of us in the beginning. Think of those we have lost. General Washington was the first. Sam Adams, then Hamilton, William Patterson, and now Jonathan making this sacrifice. There are only six of us left. Have we chosen their replacements well? What will the committee look like? No, let me correct myself. Will they think like we do a hundred years from now?" Jefferson turned to look at his fellow patriot and founder's committee member, the stress of the office and self-doubt clearly evident on his face.

James Madison looked at his old friend and fellow patriot. He had these same thoughts many times himself. "Thomas, we committed ourselves to something noble. All of us took the same vow to protect this nation. Men like Aaron Burr will always be here, interested only in their own power. We must stand in their way. If we do not, are there any that will?"

There was nothing left for either of them to say. They had already set a course they could not change or control.

The Financial Center Plaza
Newark, New Jersey
May 25, 1979

Edwin Cain's phone buzzed; his secretary Marcia Forbes knew how precious his time was. That was why she had not only worked for him for the best part of the last two decades, but was paid far better than most of his more senior account managers. Not only did she guard his time, she instinctively knew those who would waste his time and kept them from doing so. So when the phone buzzed, he knew the interruption was important. He picked up the phone and listened to Marcia tell him what someone wanted with his time. "Yes, I will see him. Go ahead and send him in."

Edwin Cain moved from behind his highly polished mahogany desk and walked toward the door of his private office. Marcia opened the door, and he heard her say, "Right this way, Mr. Stillman."

Jeff Stillman was the chairman of the Republican committee of New Jersey. His interest in coming to see Edwin Cain was to convince him to throw his hat in the ring for governor of New Jersey.

"Ed, Thanks for your time. I know how busy you are," said Stillman as he extended his hand.

"Good to see you too, Jeff. I guess I'm going to have to make a decision about the governor's job. Have a seat. Can I get you coffee or something stronger perhaps?"

"Some of that Famous Grouse would go down nicely, especially if we could toast your decision to run for governor."

"Tell me again why you think I should. The last conversation we had, if you recall, I reminded you this state has not elected a Republican governor in several years," Ed asked him as he walked to the small bar and prepared the drinks.

"Ed, the state's budget is a mess. The Democrats have spent us almost to the point of bankruptcy. The current governor can't run again. He has already served two terms, and he isn't popular. They are going to have a nasty fight in the primary. If we put you up, the others who are thinking about running on our side have said they would support you instead. That means you could start the campaign and get a positive jump talking about the issues and let them fight each other in the primary."

"Jeff, what makes you think I could win?" Ed handed the drink to Stillman and took a sip of his own.

"You were instrumental in the financing for the stadium deal. People know who you are. Name recognition goes a long way. Besides, you pulled off that deal with more private financing than public. That is golden in these days of budget woes. Getting a pro football franchise to move to New Jersey, even if they still call themselves the New York Giants, was a big deal. People will remember that."

"The stadium has been open for three years, that's ancient history. Besides, I was only involved in the financing. I wasn't the face of that deal. How is that going to help win an election?"

"Ed, trust me, you were plenty visible in that deal. The perception was it would have fallen through, and you saved it. Those were primarily union jobs that built it. We can beat them with their own playbook.

# THE COMMITTEE

I'm also going to remind you that you live in this state and so does your family. Look at what they have done to the budget and education. What legacy do you want to leave for your children? You can fix this state and leave it better for your children." Jeff knew he had him with that one. The man was devoted to his family. Ed had told him at the last meeting how his son was going to be valedictorian at Westminster. That was on the day his son had graduated. What Jeff Stillman did not tell Edwin Cain was, he was just as interested in his son's political future as well.

The Cain Home
Forrest Hills, New Jersey
Later that same day

    Trevor drove Edwin Cain home in the limousine every day. Usually, the boss was much more talkative. He was only like this when something big was happening. Trevor knew who had come to visit him at the office today; he had found that out from Marcia. He guessed his demeanor meant he had reached a decision about running for governor. Trevor also knew he would find out when "The Boss" decided to tell him.

    He maneuvered the limo down the last few blocks of the quiet street in the exclusive neighborhood the Cains called home. When they reached the mansion, he pulled into the circular drive and stopped in front of the columns that graced the entrance. He quickly stepped out of the limo and opened the rear door for the boss. Edwin was deep in thought; it was just registering that he was home when the door of the limo opened, and Trevor announced that fact. Exiting the limo, Edwin thanked Trevor and walked up the steps to the ornate door that graced his home.

    His wife, Marjorie, was in the kitchen; he could hear her talking to Nina, their housekeeper. He walked toward the study and the small bar it contained. Making himself a drink of his usual Famous Grouse, he then took it, opened the door, and stepped out onto the patio. Lost in thought, he never heard Marjorie approach. She knew he was on the verge of a major decision. Quietly, she wrapped her arms around him and rested her head on his shoulder.

Ed looked at his wife and returned the embrace. Then he asked her, "What would you think about making the governor's mansion our new residence?"

"As long as it is with you," she replied, looking up at him and smiling. "I guess this means you have reached a decision."

"Jeff Stillman came to see me today. He finally convinced me the governor's office is within reach. I told him I would run, providing you were okay with it."

"I'm always with you. Ben is going to college this fall so he won't mind. Catherine is the one we need to think about. I suppose we can arrange for her to stay in Westminster. Trenton isn't all that far."

"I have to get elected first, but it never hurts to plan ahead. If Jeff is right, there isn't supposed to be any opposition in the primary. That means I can start campaigning and worrying about fund-raisers without getting beat up before the general election. I'm not sure I'm ready for this."

"Dear, you have often said this state is in trouble, who better to fix it than you?"

"I can have all the best ideas in the world, but there is a legislature to deal with. I don't want to get too far ahead of myself. I'm not the governor yet."

"I think you will make a fine governor. Lord knows this state needs one."

The Committee
The World Trade Center
June 1, 1980

The limousines began to arrive one at a time; following their normal arrival procedures, the Committee members made their way to floor 101. As far as the employees of Atlas International knew, it was simply a meeting of the board of directors. And it was. It was just not Atlas business they were planning to discuss.

# THE COMMITTEE

Diamond, the chairman, brought the meeting to order. "Gentlemen," he began, "it appears as if the Republicans have decided to actually put that famous B-movie actor up for election this fall. He has the nomination pretty well sewn up. All that is left is the formal nomination at their convention. Our man is still the sitting president. We can still control the presidency if we get Carter reelected. I think we had best make some contingency plans if that does not happen. What are our options?"

Emerald was the first to offer a suggestion. "I think one option would be to make a deal to at least get our man on the ballot as VP. At least we would have that."

Gold, the newest member of the Committee, looked at the chairman who nodded for him to take the floor. "First of all, our efforts are going to reelection. That may be difficult. The Iranian hostage crisis is still ongoing. It doesn't look like there will be a resolution any time soon. Add to that the state of the economy, double-digit inflation and unemployment. Not to mention the oil prices. The people are unhappy and may just vote for Reagan. I think Emerald is right, at least with the VP. We would have that as a contingency."

The chairman looked to Coral. "Is that our best option? Can we arrange that?"

Coral responded, "I think we can do that. Bush got close enough in the primaries. His name has been brought up as a way to unite the party. Gentlemen, may I remind you that some of the issues that may cause us to lose this election we engineered. It was discussed if we were proceeding too rapidly with the rest of the plans. There are still too many independent-thinking Americans. We are all agreed there has never been a fixed timetable."

The chairman, looking at Coral, responded, "Let's not get too far down that path just yet. We will take this one problem at a time. I am going to remind all of us that we have been working on this as a committee since the beginning. Those of us in this room may not even be privileged to see the results of our efforts. We also have other options if it becomes necessary. Let's stay with the problem of the coming election."

Granite took the opportunity next. "If I may offer a suggestion, we have put candidates in both parties on the ballots for the primaries. Then we funded them with enough money to make it almost impossible for anyone else to win. We could create a negative campaign around any candidate that gets too close to ours. To this point, we have been relying on their campaigns to do that."

Onyx caught the chairman's eye; getting the nod, he spoke next. "Gentlemen, we do not need to do anything at this point other than getting our man on the Republican ticket as VP. The general election is still several months away. We could still win that. Even if we do not, we still have considerable influence in the House and the Senate. I will remind all of us as well, there have been gains and setbacks and patience is required in this situation as well."

Motioning to the chairman, Malachite was acknowledged. "The emphasis on one election is being overemphasized. Let's not forget the strategy. We are also working on the governors as well. Things have a way of correcting themselves. Let's wait to see what happens. Corrections can be made as we have always done. Time is on our side."

The chairman looked at the assembled committee. "I think we have a consensus on that. Moving on to other business, are the current crop of candidates progressing as we planned? We agreed that each of us would take selected candidates and have our staffs keep them monitored. Any problems?"

The remainder of the meeting was devoted to keeping the candidate pipeline filled and seeing to it that all were kept on schedule. After all, they would be needed in the future.

Montpelier
Madison's Estate, Virginia
July 4, 1826

James Madison sat in the rocking chair on the columned front porch of his home. His mind wandered to all that he had seen in his lifetime. He had still been a relatively young man of twenty-five, full of the ideals of youth, at the time of the Revolutionary War. Seven years of bitter bloody conflict had aged him considerably—the struggle in the early days just to keep the nation together, the constitutional convention that had brought so much division yet brought forth a nation, old Ben Franklin's warning about his fears of the future that had spawned the founders to form the Committee, and the dark days of the War of 1812. He had been president then and had barely escaped Washington DC ahead of the British who had burned the city and with it the White House and Capitol. If it hadn't been for his wife, whose quick thinking and use of a knife to cut the portrait of George Washington from the frame holding it, that too, would have been lost to the inferno the White House became. Oh, of course, it had all been rebuilt and in some ways the country was stronger for it. That had really been the war of Independence from the British. After that, the nation had a navy and was becoming a force in the world. The westward expansion was continuing and the nation was beginning to prosper. There were clouds on the horizon, which would sooner or later be the cause of conflict. Slavery was still a way of life in the south and many in the north didn't like it.

His old and dear friend Thomas Jefferson had tried to abolish it when he had penned the Declaration of Independence. He had been forced to remove that clause when all the southern colonies had objected. *He tried to warn us*, Madison thought. His thoughts began to wander to the committee and his, and he knew Jefferson's private thoughts if they were just in what they were doing. Their intentions were noble and their purpose was honorable; would it always be so to the ones to whom the places on the Committee would pass? That question had nagged him almost from the beginning.

His quiet reverie was then broken by the sound of a horse galloping up the road leading to the house. His gaze was drawn to it in the late afternoon sun. It was a servant belonging not to him, but his friend Thomas Jefferson. Ezekiel slowed the horse to a walk as he approached the home of James Madison. He dismounted, and with his head hanging down and a look of anguish on his aging face, he slowly walked up the steps and made his way to Madison.

James Madison almost immediately sensed what he knew Ezekiel had come to tell him. With tears streaming down his face, Ezekiel looked him in the eye, and he knew Thomas Jefferson had left this world. *He had picked the perfect day*, Madison thought. Fifty years to the day the nation was founded by his penning of the Declaration of Independence. The committee would need another member.

Montpelier
Madison's Estate, Virginia
January 1, 1832

James Madison was lost in his own thoughts. It was becoming harder for him to concentrate on the papers before him. His mind wandered from what he was trying to write. Shaking his head trying to refocus on the papers before him, he almost subconsciously began to write. Over the last several years he had been going over all of the letters, documents, and writings he had kept from his years of serving his country. He was adding notes to the edges of the letters and even rewriting some of his earlier papers. His mind drifted in and out of the present and to those times past he preferred to think about. At times, his mind was as clear and sharp as it had ever been; others, it was as if he was reliving the past. He continued his writing hardly aware of what he was putting on the paper before him.

Dolly Madison walked up the steps and down the hall toward the bedchamber of her aged husband. For much of the last year he had hardly been able to do more than get out of bed. He had begun to regain much of his strength in the last month she thought. She opened the door to his bedchamber and looked in to see him sitting at the small desk she had the servants move in for his use. What he wanted to do, she thought, was go over all of his old papers and write. It seemed to make him happy. That was worth it she thought. She walked up behind him and rested her hands on his shoulders. He took several moments to acknowledge her presence.

Smiling at him, she asked, "How are you feeling? You seem tired."

"No," he responded, "I feel fine. I am just finishing a letter to Thomas."

Dolly knew that Thomas was his lifelong friend Thomas Jefferson; he had passed away almost six years before. She knew James was aware of this. Yet even now, he still chose to write him letters as if he were still alive. She supposed there were things in his mind that he felt only Thomas would understand. She helped him out of the chair and watched him walk to the bed and lay down. She then went to the small desk and scooped up the papers he had been working on and, without really looking at them, put them in the lower drawer with all the rest. Closing the drawer, she took another look at her now sleeping husband and left the room closing the door behind her.

Montpelier
The Madison Estate
June 28, 1836

The house was strangely quiet. Dolly Madison sat in the chair by the bedside of her husband. Looking down at him, she saw the life leave his eyes. *He is at peace*, she thought. *He is now with all of the others.* Her thoughts began to replay all they had been through together. She had met him when he was in Philadelphia serving in the House of Representatives. She had been a widow, considerably younger than he was. He had been a confirmed bachelor until they met, and the whirlwind romance that followed put an end to that status. When he retired from politics to Montpelier, they envisioned living there quietly. Then Thomas Jefferson became president in 1800. He asked his lifelong friend to become his secretary of state. They were close friends with Jefferson whose wife had died in 1782. She had often helped in the White House, filling the role a first lady normally would. He had succeeded Jefferson as the fourth president of the United States, and she had become the first lady in her own right. That had been almost a quarter of a century ago.

Her gaze not leaving the face of her husband, Dolly Madison wondered what the future would hold. She knew much more of the business of her husband she thought, than most wives would. They truly had been partners in more than just their marriage. She knew of his role on the Committee and who the other founders were. The last few years, as his health and his mind had begun to fail him, The Committee had continued on with their business and out of respect had still treated him with deference. She was also aware the Committee had no idea how much of their business she knew. She would tell no one. *Some secrets*, she thought, *should stay just that*. With the passing of James Madison, the Founders Committee was now only the Committee. He had been the last of the founders.

Dolly Madison's Residence
Washington DC
September 3, 1842

    Dolly Madison heard the quiet knock on her door. She slowly made her way to door of the small cottage in which she was living. Since James had died six years before, life had been anything but easy. Like most of the other presidents, he had left office far poorer than when he entered it. Montpelier was heavily mortgaged and her son, Payne, from her first marriage had not managed it well. James had kept most of his papers from his two terms as president in hopes of leaving them for her to sell. That had not worked out as yet. There was still hope Congress would act to buy them. It would not be in time to save Montpelier.
    She opened the door and greeted the gentleman who was standing there. Levi Wilkinson stepped into the small room and cordially greeted the former first lady.
    "Good day to you, Mrs. Madison."
    "Good day to you as well, Mr. Wilkinson. Please come in and have a seat." She then turned and slowly made her way to the worn chair in the small room and sat down.
    Levi Wilkinson followed her into the small room and sat down on another equally worn armchair. Placing the small case he carried with him on the small table between the chairs, he then opened it and took a document from it.
    "I have brought you the documents. All it requires to be executed is your signature." He then handed her the document he had removed from the case.
    Taking the document from him, she realized that with her signature the last connection she had to the happy life she had with James Madison would belong to someone else. Montpelier and all that went

with it, even the furniture, would no longer belong to her or any other named Madison. She hadn't even been there in five years. All she could hope was that when she left this world, she would be laid to rest with him in the small cemetery at Montpelier. She had asked that to be put in the document she was about to sign.

She had forgotten the small desk James Madison had used and the papers it contained in the lower drawer.

The Committee
New York City
May 23, 1860

Cornelius Vanderbilt, the current chairman of the Committee, had just adjourned the meeting. He stood looking out the window of his office to the street below. *So many things to decide*, he thought. Could this nation withstand what he feared was coming? The politics of slavery was tearing the nation apart. The south refused to let go of the institution, not only because of the feared economic impact, but also they counted their slaves as population for the purpose of electoral votes. The Missouri compromise had only held off the inevitable. The storm clouds were on the horizon, and he feared there was no stopping it. The democrats could not agree on a candidate for the coming presidential election. The debates between Lincoln and Douglas in 1858 had seen Douglas elected senator by the state legislature but left Lincoln with national prominence. The committee had decided Lincoln was the best option to be president. It was likely to be the spark that ignited the country into a state of civil war.

Early on, the original founders had been trying to keep the young nation from falling apart. *History really does repeat itself,* Vanderbilt thought. The committee had evolved over the years from the patriots turned politicians into the present incarnation. The current committee was made up of the captains and kings of industry. They were determined to see the United States become an economic engine the likes of which the world had never seen. *The sad part*, Vanderbilt thought, *is the war that is going to be fought to put the blight of slavery behind.* It had the potential to destroy the nation. They had the power to put presidents in office, he thought, but not enough to stop a senseless war.

Ford's Theatre
Washington DC
April 14, 1865

John Parker stood up and stretched his legs. The chair in which he had been sitting outside the door to the presidential box was uncomfortable. He decided to step outside for a quick breath of fresh air. Nothing was happening, and the play was still going on. He stepped through the door to the alley behind the theatre. Outside was Lincoln's coachman, Timothy Sullivan.

Sullivan greeted Parker, "Johnnie me boy, what say we go get us a pint?"

Parker hesitated only briefly. "Sure, why not." The two walked around the corner to the tavern stepped inside and left the president unguarded.

John Wilkes Booth unobtrusively made his way down the corridor toward the door to the president's box. He was going to try and bluff his way past the guard; if need be, he was prepared to deal with him in a more lethal manner. Surprising him, he found the door unguarded. Reaching in his pocket he slipped a knife and a small derringer from the pocket. Placing the knife in the small scabbard strapped to his left wrist, he then held the pistol in his right hand. Placing his left hand on the knob to the door of the president's box, he paused slightly and took a deep breath.

Opening the door and stepping forward into the box, he quickly placed the pistol to the back of Lincoln's head and fired. Major Rathbone turned as Mary Todd Lincoln screamed. Major Rathbone jumped from his chair toward Booth as he grabbed the knife from the scabbard and slashed, striking the major in the upper arm. Rathbone staggered backward as Booth tried to step past him. Rathbone lunged, grabbing toward Booth as he stepped up onto the railing of the balcony and leapt to the stage. His spur caught the bunting draped over the railing, causing him to land awkwardly. He felt the bone in his left leg just above the ankle snap as he landed. He jumped up and quickly hobbled toward the exit of the stage.

Unaware he was not part of the play, the audience gasped as he jumped up and hobbled off. Ever the actor, Booth acknowledged the audience as he made his way offstage.

Lincoln was carried across the street to the Peterson boarding house by Dr. Charles Leale, a young army surgeon, two other doctors, and several soldiers who were all attending the play. He would barely make it to the next day. At 7:22 the next morning, the nation would need another president, and the Committee suddenly had business that they deemed urgent.

The Committee
New York City
May 25, 1865

Cornelius Vanderbilt called the meeting to order. "Gentlemen, we have several things to deal with. The assassination of the president is only the beginning of the problems. Andrew Johnson is not going to be able to take this nation forward in the manner in which Lincoln would have. He is a Southerner and is a man without a state. If he plans to handle the reconstruction as Lincoln had planned, Congress will fight him. They want retribution and will demand it. This is going to cause problems to our plans. We are going to have to make adjustments. Who would like to begin?"

Ezra Banks spoke first. He owned several manufacturing companies and had prospered selling war goods to the union army.

"Gentlemen, all of us in this room have prospered from this unholy conflict. It is time we began to pay back this nation. I have given this a good deal of thought. To this point, this committee has only seen to it that a strong president has been put in office. We have found ourselves without a strong president because of the actions of a group of madmen. We have to go further. If we had seen to it that we had who we wanted as vice president, we would not be in this position. We have to be more thorough in our planning."

Hamilton Reece looked over to Ezra Banks; Reece was president of the State Bank of New York and one of the most powerful men in the eastern United States. "Let me understand what you are suggesting and, I think, take it a step further. If we had controlled the process to see to it the vice president was who we wanted, we would not be in this situation. Gentlemen, what if we not only selected the vice president, let's think what would happen if we began to think of who those candidates would be ten years beforehand."

Vanderbilt turned to Reece and asked, "Are you suggesting we find candidates and groom them ten years ahead of time?"

Reece's reply brought a stunned silence to the room. "That is exactly what I am suggesting. We would not find ourselves in the situation we are currently in. Gentlemen, we plan what our companies will do with a five-year plan. The business of a nation is no different. We put a ten-year plan in place and select candidates with an eye to the future."

James D. Lockwood looked across the table to Reece. "Let us speculate for a moment that we begin to implement your suggestion. I think it will take longer than ten years. We will have to find these men and groom them. Very few will become prominent enough in that amount of time to become elected. Gentlemen, if we choose to do this, it must be done in secret. The candidate cannot even know what we are doing. If any were ever to find out what we are doing even now, the country would be up in arms."

Cornelius Vanderbilt held up his hand to stop the debate. "I am going to remind everyone in this room exactly how this committee began."

Vanderbilt paused to gather his thoughts, looking into a past only he could see. He was the senior member of the Committee. All the rest here, he thought, were younger than he by at least ten years. The original founders were all passed by 1836. The first replacement was selected at the time of Washington's death in 1799. He had been the first chairman. Jefferson had succeeded him as chairman, and Madison had followed Jefferson. There had been two others between then and now. He had been chairman almost ten years. The other men in this room had been selected, one at a time, as the Committee had vacancies created by a member's death. When the chairman passed, the remaining nine members cast votes to select a chairman from among one of their own. That was always done before the next member was selected. Potential members of the Committee were quietly screened for years, to find out if they were in agreement with the ideals of the Committee. All were sworn to secrecy upon selection and acceptance. There had never been a breach of that trust. As he contemplated what they were now considering, he realized secrecy was paramount.

Vanderbilt began, "The original purpose came about in the years it took for the Constitution to become ratified. There was much discord in the nation. Ben Franklin shared his fears with General Washington at the time of the constitutional convention. It was decided to protect this nation even from its own citizenry. The need for a strong president was recognized. Remember, gentlemen, these men were patriots. They set about to protect this nation. Look what we have just been through. This nation was almost fractured, and I suspect the healing this nation must go through will take generations. If we do what we are contemplating, what will the ramifications be? Dare we be so bold?"

There was a lingering silence in the room. The ten members of the Committee all began to contemplate what Reece was suggesting. One at a time they all began to realize they had the power to make his suggestion become a reality.

The State House
Trenton, New Jersey
January 19, 1982


Edwin Cain stepped down from the podium to the applause of the crowd. He had just finished giving his inaugural speech. He was now governor of New Jersey. Three years on the campaign trail had paid off. Jeff Stillman was beaming; they had pulled it off. Edwin shook hands with everyone around him. They all wanted a moment with the new governor. He looked around to find Marjorie. She was standing just a couple of feet away from him, Catherine by her side; they were engaged in conversation with Jeff Stillman and his wife. Ed quickly moved next to Marjorie, putting his arm around her while still shaking hands with those around him. She smiled looking up at him; he slowly began to make their way to the exit of the stage.

Ben Cain was watching his father give his speech on the television set in the commons area of his frat house. He had returned to Harvard from Christmas break just the previous week. The newscast was replaying the clip for the tenth time. Everywhere he had been on campus that day it seemed everyone knew who his father was. He had opted to stay here rather than go to Trenton to be a part of it. He wasn't really sure what he was feeling. In one sense he was proud of his father, in others, they had trouble getting along. It had been worse in high school; now that he was at college and his father had spent endless hours campaigning, they had reached sort of a truce. His father did not approve of his girlfriend. They had argued about it since high school. It may not matter anymore, Ben thought; Valerie had broken up with him at Christmas. Ben really didn't know why. All she had told him was not to call her anymore. When he had tried to call her, the phone had been disconnected.

The Newark Mall
Newark, New Jersey
October 1, 1981

Valerie Hollis punched the time clock in the back room of the department store where she worked at the mall. She then walked out of the store and made her way to the exit of the mall.

The man sitting in the car with the binoculars watched Valerie Hollis leave the mall and start walking to the bus stop as she did every day. He knew where she was going. He had been watching her for the better part of two weeks. He was going to have a talk with her; he hoped that was all it would have to be.

Valerie boarded the bus for the short ride back to her small apartment. Life had been a struggle for her most of her life. Her parents had been divorced for the last ten years, and her father was an alcoholic. Her mother had passed away from cancer last year. The only bright spot in her life had been the scholarship that Westminster school had offered. The private academy was well funded by its wealthy families and the endowments. As part of its charter, the elite academy offered several scholarships to children who otherwise would have no means to attend the school. She had earned one by her academics in junior high by and catching the eye of a former alumnus where her mother had worked. That was the only reason she had attended there. It was also where she had met Ben Cain. They had begun to date in their junior year. He had moved on to Harvard after graduation, and she had to find a job. They still saw each other every time he came home from school. She was afraid they were not going to make it.

They came from different worlds. He had a wealthy family, and his father did not care much for her; she supposed in his eyes she wasn't good enough for his son. She knew Ben loved her as much as she did him. That wasn't the problem. The problem she thought was he didn't really understand what it was to be poor. Valerie exited the bus at her stop and started to walk down the block to her apartment.

The man walked beside Valerie and began to match her pace. He looked over at her and said, "Valerie, I need just a moment of your time. Can I buy you a cup of coffee?"

Startled, Valerie stopped in her tracks and asked, "Who are you, and why do you want to buy me coffee?" She started to step away from the stranger.

He smiled disarmingly at her and replied, "I am a friend of Ben's in a manner of speaking. That's what I want to talk to you about."

Her first reaction was fear and then fright that something had happened to Ben. "Is Ben okay? Has something happened to Ben? Is he all right?"

The man replied, smiling, "Ben is all right. I just want to talk to you about his future." He smiled at her again. He had learned early on in this business to smile. People trusted him more when he smiled. He pointed to the small café in the middle of the block and said, "Why don't we go in there and grab that coffee? I'll even buy you dinner if you like."

Valerie felt relief at going in the café. She knew the owners there and often bought a cup of coffee on her way to work. The man held the door for her as they entered and led her to a quiet booth in the corner.

The waitress walked up and said, "Hi, Val, what can I get for you?"

She hesitated slightly, and the man smiled and ordered coffee for both of them. As the waitress left to get the coffee, he looked at Valerie and said, "I told you I will buy. Why don't you go ahead and order dinner?" He knew much more about her, he thought, than she would ever guess. He knew that about this time in the week her money had just about run out, and she often didn't have enough for groceries. This probably won't be difficult, he thought.

The waitress returned with the coffee, and Valerie gave in and ordered a sandwich and fries. When she left, the man began the conversation he had come here to have with her.

"Valerie, I know all about you—your alcoholic father, the divorce, and even your mother passing with cancer last year. I also know about you and Ben."

She looked at him and realized she didn't even get his name. "Who are you, and what is your name? You haven't even told me that."

"Steve," he replied. "You can call me Steve," he said, smiling at her again.

"Okay, Steve, what is it you really want? So far, you haven't told me anything."

*Right down to business*, he thought. He was beginning to like her. This one could take care of herself. That was probably why they wanted her away from Ben Cain. He never questioned his orders. His job was just to get it done.

"Okay, Valerie, let's put our cards on the table. You have been dating Ben since high school. I'm kind of surprised you two have lasted this long. He is going to have a future. Unfortunately, you will not be able to help him with that future. You come from a different world than he does. Do you want to be the reason his future is limited?"

Stunned and surprised and growing angry, she asked, "Did his father put you up to this?" She started to get up. The man reached across the table and grabbed her arm. Surprising her with the iron grip, she sat back down.

The smile that had vanished from his face just as quickly returned. He then looked at her and said, "No, his father does not know I am here. I am prepared to offer you compensation for your cooperation.

# THE COMMITTEE

What I want you to do is break up with him and go your own separate way. You will be well taken care of."

She looked at the man and realized there was more to this than he was telling her. His eyes told her she had no options. He then explained to her just exactly what was going to happen. She wondered how she was going to like Florida; she had always wanted to live there.

The man got back in his car and drove away. *It is always easier if they were cooperative*, he thought.

The Committee
New York, New York
January 26, 1877

The meeting was called to order. The first order of business was the selection of a new chairman. Cornelius Vanderbilt had passed away the eighth of January. Hamilton Reece was selected to be the next chairman. With the first order of business out of the way, the new chairman brought up the next item on the agenda. The committee needed another member. This business usually took quite a while; they were always aware of the need for like-minded men. The decision on new members was always carefully done. Each member had to approve, and the approach to the prospect even more carefully done. They usually had business dealings with them for years before the selection. While they were sounded out for their beliefs, they were also very quietly investigated. The committee took no chances. After a selection was agreed upon, the prospective member was carefully approached. They were never told everything until well after their agreement. So far the selection process had been flawless. The decision was made. The approach was made. Another agreement reached. Men of this stature were used to power. This was the pinnacle of power.

Hamilton Reece had another item on the agenda. "Gentlemen, with the selection of our new member out of the way, I have another topic I wish to discuss. We have begun to see the initial crop of candidate selections begin to enter the point at which we must begin to manage their careers. As this phase begins, they must not know they have powerful friends. We must think also of how we deal with one another. I propose that in this room we no longer refer to each other by name. We should select code names for ourselves when meeting as a committee. Then, when we conduct any business outside of here, the two worlds are kept separate. We must increase our security further."

The other members of the Committee were soon convinced of the wisdom of his suggestion. Each member of the Committee was taking an active interest in managing the careers of the candidates. It was agreed they would divide the responsibility for the candidates; each of them would need help outside the Committee; there could be no link to the others. The committee was going further underground as the power they were preparing to wield was going to dramatically increase.

Harvard University
The Student Center
Cambridge, Massachusetts
February 14, 1982

Ben Cain shoved his hands deeper into the pockets of his jacket and trudged through the snow toward the student center. *Valentine's day*, he thought, *and here I am alone. Val, where in the hell is she?* he thought. He reached the door of the student center and pulled his hand out of his pocket and pulled open the door. Stepping inside, he looked around and realized the place was almost deserted. *Figures*, he thought, *everybody else is out with their girlfriend*. He walked past the deserted tables and stepped over to the bank of pay phones along the wall. Digging coins out of his pocket, he fed them to the phone and dialed Val's number for the umpteenth time since Christmas. Once again he heard the recording telling him the number he called was no longer in service. He slammed the phone into its cradle and started to walk away; and then he stopped, turned back to the phone again, and fed it the coins. He couldn't remember the damn number. He dialed 411 and waited for the operator to answer.

"Information. How may I help you?"

"JC Penny's Department store in Newark, New Jersey, please."

"Hold for the number." Ben heard and then wrote the number down on his hand because he didn't have anything else to write it on.

He fed more coins to the phone and dialed the number he had written on his hand.

"JC Penny, how may I direct your call?"

"Valerie Hollis please."

"Do you know which department, air?"

Ben paused to think and then said, "Ladies wear."

"I will transfer your call. Please hold."

Ben waited and then heard the phone ring. It was picked up on the eighth ring. "Ladies Fashions. This is Tiffany. How may I help you?"

Ben heard himself say, "Valerie Hollis please."

"I'm sorry, sir, she isn't in this department. May I be of service?"

"Tiffany, this is Ben Cain, Valerie's boyfriend. I think we met once when I picked her up for lunch. Do you know where she is? Did she transfer?"

"I'm sorry, Ben. Valerie doesn't work here anymore."

"Do you know where I can find her? Did she change jobs?"

"Ben, I'm sorry. I don't know where she went. I haven't seen her since she left. I don't think anyone around here has."

"Is there anyone there who might know? I can't find her anywhere."

"Ben, I probably shouldn't tell you this, but I haven't been able to find her either. Sorry, Ben, I gotta go. My supervisor is coming. Bye." Then he heard the dial tone. He slammed the phone back into the cradle closed his eyes and tried not to cry.

"Damn it, where are you? Why can't I find you? Where did you go?" He turned his back to the wall, leaned against it, closed his eyes, and slid down the wall to sit on the floor.

The Arlington Arms Apartments
Newark, New Jersey
February 20, 1982

Ben had left Cambridge early in the morning, driving his three-year-old Camaro that had been his high school graduation present. He had only stopped for gas. He was going to find Valerie. He pulled his car in front of the apartment building, put it in park, and got out. He crossed the sidewalk and walked up to the building. Stepping into the small rundown lobby of the building, he took the stairs to the third floor. He walked down the corridor to apartment 312. He knocked on the door. He waited a few moments and knocked louder on the door. No one answered the door. He walked to the apartment next door and knocked on the door. He could hear the knob turning and the door opened until the chain stopped it.

Evelyn Hayes opened the door, looked out to see who it was, and recognized Ben; she closed the door enough to unlatch the chain and reopened the door.

Ben, introducing himself, spoke, "Hi, I'm Ben Cain, Valerie's boyfriend. I wanted to ask if you know where she is. I haven't been able to get in touch with her, and she didn't answer her door."

"I think she moved. She hasn't been here since Christmas or so."

Ben, visibly deflated, asked, "Do you know where she moved to? I'm trying to find her."

"I don't know where she is. She never told me anything. As far as I know, nobody has seen her."

"Did she tell you anything? Did she talk to anyone that you know of? She quit her job at the mall, and no one there could tell me anything."

"Ben, I'm sorry. I just don't know anything. One day she was there and gone the next. The movers were here and—"

Interrupting her, Ben said, "Movers? How in the hell—" He stopped himself from saying, "could she afford movers."

"I'm sorry. I didn't mean to say that. Forgive me."

Evelyn looked at the obviously heartbroken young man and smiled sadly at him. "I'm truly sorry, Ben. I just don't know anything to tell you."

Not what he wanted to hear, Ben thanked her and turned away from the empty apartment and walked to his car. He unlocked it, sat down in the driver's seat, rested his head on the steering wheel, and cried.

# THE COMMITTEE

The Committee
The Waldorf-Astoria Hotel
New York, New York
May 12, 1899

John Jacob Astor IV exited the elevator at the penthouse level of his hotel. It was literally his hotel. He had had it built. He walked down the finely decorated corridor and entered the penthouse suite. Most of the other members were already inside. They were awaiting the arrival of the chairman.

John Pierpont Morgan was the current chairman of the Committee; he had been elected to the chairmanship the previous year. He stepped out of the elevator and walked down the same corridor Astor had walked down ten minutes before. He was the last to arrive. As had been traditional for the last twenty years or so, the chairman was also known as diamond. The other members of the Committee chose the names by which they would be known. Prior to him ascending to the chairmanship, he had been known as Greenback.

Diamond called the meeting to order. As was customary, they began the meeting with the most urgent of topics and moved to the next highest priority and so on and finished with the discussion of the candidates in the pipeline. They had turned the United States into a financial empire. The current makeup of the Committee was predominately businessmen and bankers. They had begun to pass their power down almost like an inheritance. In the case of some, such as John Astor, it had been his grandfather who had passed it to him. Two or three others had been selected the same way. They were the best and brightest and the most prominent the nation had developed. The current first item on the agenda was the Senate.

"Gentlemen," Diamond began, "I would like to start with the subject of the Senate. It has been proposed we begin to place candidates in that body. The senators are appointed by the state legislatures. That will make it much more difficult. Does anyone have any thoughts on how we begin that?"

Timber, as he was known to the Committee, due to his heavy investment in that industry, began, "We have to gain influence with the legislatures. Then we could get our candidates appointed. We could start getting some of our candidates elected to the state legislatures."

Builder, who had made his fortune building bridges and skyscrapers that were beginning to dominate the skyline of New York, motioned to the chairman. With his nod to take the floor, he offered, "Let's think about that for a moment. We have begun to place our candidates in Congress by controlling the general campaign. We educate them, prepare them for office, and get them elected. We see they have enough money to win against any opponent in a general election. I propose that we think about getting the senators directly elected by the same electorate we use to get the Congress elected."

Anthracite motioned to the chairman to take the floor. Receiving his nod, he began, "That will take a constitutional amendment, which could take some time. Thinking about it, that may be easier than working the legislatures. We have no fixed time table on anything. Let me make a proposal. Let us suppose we can make that happen. The large cities in this country have most of the voters. If we concentrated our efforts there, it would have the most impact."

Diamond paused to take it all in. He had just had a staggering thought. "I have a thought I would like you to think about. What if we use the public education of the population to gradually bring them to our way of thinking? It would make it much easier to get the votes we need to get our candidates elected. We could start that and work to get the amendment to the Constitution done at the same time."

Trader, who was a major investment banker on Wall Street, motioned to Diamond for the floor. He began, "That would simplify the entire process. Think of the possibilities it would make the electorate much more predictable as well as creating the same mind-set within the candidates."

The committee continued on, and a new strategy was developed. The process to amend the constitution was started. After all, they could get the president to support the initiative.

# THE COMMITTEE

Harvard University
Cambridge, Massachusetts
February 21, 1982

Ben Cain parked his red Camaro in the small lot behind the frat house in which he lived. He had spent the night at home in Newark. Fortunately for him, his parents were in Trenton at the governor's mansion. He really hadn't wanted to see them after his search for Valerie had ended in such a frustrating way. He knew his father had never really approved of his relationship with her. His mother would go along with him while trying to keep peace between them. He really didn't understand why she had not only dumped him but left so suddenly. *What a Christmas present*, he thought. He had exhausted every place he could think of and talked to everyone who might know anything. He had found nothing; it was as if she just vanished. With no options left after spending the night at home, he had come back to school; it was better than being home.

He got out of his car and went to his room in the frat house. His buddy John Livingston had seen him come in and followed him to his room, extending a bottle of beer to him. He said, "Wow, you look down. Take this. You look like you could use it."

Ben took the beer from him, twisted the top, took a long pull, and said, "Thanks."

"What's the matter? You look like hell."

"I can't find her. I tried. Nobody knows where she went. She just disappeared. What did I do to make her leave?"

"Man, you didn't do anything. Women are strange. Don't worry, she'll be back."

"I don't think so. Her apartment is empty. The neighbor said there were movers. Man, she didn't have enough money for that. Her father is a drunk, and her mother died last year. She worked at J C Penny for god's sake. She didn't even have a car. Something is wrong."

"Come on. Let's get out of here. Let's go do something to take your mind off her."

Ben got up, drained the beer, tossed the bottle in the trash, and left with his friend trying to put her out of his mind. He somehow knew he would never see her again.

Harvard University
Cambridge, Massachusetts
May 28, 1982

The frat house was starting to empty out. Everyone was going home for the summer. Ben sat down on the bed and wondered what he was going home to. His dad was now governor of New Jersey; he was living in Trenton in the governor's mansion. Valerie was gone; he really didn't want to go to Newark, which would constantly make him think of her. He had applied for an internship to work in Washington for the summer. He hoped that would come through. Maybe it would take his mind off things for a while. He finally forced her from his mind, grabbed the last of his luggage, and made himself get up and go to his car. He tossed the luggage in the backseat, got in, and drove away. He was going to go home and hope the letter telling him he had been accepted for the internship would be waiting for him. What he didn't know was he had been encouraged to apply by someone who knew he would be accepted; The Committee was at work.

Washington DC
The Senate office building
June 23, 1982

Senator Daniel Patrick Moynihan walked through the door of his office. He was busy; this was an election year, and he was up for reelection. The new intern Ben Cain was the only one in the office. As late as it was, he was surprised anyone was still in the office; it was after ten, and the Senate had just adjourned for the night.

He looked at the young man and asked, "What are you still doing here? It's late. I thought everyone would have gone by now."

Ben looked up from the document he had been reading, realized who it was, stood up, and said, "No, sir. I just wanted to finish reading this." He held up the proposed legislation he had been asked to review.

The senator smiled at the young man and asked, "So what have you learned about Washington so far other than the newest intern gets stuck with reading all the boring stuff?"

Ben smiled at the senator and replied, "Well, sir, I have only been here a couple of weeks. I haven't had time to do much. I have learned though who gets to answer the phone."

Moynihan laughed, looked at the young man, and said, "Why don't you put that away for the night and come with me? I haven't had dinner yet, and I suspect you haven't either."

Surprised at the invitation, Ben hesitated. "Well, sir, I wouldn't want to impose. I know you have more important things do."

"Nonsense. You have to eat, and I like to get to know everyone who works in the office. Besides, I'm sure you vote, and I like to know what people think. You haven't been here long enough to tell me what everyone thinks I want to hear like everyone else around here does. Come on, let's go."

Ben stood up, put the papers in the drawer, and said, "Yes, sir." He followed the senator out the door.

Moynihan had been asked to not only look after the young man but to groom him as well. He had been told there were plans for him.

Washington DC.
The Mall
July 4, 1982

The town was shut down for the holiday. Ben had been invited to go to the party at the house of the chief of staff to the senator. It had been a cookout with all of the traditional festivities for the Fourth of July celebration. He had been surprised at the invitation; none of the other interns had been invited. It almost seemed he was the center of attention; he was having a hard time believing it was because his father was a governor. He had been introduced to some very important people. The most interesting person he had met was the gorgeous, dark-haired beauty sitting beside him on the blanket watching the fireworks. She was holding his hand and seemed to be enjoying his company. He had been introduced to her by the chief of staff himself. Her name was Marilyn Ellsworth, and he was going to try to see more of her. They had left the party and strolled around the town and taken in the sights. Now they were sitting here on the blanket watching the fireworks, and he couldn't keep his eyes off her. He planned to spend as much time with her as he could. For the first time since Christmas, his mind was on something other than Valerie.

The *Titanic*
North Atlantic Ocean
1:45 AM
April 15, 1912

John Jacob Astor stood on the deck of the *Titanic*. The list of the ship was increasing; noises made by metal under stress were coming from the ship. He watched the lifeboat with his pregnant wife, Madeleine, and her nurse being lowered from the Titanic. The young Officer Lightoller had refused to allow anyone else to accompany them. He watched the half-filled boat slowly move away from the *Titanic* and saw his young wife looking back at him. He turned and his valet, Victor Robbins, was standing behind him. They both stepped away from the rail and proceeded to move upward on the deck with the ever-increasing list. He knew the ship was going to sink, and they were not going to make it off. There were not enough lifeboats for all of those onboard.

Astor felt the ship groan beneath his feet. He lit another cigar and waited. There was nothing else he could do. As with most men when they are facing the end of their life and have time to think about it, he began to question his life. *There is much to be proud of*, he thought. He then turned his thoughts to the committee. He began to question the role the committee was playing. What gave us the right to control so much? If the American people knew how they were being manipulated, there would be another revolution. He knew what had started so nobly had spawned the corruption of the founder's greatest fears. *In the end*, he thought, *it mattered not at all. We all have the same fate.*

# THE COMMITTEE

Several minutes later, the great ship began shifting, the stern rising higher, the tortured metal screeching terribly. Titanic tore apart and began her final plunge, taking with her more than fifteen hundred souls.

John Jacob Astor's body was recovered eight days later. He was identified by the initials sewn into the back of his jacket and the pocket watch he had carried. The committee would need another member.

The Committee
Jekyll Island, Georgia
The Millionaire's Club
May 16, 1912

J. P. Morgan, also known as Diamond, decided to hold the meeting here at the Millionaire's Club on Jekyll Island. They had built the private resort over the last thirty years. And most of the committee members had invested and built cottages along with the main clubhouse. They usually wintered there. It was private and exclusive, and they controlled it. They had decided to use it rather than meeting in New York on many occasions. They were regulars here, and their arrivals were not given a second glance by anyone. The committee had business to discuss.

Diamond brought the meeting to order. "Gentlemen, things are moving forward with the process to amend the Constitution. We may have to wait until next year to get the bill introduced. However, the movement is gaining momentum. I believe we are on target with this. Another item we have to discuss is the banking system. We have begun inroads into convincing the members of Congress that a strong central banking system is needed. I need not explain why this is advantageous to us. Also there is the need to discuss a new member as we have lost one of our own. Who would like to begin?"

Builder motioned to the chairman. Given the nod by Diamond, he began, "I have been reassured the bill to amend the Constitution is gaining strength. Each of us has been working quietly with our members of Congress to see that it is moving forward. We also have been working on the banking system as well. I think we will be successful.

Remember we created and then dealt with the last two financial crises. They have come to realize a strong central bank is necessary."

The meeting continued until all of the items on the agenda were dealt with. The last item was the selection of a new member for the committee. An agreement was reached, the approach was made, and the Committee continued their quest to control the government of the United States.

The Committee
New York, New York
May 25, 1913

The committee members were all seated in the boardroom maintained by John D. Rockefeller in New York. The retired chairman of Standard Oil had been on the committee for some time. It had been a toss-up who was going to be chairman between him and J. P. Morgan the last time the committee had selected a chairman. He had been retired for some time now but was still considered a major power. He was probably the richest single individual in the world. He had been more interested in philanthropic projects than power and had deferred to Morgan the chairmanship of the Committee. With Morgan's death little more than a month before and Astor's death on the *Titanic* in 1912, the other members of the committee felt he should become the next chairman. He had reluctantly agreed. Europe was becoming enflamed, and there was fear war would erupt.

Woodrow Wilson had been elected president, the seventeenth amendment would become law before the year was out, and they had already succeeded in getting the sixteenth amendment ratified. The Committee had been busy. They were still working on the central bank issue but felt success was close. The most pressing issue the Committee faced was a new member.

"Gentlemen," began the new chairman, "as we all know, there are currently many issues before us, the most pressing of which is another selection for this committee. As we all know, we have one member who has never before been part of a selection of a new member. I will therefore explain how it works. The need for replacement members is always an issue with which we must deal. Every one of us takes an active role in finding influential like-minded men. They are quietly investigated to be absolutely sure of their political leanings, business dealings, and to determine their suitability for consideration. We then foster business deals with them, and we quietly open discussions with them to determine their true feelings on certain issues. When it is determined an individual is suited for membership on this committee, they are not approached until there is a need for a replacement. We always maintain a list of five or six possible members. At this time, I am going to circulate a list of those possible choices. We each get one vote. We must all be in complete agreement. First of all, does anyone disagree with any of our candidates?" There were no objections.

"Good, at this point, let the vote begin. If everyone will place a check mark beside the name of their choice and fold the paper and pass them to me." The papers were then handed to Diamond; he opened them one by one and smiled. "Gentlemen, it appears as though Henry Ford is a unanimous decision. Is there any objection?" Once again there were none. "The approach will be made. Now let's move on to other business. Trader, would you care to give us an update on the banking issue?"

Trader took the floor. "Gentlemen, we should have the vote in Congress on the central bank by this fall. I am expecting approval without too many problems. Once that is done, we can slowly begin to control the money supply. We can then continue on with increasing our tax structure now that an income tax is also in place. This will further our control of the monetary supply and management of the banking industry. With our increased political influence, controlling the nation's budget process should be managed within a few years."

Builder motioned to the chairman; given the floor, he spoke next, "Now that we have succeeded in getting the Seventeenth Amendment ratified, how long will it take to begin to get our candidates in the Senate?"

Diamond directed the question to Printer. Printer had been on the committee since Timber had passed in 1907. He owned several newspapers and was instrumental in pushing the Seventeenth Amendment with editorials in his newspapers.

Printer replied, "We believe the elections will be staggered. Starting next year, one-third of the Senate will be up for election every two years. The terms are six years, so it will take time. Also we will have to increase the candidate pipeline. We do not have enough to handle both right now. Also, the elections will be statewide, not just in the larger cities. This is going to take some time. Let's be patient."

The meeting continued, plans were implemented, and the business of the committee continued as it had for the last decade. The war to end all wars was just about to break out in Europe, and the world would never be the same

Montpelier
The DuPont Estate
November 1, 1984

Jason Edison began his tour of Montpelier, the James Madison estate. For most of the twentieth century, it had been owned by the DuPont family. Marion DuPont Scott, the last DuPont to own and live there, had died the previous year. She had died childless, and the estate would have gone to her brother, according to her father's will. He had died in 1965. She had bequeathed ten million dollars to the trust for National Historic Preservation to buy and maintain the estate. Her brother's five children inherited Montpelier. The legal battles were finally over. Three of the five had agreed to sell before the lawsuit to break the trust. The remaining two had lost the last legal battle, and the trust had finally bought their interests.

Edison walked through the mansion and began his initial tour. He had been hired to manage what was going to be a national historic landmark. He was also going to oversee the restoration process to turn it back into the way it was when James Madison had lived there. *There is much to do he*, thought. The original home had only been half the size it was now. When Madison had lived there, it was only twenty-two rooms. Since then, it had grown to fifty-five and had a stucco exterior over the original brick. The plan to restore it was going to take a lot of time and money. He wasn't even sure when there would be enough money to begin. For now he realized, I have to find out what is here and from what time period it had come from. Too few of the original furnishings had been saved and stored in various parts of the estate. He wished those who had owned the estate early after Madison had realized the history and saved most of the furnishings. He was almost overwhelmed with just the job to document and catalogue everything.

He opened the door to the attic storage room and walked in. Looking around, he saw several pieces of what he guessed were some of the furniture belonging to the Madison's. Greatly relieved to find out the attic storage had been well maintained, he ran his hands over a bentwood rocking chair and wondered if the president had ever used it. *No way of knowing*, he thought. They would have to do a lot of research. He spied a small desk sitting against a wall in the corner. He looked at the desk and wondered if it had perhaps belonged to Dolly Madison; too small for a former president. *He would have had a much larger one*, he thought. There were several more items of furniture that might be from the right time period he mused. Unknown to Edison, the small desk was the one Dolly Madison had moved into the bedchamber of her husband. Undisturbed in the lower drawer of the desk were the papers James Madison had been writing and rewriting almost a hundred and fifty years before.

Edison closed the door to the attic and continued on with his survey. He had no idea there were papers in the desk. It would still be some time before they were discovered, and when they were, it was believed they were nothing more than the senile ramblings of a former president.

Harvard University
Graduation
May 23, 1983

Ben Cain tossed his mortar board in the air along with all of the other graduating seniors. The cheer went up. College was finally over. Everyone began searching for their friends and family. Ben was looking for Marilyn. He spied her in the mass of bodies milling around. Moving as quickly as he could through the crowd and making his way toward Marilyn, she was the only thing on his mind in that moment. Reaching her, he wrapped his arms around her and held her close.

Separating the crowd, the three tall and muscular uniformed New Jersey state troopers of the governor's protection detail led Edwin Cain and his wife to their son. Edwin was proud of their son. They had a hard time understanding each other. *It had been rough his first couple of years in college*, Edwin thought. Things had gotten much better in the last year, especially since he had met Marilyn Ellsworth. She was much more suited to Ben, and Edwin was happy his son had met her.

Edwin walked up to Ben and Marilyn and patiently waited for their embrace to end. Catherine, their daughter, and his wife, Marjorie, didn't wait and embraced the couple. Just then Ben looked up directly into his father's eyes. It was the first time in longer than he could remember that he absolutely knew his father really loved him and saw the pride in his eyes. Suddenly it was as if only the two of them were in this place. He reached out and hugged his father and both of them knew in that moment more than words could ever say.

Edwin and Ben broke the embrace and were almost embarrassed by it. Edwin broke the silence, "Let's all go celebrate. Do you think we could find a good steak in this town?"

"I know just the place. How much of the tab are you going to pick up? If I have to pay, it's going to be McDonalds," Ben replied.

Edwin laughed and said, "I think I can take care of this one. Why don't we all go to the car and you can show us where. We will follow you and Marilyn," he said, tossing Ben a set of keys.

Catching the keys, Ben looked up into the smiling face of his father. "Are you serious?" he said as he realized the keychain had a Corvette emblem.

"You've earned it," Edwin replied.

Marjorie, Ben's mother, leaned in and whispered in Ben's ear, "I told you. Your father is proud of you."

Ben reached over, took Marilyn by the hand, and said, "Come on, Dad's buying, and you can ride in the new set of wheels."

Bennett Arthur Cain was well on his way down the path that was carefully planned for him. The next steps were already set in motion. He just thought he was going to be looking for employment.

# THE COMMITTEE

Wellington Capital
Boston, Massachusetts
June 28, 1984

Ben Cain sat anxiously waiting in the reception area, his résumé in his leather folder. He was waiting for the receptionist to call him in for the interview. He was afraid he was not going to be seriously considered. Just out of college and with no real work experience, all he had to offer was his degree from Harvard. He didn't want to work in his father's firm. He also didn't want to get a job just because of who his father was. He had been looking for the last six months or so. He had already taken the interns position again in the senator's office right after graduation. That was as much to stay close to Marilyn, who lived in Georgetown with her family. She had been in her last year at Georgetown University where she had just graduated. He had not only fallen for her, he was contemplating their future, which meant he had to get a job that would pay him well enough to be on his own somewhere.

"Ben Cain," the receptionist called. Looking up when he heard his name called, she smiled at him and continued, "Mr. Bradley will see you now." She then led him to the office where he was surprised to find James Bradley was not just a junior executive, he was an executive vice president.

Ben extended his hand and offered a very firm handshake as he had been taught by his father long ago and looked James Bradley straight in the eye. James Bradley was glad; he liked what he saw. He had plans for this young man who had just walked into his office.

Ben was sitting in a leather armchair in Bradley's office and had just handed him his résumé, and Bradley was looking it over. *There isn't much on it*, Ben thought. *Harvard and two summers working as an intern in Senator Moynihan's office.*

Bradley looked at the young man sitting in front of him and asked, "Tell me about the senator's office as an intern. What did you do while there?"

Ben explained what he had done, trying to make reading through the boring minor legislation and answering the phone as interesting as possible. What Ben didn't know and was about to find out was James Bradley knew the senator who had recommended Ben to him.

"Ben, I happen to be acquainted with Senator Moynihan, and he spoke very highly of you. It is a little unusual for an intern to be given the job of reading any legislation. That speaks well of you. Tell me why you would like to work in the business of capitol investing."

Ben was surprised at what Bradley had just told him. "Well, Mr. Bradley, as you know my degree from Harvard is business finance. I have always been interested in capitol investing and what makes some businesses thrive and others struggle. The real art is in being able to separate the good risks from the bad. Knowing the right questions to ask, talking to the right people within any business, figuring out the real numbers. I guess I learned more from my father than I thought. I worked summers in his office before the internship. I watched him figure that out more than once. I guess the best way to explain it is there is just a feeling you get when you look someone in the eye that numbers don't tell."

Bradley knew exactly what he meant. "Ben, one last item I would like to know. Why, if you have worked for your father, are you not planning on going back to work in his firm?"

Ben was expecting the question. "Mr. Bradley, I would like to work where I have to earn my own way. I don't want to be looked at as the heir apparent just because of my father as I would be if I worked in his firm. It all means much more if you have to work hard for it, and that is exactly what I intend to do."

Bradley already knew this young man was going to be hired. He was just glad Ben seemed to be made of the right stuff.

The Ellsworth Home
Georgetown
Washington DC
July 18, 1984

Ben Cain parked his Corvette on the street in front of Marilyn Ellsworth's home where she lived with her parents. He walked up the sidewalk, past the manicured lawn, to the ornate front door. Ringing the doorbell, he waited for the door to be opened. Marilyn's mother, Regina Ellsworth, opened the door and ushered Ben into the foyer. She greeted Ben warmly and led him into the family room. She really liked the young man.

"Hello, Mrs. Ellsworth, how are you doing today?" Ben asked.

"Ben, I have told you. You can call me either Regina or Mom. Take your choice. It makes me feel too old to be called Mrs. Ellsworth."

"Yes, ma'am," Ben replied.

"Ben, if you want to live past lunch, enough with that ma'am stuff too. I'm not that old yet."

Smiling at her, Ben replied, "You keep telling me that and I keep telling you my mother would disown me if I didn't show you the proper respect. Make you a deal. How about I just marry in to the family and then I can call you Mom? Would that be better?"

Regina looked at Ben and saw the look in his eye and realized there was more truth to the statement than he was trying to make it sound. "Ben, don't you tease me about something like that. I told you before I already consider you part of the family."

By the look in Ben's eye, she realized what Ben was up to. "Oh my, has it come to that? I guess you need to see Marilyn. She's upstairs. Let me get her for you."

Ben hugged her and said, "I guess I need to speak to her father first if you don't mind. I told you some things I am old-fashioned about, and both my mother and my father would be disappointed with me if I don't do this properly."

"Ben, he is in the study. Have you asked Marilyn yet, or are you going to talk to her father first?"

"You mean she didn't tell you?"

"I guess that answers that question. Go ahead and speak with her father. I'll go tell Marilyn you're here."

Ben turned and made his way to the study as her mother went upstairs. Marilyn's father, Harman Ellsworth, was sitting in the leather armchair watching television. He was a tall, dignified man in his late forties and he worked in the state department as an analyst. He stood as he saw Ben step into the room. He liked the young man who had been seeing more and more of his daughter. Offering Ben his hand, he said, "How are you doing, Ben?"

"Fine, sir, how are you?"

"I am doing well. Have a seat."

Ben sat in the armchair across the small table from Marilyn's father. He was nervous, and it showed. "What's on your mind, Ben? You look as if you want to talk about something."

"Yes, sir," Ben replied. "Mr. Ellsworth, I have been seeing a lot of Marilyn lately, and well, sir…" Ben paused, not quite knowing how to ask.

Harman Ellsworth already knew what Ben was going to ask. Unknown even to his wife, his daughter had confided in him. They had always been particularly close, and she had come in the previous weekend on top of her world, and he had seen the engagement ring she had been wearing. They had agreed not to tell her mother until Ben worked up the nerve to talk to him. She was not going to wear the ring until it was official.

Smiling at Ben, he decided to give the young man a lifeline. "Ben, if you are going to ask me for my blessing where Marilyn is concerned, I will happily give it. Just so you know, I have already talked to Marilyn, and she said you would be coming to see me. Do me a favor. Don't tell her mother I already knew. I don't think I could get away with it if she found out I already knew."

Greatly relieved, Ben looked at Marilyn's smiling father. "Thank you, sir, for making this easy for me. Just so you know, I now have a job, so I will be able to take care of her."

"It might surprise you, Ben, but I already know about that. James Bradley and I are friends, and he asked me what I thought of you. I think he would have hired you anyway, but it never hurts to have an endorsement from your future father-in-law."

Ben was surprised at that, but he was so relieved to have his blessing about his daughter, he never gave it any more thought.

The young candidate was moving nicely down the path the committee had prepared for him.

# THE COMMITTEE

The Committee
New York, New York
May 20, 1921

    The Committee members were preparing to meet in the boardroom maintained by John D. Rockefeller in New York. It was easier for them to come to meet him as he was into his eighties. There were some perks of being the chairman, one of which was to have the meetings where you wanted them. All the committee members were busy and had commitments all over the country and other parts of the world. They had agreed to try to hold the meetings in May and adjusted their schedules. There were always exceptions; Cornelius Vanderbilt had died in January of 1877 after being ill for some time. They never liked to be without a chairman and had called a meeting then to select a new chairman. They had tried to adhere to that for the last thirty years, and it had worked well.

    Things were happening in the world, and they had business to discuss. The Great War had ended three years before, and Europe and the Middle East were still in disarray. Woodrow Wilson had worked to get the League of Nations formed and had been successful; however, the United States had refused to join, the Senate had objected to article ten in the charter and would not ratify it. Wilson had won the Nobel peace prize in 1919 for his efforts, but the feelings in the United States were still tending to isolationism. Things were changing in the world, and the Committee was preparing to adapt.

    The Chairman called the Meeting to Order. "Gentlemen, we have several items on the agenda. As we all know Europe is currently in disarray. The treaty of Versailles may have ended the war, however it has caused major economic devastation in Europe especially Germany. The United States has not joined the League of Nations, and we have no influence in that body. We must prepare to deal with the fallout this will undoubtedly cause. We should be able to turn this to our advantage. I am going to suggest that we begin to get involved in Europe to prevent the chaos from spreading. Also we need to discuss our plans to further gain control of the currency now that the Federal Reserve has been created. We have been working on that for the last eight years. Who would care to begin?"

Dealer, which was the name Henry Ford had chosen for himself, motioned to the chairman. Given the floor, he began, "Gentlemen, as you know, the Great War caused devastation, and we should not have been involved. We have refused to join the League of Nations, and we should do what we must to prevent another war. Therefore, I propose that we must get involved in Europe in order to control the chaos. As far as the monetary system goes, the ideas of loans and time payment have been implemented by my company, and it has been very successful. We can use this to further our agenda to control the monetary system. We have learned the American people can be trained over time to come to our way of thinking."

Printer, otherwise known as William Randolph Hearst, motioned to the chairman and was given the floor. "Gentlemen, we must be careful not to move too fast. I have learned we can create a marketing campaign with the power of the press. Given enough time, we can create public sentiment for whatever we want. If we chose to get involved in Europe, we can make the people believe that sentiment. The more we choose to control, the more we convince the American people it is their idea. Remember what we need is time. There has never been a fixed timetable."

Trader motioned to the chairman and was given the floor. "Gentlemen, we must not move too quickly on anything. We can manipulate anything given enough time. I agree with Printer. There has never been a fixed time table. Also I think we may be straying too far from our original intent, which was to control the government of the United States and create an economy that was second to none. I agree we may have to stabilize Europe to ensure that. The economy is becoming worldwide. That is what I believe will ensure supremacy for the United States."

The debate continued, and all of the members of the committee finally realized as powerful as they were in the United States they needed influence in Europe. The decision was reached to begin to cultivate ties in Europe. The committee was expanding its operation.

# THE COMMITTEE

Saint Francis Episcopal Church
Alexandria, Virginia
June 9. 1985

"You may kiss your bride." Ben looked into Marilyn's eyes as he lifted her veil and leaned in to kiss his new bride. She smiled at him as the kiss ended, and they both heard the priest say, "Ladies and gentlemen, may I present Mr. and Mrs. Bennett Cain." The organist began to play and the happy couple made their way back down the aisle as those who gathered to watch applauded them. They stepped outside the church and were followed by both sets of their parents and Ben's sister, Catherine.

The receiving line was finally about over, and there were pictures to take and a reception to attend. Edwin Cain was looking to the dance floor where his son and his new bride were sharing the traditional dance. Jeff Stillman was standing beside him and said, "Well, Ed, looks like the governor has another daughter. That ought to be worth a few votes next election."

"Don't you ever stop with the politics, Jeff? The kids just got married, and this is their day. Is that all you can think about is how to figure out how to get votes out of everything?"

"Ed, you are the governor of New Jersey. That's how you got to be governor because I worry about things like that. Having said that, be grateful the father of the bride picks up the tab."

"Okay, Jeff, I'll give you that one. I would happily pay for it as happy as they are. Besides, how do you know I didn't pay for all this, or at least half? Harman and I cut a deal. I paid half, and he votes for me."

Jeff turned to look at Ed. He stared back at Jeff stone-faced as long as he could. "Got you with that one, Jeff." Ed laughed.

Marjorie walked up to Ed and reached for his hand and leaned against his shoulder. She was happy for their son. He had finally gotten over Valerie; Ed and Ben finally were getting along, and his career seemed to be on track. *He is more like his father every day*, Marjorie thought.

Harman Ellsworth was leaning against the bar with a drink in his hand watching his daughter dance with her new husband. He wasn't really sure he was prepared to not only give his daughter away as he had earlier in the day, but face the fact his life was changing as much as hers was. Things will never be the same. *Ben had turned out to be a good man*, he thought. His daughter had done well.

His wife walked up to him and saw the look in his eyes. She had her own thoughts about it just like he did. It was never easy to give up the way things were, no matter how much she liked Ben, and he was now the one in their daughter's life.

Ben was dancing with Marilyn, and he only had eyes for her. They were looking into one another's eyes and the rest of the party seemed to disappear. All the family and friends, the music—it was as if they weren't even there. Ben was happier than he ever had been. His world was looking up. Things were happening for him; the job was going well, and he was up for a promotion. The committee was continuing to manage their candidate.

The Committee
New York, New York
May 21, 1930

The country was in the worst economic depression in its history. The stock market had collapsed on Black Tuesday. In two days, the market had lost thirty billion dollars. For the previous decade, the wealth created was unimaginable. The Dow Jones had risen to a staggering rate. Everyone was investing in the market, and they thought the ride would never end. They had done it all with borrowed money and margin trading. It had all collapsed in less than a week. And the committee had engineered most of it.

"Gentleman," Diamond began, "the worst economic crisis the world has ever seen has been upon us for the last year. I need not tell you how we managed to create it. The manipulations we made were wildly successful beyond even our expectations. We went too far, and it has even spiraled out of control beyond our estimates. Those of us in this room protected ourselves from it because we knew what was going to happen. We were unable to put the brakes on it as we did in 1907. Our involvement in Europe is beginning to stabilize Germany, and we gain influence with every passing day. We must use this to our advantage. I doubt that Hoover will be able to manage the economy well enough to get reelected. We must plan accordingly. Trader, would you care to give us the overview of the plans you have been working on? It's time to bring this before the full committee."

Trader began to lay out the plans they were beginning to implement. "Gentlemen, as we have discussed before, the need to establish a world economy will ultimately bring about the control of nations by their economy. With the current economic chaos, the need for a strong leader to offer solutions will be demanded by the people. This will be our chance to begin to implement a social welfare structure that will allow us to extend our control further over larger sections of the electorate. In other words, they will vote for the politicians who continue to provide them with these benefits. As we begin to change their mind-set, they will look more and more to the government for these benefits. We can then begin to implement further programs that will control more and more assets. Now that the Federal Reserve has been established, we can continue our inroads into control of the monetary institutions. This will all be done under the guise of repairing the economy to bring the nation out of the depression. We are using a similar strategy in Europe starting in Germany."

Diamond thanked Trader and called on Printer to report on his progress. "Printer, would you give us an update on the marketing of the strategy?"

"We began with editorials to influence public opinion. We can report on the economic collapse and give it the spin we want. Most people have no real understanding of how the economy really works. Remember those who do are very much in the minority. When people are desperate for solutions, they are easier to influence when things get marginally better. We no longer report the news. We create it and spin it how we want it perceived. This way when we decide who should be the next president, we can get them elected by creating the perception of them we want. Then we keep repeating it every time we write an article about them. We use much the same tactic for the Congress and Senate."

Dealer motioned to the chairman. Given the nod, he began, "Gentlemen, we have worked very hard to create the circumstances we currently have. We need to take advantage of this to prevent the world ever having to go to war as happened in the Great War. If we can create the economic bond between nations out of this chaos that is to our advantage as we control the economy as well. We can create peace and control it. This will ensure we maintain control."

Inventor, as he was known on the Committee, motioned to the chairman and was given the floor. "Gentlemen," Thomas Edison began, "the world is at a crossroads, and the economic instability we created has gone even beyond not only our ability to control it but beyond our shores. We must proceed very carefully. We may be creating a situation we cannot control. Europe has still not recovered from the Great War and now this depression is upon us. The great masses will reach out to who can provide them stability, security, and in this case ensure there is food on their table. I urge caution in this area. We only have marginal influence in Europe, and the leader that offers these will come to power as the desperation of the people grow. We have not been actively grooming candidates in Europe as we have here, and we may not have the influence to control them."

Investor had been on the committee for a little over five years; he had made his fortune buying businesses that were in trouble and building them up and selling them. He knew the way government bureaucrats worked. He dealt with them every time he bought or sold a company. He firmly believed the country was a mess and would be much better off with the stability their control would bring. He motioned to the chairman and was given the floor.

"I will remind us all that we need to be patient. There has never been a set timetable. We overreached and collapsed the economy too far. The control needs to be subtle and gradual. The people need to willingly surrender their freedoms for security. We will then run things as we wish, and they will embrace it. We can use the current economic mess to create the dependence on the government. We may have to invest more heavily in Europe to foster the economic bond we need."

The discussion continued, plans were made and implemented, candidates were selected, and decisions made on who was to be president. The business of the committee continued on as the average American struggled for survival. A course was set for Europe that would set the stage for the greatest conflict the world had ever known. The committee's next selection for president would bear the responsibility of dealing with all of the world's chaos.

Wellington Capitol
Boston, Massachusetts
July 18, 1987

James Bradley stepped out of his corner office and walked to the small office that Ben Cain was diligently working in. The young man had started out on the bottom rung at the firm and had worked his way up from there. He had been given special attention and had been progressing very well. He had been promoted and had learned the inside and out of the business from his father first, and his skill was being polished by Bradley as well.

Bradley stuck his head into Ben's small office and smiled at Ben diligently working on the file he had just been given. "Ben, put that away and come with me. I have a lunch appointment with someone I want you to meet."

Ben put the file in the desk drawer and stood up. "Sure, thanks for the invite." He slipped on his jacket, pulled his tie back into place, and followed James Bradley to the elevator.

The door to the elevator opened and the two stepped inside; James pushed the button for the lobby, and when the door closed, he looked over at Ben and said, "Ben, we are going to meet a gentleman by the name of Andrew Marsh. He is a major player in the ship building industry with the spending going on to bolster defense and President Reagan planning a six-hundred-ship navy, he is expanding his shipyard. We have done business with him for years. He also is a major force in politics. I wanted to take this opportunity for you to meet him. You are going to be working on this deal, and this could help you take the next step on the corporate ladder."

The elevator stopped, and the door opened to the ornate lobby. The pair stepped through the revolving door and out onto the sidewalk in front of the building. They hailed a cab and got in the back. As the cab pulled away, James looked over at Ben and said, "Pay careful attention to Marsh. He is not the typical client we do business with. These are the type of people who make things happen, not just in business but politics as well. At this level, these are the major political donors both parties pay attention to. He also is a heavy hitter in the aviation industry. His face is not well known to the public, but to those who matter, he is very well known."

"I learned from my father about paying attention and not saying much. He always used to say something like, let the other guy talk and sooner or later you will learn what he doesn't want you to know."

James grinned at the comment; he liked Ben more all the time. "Ben, I think that is why you have done so well. You had a very good mentor. When you see him, tell your father if the governor's thing doesn't work out for him, I could use him here as well."

Laughing, Ben replied, "Little late on that one. He just got reelected. I will tell him about the offer though."

The cab pulled up in front of Ye Olde Union Oyster House Seafood restaurant that was one of the best in the city. James paid the fair, and they exited the taxi and walked toward the entrance. They were greeted by the maître d' and ushered to a small private dining room. There were more people in the room than Ben expected. One of them was a member of the committee who wanted to take a look at one of the candidates he was managing. He was the only one in the room who knew.

The Committee
New York, New York
May 23, 1932

The Committee members were gathering in the boardroom waiting for the arrival of the chairman. There were quiet discussions among two groups as they patiently waited. All of the members were powerful men in their own right and not used to waiting. In here they realized they were all equal as the Committee was structured, and it was a much different exercise of their power. Decisions made here were an agreement among powerful men. The agenda was larger than they were, and somehow they developed a different view beyond their own lifetime. They all believed in what they were doing.

The chairman John D. Rockefeller slowly made his way into the room and sat down at the head of the conference table. He was treated very deferentially by the other members of the committee. Not only was he the wealthiest and most powerful of them all, at ninety-three years of age, he was almost a dichotomy to them. He exercised great power and influence, and many could attest to his ruthlessness in business yet he used his vast wealth in the most philanthropic of ways. He was building a legacy that he hoped would be remembered forever.

Diamond brought the meeting to order. "Gentlemen, the first order of business is a new member for the committee. As you know, we lost Inventor last year, and we have not voted on a replacement as we have not met as a full committee since. We will follow the usual protocol and a replacement will be selected from the list we maintain, remember this must be a unanimous decision."

The selection of this member was almost as contentious as any they had ever made. They voted and eliminated those who received the fewest votes until a unanimous decision was reached. In the end, Joseph P. Kennedy was selected.

"Gentlemen," the Chairman began, "we finally have a consensus on the next member of the Committee. Let us pray we have made the right selection. Now let's move on to other business. Roosevelt is now president and has his hands quite full. I believe his plans to implement our social welfare agenda will begin to work as the economic depression deepens. Also on the agenda is Europe. We are beginning to make inroads there. It appears as though a leader is beginning to emerge in Germany. We have to make a decision if we will support him or if we should look elsewhere. Who would care to begin?"

Dealer motioned to the chairman and was given the floor. "Gentlemen, we must be very careful in implementing any strategy to back a leader in Germany. I am going to ask how much we know about this Hitler fellow. Remember what Inventor warned us about. We do not have the selection process in Europe as we do here. We must make a decision about those who emerge. What do we know about him?"

Printer motioned to the chairman and was given the floor. "I will remind everyone here we did not select him. What we have to decide is, do we back him? There are several things that worry me about him. He is very charismatic, and we do not know what his agenda really is. What we do know isn't very much about his early life and beliefs. He is a member of the national socialist workers party. He tried a coup in the early twenties and was jailed for a year. It is my understanding he has agreed to work within the democratic process within Germany, and the Nazi party is no longer banned. There is some speculation he is anti-Semitic and very much a believer in German expansionism. These are somewhat troubling. The other side of the coin is he may come to power with or without our support. Germany is finally beginning to come out of the chaos created by the Great War. We still have a way to go in the rest of Europe, and we must decide if we can work with him to achieve our goals."

Trader motioned to the chairman and was given the nod to take the floor. "I agree we must be very careful. I believe he is going to come to power whether we decide to back him or not. This leaves the question if we back him, do we have any influence? The Soviet Union is also becoming of major concern to us. Stalin is very unpredictable, and we have no influence there at all. Hitler may be our only chance to have any influence in Europe to counteract what we believe to be Stalin's desire for expansion. Gentlemen, we just do not know for sure. I do not like to make decisions on so little information."

Diamond let the debate continue and took it all in. What the rest of the Committee did not know was that a similar committee had been formed in Europe and was being coordinated with their efforts. He had been instrumental in forming the European version along with J. P. Morgan just before he died in 1913. That was the primary reason he had agreed to become chairman. He was the only one who knew; he had made plans to bring in the new chairman in the event of his death. The chairman controlled more than the rest of the Committee realized.

# THE COMMITTEE

Wellington Capitol
Boston, Massachusetts
July 20, 1987

James Bradley put the handset of his phone in the base setting on his desk. He had been talking to the president of Wellington Capitol, Benjamin Templeton. Templeton had just let him in on the plans the firm had for Ben Cain. Ben was bright, well-educated, and making very good progress. He also knew quite a bit about the business from his father. What Bradley found interesting was the personal attention the young man had gotten from the very beginning. When he had interviewed Ben, he had already been told to hire him; the interview was a formality. He was given specific instruction to take the young man under his wing and personally teach him the ins and outs of the business. He probably would have hired Ben regardless; he liked the young man. He had just never seen this kind of attention paid this early on to anyone at this stage. And now he was going to tell the young man the firm was going to pay for him to attend law school, get his degree, and ultimately pass the bar exam. They could hire young lawyers right from the best law schools in the nation. This was highly unusual, but orders from the top were obeyed, and his opinion had not been asked.

Bradley picked up the handset from the base, put it to his ear, and dialed Ben's extension. When Ben picked up, Bradley said to him, "Ben, I need to see you for a minute. Could you step into my office? Thanks."

Ben hung up his phone, put his jacket on, pulled up his tie, and wondered what his boss wanted. Usually, Bradley was pretty laid-back and stuck his head in Ben's office. That was one of the things Ben liked about him. This summon was a little unusual, and Bradley had sounded a little different than usual. Ben's first thought was maybe he had done something wrong with one of the clients; although he couldn't think of what it would be. His mind was churning with the possibilities as he walked to Bradley's office.

He entered the office, and Bradley smiled at him and said to Ben, "Ben, close the door and pull up a chair." As Ben complied, Bradley opened the lower drawer of his desk and pulled out a bottle of scotch and reached behind him and picked up two glasses from the small cabinet against the wall. He poured the drinks and handed one to Ben as he turned around.

Surprised, Ben took the drink as he looked into the smiling face of his boss. "Congratulations, Ben, you have made quite an impression on the old man himself, Benjamin Templeton. I just got off the phone with him before I called you in here. He has instructed me to tell you that the firm has decided to spring for you to go to law school. I don't know how you pulled that one off, but I would like to know what you have on him in case I need it sometime."

Stunned, all Ben could think of to say was "Are you serious?"

"Ben, the look on your face is priceless. You really didn't know, did you? I wondered about that."

"What brought this up? I have never talked to anyone about wanting to go back to school and get my law degree. I don't know what to say."

"Ben, sometimes the best thing to say is nothing. In this case, thank you is all you need to say. Don't worry, I'll pass it along for you. I can tell you never really expected this."

"I'm just stunned. I never expected this, I don't even think I have even talked to Mr. Templeton. I guess I'm really going to work here forever to pay this back."

Laughing, Bradley was enjoying the reaction from Ben. "Tell you what, Ben, why don't you take the rest of the day off, go tell your wife, take her out to dinner and celebrate. I hate to tell you this, but you still have to work here while you go to school. I hope you're ready for this."

"Yes, sir, Mr. Bradley. I'll do that. Marilyn is going to be as surprised as I am." With that, Ben left Bradley's office and headed home to tell his wife about this development. The committee was continuing the development of their promising young candidate.

# THE COMMITTEE

The Committee
New York, New York
May 25, 1937

    The members of the Committee gathered as they normally did; the difference was they were missing the chairman. John D. Rockefeller had passed away at his home in Florida two days earlier. He was two months shy of his ninety-eighth birthday. The Committee needed another member as well as a new chairman. Trader, as one of the senior members of the committee, brought the meeting to order.

    "Gentlemen, the first order of business is the selection of a new chairman. The second item is the selection of a new member. We will proceed as we have in the past. I will ask everyone to write the names of their selection for chairman and pass them to me and then we will see if we have agreement as to the three candidates that we will vote for."

    Each member wrote their nomination, folded the paper, and slid them to Trader. The chairman traditionally set at the head of the table and that chair was currently empty. Trader took the papers went through them and announced, "Gentlemen, we have three of us to choose from: Dealer, Printer, and Trader. If you would be so kind as to write your selection down and pass them to me, I will call out the votes. A simple majority will do for a chairman. Remember, when we select a new member, that must be a unanimous decision." Trader took the papers from the other members and looked at them. He then proceeded to call out the vote totals. "Gentlemen, we have two votes for dealer and two for Printer. The rest were cast for Trader. I thank all of you for your vote of confidence in me, and I would ask that the vote be verified." Trader passed the papers to Dealer who looked them over, nodded his agreement, and passed them to Printer. He in turn looked at them nodded his agreement and slid them to the other members. One by one they all agreed, and Trader stood and moved to the vacant chair at the head of the table.

    Diamond, as he was now known, continued with the meeting. "Gentlemen, the next order of business is the selection of a new member. As we have done in the past, I will circulate the list of names of possible members. If each of you will write the name of your choice and pass them to me." The list was circulated among the members, and they passed the folded papers with the names on them to the chairman. He opened them and announced, we have two selections John D. Rockefeller Junior, for whom eight votes were cast. There was also one vote for Howard Hughes, I will ask if the member who cast the vote for Hughes will agree to the vote for Rockefeller and that will give us a unanimous vote. If that is acceptable to everyone, we can do a verbal vote." There were no objections. The vote was taken and acknowledged. John Rockefeller Junior had succeeded his father on the Committee.

Diamond then continued the meeting with the rest of the agenda. "Gentlemen, we also have several other items on the agenda. President Roosevelt is continuing with his new deal policies of social welfare programs. His executive order to prohibit the private ownership of gold in 1933 and the subsequent seizure of it from the general public and meltdown of gold coins was successful. This begins to implement our strategy of the transfer of wealth. We own the gold, and the public are left to hold printed currency. As all of us are aware, there is no timetable for this. The overall strategy to make the public further dependent upon the government will take generations to bear fruit. Dealer, how are we progressing on the credit issue?"

Dealer nodded and took the floor. "The depression has been hard on most Americans, and those that have jobs are cautious about going into debt. However, we have convinced most that it is essential to continue to buy to spur economic growth. We are looking at the long-term aspect of creating a debt load that most do not give a second thought. That will take time. We must be very patient. Also remember our tax policy. We now have Americans paying an annual income tax bill. We can slowly increase this. Over time, we can convince them to bear an ever increasing burden."

Joseph Kennedy, also known as Importer, nodded to the chairman and was given the floor. "I would like to take this opportunity to remind the Committee that our efforts to implement control of the stock market and investments are beginning to bear fruit. The Securities and Exchange Commission, of which I headed, will be able to eventually exert control over the financial markets. This should help us further our agenda of control of investment capital. Government regulation and public acceptance of it is a key to further control and willingness of the public to trade freedoms for security."

The meeting continued, plans were discussed, decided upon, and the selection of candidates was discussed as usual. The newest member of the committee was approached and the envelope John D. Rockefeller Sr. had entrusted to his lawyer was opened upon his death. Enclosed was a sealed envelope with instructions to deliver it to William Randolph Hearst. In that letter was a key to a safe deposit box in New York with instructions to deliver the key to the next chairman of the Committee. Another letter was delivered to the president of the bank where the safety deposit box was located. Banker, as he was known on the Committee, had the other key and instructions that he and Printer were to make the keys available to the new chairman of the Committee. Some secrets only the chairman were privileged to pass to one another.

First National Bank of New York
New York, New York
June 3, 1937

    Alfred J. Barclay, president of the First National Bank of New York and Banker on the Committee, was seated at his ornate desk in his top floor office. He had a letter in front of him that he had just finished reading. William Randolph Hearst, known as Printer on the Committee, was seated across from him. Hearst was the first to break the silence. "I received that from the lawyer John Rockefeller had retained. Apparently, there are things only the chairman is privileged to know. Included with that was a key to a safe deposit box. I was instructed to turn it over to whoever became the new chairman in your presence."

Barclay laid the letter on his desk and removed his glasses. He stood up and walked to the small bar discreetly hidden behind the doors of a bookcase. He poured two glasses dark with whiskey and handed one to Hearst. They touched glasses in a silent toast to the past chairman. "I received much the same thing from a totally different firm of lawyers. The only difference is I already hold the bank's key to the box. I have no idea what is in there, only the chairman is privileged to retrieve. I cannot open the box and neither can you. Legally, we are bound to turn the keys over to Samuel Marston. He is now Diamond as you know."

"It does make one wonder just exactly what he was up to. And now we have put his son on the Committee to replace him."

"Samuel may well tell us what is in the box. He was surprised to have been informed of this when I called him to request this meeting. All I told him was Rockefeller had requested the three of us meet after his death. Rockefeller had no way of knowing who would be selected as the next chairman. The letter was sealed with wax and had been unopened. It was also written in such a manner as to make sense only to those of us who would know."

"Mine was sealed as well and was written in much the same way. The only thing we can do is turn the keys over to Samuel and see what he chooses to tell us. I have a feeling none of the other members know. Obviously, he selected the two of us from among the Committee members. There has to be a reason why. It may be as simple as the fact you control a bank with safe deposit boxes and would know what to do. I may have been chosen simply because of the time on the committee. He had to know we would be curious and also could be trusted. We can't ask Samuel either. If Rockefeller had wanted us to know, he would have instructed us to open the box. He left it up to the new chairman."

Both sat in silence and sipped their drinks, each lost with their own thoughts. Barclay was the first to break the silence. "It also could be he didn't trust any of us, and maybe he wanted us to be curious. I guess we will find out if the new chairman decides to bring us in on it. He should be here any moment. I asked you to come by half an hour before I scheduled Samuel. I thought we needed to discuss this."

There was a quiet knock on his door, and his secretary opened the door and announced, "A Mr. Marston is here to see you." Samuel Marston walked through the door to Barclay's office as his secretary closed the door after him.

"Gentlemen, it is good to see both of you. I was not expecting this meeting as I told Alfred when he requested we meet. I have no idea what this is about."

Barclay, as the host, indicated the bar and asked, "Would you care for a taste, Samuel? We started already."

Marston nodded and replied, "Some of the scotch would go down nicely. Thanks."

Barclay fixed another glass of scotch and handed it to Marston. "Gentlemen, may I propose a toast to our past chairman. May he rest in peace."

They touched glasses and each took a sip. Barclay then walked to his desk, retrieved the letter, and handed it to Marston. "This was delivered sealed to William, and I received one much the same. Neither of us has any idea of what he was up to. As you can see, we are complying with the instructions he left for us. He had no way of knowing who would be selected, and the letter states we are to meet with the replacement 'who shall be selected to follow in my position' as he put it."

Marston took the letter and took a moment to read it. His brows raised in surprise. "I wonder what the devil he was up to. I guess there is only one way to find out. If you gentlemen would be so kind as to wait for me, I will retrieve the contents of the box and come back here." Barclay handed him the key that the bank retained, and Hearst handed him the other.

Barclay looked at Marston and said, "I will send my secretary to escort you to the vault in which the boxes are kept. William and I will wait here if you like."

"Thank you, gentlemen. I will return shortly." Marston turned and was escorted to the door of the office by Barclay.

Motioning to his secretary, Barclay said, "Lois, would you please take Mr. Marston to the safe deposit box vault and sign him in. Wait for him please and then bring him back here when he is finished. Thank you, Lois." Leaving Marston with his secretary, Barclay retreated into his office and closed the door.

Lois Fowler smiled at Samuel Marston and said to him, "Right this way, Mr. Marston." She then led him to the elevator and took him to the first floor of the bank. They then walked to the desk at the entrance to the vault area. "Jenny, Mr. Marston will be accessing the box area. I will wait here for him and escort him back to Mr. Barclay's office. Thank you, Jenny."

Jenny, the keeper of the vault as she thought of her job, produced a ledger from the drawer of her desk. Flipping through the pages, she had Marston sign in as she produced a set of keys. When he was finished, she led him into the vault and explained the process. "Mr. Marston, you have the keys to the box. As you know, it takes two keys to access. The bank retains one, which you received from Mr. Barclay. I will unlock the vault area for your box. You may then use your keys to remove the box and take it into the small room over there." She pointed to one of the four rooms lining the wall of the vault area. "I will lock the door behind you while you access the box. When you are finished, you can unlock the door, and I will escort you back into the vault area to replace the box. Then I will sign you out, and Lois will take you back upstairs." She then unlocked the vault area for his box and waited while he removed the box and took it into the room and locked the door behind him.

Samuel Marston set the box on the table along the wall of the room; he then sat down in the chair and took a deep breath as he opened the box. Inside was a letter-sized envelope sealed with wax and the crest of John D. Rockefeller pressed into the wax. Removing the letter, he looked at it and thought, *Wax was used less and less, the remnants of times past.* He smiled at the thought of Rockefeller dripping the wax and pressing his signet ring into it as it hardened on the flap of the envelope. Below the letter was a small leather bound journal and below that was a letter opener. Smiling again and thinking the old man even thought to put a letter opener here knowing I would need it.

Marston took the letter opener and slid it into the edge of the flap and slit the top of the envelope, leaving the wax seal intact. He removed the letter from the envelope and began to read.

# THE COMMITTEE

From the desk of John D. Rockefeller

John D. Rockefeller
New York, New York
May 30, 1932

Congratulations, Mr. Chairman, on your selection to become Diamond. By now I am sure Banker and Printer are very curious as to the little drama with the lawyers and the keys to this box. If one of you is reading this, I am sorry. It was necessary. If it is one of the others, you may at your discretion inform them of the contents of this letter. This burden has been carried solely long enough.

In the early years of this century, Diamond and myself, before I was Diamond, J.P. Morgan held that title, had decided on a strategy for Europe. We began the implementation of the strategy to form a European version of our Committee. Europe was in chaos and both of us believed war was imminent. We had hoped to avoid that outcome and spare Europe the death and destruction which would exist. As you know, we failed in that endeavor. With Morgan's passing in 1913, I am the only one who knew. The identity of the chairman of the European Committee and the method of contact for him are in the journal. I have also detailed the actions and as much information as I have been able to gather. The discussions we have had regarding Europe were only to keep us aware of what they were doing. I have updated this journal as time has passed never knowing when the time of my own passing will be. By now that has happened, and you have been selected as my successor. I urge you not to bear this burden alone. It was hard enough to bear when there were two of us who knew. Since 1913, I have borne it alone. I would also urge you not to disclose this to the full Committee.

FROM THE DESK OF JOHN D. ROCKEFELLER

I pray that we have done the right things for this nation in our endeavors to see it prosper and maintain a status we have worked so long and hard to achieve. The outcry from the American people would be horrific if they knew what we are doing. I have always believed it is in their best interest as well. There are times when the momentum of public opinion forces choices that are not in the best interest of this nation. I have fought to prevent that. My time is now past, and I must answer to my maker for my sins of this world. May God bless you in this endeavor as you carry forward what was begun so long ago.

*John D. Rockefeller*
Diamond, Chairman

# THE COMMITTEE

Marston finished reading the letter and slowly shook his head and read it again. He was stunned. He had always believed there were no secrets among the Committee members as to their decisions. Obviously, that was not the case. He slipped the journal into his pocket and placed the letter in the envelope beside it. He returned the letter opener to the box and closed it. Rising, he unlocked the door and left the small room. Jenny was waiting for him as he exited, and he handed her the box. Smiling at her, he said, "Thank you for all of your courtesy."

"You are welcome, Mr. Marston," she replied as she returned the box to its place, locked the vault, and escorted him back to Lois.

Marston followed Lois to the elevator, his heels drumming in his mind the sound they made on the marble floor. They stepped into the elevator, and it carried them to the top floor. Marston was still lost in thought as he followed Lois back to Barclay's office. Lois opened the door to the outer office where her desk was and led Marston to the door of Barclay's office. Turning, she looked at him and said, "Let me know of anything else I can help you with."

"Thank you for your kindness. I can't think of anything at the moment." Marston walked through the door of Barclay's office and closed it behind him. Printer and Banker were patiently waiting for him and were still working to diminish the level of the whiskey in the bottle that sat on the desk between them.

"I could use another one of those if you don't mind," Marston said. Banker refilled the glass he had left and handed it to him. Neither he nor Printer had said a word; they were waiting on him. Diamond took a healthy sip of the whiskey and removed the letter and handed it to Banker who proceeded to remove it from the envelope and began to read it. His eyes went up as he took the letter and handed it to Printer who began to read it.

"I will be damned," Printer said as he took his eyes from the letter and looked at Diamond. "The old SOB could keep a secret, couldn't he?

Banker laughed and said, "Yes, he could, and I suppose all of us will have to. I don't think this is something the rest should find out about, is it?"

The three Committee members agreed to keep this a secret only they would share. The world was preparing to finish what had been started in the Great War, and the rumblings were already beginning. No one yet knew how much the world was about to change.

Montpelier
The Madison estate
November 3, 1987

The moving van pulled up in front of the estate, and Eddy, the crew leader, jumped from the cab. He preferred to ride with the driver rather than in the van with the rest of the crew. Dave, the driver of the rig, set the brake and shook his head and grinned to himself at Eddy—strong back, weak mind, but he's the crew chief simply because he had worked for Archer Moving for five years. *At least I get to drive the rig by myself after it gets loaded and he has to ride back with the manual labor*, Dave thought.

Eddy walked up to the door of the mansion as the door was opened, and Jason Edison stepped out with a clipboard in his hand. "Hello, I'm Jason Edison, director of Montpelier." He offered his hand to Eddy who grinned as he shook hands.

"I am Eddy, crew chief, and these guys are my crew. Dave is the driver of the rig, and I understand you have items for us to move to storage for you."

"Yes, Eddy. We are going to restore the estate to its original floor plan and appearance as the home to President Madison. The first order of business for you and your crew is to remove the selected items of furniture for storage. I would like to remind you that all of these items are of great historical significance. Many are quite delicate and need to be handled very carefully. Everything is tagged and to be moved in a very specific order." Edison handed the clipboard to Eddy to show him the tagging system he had devised to keep everything in order.

"Yes, sir, me and the crew will be real careful. We don't wanna break anything. The boss wouldn't be real pleased."

Edison smiled at Eddy and vowed to himself to watch over everything they did. Two-hundred-year-old furniture could be destroyed by Eddy and his crew. "Okay, Eddy, let's go inside and get started. The larger items first and then we will move upstairs."

Eddy returned the clipboard to Edison and motioned for his crew to follow them inside. Eddy as usual directed the crew who began loading the furniture. By lunchtime, they had most of the first floor loaded under the watchful eye of Jason Edison. After they had come back from lunch, Edison moved with them to the upstairs. As the first trailer was almost full and only a few smaller items could fit and the second trailer was not yet here, Edison directed them to attic storage space where the small desk used by James Madison still sat. It had been there undisturbed since it was put there shortly after his death. The previous occupants had taken care of many items of furniture and had maintained the storage spaces and the small desk was still reasonably sound. Eddy and his crew began moving the other smaller items of furniture and loaded them until they got to the small desk. Two of his crew went to the small desk and picked it up under the watchful eye of Jason Edison. As they carried it across the attic and stepped through the door, one of them tripped on the threshold and momentarily lost his grip on the desk. The edge of the desk caught on the doorframe and it jarred and slid out of his grip. The jolt, as one end hit the attic floor, caused the drawers to slide out and fall out of the desk.

Jason Edison, horror-struck as he envisioned the desk breaking, moved in to examine the desk. It was when he bent down to examine the desk that he noticed the papers in the drawer. After finishing an exam of the desk and breathing a sigh of relief at the lack of apparent damage, he turned his attention to the contents of the drawer. Reaching in and gently lifting the top of the papers, he realized he was holding writings of the fourth president of the United States. He ordered the crew to leave the desk where it sat until he could remove the papers from the desk. Stepping around the desk, he went downstairs to find a box to put the papers into. As he made his way downstairs, his mind began to work on what to do with the discovery.

Returning upstairs to the attic storage space with a box in his hand, he gently removed the entire stack of papers from the drawer and placed them into the box. Placing the lid on the box, he picked it up and took it with him as he left the attic storage.

The crew leader, Eddy, replaced the drawers in the desk and vowed to let his crew have it for almost breaking the damn desk and embarrassing him. Jason Edison was debating what to do with the papers since the renovation wasn't even scheduled to begin. The money for it still had yet to be raised, and he couldn't properly store them. Just then the thought struck him to contact his friend at the University of Virginia. He would donate them to the library there where they could be properly cared for and catalogued. Any curiosity at what might be in the papers never entered his mind. He was mainly concerned with their preservation. He didn't know the box containing the papers would languish unopened for years until someone finally remembered they were there. The bombshell they contained was still waiting to be discovered.

The Governor's Mansion
Trenton, New Jersey
July 25, 1987

    Ben Cain and his wife, Marilyn, walked up to the front door of the governor's mansion, which his parents had called home for the last six years. There was a very large and muscular state trooper escorting them to the door. Ben wasn't really sure how he felt about having them around his parents all the time. It seemed there was a reason for their presence that worried him sometimes and the lack of privacy that came with it for his parents. Visits here were not like it used to be when home was the Forrest Hills mansion his parents owned. He had grown closer to his father since he graduated from college. He now understood the old saying that "When you are six, your father is the smartest person you have ever seen. When you are twelve, he isn't that smart. When you are sixteen, he has to be the stupidest person you know. And when you are twenty-five, he is the smartest and wisest person you have ever met." Ben was now twenty-six, and his father was probably one of the smartest individuals he knew. His three years working at Wellington Capitol had further reinforced that belief.
    The door to the mansion opened, and Marilyn walked through with Ben following his wife. The security guard greeted Ben and Marilyn warmly; he really liked the Cain family. He had been around a lot of politicians over the years and most treated the staff as part of the furniture. The Cains always spoke and acknowledged the service they

provided. Edwin Cain was the only one who had ever asked about his family and remembered them at Christmas with a gift and thanks for what they did. Ben was much the same as his father and greeted him by name.

"Hello, Mark, how are you? I hope the family is well," Ben asked as he shook hands with the security guard.

"I am fine, Mr. Cain. The family is doing well, and I hope you are as well. Marilyn, you look wonderful as usual. Your father is in his office, and your mother and Catherine went shopping and should be home soon. I will see to your luggage, and your father said for you to go on in when you got here."

"Thanks, Mark, I appreciate how you take care of us when we visit and for taking care of my parents as well."

"Mrs. Cain, if you would like, I will show you to your room."

"Thank you, Mark. I need the ladies room first, and I think Ben would like some time with his father." Marilyn followed Mark to the guest room, and Ben headed to the governor's office of his father.

Edwin Cain looked up from his desk and the paperwork he had been reading as his son walked through the door of his office. Standing up, he quickly walked around his desk and shook hands with his son. The handshake quickly turned into an embrace as father and son greeted one another.

"Ben, I'm glad you called and wanted to visit for the weekend. I have missed you, and I know your mother is looking forward to seeing you and Marilyn. You look great. Everything must be going well in Boston."

"Dad, you look good. Yes, everything is going well. That's one of the things I wanted to talk to you about. Talk about surprised, the firm is going to spring for me to go back and get my law degree. I have to work and do it at the same time, but they brought it up and I was highly surprised."

"Well, you certainly must be doing something right. That is a little unusual, but then again top-notch talent is very hard to find. If I have to say this myself, I think you are top-notch talent. Obviously, I'm biased."

"James Bradley also said to tell you if the governor's job was getting boring, he could use you there as well."

Laughing, Edwin replied, "Ben, of all the things this job is I don't think it qualifies as boring. Come on over and sit down. How about a little something to cut the dust?" Ed walked to the small bookcase in which he kept a bottle of his Famous Grouse and several glasses. Taking two glasses and the bottle, he walked over to the armchair in which Ben had sat and handed him a glass. Pouring the whiskey in Ben's glass and then his own, they touched glasses and took a sip. Ed sat on the couch across from his son and once again thought of how proud of his son he really was.

Taking a sip of his drink, Ben looked at his father and decided to go ahead and let his father in on the news. "I may as well go ahead and tell you if you promise not to tell Mother and Catherine I told you first."

Edwin looked at his son and had a sudden insight into what his son was going to tell him. "I will keep your confidence of course, but it might be difficult."

Smiling at his father, Ben looked him in the eye and said, "I wonder how you are going to like being a grandfather."

"I am going to take to that role gracefully. I just wouldn't use the term grandmother when you tell your mother. I don't think she will be all that unhappy though. Now Catherine might just decide to move in with you." The two shared a laugh and the bond between father and son continued to grow stronger. Ben was going to rely on his father's wisdom more than he would ever realize.

Pearl Harbor
Hawaii
December 7, 1941

Joseph Lockwood hung up the field telephone and shook his head as he looked at the other member of the squad manning the radar. "They said not to worry about the contact. It was just a flight of B-17s coming in from the mainland. Let's go ahead and shut it down. It's time to head back to base." The crew shut down the mobile radar unit they had been manning and loaded up the truck and started to make their way back to their base.

Mitsuo Fuchida slid the canopy of his Kate torpedo bomber into place and ordered his radio operator to send the code, "Tora, Tora, Tora, back to the carrier group." This signaled the complete surprise they had achieved as he led his group to begin the attack on the American fleet that lay at anchor below. He had worked long and hard to plan the attack with Minoro Genda, and now the surprise they needed was theirs. He banked the plane toward the battleships and released the specially modified torpedo and watched the wake it made as it streaked toward its target. There wasn't even any antiaircraft fire to avoid yet. He pulled back on the stick and climbed away to direct the rest of the air group as they attacked.

The modified naval shell turned into an aerial bomb screamed toward its target after it was released from the bomber. The battleship *Arizona* lay at anchor below. Her crew was just beginning to fire the first few rounds from the machine guns when the bomb struck the forward deck. It penetrated through the deck and the armored magazine before it detonated. A million pounds of gunpowder exploded, causing the sympathetic detonation of all the shells stored in the forward magazine. The fourteen-inch guns and the turret that contained them lifted straight upward from the force of the explosion. A massive fireball engulfed what was left of the dying battleship. The oil in the water ignited, and men tumbled into the water. Admiral Kidd, who had been standing on the bridge gripping its railing when the fireball erupted, was instantly incinerated. All that would ever be found was his ring from the naval academy welded to the railing. A total of 1,177 men on the *Arizona* died almost instantly. The ship took only nine minutes to sink.

The US pacific fleet at anchor at Pearl Harbor had almost ceased to exist. All eight battleships were either destroyed or badly damaged. The harbor would have been unusable if the battleship *Nevada*, the only ship to get underway, had sunk in the channel. Her captain had managed to run her aground at Hospital Point. There were over 2,400 casualties, 1,282 wounded, and a massive loss of aircraft. Not one of the US aircraft carriers was in the harbor.

The Japanese had achieved a complete surprise in their attack on Pearl Harbor. The United States was now involved in World War II. Franklin Delano Roosevelt had wanted the United States to come to the aid of the British against the might of the German army that now controlled most of the European landmass. The war in Europe had been raging since 1939. The European committee that had brought Hitler to power was now powerless to stop him. They had not planned on Hitler becoming a maniac they couldn't control. When they had fled Europe, their only recourse was to turn to the Americans for help. The Committee had prepared the way for the United States to enter the war.

The Empire State Building
New York, New York
December 8, 1941

Samuel Marston had just finished listening to President Roosevelt deliver his speech to Congress asking for a declaration of war on Japan. His chest suddenly felt very heavy. The Committee had wanted to get the United States involved in the war. None of them had believed Japan was capable of what they had achieved at Pearl Harbor. They had expected an attack, possibly even against the base at Pearl Harbor. They had badly underestimated what the results would be.

Marston stood up and walked to the small bar against one wall of his corner office. The pain in his chest increased as he poured a glass of whiskey and put it to his lips to take a drink. The lights in the office began to dance before his eyes, the glass slipped from his hand, and he couldn't seem to focus. His left arm didn't respond to his request for it to move. He tried to reach his desk and the phone sitting on it. He stumbled as he tried to take a step and crashed to the floor, striking his head on the floor as he fell. Diamond's heart stopped beating and began to quiver as the heart attack he was suffering caused him to lose consciousness. He was dead within minutes; he would not be found until his secretary brought in paperwork for him that would never get signed. The committee would have to select another chairman.

# THE COMMITTEE

The Committee
Rockefeller Center
New York, New York
January 16, 1942

    The members of the committee began to arrive one at a time. The meeting had been called because of the need to replace the chairman. Samuel Marston, Diamond, had dropped dead of a heart attack in his office on the eighth of December, the day after Pearl Harbor. Banker brought the meeting to order as Trader had on the previous occasion the Committee had found itself without a chairman.

    "Gentlemen," Banker began, "we once again find ourselves in need of selecting a chairman and of course selecting another member. We will do this as we have in the past, selecting a new chairman from the nine of us in this room. After that is done, we will then select a new member from the list of potential members. I will remind everyone that the vote for chairman requires only a simple majority. However, a new member must be a unanimous selection. I will ask that each of us write their preference for chairman, slide them to me, and I will see if there is a consensus."

    Each of the nine members took a moment to decide who should become the new chairman. One by one they wrote their choice on a sheet of paper, folded it, and passed them to Banker. He opened them, and as he read them, he placed them in four separate piles in front of him. "Gentlemen, we have one vote for Banker, two votes for Dealer, three votes for Importer, and the remaining three for Printer. As we have done in the past, we will remove those with the least votes and vote again. Let's cast our votes again to decide between Importer and Printer."

    Each of the nine again wrote their choice, folded the paper, and slid them to Banker. He repeated the process of reading them and dividing them. This time there were only two stacks. One stack only contained three sheets of paper and the other six. "Gentlemen," Banker said as he picked up the stack of three, "we have three votes for Importer and six for Printer."

William Randolph Hearst, formerly Printer, stood up and made his way to the vacant chair at the head of the table. Diamond, as he was now known, brought the meeting to order. "Gentlemen, with our first order of business out of the way, we must now turn our attention to a new member for the Committee. Banker has already reminded us that our next selection must be unanimous. I will pass around the list of potential members for each of you to review. We will then vote in the same manner as we have before. Each time, the candidate with the fewest votes will be removed until we can agree on a consensus. Let us begin." With that, he slid the names to Banker who read them and passed them on until all of the committee members had read them.

"Now that we have seen the list, it is time for us to vote." It took five rounds of voting until there were only two names remaining. Diamond looked around at the other members and announced. "We have two choices, Howard Hughes has six votes and Elliot Spivey has three. At this point we must have a unanimous decision. I will ask if the three who voted for Elliot Spivey will agree to the selection of Howard Hughes. Are there any objections?" None were voiced. "Gentlemen, we have selected Howard Hughes. The approach will be made as it has been done in the past."

Banker nodded to get Diamond's attention; given the floor, he addressed the committee. "Gentlemen, I have given some thought to several items I wish to bring before the committee. The first item is the use of the names we have chosen for ourselves on this committee. I have some concern we may be giving too much of a clue as to our identity if we ever have a security breach. My identity as Banker would tell anyone exactly what profession I am in. Printer would also give too much away as well as Importer. To this point, we have never had a security concern. I do not wish to be complacent as we accelerate our strategy. I am suggesting we use the names of minerals and establish ten permanent names, and new members will be given the name of their predecessor."

Importer raised his hand and was given the floor by the Chairman. "Are you suggesting we all change our names or simply give these to new members as they come in? I am not nearly as concerned about our identities being discovered as I am a security breach as to our intentions being discovered as we implement our plans."

Banker looked at Importer and responded, "One of the reasons I am suggesting this is the need to constantly be aware of security. The second reason is another item I have given a great deal of thought. This nation is now at war, and we will be massively converting our industries to war production and huge spending increases in defense. There will be very little oversight in the procurement process, and we control several key industries. I am proposing that we use this to fund our activities. To this point, we have used our own money. That well could eventually be drawn down and make it harder to implement our strategy. We are serving this nation, and this nation should pay for that service."

Dealer motioned to the chairman and was given the floor. "I would like to remind this committee the massive amounts of money we have spent so far, and I have had to spend a considerable sum to convert from the manufacture of automobiles to war materials. I am very much against the idea of nations going to war. Having said that, we were attacked and have no choice. I know that Europe is in a terrible situation, and we have no choice. We should use this opportunity to repay our investments."

Diamond held up his hand to stop the debate. "Gentlemen, I think that Banker has brought up a very valuable strategy. I would like to expand on that. I believe we could not only profit from this, I propose that we use this opportunity to start a corporation to take care of the committee business. This would remove us one step further from our activities and make it harder to bring it back to us. We could not only turn a profit, this is the time to do so when there will be much less oversight. There will be many times in the future this would be to our benefit."

John Rockefeller Jr., known on the committee as Developer, who actually owned the development in which they had built their headquarters, Rockefeller Center, raised his hand for acknowledgement. Given the nod by Diamond, he began to speak, "Gentlemen, I think these proposals have a lot of merit. One area of concern that I've had for some time is that we will find ourselves in need of our own security specialists to take care of situations that may arise. We as businessmen sometimes have to deal with situations that may not be pleasant. The stakes we are playing for have increased dramatically since our entry into this war. The world will never be the same when this is over."

There was silence for several long moments. The Committee members began to realize the world would indeed be changed, and they had to adapt with it. The committee had adapted to every challenge they had faced for the last one hundred and fifty years or so. With that, a new strategy was begun that would change not only the nation but a new world order.

Wellington Capitol
Boston, Massachusetts
March 18, 1990

Ben Cain looked up from the file he had been working on for the better part of the last two months. Trying to get this kind of a deal done was a lot easier before the economy had turned. He rolled his neck and rubbed his eyes. The last three years had been a bitch. He had a son that was almost three years old; he had held down working full time and managed to get through law school in three years. His graduation was going to be in May. God was he tired. Ben looked at his watch; it was almost five thirty. He had learned from his father that there were times no more work could be done when the words blurred together or they didn't make sense. He had found it was true; he spent far more time than what he accomplished was worth. He put the file away and stood up and grabbed his jacket from the back of his chair. He slipped it over his arm rather than put it on. He stepped around his desk and headed out his office door, most of the office had left already. James Bradley caught him just as he reached the lobby. *Damn*, thought Ben, *the one time I try to leave before seven he catches me.*

"Hey, Ben, got a minute?" Bradley asked.

"Sure, Mr. Bradley. I was just about to head home early for once. What's on your mind?"

"How about we go grab a quick drink on the way?" Bradley asked.

Although it was the last thing Ben wanted to do, he decided it wasn't wise to turn his boss down. "Sure," Ben replied.

"This won't take long, Ben. Around the corner at the pub okay with you?" Bradley asked.

The two left the office and entered the elevator where Ben slipped on his jacket. "There is someone waiting for us I would like to introduce you to. He is in the pub around the corner already and asked if I would bring you by. Ben, I don't think you have officially met Benjamin Templeton have you?"

Surprised at the invitation at all, Ben was really surprised that the founder of the firm who was now chairman of the board wanted to meet him. "Met him, no. Wait, I think he was at lunch once when we did the Marsh deal. That is the only time I recall. I don't think I actually talked to him. We were just introduced."

"Well, Ben, believe me he knows who you are. He has taken almost a personal interest in your career development since you started here." Bradley was still surprised at Ben's reaction, the look on his face told it all. *Damn*, he thought. *Ben really doesn't understand the special amount of interest that's been paid to his development.* Sometimes Bradley didn't understand it. Granted, Ben was special. It wasn't every day someone with his background, work ethic, and connections landed in your lap for a job interview. *However*, Bradley thought, *there is something way beyond the norm with the attention paid to Ben. Maybe, just maybe, I can get some insight into what is going on*, Bradley thought.

The pair arrived at the door to the pub, aptly named the Corner Pub, and Ben opened the door and held it for Bradley and followed him in. Bradley quickly scanned the room and found Benjamin Templeton sitting in the corner booth. He motioned for Ben to follow him as Templeton stood and extended his hand to Bradley and then to Ben. Ben was surprised at the almost fiercely strong handshake. He had learned from his father to look someone straight in the eye and evaluate them while delivering a very firm handshake. Templeton who was well into his sixties did exactly the same while a smile crossed his face as he peered into Ben's eyes.

Bradley, no stranger himself to the practice, introduced the pair. "Mr. Templeton, I would like you to officially meet Ben Cain, who I know you have heard a great deal about."

Templeton, still eying Ben, thought to himself, *I know much more about him than either of you suspect.* He replied, "I have heard all good things about you, Ben. I'm pleased to finally get the chance to meet you when other business isn't the topic of discussion."

"I am very much honored, sir, to meet you and thank you for all you have done for me since I joined the firm."

"Why don't you have a seat and drink, and we can discuss why I wanted to meet with you. What will be your gentlemen's pleasure?" Templeton motioned with his right hand to Rick Evans, the owner of the pub.

As Ben sat down, he realized the owner of the pub was hovering in the corner to take their order. *Wow,* Ben thought, *I've seen the guy a dozen times coming in here and have never seen him take drink orders before.*

"What can I get you, gentlemen? Famous Grouse for you Ben, right?" Evans asked, smiling.

"Sure, that will be fine," Ben managed to reply, stunned that the owner who had been pointed out to him but whom he had never met would know his preference.

Evans returned with the drinks so quickly Ben realized they had to have been made while they were walking to the table. Also, Ben thought, Bradley and Templeton hadn't even ordered. Obviously, he knew all of their preferences. Evans placed the drinks on the table and quickly retreated, leaving the trio alone.

"Well, Ben, what should we drink to? How about a bright future for our rising star?" Templeton asked and held up his glass. They quickly followed suit, and each took a sip of their drink. "Ben, you must be aware that I have taken a personal interest in your career. It isn't often we land someone with your talent and knowledge of our type of business. I have been very pleased with your progress so far. I would also like to tell you the great things we expect from you."

"Thank you, sir," Ben managed to reply. This was almost moving too quickly for Ben.

"James, I would like your evaluation of Ben's progress in learning the laws as they apply to our business and an evaluation of his overall progress so far."

"Well, sir, Ben's grasp of the banking laws was far ahead of where most start. As you know, he has completed law school and will graduate in May. I also think he learned far more from his father than even he realizes and shows a very good aptitude for the subtleties of evaluating people that can't be taught."

"I am making a judgment here, gentlemen," Templeton stated. "That you think highly of Ben personally as well as professionally, would that be correct, James?"

"Yes, Mr. Templeton, I think very well of our young Mr. Cain. There aren't very many of his age and background who have done as much on their own. Most prefer to take advantage of their family wealth and status. Ben, if you haven't already figured it out, I not only like you, I admire your commitment and work ethic."

"That is my impression of you as well, Ben. I'm pleased to hear James's evaluation of you agree with everything everyone I talked to about you thinks. Now let me get to the heart of what I wanted to talk to you about." Templeton paused to take a sip of his drink. He then looked Ben in the eye and appeared to gather his thoughts. "Ben, as you know, in the world of finance, we deal with banking laws and all sorts of different regulations, most of which you are familiar with. The one thing all of these have in common is they are all written and passed by politicians, most of whom have no real understanding of business. Let's be honest, what they are mostly interested in is getting reelected. We spend a good deal of money hiring lawyers to deal with these sometimes ridiculous regulations. We also make very large political contributions to them in the hopes of getting favorable legislation. I have given this a great deal of thought the last few months. With your background and now that you have completed law school, have you given any thought to entering the political arena?"

Ben sat in silence for a moment. He hated to admit it, but since his father had been governor of New Jersey, he had wondered if he could do what his father had done. "I never gave it a lot of thought, but

I have to admit watching my father handle the governor's job as well as he has made me wonder how I would have done."

Templeton smiled inwardly; he knew he had him. "Well, Ben, I'm glad to hear you answered that honestly. I happen to know all of us think we can do better than the politicians do. We need laws, of course, to govern what we do, but we need sensible laws. What I would like you to consider is a run for the state legislature. There is going to be an open seat the next election, and I know the chairman of the Republican committee in this state is having a hard time finding a suitable candidate. That is when I thought of you. You have the perfect background. You will have passed the bar by then and having your father as a very successful governor is the icing on the cake. You will still be able to work for the firm of course, and we gain someone to look favorably on sensible legislation. Why don't you take some time to think about it? Go home and talk to your wife and your father perhaps. We have plenty of time."

*The meeting had ended well,* Templeton thought. *It is only a matter of time until our candidate takes the first step. He has been well groomed.* Malachite smiled to himself.

Hotel Del Coronado
San Diego, California
March 18, 1942


Howard Hughes strode through the door of the Hotel Del Coronado. It was one of the few that had not been completely taken over by the armed services for the duration of the war. The owners had managed to convince the government all of the rooms they needed would be made available. This left it still in private control and one of the few places Hughes felt reasonably comfortable in staying but also where he could get a drink in the gentlemen's bar and not be run over with the overflow of rowdy sailors. Howard was tired; he had been working with Lockheed on the development of the new *Constellation*, which he knew was his airliner of the future. Right now the first unofficial flight had taken place, and it was to be used as a transport. There were no other aircraft like it. It could cross the oceans as well as the continents and do so as fast as the best Japanese fighter. He liked to look to the future. This war would not last forever, and he was already making his plans to be on top of the airline business. Making his way into the bar, he sat down at one of the out-of-the-way tables. He wanted nothing more than to have a quiet drink, go to his room, take a shower, and get some sleep. The waiter approached and took his drink order and quickly returned, with not only the drink but the bottle and a bowl of pretzels and mixed nuts. He was well known after all.

Staring out onto the gently moving waters of the bay, Howard never noticed the two well-dressed men as they came in and set down. Far enough away not to be intrusive but close enough to be sure the meeting that Hughes didn't yet know about was undisturbed. William Randolph Hearst approached through the doors of the bar and made his way to the table Hughes was sitting at alone. "Mind if I join you, Howard?"

Hughes looked up into the smiling face of Hearst, stood up, offered his hand, and said, "Help yourself. I may not be good company as tired as I am."

"Howard, you are always good company. The dashing aviator and movie mogul. Who wouldn't want your company?"

Laughing, Hughes shook his head and said, "If you only knew how far from the truth and glamour it all really is."

"Oh come now, Howard. You really are a self-made man who has done things the rest of us only dream about. For example, getting Lockheed to spend massive amounts of money, building during wartime what really is an airliner, justifying it because it can be used as a transport. That should set you up quite nicely when this war is finally over."

Surprised that Hearst knew about the *Constellation*, Hughes looked at him with a hard look and began to suspect his appearance was not quite a coincidence. "All right, William, you have proved your point. Somehow I suspect you being here isn't accidental. Now tell me what you really want. I'm tired and not in the mood for bantering around the point."

"Howard, there are some things that have to be dealt with quite delicately, wouldn't you agree?"

"William, what kind of game are you playing with me? I told you already I am tired and not in the mood. Get to the point."

Hearst returned the hard look Hughes was giving him and knew he was among an equal. This was the type of man to be reckoned with; the committee had chosen well. "All right, Howard. You have been selected to become a member of a very exclusive club. One to which I am sure you have no idea you were under consideration for. This is not the place to begin the discussion of just exactly what we do. Let's just say it is made up of just a select few members of like-minded men who have the best interest of our nation at heart."

"William, I have no idea what you are referring to. What makes you so sure I will want to be a member of your exclusive club?"

Hearst looked at Hughes and took a long moment and said nothing. When he finally broke the silence there was no doubt the message he was sending. "Let's just say that an invitation has never been refused. You have been selected and are about to be trusted with things that are much larger than any one of us. This goes back to the very founding of our nation and has been carried on from then to now with no breach of that trust and security. There are very few who have been honored to become selected. When you find out just exactly what we do, I am sure you will feel the same way. I will say I felt much as you do now when I was selected. There are some things I am not at liberty to discuss in these surroundings." Motioning with his hand to the gentlemen's bar, it took Hughes by surprise that it was empty except for the two of them and the two well-dressed gentlemen sitting at tables discretely away from them. The doors were closed with a sign announcing that fact and two rather large individuals stationed by the doors to keep the curious away. Hearst smiled at Hughes and simply said, "Welcome to the club, Howard."

# THE COMMITTEE

The Committee
Rockefeller Center
New York, New York
May 18, 1943

    The committee was assembled around the large oval-shaped conference table in the boardroom of the space they maintained in Rockefeller Center. Diamond brought the meeting to order. "Gentlemen, we have several items on the agenda. First, I would like to begin by welcoming our newest member of the Committee. I am sure he is known to all of you and will be known as Gold to the Committee. Let me also remind us of the rules. Remember, nothing written leaves this room. We refer to each other in here by our Committee names. When we leave, those personas remain in here. We meet as a full Committee once a year unless something else requires our scheduling a meeting. We seem to have had several of those in the last couple of years. We will conduct our business as we have in the past with each of us taking areas of responsibility. We then handle that area without the interference of other members unless it is a joint effort or help is needed to make something happen. This is to isolate everything we do to ensure it is not connected to our overall strategy. I will also remind all of us once again there is no fixed timetable. We have adjusted everything we do to our ability to control certain aspects and to react to others beyond our control. I would like to begin with the decision to start a corporation to take care of our interests. Dealer, you are spearheading that effort."

    Henry Ford, also known as Dealer, had the floor. "Gentlemen, we decided a corporation was the best option to further remove our activities one more layer from being identifiable to us. It has been decided that several corporations should be started. That will give us the ability to further separate what we do and make sure it is not connected. Several of us can control different boards of directors with the influence we have. It was also decided to begin to pay back our personal investments. With the war industries in full production and all of the cost plus contracts, it is quite easy to inflate the cost of the material and the excess profits quietly going to where we need them. We have managed to do this in our own companies, as well as the new ones we started. If it is ever looked into, we have covered ourselves quite well, and it will be looked at as nothing more than cost overruns, confusion, and some poor management decisions to meet deadlines. It has been effective beyond our best estimates. The agencies who might have an interest in looking into this are occupied elsewhere right now. We are also being quite subtle about it. I believe this practice can be carried forward into the future long past this war."

"Thank you, Dealer. Importer, would you care to bring us up-to-date on the currency situation?"

Joseph Kennedy, also known as Importer on the Committee, now had the floor. "As you know, we began with the implementation of the Federal Reserve. This allowed us control of the banking system. We can now decide what interest rates are, which banks will be successful, and further our control of the monetary system. With the beginning of the income tax during World War I, Americans began to expect a tax bill annually. We convinced them now that weekly withholding is necessary to fund our war effort. Deficit spending to fund the war has also greatly increased. The public has accepted it as their duty to buy war bonds. We continue to control the hard assets such as gold and leave the public holding paper currency. It may take several decades and more economic downturns to gain complete control."

Howard Hughes sat and listened to the Committee at work. As powerful and successful as he was, even he was stunned. He had never imagined manipulations on this scale. When the business of the candidates came up, he was even more surprised to realize the Committee had been doing on a national scale what businessmen had been trying all along with bribes and coercion. This took it to a whole new level. He had to admit he was impressed.

The meeting was finally adjourned. Howard Hughes was leaving the conference room and heading to his car where his driver was waiting. William Randolph Hearst called out to him, "Howard, wait a moment. If you don't mind, I need a few minutes of your time." Hughes turned and nodded his acceptance while Hurst finished talking with Joseph Kennedy. Taking his leave from Kennedy, Hurst made his way toward Hughes.

"Well, Howard, now that you are fully welcomed into the club, was it everything I promised it to be?" Hurst smiled at the expression on Hughes's face.

"Let's just say I am suitably impressed. Things you can only dream of controlling are in the Committee's grasp."

"Howard, this is larger than any of us. This really does go back to the founding of our nation. The founders learned early on the will of the people is not what is always best. Look at the world today, torn by war. Millions will be dead before this conflict is over. We can control it, stop the madness, and make it a much better and prosperous world."

"Tell me the overall strategy again. It moved pretty quickly, and I am not up to speed on all of this yet."

"Let's take a walk while I give you my viewpoint." The two left the conference room and exited the elevator on the ground floor. Walking around the streets of Rockefeller Center, Hurst gathered his thoughts for the discussion with Hughes.

"Howard, I am sure this is all quite surprising to realize this has gone on from the beginning of our country's founding. George Washington was the first chairman of the Committee. Early on, they began to realize the average American had no idea what it was going to take just to ensure the country would survive. Most were and still are uneducated in the true ways of the world and business. Even now, many are illiterate in the remote regions of a country as prosperous as the United States. We are barely removed from actual slavery, only eighty or so years from it. That legacy alone will haunt us for some time to come. Decisions as important as who our president is, much less the Congress and Senate, do you feel comfortable trusting the direction—not just this nation but this world takes—to the uneducated masses of voters?"

"I see your point, William. I just wonder what will happen if it is ever found out. What I really want to know is just what exactly our endgame is going to be. Do we really have a plan, or are we doing this just for the sake of control? Will the world be better off for what we are doing?" He stopped and looked Hearst straight in the eyes.

Meeting his gaze, Hearst smiled and replied, "Read history, Howard, there has never been a great empire to survive. The Romans were probably the closest. Eventually, the depravity of the people caused them to fall. Do you realize there still was a holy Roman emperor when Washington became president? Look at it now, Hitler devastating Europe, Mussolini invading Ethiopia in the thirties, killing hundreds of thousands with chemical weapons. Now he has brought Italy to the brink with his alliance with Hitler. Japan brutally killing millions of Chinese then attacking us. What I want, Howard, is a way to stop it all. A legacy we can leave this world. Individuals cannot be trusted. They must be guided and directed. That is all we are doing, providing this world with some badly needed direction and control."

"William, I understand where you are going with all of this. All of us at one time or another believes we can save the world. We are small pieces passing through. What will it all be fifty or a hundred years from now, will we make a difference?"

Hurst laughed. "Howard, I have asked myself those same things. If we don't do this, what is going to happen? Throughout history there has always been a conqueror or a dictator who wants to take control for selfish purposes. At least with the Committee we have reasonable business people making business decisions about where we are headed. I much prefer that to chance."

"Perhaps, William, you are right. All we can do is our best." The two continued walking toward their cars where their drivers waited, neither convinced nor realizing that they too were part of the masses.

The Cain Campaign
Boston, Massachusetts
November 6, 1996


The election coverage was being played on the large screen television and was being projected onto the large screen behind the podium. The election results were being predicted and the races called by the network news anchors. The Massachusetts congressional districts were coming in. Ben Cain and his wife, Marilyn, were surrounded by campaign staff and the wealthy donors who had generously funded his campaign. He had served in the state legislature for four years and had thrown his hat in the race for Congress. He had once again been encouraged by the chairman of Wellington, Benjamin Templeton. It all seemed to have happened so quickly. Everyone in the room was glued to the screen as the anchor called the race. "With 62 percent of all precincts reporting, we are calling the twelfth district for Republican, Ben Cain, 53 to 47 percent."

The crowd broke into cheers and congratulatory handshakes as Marilyn hugged her husband. Ben found himself being pushed toward the podium. The crowd wanted a victory speech from their new congressman elect. Ben found himself standing at the podium with his wife by his side. The cheering was still ringing in his ears as he began to speak. "Thank you. I can't begin to tell you how much your support has meant. We would not be where we are taking our message to Washington without all of your tireless effort to make this happen." Ben continued speaking hardly aware of what he was saying. Across the room, Edwin Cain stood with his wife, Marjorie, by his side. He was having a hard time controlling his emotions. He was proud of his son. He had tried to set an example for both of his children. He had never dreamed his son would enter into the political arena.

Edwin Bennett Cain had served two terms as governor of New Jersey. He was proud of what he had accomplished. He had taken the budget and fixed all of the waste and gotten them on track financially. He had fought long and hard using persuasion and reason to get education reform through.

He did everything he could to streamline the state agencies, cut waste, and even push for tax reform. He had retired from public service after two terms rather than run for senator as he was being pushed to do.

Edwin was now sixty-six and happy with the life he had worked so hard to build. Ben was obviously doing well. Catherine had pursued a career in business and surprising him had taken over the day-to-day operations as president of Atlantic Holdings. He had been happy to relinquish that role to his daughter and continue on as chairman of the board. Looking at his son delivering his victory speech, Ed knew Ben was somehow going to go farther than being just a congressman.

Benjamin Templeton was sitting in the leather armchair in the den of his home in the gated security-patrolled estate he owned overlooking the Delaware River. The television he was watching was playing the same network coverage calling the congressional races that was being projected onto the screen behind the podium where Ben Cain would give his victory speech. He was keeping score; his candidates were having a good night.

The Little White House
Warm Springs, Georgia
April 10, 1945

    Lucy Mercer Rutherford tossed the covers back on the bed in which she had spent the night with the president of the United States, Franklin Delano Roosevelt. He was still asleep. She had been his mistress longer than she cared to think about, even when she had married. Leaving the bed, she smiled sadly as she looked at the sleeping president. *Things were not always what they seemed*, she thought. Oh yes, she supposed in his way he cared about her. She wondered if he really cared about anything other than his own power and prestige. She knew much more about how his power had come about than anyone realized. Because of this, she had been recruited to do something she had no choice but to do. She realized long before there was something unusual in the way he had come to be elected. Over the years they were together whenever they could and there was always someone following her, and she was never in doubt they were keeping an eye on her. At first she thought they were Secret Service. Later she realized it had started before he was president. She had confronted them once and found out quickly they were playing for keeps. The only reason she hadn't had an accident was the problems it would have caused them. When you can control someone, they can be more useful than if they are dead. They knew everything about her; she had no choice. She had been paid a visit before this trip to Georgia. Decisions had been made. She was told she had no choice but to implement that decision. She had been given a vial of something; she didn't know what it was. Over the past two days she had been putting several drops in whatever she could get it into that the president would consume. He was already sick; she wondered how long it would take. *Some things*, she

# THE COMMITTEE

thought, *you have no choice but to do*. She knew there was power behind him larger than what anyone realized. Somehow he had scared them. *Perhaps*, she thought, *he no longer thought they could control him*. She knew they could control all of them.

Leaving the bedroom where Roosevelt was sleeping, she made her way to the room she stayed in on those infrequent times she visited here. The Secret Service agents acted like they never saw her. *They know*, she thought. After all, it was one of them who had seen the vial in her purse and acted like it wasn't even there. It was Franklin's daughter who had arranged for her to be here to see her father. *If she only knew what I am being forced to do.*

It had been one of those faceless men that had always followed her. He had approached her when she had left to come here and told her exactly what she was going to do. He made it very clear she had no choice. She wondered how long she would survive after this.

Hearst Newspapers
Corporate Headquarters
Los Angeles, California
April 12, 1945

William Randolph Hearst was sitting in his office staring out the window overlooking downtown. The door to his office opened, and his secretary rushed in to his office, a pained expression on her face. She was holding a sheet of teletype paper out to him. She didn't say anything; she handed him the paper and practically ran from his office trying to hold back the tears. Looking down at the paper, he highly suspected what it was going to tell him. This one was personal.

Reading the teletype that announced the death of the president of the United States, Franklin Delano Roosevelt. He smiled to himself. Roosevelt had been selected long before he came to be Diamond. The Committee had seen to it Roosevelt was not only elected but reelected three more times. He had been one of the members then and not powerful enough to have enough influence to have someone else selected. He had ascended to the chairmanship in early 1942. He had decided he was going to even the score. Roosevelt had gone after anyone he had decided was his enemy. He had personally instructed who he had wanted investigated for tax evasion. Had FDR known who he was going after, Hearst thought, he would not have done so. No president ever knew who the Committee was made up of. None of their candidates did. They could never allow it. They had ways of controlling them and letting them know exactly what was required of them.

Roosevelt had crossed the line and begun to believe he really was as powerful as his ego was telling him. Since Hearst had come to hold the chairmanship of the Committee after the United States had entered the war and Henry Wallace was his vice president, Hearst had to wait. FDR had gone after him for taxes in the thirties. He didn't know Hearst would play for keeps. You never ever cross him. Roosevelt may have been ill and would not have lived out the year anyway, but Hearst wanted the personal satisfaction of taking him out. You never crossed the Committee or Diamond in particular. Even presidents could be replaced.

The Committee
New York, New York
September 27, 1951

The members of the Committee each made their way to the building they maintained in Rockefeller Center. They were careful not to arrive at the same time or to be seen going into the building the same way. They were each very careful and had plenty of security to see they were not followed. William Randolph Hearst had passed away in August, and the Committee was without a Chairman.

John D. Rockefeller Jr. called the meeting to order. Developer, as he was known on the Committee, began, "Gentlemen, as we all know, we have the need to select a new chairman and a new member for the Committee. We will proceed as we have in the past, selecting a chairman from one of us in this room. A majority is enough for this. For the selection of a new member, the vote must be unanimous. If each of you will write your selection for chairman and pass them to me."

There was silence as the members of the Committee contemplated who they wanted as chairman. There had been several chairmen in little more than ten years; several of the newer members were thinking the time of the old guard was past. They wanted one of their own. They had been planning their moves carefully. Their time was now. In the end, it had come down to a choice between Howard Hughes and Everett Sloan. Sloan was selected five votes to four. Everett Sloan had been chosen to replace Dealer when he had died in 1947. Everett Sloan was a self-made man. A distant relative of the Sloan plumbing family He had managed to leverage that into several lucrative business deals. Investing in war industries had been vastly more profitable than real estate. He had a knack for knowing not only the right deals but the wrong ones and managing to stay away from them. The fact that he was totally ruthless and would do whatever it took ensured his success. There was a trail of broken business opponents to prove it.

Obsidian, as he had been formerly known, stood and made his way to the vacant chair at the head of the conference table. The moment he sat down, he was Diamond. The most powerful of the most powerful; the Committee would never be the same. Looking down the table at the other members of the Committee, he took a long moment to savor his victory. Making eye contact with each and every single one left no doubt who was now in charge.

"Gentlemen, the next item is of course selecting a replacement to fill the vacancy we now have." Moving forward, not even thanking them for their vote of confidence, Diamond continued with the business at hand. "I will circulate the list of potential members. We will nominate three to choose from. The final choice must be unanimous." Sloan was doing things his way.

Taking nominations from the Committee members, Diamond announced, "We have three to choose from: J Paul Getty, H. L. Hunt, and Howard Ahmanson Jr. If you will write your selections down and pass them to me."

The selections were written down and passed to the chairman; the votes were tallied. "We have two votes for Hunt, two votes for Getty, and the remaining votes for Ahmanson. This leaves us with a bit of a dilemma. I have decided the way to handle this is to revote for the two with two votes each and the winner facing Ahmanson in another vote."

The committee members were stunned; this wasn't how it was done. Now that he was Diamond, Sloan was letting the rest of the committee know he was in charge. The vote was retaken, H. L. Hunt was then put up against Ahmanson, another split vote, more arm twisting, and Ahmanson was finally selected to fill the vacancy on the Committee. The remaining business was handled and the meeting was adjourned.

Alfred J. Barclay was waiting on Howard Hughes as he left the building where the committee had just met. "Howard, walk with me if you don't mind." The two made their way toward where their limousines were waiting. Barclay, one of the elder statesmen on the Committee, was in his early seventies. "Howard, I'm concerned at what went on in there. That's not the way we run our business. I'm afraid Sloan is going to run his own agenda just for personal power. We are all agreed that is not what we are trying to do."

"I rather got that impression myself. The question then becomes what we are going to do about it. There seemed to be a pretty clear divide of those who wanted him and those that didn't."

Barclay stopped, turned to Hughes, and looked him in the eye. "Howard, the committee was never about personal gain. It all started among honorable and noble men who had the best interests of this nation at heart. As I have gotten older, I have begun to realize just how far we have strayed from that purpose. We are all powerful, well-educated, and wealthy. We believe we know far better what is best than the average American does. We even figured out how to control their votes with marketing campaigns. We are only educating them to the point they can work and be productive and not threaten our control. We even began to steal from them with how we figured out how to build cost overruns and funnel tax money into where we control it. We are manipulating and controlling them, and they are unaware. My god, what have we done?"

Stunned at the candid admission, Hughes was at a loss as to what to tell him. "Alfred, between us, I have thought much the same thing. I've been troubled by this almost from the start. When I was a young man, I had to fight for what was mine. The problem is we don't have any allies in there."

# THE COMMITTEE

"We have some time, Howard, to figure out how we can deal with this. There are some things we need to talk about. There were things done, not even the entire committee knows about. As the new chairman, he is about to find out how much more power he really has."

The two had reached the area where their limousines were parked. They parted ways, each with their own thoughts knowing something had to be done. The first cracks were developing in the Committee.

The University of Virginia
The Law Library
March 2, 1999

Chris Evans stepped out into the rain. He had forgotten his jacket this morning when he had left for class. The weather had changed for the worse since then. He had a lot to do, and his mind was on everything else. He was working on his research for his doctorate. Holding his briefcase over his head, moving as quickly as he could across the campus, he was on his way to get his jacket when he realized he was close to the law library. Making a quick decision, he ducked inside. He didn't think the rain would last much longer. He still had plenty of research to do, and he could get in a little time here in the library and maybe avoid getting drenched.

Stepping through the lobby, he stepped up to the desk where the librarian was sitting. Smiling at the cute blonde behind the desk, he thought sometimes an unplanned diversion might bring a welcome opportunity. "Hello, I wonder if you might be able to help me."

Looking up, Pam Oliver smiled at the nice-looking guy standing in front of her desk. "What can I do for you?"

"I am working on my paper for my doctorate. The subject is kind of boring, but I'm trying to find information on some of the founding fathers, relating their writings and beliefs against some of the recent Supreme Court decisions. I have found quite a bit on Jefferson, but I still need some stuff on James Madison."

"Let me get one of our senior librarians to help. Jared Conley is our resident expert. He can tell you where all that stuff is hidden. Hang on while I call him." She picked up the phone, dialed an extension and then explained what she needed when the phone was answered. She hung up on the phone, smiled at Chris and said, "He will be out in a minute."

"Thanks for all of your help. By the way, I don't think I properly introduced myself. My name is Chris Evans." Extending his hand and smiling as she took his hand to shake it, the moment was interrupted when Jared Conley walked up.

Jared Conley smiled to himself as he noticed the look between the two. "Hello, I'm Jared Conley. I understand you are interested in writings of James Madison," he said as he extended his hand toward Chris.

Letting go of the hand of Pam Oliver and extending his hand to Conley, Chris began to explain what he needed.

Conley thought over the request and said, "Let me get you started with what we have in the main library, and we will go from there." He then led Chris to the area where all the Madison material was kept.

Three and a half hours later, Chris rolled his neck and rubbed his eyes. It was still raining outside, and he still hadn't found quite what he was looking for. Most of Madison's writings were in Washington DC in the library of Congress. Jared Conley walked up and asked, "Find anything useful yet?"

"Not quite what I'm looking for I'm afraid. Most of his writings are well known. I need something that reveals his personal feelings."

Conley thought for a moment and said, "Well, that is most of what we have here. As you know, most of his writings are in DC. Let me think. There was something we received quite a while back. I don't think it has been completely catalogued yet. You would have to be quite careful with it. These are the originals. They are writings from his later years I believe. I received them from a friend of mine when Madison's home was being restored. I very briefly looked them over, and most of them are from when he was senile in his later years. I never completely went through them. If you promise to be extremely careful, I will let you look through them."

Conley left to retrieve the box he had received from Jason Edison over a decade before. Returning about ten minutes later, Conley set the cardboard file box on the table. "There's not a lot new. From what I remember, most of them are copies of other documents with handwritten notes in the margins. I will leave them with you until we close, and I must collect them then."

Chris looked at the small stack of papers in the box and looked at his watch. Deciding he may as well get it out of the way, he thanked Conley and began to sort through them.

Pam Oliver was finishing her shift in the library and decided she would look in on the interesting young man who had come in earlier. Walking into the study room where he was sitting at the table with all of the papers spread out before him, Pam approached the table and smiled when he looked up. "Hi, I was finishing up and thought you might still be here. Find anything interesting?"

"Not yet, most of this stuff I have already been through. He just brought another box that hasn't been catalogued. I'm trying to decide if I want to go through it all."

Looking at the small stack of paper in the box, Pam had a sudden insight in how to get to know Chris a little better. "There doesn't seem to be a lot of them. How about I give you a hand going through them, and you can buy me coffee afterward?"

Looking up into the smiling face of Pam Oliver, Chris decided God was being kind to him. "That is the best offer I've had. I would even be willing to throw in dinner."

Pam sat down and reached into the box and gently pulled the yellowing stack of papers from it and began to divide them up. Taking one stack and giving them to Chris, she took the other and the pair slowly began to go through them. Fifteen minutes later, Pam picked up the letter James Madison had penned to his deceased friend Thomas Jefferson one hundred and sixty-seven years before.

My dearest Thomas,

As I write these lines to you, I realize you will never read them. Many years have gone by since you have passed, and I became the last to carry on. You are the only one who will understand the burdens we carried so long. The chairmanship passed to me when you were taken from this world, and I have tried to live by the principles with which we founded this nation. I fear as time passes those to whom we entrusted positions on the committee will no longer abide by the guiding principles of faith the founders sought to live by.

    I know you and I shared the same self doubts if we were right to form the committee. Our purposes noble and our intentions honorable, we did not trust our citizens to make the right decisions of leadership this nation has needed. We chose to implement our will by choosing who those leaders would be. Those of us who fought to bring this nation forth may have understood our concern for those Americans who were never willing to fight for their principles of faith, freedom, and liberty. Yet these have been our guiding light. I fear it will not always be so to those who follow. We have given them the power to decide the fate of this nation. As the years passed and we lost the original members of the Committee, General Washington, Samuel Patterson, Jonathan who sacrificed so much, all the others, to Alexander who was struck down by the madman Burr. I am the last, and the power has passed to those that we chose. I pray we have chosen wisely, and I fear we have not. The course they choose will determine the fate and freedoms we cherished and sacrificed to provide yet may be the cause of their demise. I will answer for my sins of this world when I meet our creator. It may not be far in the future for me now. They have set me aside and treat me with respect, yet I fear they seek power never intended. May God forgive us for what we have sown, and I pray what we feared shall not come to pass. I am powerless to stop them. History will tell what our decisions have wrought. May God forgive us and bless this nation and protect it from the committee with which we so inadvertently burdened it.

James

# THE COMMITTEE

Pam reread the letter, stunned at its implication. "Chris, you need to read this." Handing the letter to Chris, Pam was at a loss for words.

Chris took the letter from her and as he read the words James Madison had penned, Jared Conley's words came to mind, "Most of them are from when he was senile in his later years."

Finishing the letter, Chris shook his head and said, "Boy, he wasn't kidding when he said Madison was senile." Laughing, Chris spoke the irreverent thought that popped into his mind, "Man, he really nailed Congress, didn't he?"

Pam extended her hand and took the letter back from Chris. Somehow she knew that wasn't what Madison meant, but she also thought Chris would never take it seriously. "Yeah, I suppose you're right. Let's finish going through these. You still owe me dinner."

Turning his attention back to the papers he was going through, Chris never saw her slip Madison's letter into the folder she had. Pam knew just who would take this seriously.

The Oliver Home
Richmond, Virginia
March 15, 1999

Pam Oliver put the gearshift into park and got out of the driver's seat of her Mazda Miata. The bright red convertible had been a high school graduation present from her father. Her mother had passed away when she was twelve from breast cancer and her father had never remarried. They had always been close and that had only made them closer. Letting herself into the house she had grown up in, she was thrilled to see her father. "Hi, Dad, I'm so glad to see you." Hugging her father always made her feel better.

"Hey, sweetheart, I'm glad to see you too. I was kind of surprised you called and said you were coming home. Why aren't you going on spring break with the gang? It's your last one."

"Because I wanted to see my dad. Besides, I've got something to show you."

Dan Oliver knew his daughter well enough to know there was more to it than that. Not only did they share almost everything, he had been an FBI agent longer than he cared to think about. Nine years before he had to take a desk job in the Richmond Virginia field office when his wife had passed. His daughter was the single most important person in his life. He had never remarried; in his mind, he never wanted anything to compete with his daughter. The lady he had dated for the last three years understood. She had two kids of her own and had lost her husband around the same time she had come to work in the field office. They had kept it quiet. When he retired after his daughter finished college, it wouldn't matter anymore. He was counting down the days.

"What could possibly be more important than going on your last spring break?"

"I found something in the archives at the university. Let's just say I was surprised, and I think there's something to it." Moving into the kitchen, which had become their favorite room in the house when they were home together, they sat down at the kitchen table. Unspoken was it reminded both of them of her mother. Lifting her bag to the table, she removed the small leather folder and the letter James Madison had penned so long ago.

Taking the letter from her, Dan Oliver raised his eyebrows when he realized how old it was. "Don't you really think you should have copied this and left the original?"

"Dad, there's something to this. I think you need to read it and then you may understand why I didn't leave it."

Dan saw the look in his daughter's eyes; they were both highly intelligent and shared conversations on a level way above normal. Dropping his eyes to the faded writing, he read the letter slowly and carefully. His instincts were kicking into high gear. Reading it again to make sure he understood what he was reading, Dan knew why his daughter had taken the original. "Okay, who else knows about this?" In an instant he became the FBI agent.

Pam instantly recognized the change in her father; she had seen it before. "The only person I know that saw it was the guy who came in to work on his doctorate, Chris Evans. I showed it to him right after I found it. I doubt anybody else knows. It was in a box of documents that had been sent to the university, and it had been there for some time."

"Do you know where the documents came from?"

"Jared Conley told Chris they were discovered when they began the restoration of Madison's estate. Apparently, a friend of his found them and sent them to him at the university." Pam never noticed her father had begun to take notes.

"What did Chris say when you showed it to him?"

"He made a smart-ass remark about Madison being senile and really nailing Congress. I don't think he took it seriously."

"Does anyone know you took the letter?"

"I slipped it into my folder when Chris gave it back to me, and I returned the document box to Jared when the library closed. Nobody knows I took it."

Pausing to gather his thoughts, Dan drummed his pencil on the small notebook he had been using to take notes. "Does Conley know the letter was in the documents?"

Pam looked down at the notes her father was taking. She realized the whole conversation had turned into a very skillful interview. "He told Chris he had never finished cataloguing them, that he had briefly looked through them and they were from the latter stages of Madison's life when he was senile. I don't think he thought there was much worthwhile, or he would never have let the originals out."

"Okay, what we have so far is Madison wrote a letter to his deceased friend Thomas. That has to be Thomas Jefferson. He knew he was dead. So I don't think he was as senile as everyone thinks. Maybe he was having a period of clarity. What I find interesting is the reference to 'You are the only one who will understand.' Obviously, there wasn't anyone else he felt he could tell. He also made reference to the other original members of the Committee. General Washington is obvious and so is Samuel Patterson. Jonathan is only a first name. It probably won't take much to figure out who that is. Alexander has to be Alexander Hamilton. Remember he was killed by Aaron Burr in a duel. All the others mean there were more than those he named. He also referred to himself as the last. That has to mean the other founders, as he referred to them, died before he did. Pay attention to the line 'The power has passed to those we chose.' That says to me others were chosen to replace the members when they died. He also says they treated him with respect and set him aside. He also says they didn't trust the citizens to choose the nation's leaders so they did it. Whatever they set up was continuing, and he was concerned they were expanding the power that was passed to them. He also said he was powerless to stop it. Does that mean he tried?"

Pam was fascinated at her father's reasoning. She knew he was good at what he did. She had seen him work but had never been "interviewed" by him and witnessed his reasoning this fast. She had to admit she was impressed. "Dad, the big question in my mind is, still whatever they set up are they still at it? Does this Committee still exist?"

"Let's think about that for a second. Madison died when? Had to be quite a few years after he was president, if I remember my history. He was president during the war of 1812 and after. So this was written several years after Jefferson died but before he did. Those dates will be easy to find. The problem is he made no reference to any names of who they chose as successors. All we know is they continued on."

"So this is nothing but a dead end?"

Her dad grinned at her. She knew he had an idea. "No, this is only the beginning. We don't have to worry too much about what they did from then on. What we can concentrate on is if they are still doing this. There's going to be a trail."

"Dad, I'm lost. How can there be a trail after more than a century?"

"Sweetheart, think about it. What Madison referred to was they didn't trust the citizens to pick the nation's leaders, so they did it. What does that tell you?" Smiling at his daughter's reaction, Dan Oliver knew she had figured it out.

"My god, Dad, they were selecting the president of the United States!"

"That's how I see it. Now think about what expanding their power meant."

"They wanted to control the entire government." Pam was so stunned she couldn't say anything more.

"Now you know why I was so concerned about who knew about this letter. If they are still doing this, you can bet they play for keeps. Sure explains some things, doesn't it?"

The two sat and looked at each other. Dan knew his daughter had no idea what she had stumbled onto when she took the letter. His retirement had suddenly been put on hold. This was one investigation that would have to be deeper and quieter than he had ever done. No one could know. He had long suspected the government wasn't quite as transparent as they wanted the public to believe. He was astounded it may have gone on from the beginning. This one would have to be done solo.

The Oliver Home
Richmond, Virginia
March 20, 1999

Dan Oliver hugged his daughter; it was hard for him to let her go. Yet he knew she had her own life and the dreams that went along with it. He had worked very hard to take care of her and had given up on the chance to become head of a field office for the FBI. It had not been easy being a single dad with a twelve-year-old daughter. He missed his wife, Elaine, terribly. Pam was more like her with every day that passed. Closing his eyes and giving her one more squeeze, the embrace finally ended. "You drive carefully. Let me know when you get there. The old man still worries about you."

Pam looked up into her father's eyes. The look that passed between them said it all. "Dad, you be careful too. I'll call you when I get in." Sliding into the driver's seat of her Miata, clicking the seat belt, she felt her father's eyes still on her. Looking up and smiling at him, she knew the look in his eyes. She had seen that look of steely determination before. Starting the car, she backed out of the driveway and began her return trek to school.

Dan waved to his daughter as she pulled away. He stood there until her car turned the corner and was out of sight. He knew what he was going to do.

Dan Oliver had been an FBI agent since he had graduated college with a degree in criminal justice in 1970. He had been recruited in his last year of college. Going to the FBI academy at Quantico, Virginia, he had met Elaine while he was there. She had followed him around the country, to all the assignments junior G men, as he thought of himself, back then were given. They would have been married twenty-seven years this fall. The breast cancer, which no treatment they tried could stop, had finally taken her from both of them. Pam missed her as much as he did.

Turning, Dan went back into his house. He was going to think this one through very carefully before he started. The one thing he was not willing to risk had just left on the drive back to college. He had often thought that there were certain things that happened with the government that weren't just coincidence. Some of the politicians he had met over the years weren't smart enough to not only get elected but to wield the immense power they seemed to have. He had become an expert over the years in following the trails of corruption and money.

More than one investigation he had been working had been suddenly stopped in its tracks. He had always been smart enough to not let on he suspected something. One thing they didn't know was when he had been told to turn everything over, "that he was no longer on the case," the notes he turned in was not all there were. The first time it happened he had screwed up and given them everything. They had even asked for the notebook he kept in his pocket.

Somehow that didn't sit right with him. A couple of questions he had asked later about the case had gotten him a stiff dressing down from the agent in charge of the field office and a transfer he hadn't asked for. He'd learned his lesson. Since then, there were notes he kept only he knew he had. They were not kept in his home. The second time it happened, he had smiled, given them everything they wanted, and shut up. Over the years it had happened several more times. He had learned to keep his notes on everything he did. At the time he hadn't seen a pattern. It just didn't feel right. It had always been in the back of his mind.

When he had married Elaine two years out of college and Pam had come along six years later, Dan worked hard to get his shot at moving up the ladder. It finally came when he was made the assistant special agent in charge or ASAC as it was known in the Bureau. The promotion had seen the move here to Richmond. He had turned down the next promotion because Elaine was sick by then. Three years later, Elaine had passed away. It was tough having a twelve-year-old daughter you had to raise by yourself. The Bureau didn't care. He knew this was his last stop. He was going to put in for retirement when he had his thirty years in. That was before Pam had come home with the letter from James Madison.

The game had just changed. Dan unlocked the room in the back of his basement. Going in to his private home office, he sat down in the chair at his desk. The short-term location where he kept his notes now contained the letter of James Madison. It wouldn't stay there long. Someone who knew what they were looking for could find the floor safe under the carpet of his basement office. He was going on vacation for a couple of days. Soon the letter would be with his notes where nobody could find them. Five years before his wife died, Dan had set up his safe house; Elaine hadn't even known where it was. He never knew why he had the urge to set it up. Being honest, too many things he had seen and experienced had seemed more than just coincidence. By itself the one-hundred-and-fifty-plus-year-old letter wasn't proof. Everything else he had now made a whole lot more sense.

Opening the lower drawer of his desk and retrieving a key ring, Dan closed the drawer and turned to the locked steel cabinet in the corner. Unlocking it, he reached in and pulled out the box with the 1911 Colt .45 auto. Ejecting the magazine, he worked the action and caught the round as it flew out of the weapon. Putting the round back in the magazine, he put it back in and worked the action, making sure the safety was set; he put the gun down on his desk. Reaching back in the cabinet, he pulled out the holster that went with it and several extra magazines. Setting those down beside the pistol, he turned back to the cabinet once more; reaching in, he removed a leather billfold, a small stack of currency, and a passport. Opening the passport and setting it down on his desk, he then opened the billfold and set it down beside the passport. Comparing the driver's license with the passport, both had a completely different identity from his own. Reaching back in once more, he took the leather folder with the special agent badge and ID that matched the passport. Closing and locking the cabinet, he then reached under the desk and picked up a leather briefcase. Placing it on the desk, he placed the pistol, the magazines, the passport, the currency, and the billfold into the case. Later, the documents in his safe would go in. After he disappeared for a couple of days and the letter, along with the documents he had, made it to his safe house where no one could find them, Dan was going on the hunt, quietly.

The Kennedy Compound
Hyannis Port, Massachusetts
June 28, 1955

    Joseph Kennedy was getting on in years; he was having trouble with his health and was having a hard time admitting it was true. Things were changing; he still wielded immense power. His position on the Committee had given him the opportunity to set up his own personal dynasty. For him, the sad part was the death of his oldest son Joseph in World War II. He would have been president by now. He had come close to losing his son John in that war as well. Fortunately, he had not only survived, he had become a true hero. His exploits commanding a PT boat in the Pacific had become legendary. John still did not know how his father had arranged everything. The Committee had made it all possible.

    Joseph had never gotten over being passed over for the chairmanship. He couldn't afford to let it show. The legacy he was building for his sons would live far beyond him. They had powerful friends. Joseph would use his position on the Committee to see they all would be president.

    Taking a walk on the beach was solace to him. He stopped and turned his gaze toward the ocean, enjoying the brisk breeze on his face and the smell of the salt water soothed him. He would live his dream for power through his sons. What he felt should have been his would belong to the Kennedys for a long time. The sun was warm on his face as he turned and walked toward his home. He was aging, but he would see to it the Kennedy legacy and power would be ageless.

# THE COMMITTEE

On the dunes overlooking the beach, the chief of the security detail scanned the beach and all the surrounding area with his binoculars. There were currently six security specialists on duty right now. It was their job to see all the Committee members were well protected. Not one of them knew who they all were or even what they did. They were professionals—efficient, quiet, and invisible. Not only did they protect the Committee, they did the dirty jobs that had to be done. He watched as Joseph Kennedy walked toward the house. He knew much more of what Joseph Kennedy was doing than he let him know. The reports went straight to Diamond; he didn't know that code name or even the existence of the Committee, at least not that he would admit. He was too professional. The Committee wasn't as perfect as they believed themselves to be, some of them didn't even trust each other.

As Joseph Kennedy entered his home, the detail chief lowered his binoculars. He hated this type of job and all that went with it. He was too much of a professional to let it show. He did every job, and he was good at it. In this business, if you weren't, you didn't survive. Every detail was recorded in his almost photographic memory. Nothing was ever written down. Leaving the dune, he didn't bother to tell the rest of the detail what to do. They were professionals too; they knew what to do and the price of failure. He got in the pickup truck and left the area of the Kennedy compound. He had a report to make in person.

The Texas School Book Depository
Dealey Plaza
Dallas, Texas
November 22, 1963

Lee Harvey Oswald rested his rifle on the edge of the windowsill on the sixth floor window where he had set up his sniper's perch. He didn't have much longer to wait. The presidential motorcade was turning onto the short one-block part of the route toward the school book depository where he worked and was now waiting with his rifle. The part of the plan he didn't like was not taking the shot until the motorcade turned in front of him. They had insisted; he had argued it made more sense to take the shot as the motorcade drove straight toward him. He would only have to compensate for the elevation, not track left to right when he made the shot. Once they were moving parallel to and away from him, it was a harder shot to make. Also the foliage of the tree was a potential problem. He could make the shot either way. It was easier to miss this way. They had argued not to make the shot until after the turn in order to place the motorcade between him and the other shooters. He had argued if he took the shot he wanted, they wouldn't need more shooters; besides, the motorcade could only go forward into the killing zone. He lost the argument. They told him if he did it his way he was on his own; the extrication wouldn't be forthcoming. He planned to survive this; otherwise, he would be just a crazy assassin. He knew he would be a hero if he was alive to help create his socialist utopia.

The motorcade was just beginning the turn; he peered through the scope, tracking his target. Taking a breath, letting half of it out then holding his breath, he gently squeezed the trigger; working the bolt, he fired again, worked the bolt, and fired a third shot. He had seen the president's head explode; he told them they wouldn't need the backup shooters.

Rising from his shooter's position, he hid the rifle and moved away as quickly as he could toward the planned extrication. Going down the stairs as fast as he could without attracting attention, he exited the building on the ground floor.

The Secret Service agent in the follow car heard the report of the rifle and saw the president lurch forward, throw his hands toward his throat, and then he lurched again. Clint Stevens jumped off the running board and ran toward the presidential limousine and jumped on the back as fast as he could. Mrs. Kennedy was crawling on the trunk, trying to retrieve part of the president's skull. Stevens pushed her back into the backseat as the car speed up. Sliding into the backseat, he looked at the president's head and knew it was too late.

On the overpass, the motorcade would have to go under; the second shooter watched the president's head explode. Fortunately, he didn't have to take a shot. He looked toward the small knoll where the third member of the team was leaving. They would only have had to shoot if Oswald had missed. Fortunately, he hadn't; it was much better this way. The rest of the plan to deal with Oswald was now in motion. Oswald thought it was just his extraction. The plan was never for him to survive the assassination as they had led him to believe. Manipulating him was quite easy. They had set it up for a police officer to be his way out. What better way to get out of an area swarming with law enforcement. They would deal with him after that. The setup was perfect. It would look like he was a lone assassin who would leave his manifesto and take his own life.

The police radio in Officer J. D. Tippet's car came to life, and the excited voice of the police dispatcher reported the shooting of the president. Tippet listened as the description came over the radio. He hadn't bargained for this. He was just told to be at a certain location to meet someone and get them out of the area. Now he knew why. Stepping out of the cruiser, he motioned toward the man on the sidewalk and motioned him toward the car. Moving his right hand slowly toward his service revolver, he started to pull it from his holster. Lee Harvey Oswald approached the patrol car; this was his way out. Noticing Tippet moving his hand toward his holster and trying to draw his revolver, Oswald already had his hand on the pistol in his jacket pocket. Pulling his hand with the pistol out of his jacket pocket, he pointed it and fired four times. Tippet crumpled to the ground with a surprised look on his face, Oswald turned and fled. The plan was coming apart.

The motorcade had made it to Parkland Hospital. The governor of Texas, John Connally, had been wounded and was in surgery. The president was still in the trauma room. There was no hope for him. The Secret Service agent walked down the corridor where the gurney John Connally had been wheeled in on was sitting unattended. He took a quick look down the hallway, He was alone. Reaching quickly into the pocket of his jacket, he took the small bag with the fired bullet and dumped the bullet onto the gurney. Stuffing the bag into his pocket, he left as discreetly as he could. He had already seen to it someone would begin to attempt to clean up the presidential limousine. His job was to see the evidence pointed where they wanted. There would be no autopsy in Dallas. LBJ had already been told to get the body on Air Force One and back to Washington. It was amazing what some politicians would do when they were promised certain things.

Walking through a side door of the hospital onto the street, the agent's job was now done. He didn't think Johnson was in on it. As soon as he could after the assassination, while Kennedy was still on the way to the hospital, he had told Johnson what he was expected to do. It seemed the soon-to-be president was shocked at what had happened. *He shouldn't have been*, the agent thought. *He had been around a long time. He should have known what happened if you crossed the Committee.* The agent walked down the street. He had a report to make to his other employer, and the rest of the problems would soon be dealt with.

Johnny Brewer, the manager of the shoe store, heard the news on the radio. He was as shocked as everyone else at the news of the shooting of the president. A description of the suspect had been broadcasted. Looking out the front of the store, he noticed a man matching the description. What really caught his eye was the way he was acting; he had ducked into the doorway of the store then he had quickly looked around, scanning the street before moving on. Johnny watched as he walked down the street. Stepping through the door, Johnny tried to keep his eye on him. He saw him duck into the Texas Theatre without paying. Following him, but not too closely, Johnny then walked up to the box office, told the attendant what had happened, and had her call the police. Shortly thereafter, several officers had shown up, covered all the exits, and emerged with a handcuffed Oswald. The handcuffed Oswald was screaming, "I'm just a patsy," over and over as they loaded him in the back of the police car.

The plan to deal with Oswald had fallen apart. They would handle it; Oswald could not be allowed to survive, and they were the professionals. Oswald was the part they had planned to expend. It would still happen. The Committee left no loose ends.

The Carousel Club
Jack Ruby's Office
November 23, 1963

Jack Ruby was in his nightclub office watching the news reports of the assassination of President Kennedy. He liked this president. It was a damn shame some wacko had taken him out. *All the good ones,*

# THE COMMITTEE

he thought. The door to his office opened; the man stepping through the door nodded to Ruby. Jack knew his face; he'd had dealings with him before. Jack never could figure out how he could get in. All the doors were locked and so was his office. Jack was the only one here. The people he worked for you didn't screw with. Ruby had paid them everything he owed. He wondered what he was doing here; it usually wasn't good news.

"Hello, Jack." The smile was as cold as ice.

Ruby didn't know his name; when he had asked, he had been told he didn't need to know. That it was better that way. "What do you want?"

"You are going to do us a favor."

"I paid everything back. I don't owe them anymore."

"Jack, you knew the rules when you borrowed the money. One of the rules Jack is that you have to do the favors we ask. So far we haven't asked anything of you. This one will square it all. We won't ask anymore, and we will go away." He gave Jack Ruby a look that told him he had no choice.

"What is it you want?" Jack Ruby knew he had no chance of survival if he refused.

"You saw the news and what happened. We need you to fix the problem that caused it. We can't let it go unpunished."

"What do you mean fix the problem?"

"Oswald can't get away with shooting our president, Jack. He crossed the line, and we are not going to let him run his mouth. You're going to fix it for us, Jack."

"I don't have a choice, do I?"

"There are always choices, Jack. One you survive and one you don't."

"What do I have to do?"

"The Dallas police are going to move Oswald tomorrow. We will tell you when and where. You can get access to him. When you do, you have to use this." The man placed a revolver on the desk in front of Ruby. "And don't miss, Jack. It won't go well if you do." He then tossed a box of cartridges for the pistol on the desk. "Be sure the rest of these are here where they can be found." He turned and opened the door to Jack Ruby's office. "I'll be in touch, Jack." The door closed behind him.

Jack Ruby would do what he had been told. Life in prison would be a better alternative than what they would do to him if he didn't. The Committee never left any loose ends.

The Everett Sloan Residence
Chicago, Illinois
November 24, 1963

Everett Sloan was sitting in the leather chair behind his mahogany desk. Across the room the television anchor was describing what was going to happen as the Dallas police were preparing to move Lee Harvey Oswald. They were moving him from the Dallas police headquarters to the Dallas jail.

Sloan had been told the problem would be resolved; after asking when he could expect to know for certain, the response was a smile and "Watch when they move him." Sloan just expected what he wanted to be done to happen. Joseph Kennedy had been told he wasn't going to set up his own personal dynasty. The bastard had tried it anyway. Sloan had personally told him that if he continued there would be consequences. This was just the first. There was nothing any of the members of the Committee did that Sloan didn't know about. The security they all had answered to him.

He returned his attention to the television; the announcer was saying that any moment Lee Harvey Oswald would be coming out the doors behind him. The camera panned to the door as it was opened by two Dallas police officers. Two detectives were on each side of the handcuffed Oswald, two more followed. As the pair holding the door let them close and moved to follow, the pair on either side of Oswald moved through the parking garage toward the armored van they were going to transport him in. The crowd parted in front of them. Just then, a man wearing a suit and a hat on his head stepped forward toward Oswald. Before anyone could react, he shoved the pistol he had been holding directly into Oswald's' midsection and fired. The police reacted, wrestling him to the ground. Jack Ruby had done what he had been told. Now all he had to do was tell the story he had been told to repeat and shut up about everything else. It had been made clear to him that bad accidents could be arranged in prison as well.

The loose ends were being cleaned up. There would be speculation and wild theories for decades to come. *That was all the better*, Sloan thought. The Committee could use it to their advantage.

The Kennedy Home
Hyannis Port, Massachusetts
March 20, 1964

The two-car convoy, made up of a dark four-door sedan and a black limo following, drove down the road toward the Kennedy compound. It was passed through the security and never stopped until it reached the front of the main house. The doors of the front car opened first. Two well-dressed men got out, scanned the area, and nodded to the limo. The front doors opened and two more well-dressed men got out of the front of the limo and one opened the rear door. Everett Sloan got out of the back of the limo, flanked by the four men he walked straight into the home of Joseph Kennedy. Even though he had never been in the house, he knew where to go. He went straight to where Joseph Kennedy was sitting in his wheelchair. The house was otherwise empty; when he wanted a private meeting, he could set it up.

Joseph Kennedy had suffered a stroke in December of 1961 that left him unable to speak. He was regaining some of his mobility. Everett Sloan hoped the bastard would never be able to talk. Not one for small talk, Sloan got straight to the point.

"I told you what would happen if you ignored me, Joe. You should have paid attention. I thought I made it clear senator or governor was as far as he could go. There are consequences for ignoring me."

All Joseph Kennedy could do was meet his gaze and try to tell the arrogant bastard what he thought of him. The grunting noise he made brought a smile to Sloan's face.

"That's right, Joe, you tell me. Let me make this as clear as I can. If you try to make one of your remaining sons president, or if they try it on their own, the result will be the same. I don't give a good goddamn if you can't tell them yourself. Those are the rules, Joe. I thought I made it clear. If any more of your sons have to die, it will be your fault."

Everett Sloan gave Joseph Kennedy a hard look. Turning and walking out the door, he heard the grunting noises again. *The bastard deserved it*, Sloan thought.

The Barclay Residence
New York, New York
August 12, 1965

Alfred J. Barclay wasn't feeling well. He was now in his late eighties; the last several years had been difficult. The Committee had changed over the years since he had been on it. The current chairman was running it like he wanted, more like a dictator than a director of a business. That was how they had always done it, like a business. He had tried to do something about it; quietly, he had been working with Howard Hughes to try and keep him in check. They were now at the point something more drastic might have to be done. His private opinion was the Kennedy assassination had brought too much attention that could lead to them. He had opposed it. The chairman had done it anyway.

Howard Hughes was setting up his own security. He had told Barclay they couldn't move on the chairman until then. Barclay didn't think it would be soon enough, at least not for him to see it. He had been feeling worse over the last several weeks, and the doctors couldn't tell him what it was or make him feel better. He would have been surprised to know his own security was slowly poisoning him. The chairman wanted him out of the way, and Everett Sloan got what he wanted.

Barclay slowly made his way toward his kitchen where his medicine was kept. His wife had passed away several years before, and he was living here alone except for the security that was constantly here. His two sons had their own careers and had no idea about his involvement with the Committee. Some things you were not at liberty to share. As he stood at his kitchen sink and filled a glass with water, his hands started shaking, and he couldn't seem to focus on the task at hand. The glass slipped and his world went dark. He slowly crumpled to the floor.

The security agent that was in the house heard the noise as the glass broke in the sink. He shook his head at the thought the old bastard had made it this long. He decided now would be a good time to inspect the grounds for an hour or so that way the old man might be dead when he finished. He was tired of this job.

Coming back in to the house an hour later, he walked into the kitchen and found Barclay lying in the floor in front of the counter. Reaching down to check for a pulse that wasn't there, the agent confirmed that Barclay was dead. He went to the telephone hanging on the wall. He picked it up, dialed a number, and waited. After three rings, the phone was picked up and answered with one word, "Yes."

"Confirmation" was the one-word reply the party on the other end of the line was waiting for.

"Clean it up" was all he got in reply as he heard the phone being hung up on the other end.

Hanging up the phone, he picked it up again and called in the emergency, acting as distraught as he could. He then went outside to wave the other agents away; they were already in the car. All he had to do was wait to make sure he was loaded into the ambulance and then he could disappear. The chairman was at work, and the Committee would need another member.

The Congressional Office Building
Congressman Cain's Office
December 12, 2000


Congressman Ben Cain was sitting at his desk. He was reading through the legislation that would be coming up for a vote in the next few days. Unlike most of his peers, he actually read through all the bills he was going to vote on. He felt he owed it to the voters that sent him here. Hearing the tap on his door, he glanced up at the clock on the wall. It was after nine. *Where had the day gone?* he wondered. The door opened, and Steele Davis was standing in it smiling at him.

"Ben, you really are going to have to learn to let your staff go through that stuff." Steele Davis was the head of the Republican party.

"Steele, if you don't mind me asking, what the hell are you doing here this time of night? Don't you have anything more important to do than visit a junior congressman?"

"Haven't you ever heard that some pigs are more equal than other pigs?" Davis smiled at the expression and shake of the head Cain gave him in response.

"Obviously, you have something on your mind or you wouldn't be here this time of night. The staff has all gone home, or you would have been kicked out and not gotten to the door of my office." Ben Cain reached into the lower drawer of his desk and pulled out a bottle of Famous Grouse. Setting it on his desk, he stood up and went to the small cabinet and pulled out two glasses. "Grab a chair and tell me what's on your mind."

Steele liked the young congressman. There weren't many with only two terms behind them who were going to be offered what Steele was preparing to give Ben Cain. As Ben poured the drinks, Steele decided to get right to the point. "I wanted to be among the first to offer my congratulations on your reelection for a third term."

Ben took a sip of his drink and wondered what the hell he really wanted. To say a visit like this was unusual was an understatement. "Thanks, now would you mind telling me what you really want."

Steele laughed. "Before we get down to business, Ben, how are Marilyn and young Edwin?"

"Thanks for asking. Both are very well, and Edwin is the apple of his grandfather's eye."

"Glad to hear it, Ben." Taking a sip of his drink, Steele bought another minute before broaching what he came to talk to Ben Cain about. Setting his glass down, Steele looked Ben in the eye. "Ben, have you given any thought to taking the next step in your political career?"

"I was just reelected to Congress. For the next two years, I will be right here."

"In two years, you are going to be up for reelection. Instead of running for Congress again, how about running for governor? The job is going to be open then."

# THE COMMITTEE

Ben Cain looked into the smiling face of Steele Davis. The candidate was on his way.

The Ambassador Hotel
Los Angeles, California
June 4, 1968
11:15 PM

The two men in the front seat of the sedan parked outside the Ambassador Hotel's service entrance and turned to the young Palestinian in the backseat. The driver spoke first. "He should be speaking about eleven forty-five. That should be about fifteen minutes after the news calls the race. From there he is scheduled to meet a group of supporters and then a press conference at midnight. We will see he is directed through the kitchen on his way to the press room. You just have to be in the loading area just off the kitchen."

The second man in the front seat opened the glove box and took from it a .22 caliber pistol. Handing it to the Palestinian in the backseat, he then reached back in the glove box and removed a box of cartridges and passed them to the man in the backseat. "This is small enough to conceal. Don't fire until you are close. Remember, go for a head shot. We have to be sure. We will be directing him to you. Try to create as much confusion as you can. That will make it easier to get you out. This is our best opportunity."

Sirhan Sirhan took the small pistol from the man in the front; opening the cylinder, he removed the cartridges from the box and loaded them one by one. "I told you I won't miss. He must die. He supports the Zionists who occupy our homeland. Allah will guide my hand."

The driver turned back to him and said, "You guide your hand. Just be sure you don't miss. If we have to shoot him, we can't get you out. There is very little security here. There may not be another chance."

"Allah will not allow me to miss. He must die. It has to be now."

The second man checked his watch, 11:20. "You stay in the car until 11:45. You can't afford to be seen too soon. After it's done, get back out here as fast as you can. Got it?"

"We have been over this. I know what to do."

The driver nodded at him, opened the door, and got out of the car. The second man waited five minutes and exited the car. They would see it all came together. The young Palestinian was the expendable part of the plan.

Robert Kennedy had just finished speaking to the cheering crowd in the ballroom celebrating his primary win. It was just after midnight. Stepping down from the podium smiling and shaking hands with his supporters who all wanted a moment of his time. His campaign aide Fred Dutton looked at his watch and shook his head. They were late. The reporters were all anxiously waiting for the senator who hoped to be president. Leaning in and whispering and receiving a nod from the senator, Dutton ushered Kennedy away from the crowd and motioned for him to follow. Dutton and William Barry, Kennedy's security guard, led the small procession through the doors in the back of the ballroom into the kitchen, taking a shortcut to the waiting reporters. The two men carefully maneuvered the separation of Kennedy from following Dutton and Barry. Getting hemmed in by the well-wishers, Kennedy lagged behind. The maître d' Karl Uecker motioned for him to follow and led him through another exit toward the kitchen. No one realized how carefully the misdirection had taken place.

The pair started down the corridor with Kennedy, stopping to shake hands with everyone. As he shook hands with the busboy, a man rushed past the crowd and, brandishing a pistol, began firing. Those around Kennedy rushed the gunman and began to wrestle him to the ground as he continued firing wildly. Kennedy fell backward onto the floor still clutching the young busboy's hand. The two men had successfully maneuvered Kennedy into the gunman's path. Assuring themselves the young Palestinian was going to be captured, the pair separately exited during the confusion. One exited toward the car in the parking lot while the other simply walked down the block. The car pulled out of the lot and drove down the street until the driver saw his partner. Slowing and pulling to the curb, the driver waited while his partner got in the car. Pulling away from the curb, the car disappeared into the night. In the excitement, no one paid any attention.

# THE COMMITTEE

The crowd parted as the medical team from the ambulance made their way through the kitchen with the gurney toward the senator still lying on the floor. Ethel Kennedy, still by her husband's side, watched and tried to maintain her composure as he was loaded onto the gurney. The stunned crowd was herded back into the ballroom by the police as the investigation began. The shooter was loaded in the back of the police cruiser and taken to police headquarters for questioning.

Twenty-six hours later, another Kennedy had been taken from a stunned nation. The chairman had kept his promise to Joseph Kennedy.

The Desert Inn
Las Vegas, Nevada
June 6, 1968

Howard Hughes was watching the television in the ninth floor suite of what was now his hotel; he had bought it last year. He had moved here in 1966, and the owners had been trying to get him to leave. Buying the hotel had resolved the conflict. He had carefully crafted the image of a crazy, delusional eccentric.

Since Kennedy had been shot, that was all the news was covering. Now that he had died, it was nonstop. This was the second Kennedy to be assassinated. The news was making all the comparisons and reminding the nation of what had happened to JFK. He was one of the few people who really knew who was responsible. The crazy bastard had taken out both of them.

He highly suspected the chairman was responsible for more than just the two assassinations of the Kennedy's. Alfred Barclay had died three years before, and while he was in his eighties, he had been in excellent health. The chairman was doing what he wanted, and murder had never been condoned by the rest of the Committee. Howard had finally gotten rid of the security that had been set up and gotten his own in place. It hadn't been soon enough to save Alfred. The real protection he now had was being crazy. He was going to have to deal with the chairman. He was the only one who could. He was the only one with the resources, and he had spent four years setting everything up.

Thinking back to his years on the Committee, his interest had really been making the United States strong with an economy envied the world over. Everything had begun to change when Sloan had become Diamond. He really wanted to control it all; the ruthless bastard would set himself up as a dictator if he could get by with it. Howard Hughes was a lot of things; he was not a murderer like Diamond had turned out to be. He was perfectly willing to make an exception in the case of Sloan; when you made a deal with the devil, as he felt Sloan had, you deserved what you were going to get. It would take some time to get it all set up. The bastard had brought it on himself.

Chappaquiddick Island
Massachusetts
July 18, 1969

The party was in full swing. Ted Kennedy took another sip of his drink and scanned the room. The party had reunited the girls known as the Boiler Gang along with other members of his staff and those of his late brother. Everyone was having a grand time. Ted was beginning to feel really loose; the alcohol was having the desired effect. He had been making time with the gorgeous redhead who had just excused herself to go to the ladies room. That was his cue to move to the private balcony overlooking the pool. She had whispered in his ear to go there and then announced she was going to the ladies room. Ted slipped away from the great room where the majority of the party was taking place.

Across the room, Mary Jo Kopechne was drunk. She grabbed one more drink and took a sip and stepped outside to grab some air. She was just about to pass out when she decided to open the door of the car she was beside and sit down to gather herself. Trying to take a final sip of the drink, she let it fall from her hand as she slid down the seat onto the floor and passed out. The two security agents that were there to keep an eye on things noticed Mary Jo get in the car. This might work out better than they planned. Unknown to them, their employer was the chairman of the Committee, Everett Sloan. They had been told to look for a way to contrive a situation that would be devastating to the senator's career. Sloan had decided killing a third Kennedy would bring too much unwanted attention. He had decided to destroy any chance he had to run for president.

The two walked to the car Mary Jo had passed out in. The first checked to see if anyone was about that might see what they were doing. Satisfied, he looked at his partner and said, "Check to see if she is passed out. If she is, let's get her over to the senator's car and put her in the back." The second agent opened the door and checked on Mary Jo.

"She's out cold. Give me a hand." The pair picked up Mary Jo and carried her to the Oldsmobile that belonged to Ted Kennedy. Opening the back door, they deposited her on the back floorboard and closed the door. Now all they had to do was wait and watch for the senator to leave.

Ted Kennedy quietly exited the great room and headed toward the bedroom with the balcony where the redhead was waiting. Closing the door to the bedroom behind him and stepping onto the balcony, Ted felt her arms reach out and pull him to her.

Elizabeth Perrin, the wife of one of the businessmen who was a major contributor to the Kennedy campaign, wasn't as drunk as she had let on. She pulled Kennedy closer and kissed him and felt his tongue on hers. Reaching her hand to the senator's groin, she felt him grow stiff in her hand. Putting his hand under her skirt, the senator felt the lace panties and slipped his hand inside. The pair continued to kiss and grope one another. Moving her mouth from his, she whispered into the senator's ear, "Not here. Let's go down to the beach. I know where we can go where we can be really alone. You slip out and get your car. Pick me up around the side." Giving him another squeeze, she let him know exactly what she had in mind.

Ted kissed her one more time and left the balcony to slip out the side door to his car. Reaching his car, he opened the door and slid into the driver's seat. He never noticed the passed out Mary Jo in the back floorboard. Starting the car, he slipped it into gear and pulled to the side of the estate to the waiting Elizabeth Perrin.

Stopping the car well out of the light, Ted watched as Elizabeth slipped away from the doorway and slid into the front seat of his car.

As he pulled out of the drive of the estate, she slid over the seat and kissed the side of his neck as her hand slid to the zipper of his trousers.

The two agents watched the senator's car stop and Elizabeth Perrin get inside. The first smiled at his partner. "This might work out better than we hoped. Let's go." The pair quickly got in their car and followed the Oldsmobile down the road that led from the estate. Keeping the headlights off, they continued to follow until the Oldsmobile made the turn toward the beach. As the car approached the small bridge, they were right behind as they turned on the headlights to full bright. Speeding up, they tapped the back of the Oldsmobile, causing the back to sway and watched as it missed the bridge and turned over into the canal. The pair sped away and disappeared down the road.

Ted Kennedy was blinded as the lights came on from behind; to say he was distracted by what Elizabeth was doing to him in the car was a massive understatement. Unable to control the direction the car was going, all he could do was throw his arms up and try to stop Elizabeth from hitting the windshield as the car clipped the guardrail and went airborne.

The car was upside down in the water as Ted managed to get his window open so he could try to open the door. Finally managing to open the door, he reached in and grabbed Elizabeth and pulled her from the car. Neither ever knew Mary Jo was in the back floorboard wedged against the seat. Rising to the surface of the water, Ted dragged Elizabeth onto the shore.

Breathing hard trying to catch his breath, Ted collapsed onto the ground beside Elizabeth. As the two came to grips with what had just happened, Elizabeth was the first to regain her composure. "My god, they ran us off the road and disappeared. I can't afford to be caught out here, and you can't afford to be caught out here with me. I have to get out of here." Getting up, she started to walk down the road away from the bridge. Ted struggled to his feet and went after her.

"Let's get you out of here and into some dry clothes. Then I'll call for help. Nobody has to know you were here." The pair left, never knowing Mary Jo was slowly suffocating in the diminishing pocket of air in the car.

# THE COMMITTEE

Chappaquiddick Island
Massachusetts
July 19. 1969

The lights of the emergency vehicles and the police cruisers from the county sheriff's cars were flashing, and the emergency personnel were milling about. The press was being kept back from the scene; fortunately, it was only the local press. This hadn't made the national news as yet. The tow truck operator was trying to explain to the diver, who had just come out of the water, what they had to do to get the car out. They were probably going to need a crane because the car was upside down.

Ted Kennedy was still in the back of the unmarked cruiser the sheriff used as his personal duty vehicle. The sheriff, Ray Walker, got out and walked to the back of the cruiser and opened the door and motioned for the senator to get out. "Senator, I know we have been over what happened, with everybody here. Do me a favor and don't say anything to anybody. As far as any of them know right now, it's just a single car accident with only you as the driver. Once we get the car out, we can make this all go quietly away."

Exiting the cruiser, Kennedy nodded to the sheriff. They still had a lot of power and influence. He knew the sheriff would do as much as he could to help. So far the only one who knew Elizabeth Perrin had been anywhere around was the sheriff. He owed the Kennedy family. He would keep it quiet. "Thanks, Ray. I know you'll do what you can. Let's get the car out of here so we can get the vultures out of here." Kennedy motioned toward the area the press and curious were being kept behind the police tape.

The senator and the sheriff walked over to where the diver and the tow truck operator were discussing the options. The sheriff was smart enough to let the experts make the decisions. Charlie, the tow operator, was explaining to Ken, the diver, with what they had here they had to turn the car over before they could pull it out. "Ken, if you can find a place to attach the tow cable, we can turn it upright, and then move the cable and we can pull it out. Otherwise we're going to need a crane. Is there anything in the way that would prevent it from rolling back on its wheels?"

"I think we can do that. It's not completely on its roof. Fortunately, we can attach the cable to the frame and roll it away from the bridge. After that, I'll have to go back in to move the cable and then you can winch it out."

"Got it. Let me move the truck and then we can set the cable." Charlie left to move the truck as Ken prepared to go back in the water. Both knew their business; it only took fifteen minutes, and they were ready to pull it out now that it was back on its wheels.

With everything set and ready to go, Ken came out of the water and motioned to Charlie. The slack was taken out of the cable, and everyone watched as the water churned muddy ahead of the car appearing. The Oldsmobile broke the surface and was pulled up over the bank and back onto the road. The cable went slack and the car stopped; water poured out the open driver's window. The sheriff walked up to the car with two of his deputies as everyone watched. He opened the door to speed up getting the rest of the water out of the car. Looking into the car, the two deputies heard him say, "Oh shit, what the hell?" The sheriff opened the back door of the car, and Mary Jo Kopechne's arm fell through the open door. There was dead silence as everyone that was in view saw what was in the backseat of the senator's wrecked and soggy Oldsmobile. The sheriff walked away shaking his head and went over to his cruiser and got on his radio to call the medical examiner. Senator Ted Kennedy stood stunned at the realization; he never knew that Mary Jo Kopechne had been placed in his car. The chairman had succeeded, in spades, of destroying any ambitions Ted Kennedy had of running for president.

Meigs Field
Chicago, Illinois
January 12, 1970

The private Gulfstream jet was waiting on the tarmac. The snow was starting to come down heavier, and the wind was beginning to pick up. The captain for this flight had just finished the walk around. The aircraft was ready to go. As he opened the door of the private jet, one of the ground crewmen that had just finished fueling the aircraft walked up to the captain with a clipboard in his hand and extended it for his signature. The captain took the clipboard and the extended pen; as he began to sign, the ground crewman pulled a pistol out of his pocket and pointed it at the captain. "Keep your hands where I can see them. Slowly walk toward the fuel truck and get in and don't say a word."

The startled captain had no choice but to do what he was told. He began walking toward the fuel truck; the other two members of the ground crew were holding pistols and motioned for him to get in the truck. One of the ground crew took a pair of handcuffs and put them on the captain's wrists. The other took a weighted sap and struck him behind his left ear.

The fuel truck pulled away from the jet and pulled next to the adjacent hangar. The door opened and the two ground crewmen pulled the unconscious captain from the cab of the fuel truck and dragged him into the hangar. Howard Hughes and two other men dressed in the same uniforms as the unconscious captain left the hangar and entered the Gulfstream. They waited for the chairman to arrive. Everett Sloan was scheduled to take the private charter to a meeting in Mexico. This was the chance Howard Hughes had been waiting on. The chairman wouldn't make his meeting.

The chairman's limo pulled directly up to the waiting gulfstream as the two ground crewmen pulled the wheel chocks. The door of the gulfstream opened, and the stairs dropped into place. The front door of the limo opened and the security guard looked around and then opened the rear door of the limo. Everett Sloan stepped out and made the short walk to the stairs of the gulfstream. Before the guard could follow him onto the stairs, one of the ground crew stepped behind him and hit him behind his left ear with the weighted sap. The other ground crewman reached into the door of the limo and pointed a pistol at the head of the driver who was reaching inside his jacket. "Pull your hand out slowly or die" was all the driver heard as he slowly pulled his hand out of his jacket and held both of them in the air. The first ground crewman unceremoniously dumped the guard in the back of the limo and hit the driver with the weighted sap. He then pulled him into the backseat and began to tie up both of their hands. The second ground crewman slid into the driver's seat and put the limo in gear and drove away.

Two more of the ground crew who had been waiting on the other side of the gulfstream went into the aircraft, pulled the stairs up, and closed the door. The idling jet engines spooled up and the jet began to move toward the taxiway. Everett Sloan began to sense something was wrong when his security guard didn't follow him up the steps. The two ground crew inside the jet walked toward Sloan as the cockpit door opened, and Howard Hughes stepped from the cockpit into the passenger compartment. Everett Sloan stared at Howard Hughes as he walked back toward Sloan. "Taking a trip, Everett?"

"You really don't expect to get away with this, do you, Howard?"

"You are going to die Everett. I want you to have plenty of time to think about that. When I face my judgment, I will be able to answer for my sin of making that happen. How many have you killed, Everett? Alfred, both of the Kennedys, how many more are there, Everett?"

"You arrogant crazy bastard. Do you really think this solves anything?"

"There will always be those like you, Everett. At least you won't be able to kill anyone else, you egotistical psychopath." Howard Hughes turned and walked back into the cockpit and closed the door. The two crew men walked to Everett Sloan and placed handcuffs on his wrists. The terrified Chairman was then strapped in the seat as the jet began its take off roll.

The Gulfstream followed the flight plan until it crossed the border into Mexico. As soon as it was no longer the concern of the U. S. air traffic controller, it dropped down below the radar coverage and headed toward the airstrip on the west coast of Mexico that was favored by those that preferred to avoid the authorities.

The gulfstream landed and turned at the end of the runway and taxied to the waiting helicopter. The rotors were already turning as the doors of the jet opened. and Everett Sloan was hustled down the steps by the two men who had posed as the ground crewmen. Howard Hughes followed them into the open side door of the helicopter; as soon as everyone was aboard, the door closed and the helicopter lifted off and headed toward the ocean.

An hour later the helicopter was well out of the shipping lanes and dropped down and hovered fifty feet over the emptiness of the Pacific Ocean. The door opened, and the chairman—his hands still handcuffed—was led to the open door. One of the two men produced a length of chain and began to wrap it around his waist and secured it with a lock. Howard Hughes stepped up behind the chairman and unceremoniously kicked him out of the open door of the helicopter. The door closed and the helicopter rose and turned back toward the Coast. The Committee suddenly had need of a new chairman.

El Rosario, Mexico
January 12, 1970

The helicopter touched down on the airstrip it had left a little more than two hours before. The sun was beginning to set, and Howard Hughes knew they had to be airborne again before it did. The airstrip was not lighted, and it was one that the local authorities didn't want to know was there. The drug lords and smugglers paid them well to look the other way. Those who didn't wouldn't survive long. The price for using the airstrip was the gulfstream jet Howard needed to make disappear. It had already been flown out by the drug cartel as soon as the helicopter had been airborne on the way out over the ocean. The use of the helicopter had been part of the deal. As soon as he stepped down from the helicopter with the two men he had brought with him, the helicopter took off and disappeared. Howard Hughes had hated to do what he did; killing the chairman wasn't the part he disliked. The deal with the drug lords was the problem. Getting rid of the bastard was worth it. The plane would be reported crashed in Mexico, and there would be wreckage and bodies to prove it. He didn't want to know who they had wanted out of the way. Sometimes the end justified the means.

The plane he would take back to Las Vegas was just approaching. He would have to fly to Mexico City first. They had stopped here on the way from San Diego and would only be on the ground just long enough to pick him up. He would spend a couple of days in Mexico on business he had arranged as cover for this little side trip. As soon as he could, he would be back in Vegas before the news of the crashed plane hit the States and the rest of the Committee found out. He had learned to cover his tracks. Hopefully, none of the others were any sorrier to see the chairman dead than he was. He was the only one with enough connections and the balls to pull it off. They would pick a new chairman, another member, and go on as they had. He privately thought they would breathe a sigh of relief and not ask. Not one of them really wanted to know.

The business jet touched down and turned at the end of the runway. As soon as it stopped, Howard Hughes and the two of his employees boarded the jet, the door closed, and it began to take off. It had been on the ground less than two minutes. Hopefully it had all been unnoticed; if not, he would deal with it. At least the bastard was dead.

The Committee
Rockefeller Center
March 15, 1970

The three-car convoy stopped in front of the building where the Committee maintained their offices. It was a meeting of the board of Atlas international trading. The Committee had started several corporations over the years since they had started the practice during World War II. It was then they began to funnel money to fund their manipulations. They had started Atlas only five years before. The cost overruns built into government contracts had given them billions of dollars since they started. With enough money, they could create a marketing campaign to sell their candidates second to none. They had started Atlas to create another level of separation from the sources of the money to where it ultimately ended up. Atlas had no direct business dealings with the government. They were continually refining their model.

The front car stopped, and the security agents exited the car and scanned the area. Two more agents got out of the last of the three cars and a cordon was formed by the rear door of the center limousine. Howard Hughes exited the rear of the limo and was escorted into the

# THE COMMITTEE

building. The cars pulled away from the curb and would return when the meeting ended. Walking down the hallway toward the conference room, Howard Hughes decided he was going to take charge of this meeting.

The rest of the committee members were already in the room, and he was the last to arrive. Striding into the room, he was immediately the center of attention. His reputation as an eccentric had played well. "Gentlemen, let's get this meeting started. We have business to discuss." The Committee members began to take their seats with the chair at the head of the table usually occupied by Diamond left empty.

All eyes turned toward Howard Hughes. "Gentlemen, as you have all found out by now, we have need of a new member and a new chairman. Before we start that part of the business, I am going to make this perfectly clear. The way this Committee has operated in the past is now behind us. It is now time to refocus our efforts on taking care of this nation. Personal agendas will no longer be tolerated, or it will end as our last chairman did. I will not be nominated for chairman. We will now run this like a business and proceed as the board of directors would. Are there any questions?"

There were none. "Good, then let us proceed with the nominations for chairman. As has been the tradition, we will select a new chairman from those of us in this room. As I stated before, I will not be up for consideration."

With this selection, the Committee had turned a page and closed the chapter of Everett Sloan. All the members of the Committee knew Howard Hughes was responsible for dealing with Everett Sloan. Privately, they were glad it was over. Reginald Holbrook, formerly Obsidian, was selected as the new chairman. Rising from his chair, he made his way to the head of the table and sat down. He was now Diamond. "I thank you, gentlemen, for your trust at this critical time of our venture. The next order of business is the selection of a new member. As we have done before, I will circulate the list of potential members. This must be a unanimous decision."

There was an unspoken agreement among the members that the new member would not be one of those that were associates of the previous chairman. In the final vote, it was agreed Stanley Hawthorne would fill the void and was now known as Obsidian. The business of the Committee continued as it had for the last one hundred and eighty years.

The Cain Home
Forest Hills, New Jersey
December 25, 2000

Edwin Cain enjoyed having everyone home for Christmas. Ben and Marilyn and their son Edwin, his namesake; Catherine and her husband Marshall and their two children were home. It didn't happen often anymore. Everyone was having a grand time. Ben walked over to his father. "Merry Christmas, Dad. You look like you're enjoying this." Ben gestured toward the family in the great room.

"I am. It doesn't happen much anymore. It isn't often all of us can be together. You have to spend most of your time in Washington, and Catherine is now chairman of the board, and I have retired. Seems like I'm the only one with enough time to visit."

Ben laughed. "Dad, you seem to have forgotten all those years you spent traveling working all those deals. In fairness though, you did take us with you in the summers. I got to see a lot of the world while you financed it."

Edwin laughed. "I suppose you're right. I have to admit being retired does give me a lot more time, which I now prefer to spend with my family whenever I can."

"Dad, let's go in the office for a minute. I have to talk to you, and now is as good a time as any." The two left the family room and walked down the hall to Edwin's office. Stepping inside, they closed the door, and Edwin went to the small cabinet and pulled out a bottle of Famous Grouse and two glasses. He handed one to Ben and poured an inch in Ben's glass and then his own.

He held up his glass and said, "To family. It's the best gift God gives us." They touched glasses and looked each other in the eye as they each took a sip. "Okay, Ben, what's on your mind?"

"Dad, tell me what happened when you decided to run for governor."

# THE COMMITTEE

"Well, I decided to run for governor and won the election. The rest as they say is history." Looking at Ben, he realized there was more to the question than simple curiosity. "Ben, do you remember Jeff Stillman?"

"Yeah, he was head of the state Republican party, wasn't he?"

"That's right. He started working on me for over two years before the election. I reminded him this state hadn't elected a Republican governor in how many years. He finally convinced me I had a shot to win. What made it easier was the deal he somehow worked that I went into the primary unopposed. I don't know if I could have won otherwise." Knowing his son as well as he did, Edwin had an insight into what was on his mind.

"Steele Davis came to see me a couple of weeks ago. They want me to run for governor. I haven't given him an answer yet. I want to know what you think about it."

"Ben, you have to decide for yourself. My reasons for running had to do with wanting to make a difference. The state's budget was a disaster, education wasn't working, and for that matter a lot of people weren't working. You were going into college and Catherine was still in high school. We had double-digit unemployment; interest rates were pushing 20 percent, and the state was broke. I have been very successful. I worked very hard to get where I am. I never took any of it for granted. Ben, I'm proud of you. I hoped and prayed that I taught you well the values and responsibility I try to live by. I think you would be a very good governor."

"Dad, have I ever told you how proud of you I am? I need a refill. This glass must have a hole in it." Holding up his empty glass, the two shared a laugh as Edwin refilled their glasses.

"Ben, I will tell you this. Politics is a dirty business. Not that you haven't figured that out. I only went through two elections. You have already been through and won more elections than I have. Being governor is different from Congress. A governor is the chief executive. When you hold that job, you make a lot of decisions. You also have to be a good leader. There is a legislature to deal with, and you would be up against the same thing I was. They will be controlled by the other party. Learning how to work with them and the art of compromise is a must. Having said all that, there are times you have to take a position because it is the right thing to do. Knowing when those times are and, more importantly, how to make your argument without being argumentative, that isn't easy."

"Are you trying to talk me into running or talk me out of it?"

Ed laughed. "That's up to you, Ben. I wish someone had told me what I was getting into that's all."

"I knew I could count on you to give it to me straight. Let me ask you this, any regrets?"

"No regrets. I served and did my job and left this state in much better shape than I found it. Thomas Jefferson said it best, 'Go and serve and then go home and be served.' That's what I did. The best advice I can give you is to remember why you are there and never forget where you came from. You also have to remember you are not the average citizen. You have had a privileged life. That is something that the opposition will use against you. Ben, you can go as far as you want, but if we don't get back to the family, they will become like angry voters. Come on, let's go." The two walked back to the family room where the rest of the family was still gathered. The conversation with his father had convinced Ben; the candidate was on his way.

Hawthorne Energy
Houston, Texas
May 23, 1970

Stan Hawthorne looked up as the door to his office opened; his secretary, Luanne, was standing in the door. "Mr. Hawthorne, sorry to interrupt, but there is a Mr. Holbrook to see you. He said he has an appointment."

"Did he happen to say if his first name was Reginald by chance?"

"Yes, he did. He is not on your schedule. Would you like me to tell him you're in a meeting and will have to reschedule?"

"Luanne, do you know who Reginald Holbrook is?"

"I've heard the name, but I can't remember where."

"Reginald Holbrook is the chairman of the board of Keystone Holdings. They own, among other things, several of the largest newspapers and radio stations all over the United States. In addition to that, he happens to control several other industries, one of which is the tankers, which happen to move all of that oil we extract and ship all over the world. Those are just the two I can think of off the top of my head. Keystone Holdings is not a household name. It just happens to own most of the companies that are household names. He knows damn well he has an appointment with me whenever he wants. Show him in."

"I had no idea."

Stan Hawthorne chuckled at his befuddled secretary. "It's okay, Luanne, not too many people know who he is. I also happened to go to high school with him. Let's not keep him waiting."

Luanne left his office and escorted Reginald Holbrook in to see Stanley Hawthorne. "Right this way, Mr. Holbrook."

Stan Hawthorne stepped around his desk and warmly greeted his former high school friend. "Reggie, you do know how to make an entrance. You could have called. I would have been happy to come and see you. Pull up a chair. What's your pleasure by the way?" Opening the cabinet against the wall and taking two glasses from it and motioning to the selection of bottles, Stan selected a whiskey for himself.

"I'll have the same, Stan. My tastes haven't changed that much since we grew up."

Handing him the drink, Stan touched glasses with Reggie, and they each took a sip of their drinks. "How long has it been since we were those young kids? Reggie, that was a long time ago. I haven't seen you in almost ten years, and you show up in my office. All you've done in all that time is call me. How much business have we done together? What gives, Reggie?"

"Nice to see you too, Stan. Can't I stop by to see an old friend?"

Laughing, Stan looked at Reggie and shook his head. "You're killing me, Reggie. I have made how much money with you, and I could never get an appointment. Nice to know after all this time you didn't forget me."

"How secure is your office, Stan?" Reggie's demeanor changed like flipping a switch.

Surprised at the question, Stan replied, "I have as secure an office as anyone else in this business, no better than most. I had it soundproofed when we moved in, and security keeps everyone out when I'm not here. Even the cleaning people are checked and escorted when my office and other places sensitive data is kept. The oil business has gotten competitive, and I don't take chances. I gather from that question this isn't a social visit."

"You always were perceptive. No, this isn't a social visit. Stan, you have been selected to join a very select group of individuals I need to explain exactly what we do. Let me just say this, we will have plenty of time to get into the details later. For now, I don't want to say more until we can talk somewhere really secure. No matter how good your security is here, it's not up to the level this conversation requires."

Perplexed at his suggestion, Stan shook his head. "I must admit I'm intrigued. I always suspected there was more to you than just a high school buddy."

The expression on his face told Stanley Hawthorne more than what he was saying. "I will tell you this much, the business this select group of individuals does will go beyond whatever expectations you have. Clear your schedule for the rest of the week. I need your undivided attention when I explain what it is we do. There are not many to have this invitation extended. There will be a Gulfstream waiting for you in the morning along with all the required security. There will be a car to pick you up at nine at your home in the morning. I will be on the flight with you. and we can chat some more. This is quite an honor, Stanley. There are very few selected." The Committee had its newest member.

William P. Hobby Airport
Houston, Texas
May 24. 1970


Stan Hawthorne had to admit he was impressed. Everything Reggie had done was first class. The limo was new with a full service bar, two rather large and well-dressed men, obviously security, had escorted him in the limo right onto the tarmac next to the waiting Gulfstream. As Stan entered the private jet, the door closed behind him and was secured by one of the two security agents that had picked him up. The jet was new and plush. The interior was not standard executive jet seating. There was a private compartment in the back and the rest resembled a conference room more than an airplane interior. In the center was a conference table with six seats around it. They were airline seats in leather mounted on a swivel so they could be turned away from the table. Just behind the cockpit was a small service kitchen staffed by a very pretty attendant who smiled at him and asked what she could get him.

Stan was seated at the table and strapped in and the engines spooled up as the jet began its takeoff roll. Once the jet was at cruising altitude, the door to the compartment in the back opened, and Reggie Holbrook waved Stan inside.

"Well, Stan, I promised you would be well taken care of and that our security would be airtight."

"I have to admit I am impressed. Needless to say, I am just a little curious. I don't think this is the standard treatment you give to all of the people you do business with."

Reggie chuckled at his comment. "Let's say this is how I like to travel, and no, not everyone gets this treatment. "

Stan looked around at the small compartment. Along one side of the aircraft was a desk with two plush swiveled aircraft seats on one side and an even plusher swiveled seat on the other. On the other side was a leather couch that folded out to a bed with a small table in front. Reggie motioned for Stan to take one of the two seats as he set down behind the desk. "A little early for me to have a drink but whatever you want we have."

Stan shook his head and said, "I have a feeling a clear and sober head might be in order, and it is a little early. How about a cup of coffee?"

Reggie laughed and said, "I thought you might feel that way." He pushed an intercom on the desk and ordered coffee. Almost instantly, the door opened and the attractive attendant brought in a service and set it on the desk between them. After pouring coffee for both of them, the attendant left as quickly as she had come in and closed the door behind her.

Stan shook his head in amazement. "It all seems so unreal." Looking over at Reggie, Stan realized his demeanor had again changed, and it was obvious he was ready for business.

"Stan, there are things that happen at this level of business that still seem unreal to me even now. My reaction when I was selected was much like yours. What you are now a part of is bigger than you can ever imagine. This has gone on from the very founding of this nation. Very few are privileged to be selected. Whether you know it or not, you were selected several years ago along with others, and we have checked you out and done business with you since then. That's one of the reasons your business has prospered as much as it has the last ten years. Certain things were steered your way. The contract with the navy for all that aviation fuel. Of course you wouldn't have been able to provide it without that deal for the refineries ten years ago. From what I understand, that makes a nice profit for you."

"How could you possibly know about all that?" The shocked expression on his face would have caused Reggie to laugh if it were not for the topic under discussion.

"Stan, I told you, we keep up with everything of those under consideration. We know everything about you, even that evening you spent with the lady you met at the convention in Vegas. That is one of the reasons you were selected. Your discretion is admirable. No one other than us knows."

"Reggie, how in the hell do you know all that, and may I ask why in the hell is it any of your business?"

"Stan, relax. I told you we keep up with everything about those under consideration. Besides, both of us have lifted a few skirts over the years. Let me get to the bottom line of what we do. Let me give you the background first. Around the time the Constitution was ratified, the nation was in trouble. The old form of government wasn't working, and the constitutional convention was quite contentious. The founding fathers of this nation set up a committee. There was quite a bit of concern that the citizens who wouldn't fight for their freedoms could be trusted to pick the leadership of this nation. So they set up the committee to pick those leaders. As we both know, there is still concern the citizens of this nation could pick a good president. Most of them have no idea how business works. Let's be brutally honest, Stan. The average American pays no attention to a damn thing that goes on. Hell, most of them don't even vote. Do you really think they can be trusted to pick the leader of the free world?"

"Reggie, what in the hell are you trying to tell me? That this committee decides who our president is?"

"Now you understand the reason for all the security."

"You're serious, aren't you? Jesus Christ this is hard to believe."

"Think about it, Stan. The United States has been wildly successful. You don't believe that was all by chance, do you? We have made the United States what it is. The American people owe us for that. Let me expand a little more. We also are working on control of the Congress and Senate. That has taken some time. We are not quite there yet, but we will be in another twenty years or so."

"How in the hell is all that possible? I don't see how you can make all that happen. I'm having a very hard time believing all this. I've known you since we were kids. You're not kidding, are you?" The look on Reggie's face and the smile spoke volumes.

"Let me explain just how all this happens. Candidates are selected while in high school or college. We see they are educated to think the way we want. Their career is carefully arranged. When they are ready, we get them elected to a local or state office. Then we manage their rise to Congress or a governor. We see they have enough money to run a successful campaign. Sometimes it's necessary to arrange an event that will help us control them. It's incredible what their lust for power does to them. We control enough of the media to create a marketing campaign to make the voters think the way we want."

"Stop for a minute, Reggie. I'm having a hell of a hard time believing this is possible. How in the world can you have money to do all this?"

Reggie laughed. "That's the really interesting part, Stan. Tell me, do you think all those budget deficits and cost overruns and all those poorly managed government contracts are an accident? That is all carefully controlled. We see the money is funneled to where we want it. Not to mention getting all those wealthy campaign donors to write large checks. Influence goes a long way in Washington and it's expensive. We have set up several corporations to control it. The beautiful part is none of them realize they are being controlled."

"Are you telling me all this is in place?"

"Congratulations, Stan. You are now a member of the board of directors of Atlas International."

FBI Field Office
Richmond, Virginia
June 8, 2003

Harlan J. Starks, the special agent in charge or SAC as it was known in the bureau, picked up the receiver of his phone and dialed the extension for his ASAC Dan Oliver. The phone was answered on the second ring. For all of his faults as Harlan saw them, the one thing he could say for his ASAC was that he always was available. Personally, he despised Dan Oliver. The man hadn't shown him the proper respect he deserved. Even the way he answered the phone annoyed him, using only his last name. "Oliver" was all he ever said when he picked up.

Dan Oliver looked up as the phone on his desk beeped the signal for an internal call. It was Harlan J. Stark's extension. Dan knew it annoyed him when he used only his last name when he answered his phone. That was why he had started it. "Oliver."

"Could you step into my office, Agent Oliver?"

"Be there in a moment" was all Dan responded with and hung up the phone. Starks was a really self-important pompous ass. He had been named SAC two years ago after a stint as ASAC in Cincinnati. He was an ass kisser, and Dan hated the type. He got up from his desk and headed to the men's room. Anything to make him wait, Dan finished washing his hands and walked down the corridor toward the asshole's office as he thought of him. He was the only SAC Dan had ever worked for that had his secretary make him wait while she picked up the phone and announced him. What the hell for? After all, he called me in here.

The one thing Dan had going for him was that Starks had picked Rebecca as his secretary. She had worked in the office for a little over six years. What Starks didn't know was Dan had been seeing Becky almost since she had been working there. No one in the office knew.

# THE COMMITTEE

They were both extremely intelligent people and had been attracted to each other right from the start. They both knew how to keep it quiet. Dan knew everything that went on in the office. He had the right as ASAC anyway. Starks didn't see it that way. He almost treated Dan as the enemy. The last four years Dan had been looking into some things no one else knew about. He had more than anyone knew.

Dan opened the door to Starks outer office. Becky was at her desk and looked up when Dan walked in. She gave him the signal there was someone in the office with Starks and that she had no idea what he wanted. She picked up her phone as Dan acknowledged what she was telling him. They had gotten very good at nonverbal communication over the years. It was all so subtle unless you knew you wouldn't pick up on it. "Mr. Starks, Agent Oliver is here to see you." Looking up at Dan, she said loud enough for Starks to hear as she opened the door "He will see you now ASAC Oliver." She winked at Dan because they both knew it irritated Starks to be reminded Dan was his ASAC.

Dan walked into the office of the pompous asshole and raised his eyebrows as if to say "What you called me?"

"Agent Oliver, this is special counsel Flory of the Justice Department." The two sized each other up as Dan offered hand. "Would you bring us both up to speed on the Taggart investigation?"

Because he knew it would annoy him, Dan looked up to the ceiling and took a deep breath like he was deep in thought and needed to gather his thoughts. After a long pause, he looked at Starks and began, "The congressman is being investigated for irregularities in his campaign contributions. The filings he made don't add up to the total amount of contributions he received. Some of the payouts seem to be going somewhere other than campaign spending, and there is a rather vague description. We are running down the money trail. The congressman has not been very forthcoming with information we have requested. It is going to take some time to find all the documents and the money."

Starks looked at Dan and simply said, "The justice department is taking this over. Would you please fully brief Councilor Flory and turn over everything we have. Thank you, Agent Oliver, I will send him to see you when we are done."

Dan just turned and walked out of Starks's office. He motioned to Becky what had just happened and never slowed as he walked by her desk. One more investigation that had been taken away. It was becoming all too regular. He had known it was going to happen. He had prepared for it.

Returning to his office, Dan knew his extension would ring once when Flory left Starks's office. Becky would see to that. He had enough time. He reached into his briefcase and removed the CD and slipped it into the drive of his computer. If anyone got too curious and looked at the CD, it all had rather benign information on it. The background program that was its primary purpose had been written by one of the best covert programmers there was. He thought of it as "The Mole" he was preparing to put his papers in for retirement. His other investigation was getting very interesting, and he was going to have to be very, very careful. "The Mole" was going to give him covert access to not only the FBI computer system but every other system it was introduced to. He was preparing to put everything he had on the Taggart investigation onto CDs for Flory, "The Mole" would go with it. It would send out the access codes he needed to get into any computer system it was on and only he knew how to access it. Then it would wipe out any trace of what was accessed. Dan was going to need everything he could get. The bastards he was looking for had control of more resources than you could imagine. His advantage was no one had ever looked for them, till now. He would find them, all of them. He had resources no one knew he had. He had found enough to know they were out there. It was only a matter of time. The question he had in his mind was, would they find him first?

The Holbrook Residence
New York, New York
Election Night
November 4, 1980

Reginald Holbrook was sitting in the leather armchair in his private study. The news was reporting the results of the presidential election; it wasn't even close. Ronald Reagan was racking up one of the largest landslide votes ever. The electoral vote was 489 for Reagan and 49 for Carter. They had thought it might happen. What surprised Diamond was the landslide. They hadn't been as successful in changing the mind-set of the American people as they had believed. They were still too damn independent. Reggie turned off the television and poured himself a drink. They had lost ground; the Senate had even changed hands for the first time in twenty-eight years. Reagan and the Republicans had quite a night. They didn't have enough candidates to cover all of the races. They had concentrated on the Democratic candidates for this election. History had shown they would continue to hold both the House and the Senate. They had even moved some of their candidates to cover races they didn't have control of before. They had rolled the dice and lost. They would not make that mistake again.

Reggie took a long pull of his scotch; the phone ringing brought his thoughts back to his surroundings. When he was in his study, everyone in his family and his staff knew to leave him alone. It was the secure phone ringing. Reggie rose from his chair and walked over to his desk; the phone was more secure than any phone anywhere in the world. The Committee had better security than anyone else in the world, even the government of the United States. They controlled the contractors that provided everything to all the intelligence branches of the government and the military. They were always one generation ahead of the technology they allowed the government to have. Not only was it scrambled and double encrypted, it randomly changed frequencies over the phone lines it used. There was nothing quite like it anywhere in the world. And it looked like an ordinary phone.

Reggie walked over to his desk, pressed the sequence of buttons for his security code, and picked up the handset. "Yes" was his one word answer. Only the Committee and the head of security had access to these phones.

The security chief was the one on the other end. "Should we proceed with the contingency preparations?"

"Where do we stand?"

"We have begun to program a potential selection. It will still take some time to get him completely ready. We need another sixty days to finish the programming. There is no firm schedule for the target yet. Once a location is selected, we have to have at least thirty days to prepare. I calculate a six-month window after the programming is finished, the shrink estimates he won't be able to hang on longer than that. Taking all of that into consideration and allowing a thirty days window, a go decision needs to be made no later than five months from now."

"Continue with the preparations. Do not go without my specific orders. Maybe we will get lucky, and he will have a heart attack before then. I'll be in touch." Diamond hung up the phone, took the last swallow of his scotch, and contemplated his options. A president had died in office every twenty years since the beginning, one more might be needed.

The Hilton Hotel
Washington DC
The Cain Fund-raiser
August 26, 2001

The five-thousand-dollars-a-plate fund-raiser for Congressman Bennett Arthur Cain had been a huge success. Almost half a million dollars was going into the war chest for his run for governor. Congressman Cain had just finished speaking at the podium. It was now the part of the event he had gotten very good at, mixing with the well-heeled donors. They expected a few minutes with the soon-to-be governor for parting with a hefty donation to his campaign.

Almost three hours later, the night was beginning to wind down. Ben was talking to Dr. Crandall, a cardiac surgeon who had made a lot of money doing heart bypass and transplants. Someone took the empty glass from him and put another drink in his hand. Almost absentmindedly, Ben took a sip. He was really starting to get tired. He didn't pay any attention to the slightly off taste and imperceptible cloudiness. He had spoken to every single one of the guests. The private security was beginning to usher them to the doors. Ben was tired. It had been a very long week; this was the third fund-raiser in the last five days. All he wanted to do was get some sleep. As he bade Dr. Crandall and his wife good night, he finished the last of the drink and placed the empty glass on the tray the waiter held out for him. He left the ballroom and headed toward the elevator. They had booked him a room in the hotel so all he had to do was head upstairs; it was almost one in the morning. He was not up to the drive home tonight. He must really be tired; he was starting to feel light-headed.

He shook his head to clear it as he waited for the elevator. The elevator chimed as the door opened, and he stepped inside. Just before the door closed, a tall willowy brunette in a black evening dress stepped in the elevator with him. He vaguely recalled seeing her at the fundraiser; he couldn't remember her name. She obviously knew him as she said to him, "Hello, Ben."

"Hello" was all Ben could think to say. He was lost in her smile, and his head seemed to be spinning faster.

She moved closer to him as the elevator began to ascend. "Are you okay? You look a little flushed."

"I seem to be unusually tired tonight." His voice sounded funny to him almost like it was someone else speaking.

The elevator stopped at the top floor and the chime sounded again, and the doors slid open. "Let me help you to your room" was all Ben heard as she led him out of the elevator toward the penthouse suite. Later, Ben would never remember he never handed her the room key card. Somehow the door was opened, and Ben found himself in the bedroom of the suite.

"Why don't you let me help you with your jacket?" Ben felt his jacket slide off as her lips met his. Her dress slid off of her hips and landed on the floor, and she stepped out of it. Ben was barely aware of what was happening; it all seemed like a dream. He felt her hands undo his belt and then work the zipper of his trousers. The last thing Ben would remember was the black lace thong sliding down her legs and her pushing him back on the bed. The congressman and gubernatorial candidate passed out.

She gently laid his head on the pillow and, not even bothering to put her dress back on, walked out of his bedroom and went to the second bedroom of the suite and opened the door. The two men inside never said a word as they went into the bedroom with the passed-out congressman on the bed. She followed them into the room and got onto the bed with Ben. She finished taking his clothes off as one of the two men produced a camera. She reached down and began to position him and crawled on top of him. The man with the camera began to take pictures. She moved again and made sure his face was plainly visible in all the pictures that were taken. The whole process had been completed in less than fifteen minutes. The two men left the suite, never having said a word. She would be well paid for her performance. She decided this one was worth it after all, and she may as well stay and enjoy it. The congressman was a nice-looking guy. The drugs they had put in his drink would only last for a few hours. If she timed it just right, she could arouse him just before he woke up and give him what they had paid her for. Sometimes she wanted to control things herself; this one was too good to miss.

Ben felt like he was dreaming; he felt her body going up and down on him as he began to regain consciousness. He opened his eyes and saw two perfectly shaped breasts right in front of his face. He still couldn't move. The drugs they had slipped him were still doing their job. She felt him convulse inside of her; she continued moving up and down on him until she achieved want she wanted. Ben passed out again. She got up from the bed, put her clothes back on, and left. She had left the black lace thong for him to find. If the drugs did their job, he wouldn't remember much of what had happened.

Ben Cain woke to the sunlight streaming through the window of the bedroom in the penthouse suite. His head hurt; he put his hands to his temples and gently massaged them. He sat up and swung his legs to the side of the bed and put his feet on the floor. He took a long moment trying to remember where he was. He didn't think he'd had too much to drink. One thing he tried to do was never to get drunk. You couldn't afford it in this business of politics. The last thing Ben remembered clearly was talking to Dr. Crandall and his wife. He had really had a strangely vivid yet hazy dream last night. Ben threw the covers back as he stood up and realized he was naked. He shook his head as he saw the black lace thong on the floor. Oh god what had he done. He reached down and picked it up and realized it wasn't a dream. What was worse, he really couldn't remember what had happened. That had never happened to him before. Ben stepped into the bathroom and dropped the lace thong in the trash and turned the shower on. How in the hell had this happened? He didn't even know who he had been with. He stepped into the shower and prayed he would not ever be in this position again. Little did he know, the Committee had their way of controlling their candidates, and he had been masterfully set up.

The Washington Hilton
Washington DC
March 30, 1981

Ronald Reagan finished his speech and stepped down from the podium to the applause of the crowd. The Secret Service agents began to close ranks around the president. He was not going to be here long; it was a very short luncheon speech to the AFL-CIO. Jerry Parr, the head of the detail, spoke into his microphone, "Rawhide is moving. Bring the car to the front." Reagan made his way through the crowd shaking hands, exchanging pleasantries, and giving his famous smile to everyone. It took a few minutes to get him out of the ballroom through the corridor to the exit toward the "president's walk" the covered walkway installed in 1963. This short trip was considered so short none of the agents had bothered to wear their bulletproof vests. For some reason, the president wasn't even wearing one on this occasion.

Just outside of the exit there was a small crowd gathering behind the security rope. Normally, any crowd would have been screened if they were allowed this close to the president. The Secret Service hadn't bothered this time; there was only a thirty-foot walk to the presidential limousine and motorcade. John Hinckley Jr. was standing in the crowd. He had been programmed carefully for this moment. He felt the .22 revolver in his jacket pocket. He was convinced his actions would impress the target of his affection.

The doors opened and the Secret Service agents stepped out and quickly scanned the crowd. The president was ushered through the doors toward the waiting limousine; there were several DC police officers watching the crowd as the president turned to wave. John Hinckley Jr. pulled the small revolver from his pocket, stepped forward, and began to fire.

The first bullet hit James Brady, Reagan's press secretary in the head. As he fell to the sidewalk, DC police officer Thomas Delahanty tried to step in front of the president; for his efforts to protect him, he took a bullet in the back of the neck. Hinckley continued to fire all six bullets in the revolver. Agent Parr pushed the president in the back of the limousine as agent Timothy McCarthy stepped in front of Reagan and spread himself as far as he could. Another bullet hit him in the abdomen. Hinckley was wrestled to the ground as the limousine and motorcade sped away.

In the back of the limousine, Agent Parr spoke into his microphone "We are going to Crown." He began to check the president over. Reagan coughed and bright frothy blood began to come up. He looked at Parr and said, "I think I broke a rib when you shoved me and I cut my lip."

Parr looked at the bright blood spilling from the president's mouth and realized he probably punctured his lung with the broken rib. Instantly, he decided they had better go to George Washington University Hospital. He spoke into his microphone again and said, "Divert to George Washington. The president needs medical attention."

The limousine sped away with the injured president losing blood into his chest cavity. As soon as the limousine stopped in front of the emergency room, Reagan stepped out and walked into the hospital unassisted. Stumbling once he was inside, Reagan dropped to one knee and remarked, "I can't seem to catch my breath." Parr and the others quickly grabbed the president and hustled him to the emergency room. It took the attending medical staff several minutes to even realize they were working on the president of the United States. Within thirty minutes, they had him stabilized and headed to surgery.

Benjamin Aaron, the chief of thoracic surgery, finally found the bullet in the president's lung; it had taken a lot longer than he liked. It had hit the door frame of the limo and flattened and struck under his arm and ended up in his lung. It would later be discovered the bullets were explosive and would have become toxic if it would have been left in. They finally managed to stop the bleeding; the president had lost almost half his blood volume during his time in the ER and surgery. Rawhide had survived the assassination attempt.

# THE COMMITTEE

Hinckley was taken to jail and interrogated, and his carefully programmed mind began to reveal the details that were so carefully tucked away in his memory. The Committee had learned their lessons from the Kennedy mess. There would be no evidence of any organized attempt. They had refined their technique. It was much better this way. Diamond hadn't counted on the fast decision of Agent Parr and the quick work of the ER staff and the trauma surgeon. There had been many setbacks over the years.

The Holbrook Residence
April 5, 1981

Diamond turned off the television. The news was reporting how well the president was doing and the outpouring of goodwill from the nation. He had badly miscalculated. They had gambled on the election, betting the Democrats would retain control of both the House and Senate. They had shifted the available candidates accordingly. They would have to increase the pipeline to get enough candidates to cover both parties in more of the House and Senate. The Republicans had seemed to be the weaker party, and they had concentrated their Republican candidates only where they seemed to have stronghold seats. Carter had lost the election to Reagan, and the best they had done was cover the VP slot. The attempt on Reagan was only to get control of the White House again.

Reggie realized he was pacing; he hated being this worked up. His miscalculation had set them back by at least twenty years. He had forgotten the lesson of patience. The American people weren't far enough down the road of dependence as he had thought.

The secure phone rang. Reggie picked it up entered his code and said, "Yes."

The security chief was on the other end. "Obviously, it didn't go as planned. The good news is the programming of our selection worked as we hoped. There will be no connection. They believe he was fixated on gaining the attention of the actress Jodie Foster. We have no worries there. Should we plan anything else, or do we wait or do nothing?"

"What went wrong?"

"We had him programmed for a lot of things. One was he had to get the gun. He picked a .22. It wasn't a large enough caliber to do the job properly. He wasn't a trained marksman. We couldn't risk training him. We had it set up so the target didn't have to wear the vest. The agents didn't either. We were just unlucky. I don't think it would be a good idea to try again at least not soon."

"We have other priorities. Sometimes things that don't work have a reason. We have to be patient. At least we know the programming worked. The one thing we can't afford to be is reckless like my predecessor was. There are no real questions being asked about this attempt. I do not want anything like the mess around the Kennedys. That still hasn't faded. Remember, no other members need to know about this. This area is only my responsibility."

"They don't even know who I am or the other members of the special team. I have at least three members of each of their security team that reports to me. They don't know about each other. Even they don't know about the special team, and the special team only knows they work for me. None of them know anything about anyone except the one member they cover, and they are only for protection. The security is fully intact."

"What about the shrink?"

"That's covered. He had a heart attack a month before the attempt, and unfortunately, he didn't survive."

"Others are available if needed I assume."

"We are covered if we need it."

"Okay, shut it all down for now. We won't need them for a while. Just keep them trained and ready."

"They always are anything else?"

"No, just continue with normal operations. I'll be in touch."

The chairman hung up the phone. He had learned his lesson. He had to remind himself there was no timetable. They had worked on it for almost two hundred years. Time was on their side.

# THE COMMITTEE

The Committee
The World Trade Center
May 10, 1981

    The limousines began to arrive in the private security parking garage, and the members of the Committee took the private elevator to the 101st floor. They never all arrived at the same time. Within an hour, the board of directors of Atlas International was assembled in the boardroom, and Diamond brought the meeting to order.
    "Gentlemen, as you are all aware, we have taken quite a setback in the last election. I think it's time we reevaluated our time frame. We took a chance in concentrating too many of our candidates in a single party. We are going to have to increase the number of candidates in the pipeline. I never expected that the Republicans would gain control of the Senate. We have a lot of ground to make up."
    Malachite motioned to the Chairman and was given the floor. "I am going to stress again there has never been a fixed timetable. We have always had to expand the pipeline just to cover the increase in congressional seats as the population increases. That's why we plan so far ahead. We have to expand our recruitment and double up on the regional strategy. That's ten years out before the current recruits are going to be ready."
    Obsidian, deep in thought, looked over at Malachite "So far we have only used Atlas International to track and control the candidates and the money. I am thinking of this in business terms as if it were an investment. What's the one thing we were always taught? Diversify. I propose we start several more corporations each with the same objective. We have enough experts in Atlas to break them up and let them each control their own little domain. None of them know who the others are within Atlas. Each of us has how many that think they are the only one. We would have to do the approaches individually after we get the startups done. Three to five years and we could easily double the number in the pipeline."
    Jade motioned to the chairman and was given the floor. "We are going to have to be very careful if we start too many more corporations like Atlas. I think it is a good idea. I propose that we leave Atlas in place

and start up regional corporations as we begin to start each region. We could each sit on several of the boards of directors so that no two are together on all of them. I do not want to bring in any others to the boards to be in a position to ask questions."

Granite leaned back in his chair as an idea began to blossom in his mind. Motioning to the chairman, he was given the floor. "What we are thinking is duplicating what we are doing with Atlas. I think that is too dangerous. Leave Atlas in place. Let's use it to train others as we are already doing and then move them to fill a spot we create in corporations we already control. I think a new office in a defense contractor that gets a new government contract would raise no suspicion. Reagan stated during his campaign he wanted to increase military spending. That will play right into our hands. Let's use what he wants to do to our advantage."

Coral was next and motioned to get the floor. "I like the idea. Something else I have thought about is the reaction to the Iranian hostage situation. It has created a sense of public anger. What if we can change that to fear? The Israelis have dealt with terrorists since the inception of their nation. The American people have not. Think of the reaction to all the airplane hijackings and the '72 Olympics and the killing of the hostages. We can use that as a means to speed up the dependence on government we are creating. They will demand the government protect them."

Gold leaned across the table and looked Coral in the eye. "Are you suggesting we recruit terrorists?"

Coral laughed and said, "No, that's not what I am suggesting. We can funnel money to these terrorists and let them create chaos. Over time, we can gain control of the leaders and then when they have served their purpose we can eliminate them again with the purpose of creating the dependence we want."

Diamond held up his hand to stop the debate. "Let's put that on the back burner for right now. What I think we have to concentrate on is reversing our failure in the past election. We need more candidates to cover both parties. Let's figure out how we do that without making any connection to us. I would rather expand existing operations than start new ones. While we do that, we can look into using the terrorist angle."

# THE COMMITTEE

Onyx motioned for the floor; given acknowledgement, he began, "Gentlemen, we have suffered a setback but that doesn't mean we have to overreact. The original strategy is sound. Patience is required. We can increase the pipeline without additional risks. There are a variety of things we can do. It does not have to be a single solution. Over the next several years as the budget is increased and we can funnel off more funds to our existing government contractors, we can use both solutions."

Emerald, deep in thought, was the only one who hadn't taken part in the discussion. As the ideas were tossed around among the committee, he sat there and took it all in. He had the reputation as a deep thinker and a brilliant strategist. He leaned forward and motioned to the chairman. Given the floor, he looked around the room at the other members before he began to speak. "All of the ideas we have discussed have merit. We prioritize them and decide which we do with the available resources and work on obtaining the resources we need. I do not think a sudden increase in any one area is desirable. I also think we need to create more political action committees as well. Let's use them as a diversion to take the heat while we work behind the scenes and implement both of the strategies. If we do that slowly and carefully, it will not be noticed. One other area we have not done is to gain control of some of the newer members of both the House and Senate."

Ebony asked the question the others were thinking. "Wouldn't that be a huge risk?"

Emerald shook his head in the negative and responded to the question. "Gentlemen, almost all of them have a weakness. What we have to do is find it. They haven't gotten this far in politics and remained squeaky clean. Remember even our own candidates don't know they are being manipulated much less who we are. We have the resources to find each of their weaknesses. They all will do whatever they can to avoid a scandal."

Diamond had let the discussion go; as usual, they had come up with several options. The rest of the meeting was focused on the implementation of the selected strategies and candidate selection. As the meeting was adjourned and they began to leave, the chairman found himself alone with Onyx and was surprised with the question he was asked.

"Are you planning another attempt on Reagan?"

"What makes you think I was responsible for that? I thought it was just a sick young man trying to impress an actress."

Onyx laughed. "I have been on this Committee long enough to know certain things. I don't think it would be wise to try again. We don't need to revive any lingering questions about our past actions. I know about the special security we each have and the special team we have under your control. I am relieved you are not as reckless as our past chairman was. I highly suspect most of the others know as well. We do not need a repeat of the past mistakes."

Diamond smiled at Onyx. "Don't worry, I'm not planning another attempt. We can afford to wait him out. It was worth the try."

Onyx gave the chairman a hard look. "Good, I like to believe you really are smarter than that." Onyx turned and walked away toward the private elevator, leaving the chairman to wonder how much more he really knew. There were some things he didn't want any of them to know. He was going to have to find out.

The World Trade Center
Atlas International
New York, New York
October 23, 1983

Onyx was sitting at his desk in his office suite on the 101st floor of Tower One. Atlas International occupied both the floor above and below. The members of the Committee used the offices each had on the floor. They did not want to draw attention to the fact the floor was exclusively for Committee business, and they had decided to use them when any of them were in New York. He had officially retired from his other position as president of a major defense contractor earlier in the year. He was still in his midfifties and had taken their board by surprise with the announcement he was stepping down. He was still on their board of directors and was slated to be chairman early next year when the new board of directors for McAllister Halstead was seated. The

# THE COMMITTEE

members of the Committee each sat on several different companies' boards. This was what they did outside of Atlas and their work on the Committee. Each one controlled major business interests, and it was not at all unusual at this level of business.

The television across the room was showing footage of the smoking remains of the marine barracks at Beirut International airport. Two truck bombs had been detonated at both the French and American compounds. Two hundred and forty-one American service members and fifty-eight French members of the international peace-keeping force had been killed. Islamic militants might have been responsible for the suicide bombings and other acts of terrorism that had happened, but Onyx knew who had funded them. This part of their strategy bothered him. He had served in the army as a young officer right out of college. There was a brotherhood of arms. He didn't like to see young servicemen killed for what he considered political reasons.

He pushed his chair away from his desk stood and turned to stare out the window at the New York skyline. Taking a sip of the scotch, he began to think of his time in the service of his nation. He had been in Korea for the last two years of what was officially called a police action. Taking another sip of his drink, he thought what he always had. The politicians could call it what they wanted; it was still a war. He had seen buddies of his die. Now whether he liked it or not, he was responsible for those young marines' death. He had been the only one on the Committee to express reservations about funding terrorists. None of the others had served or seen combat; this was making him question what the committee was doing. Things were not going the way he had envisioned. Controlling the government was one thing, purposely killing your own citizens especially those who had volunteered to protect the nation was something else. Privately, he was glad Reagan had won the election. He wouldn't share that with any of the others. He hadn't liked what Carter had done to the military. Helicopters so poorly maintained they crashed in the desert trying to rescue the hostages held by the Iranians after they had overrun the embassy, more soldiers dead. What he really wanted was to make the United States the leader of what they were trying to engineer. The rest of them were happy to destroy it if they could run the world.

The door to his office opened and Gold stepped in. Onyx turned from the window and tried to hide his surprise. He was the only one using the office regularly since he had retired.

Gold gestured to the television and said, "I guess you have seen the news. I don't like that very much."

"Neither do I. Dying in combat is one thing. At least there we had a chance to defend ourselves. These kids never saw it coming." Onyx gestured to the bottle sitting on his desk. "Help yourself if you like."

Gold picked up the bottle of scotch and moved to the small bar against the wall, took a glass, poured an inch, set the bottle down, walked to the window, and stood beside Onyx who had turned and was staring at the skyline again. "I'm not comfortable with this whole terrorist thing. We don't really have any control over what they do. We are going to have to do something."

Onyx turned to look at Gold. "What do you suggest?" He wasn't really sure where this was going.

"The problem is I don't know. I don't think the rest of them will go along with stopping the funding."

Onyx couldn't stop himself from saying what came to his mind. "The Committee hasn't ever been wrong. I thought you knew that."

"I haven't been around quite as long as you. This wasn't part of what we set out to do. Control is one thing, mass murder is something else."

Onyx was trying to gauge if Gold was sincere. He decided to take a chance. "You are aware Diamond was responsible for the attempt on Reagan?"

Gold looked Onyx straight in the eye. "I thought as much. I highly suspect he has a larger agenda than the rest of us do."

Onyx wasn't sure if he was being tested or trusted. He decided to take another chance. "The strategy has changed from the original intent. I was foolish enough to believe we were preventing the uninformed masses from destroying this nation, and we were putting the United States in a position of dominance and control over the rest of the world. It appears we have decided to destroy it to set up something else that will control the rest of the world. I am beginning to doubt that wisdom."

"That is at least two of us. I think we are the only ones."

"What is the old saying? Power corrupts and absolute power corrupts absolutely. I have always thought I was above that. It is humbling to learn I'm not. If the founders of this nation could see what we are doing to it…" Onyx shook his head as the realization of his own responsibility for it hit him.

Much as Jefferson and Madison almost a hundred and eighty years before, the realization of what they were doing reached out from the past and settled on them. They were also powerless to stop it.

The Holbrook Residence
Election Night
November 3, 1992

Reginald Holbrook was sitting in his study watching the election results come in. It really didn't matter much who won. This was the first election both of their candidates were facing each other. The wild card was the crazy bastard Ross Perot. He had gotten into the race as an independent and had done better than anyone would have given him credit for. It had been interesting to say the least. They had tried to get him out of the race; their initial threats against his family had seen him withdraw and then get back in. They could not risk nor had they planned to do anything, just making him look slightly crazy was enough. What worried the chairman was he actually got almost 20 percent of the popular vote.

Diamond felt it indicated too many Americans were still too damn independent. He took a sip of the scotch he was drinking and turned his attention back to the television. Clinton was going to win. The real surprise to him was the electoral map. The south was beginning to lean toward the Republicans more. He smiled to himself; it had taken twelve years to increase the candidate pipeline enough for their candidates in both the House and Senate to face each other in certain races. Those they could not lose no matter what happened. They had begun to outsource control of some of the operations to offices in defense contractors first and then other corporations they controlled. It was working flawlessly.

The secure phone on his desk rang; picking it up, he didn't even have to use access codes anymore. This latest version had voice recognition built in. Anyone other than him or one of the other members or the security chief would get a dial tone as if the other party had hung up as soon as they spoke.

Reggie reached for the phone. "Yes."

Malachite was on the other end. "I would say overall it has certainly been a very productive evening,"

"Interesting as well. Did you pay attention to the numbers Perot put up?"

"Yes I did. I also noticed the trending in the south. I think we are going to have to make sure we have enough candidates to cover the changing demographics."

"I don't like the numbers there. We have to invest more in the education and marketing, or we are going to have to have a lot more candidates."

"The latest group is now beginning to enter into the State races. We are six to eight years out to have them ready for the next level. On an even better note, our recruitment is really beginning to bring in increased numbers that are still in high school and college. That puts them about ten to twelve years from beginning the state and local levels."

"I spoke with Obsidian earlier; he assured me that we are making progress with the targeting of several more incumbents that we have targeted for control. The effort we have made is beginning to give us control back. Another election or two and we are back on track."

Malachite laughed. "Patience pays off. It won't be much longer, and we can begin to implement the next phase. "

"When we begin the marketing for that, it will really tell us where we stand with the American people. If that works, we are less than twenty-five years away."

"Let's not get too far ahead of ourselves. I remember an election twelve years ago that didn't go as planned. Patience."

Diamond laughed. "I have learned my lesson. We have all the time we need. Human nature will take us the rest of the way. It's inevitable. All we have to do is continue with the rest of the plans."

Malachite's tone changed. "I really hope you have learned your lesson. We are progressing too well for you to do something stupid. Keep your impulses under control and the special team idle."

*Another one*, Diamond thought to himself. "Don't worry about what I do. You need to do your part just as the rest need to do the same. We still have a long way to go."

"I will as I always have. We can't afford to be careless now. It won't take much longer and the massive increase in spending will start. We don't want any questions."

"Don't worry, there will be enough distractions and diversions. There won't be enough of them that pay attention to make a difference."

"All it takes is the wrong ones to pay attention and something could go out of our control."

"We just have to see that doesn't happen. We are too far down the path now. It's inevitable."

Malachite was silent for a long moment. "I think we need to be careful. Too much is at stake."

"Let's not be too timid either. We can be careful and still make everything happen the way we want."

"As long as we are not careless, I think we agree on that. "

Malachite ended the conversation with Diamond and hung up the secure phone. Pushing the chair back from his desk, Benjamin Templeton stood and walked to the floor-to-ceiling windows in his private study that overlooked the Delaware River. He knew he wasn't the only one of them who worried what the chairman might do. The mistrust in the Committee was growing with every day that passed.

The White House
January 15, 1998


The limousine was passed through the security check and directed into the underground parking garage. The entrance to the garage was not all that close to the White House. There were visitors that wanted their business not to be the lead on the evening news. The security was airtight. The entire garage area along with the building where the entrance was located was under constant view of cameras located throughout the entire route. The garage could be pressurized or depressurized almost instantaneously in the event of a chemical threat. Doors were kept closed and opened only to allow the limousines to enter and exit. There was even an immediate response team ready for anything.

Two men exited the front of the limousine and, never taking anything for granted, scanned the area before opening the rear door for their passengers to exit the limousine. They had no concern here for their security; their concern was for the secrecy of the discussion that was about to take place.

Instead of going into the White House itself, the two men and the two security specialist got into the elevator and headed down to one of the secure levels below the White House. They were passed into the small conference room where the others were waiting. The power they wielded was absolute.

There was silence from the others seated in the room as the group entered. The meeting was not going to start until they had arrived. Seated around the conference table was the head of the Democratic party, the House minority leader, and Senate minority leader. Sitting alone at the end of the table was the first lady. The president had not been invited.

"Now that everyone is here we can get started. What the hell is going on?" The first lady was the first to say what the rest were wondering.

The two men exchanged looks. They had already decided who was going to start. "Right to the point, that's what I like about you. Sometimes you really aren't as smart as the public is led to believe. You can be quite the bitch, that won't work here. Let's get this straight. You need to shut up."

Enraged, the first lady stood up and started to walk toward the door. "You can't talk to me like that. I'll have both of you thrown out of here."

The laugh stopped her dead in her tracks. She turned to look at the senator and congressman for help. They both looked at her with contempt in their eyes. The senator was the first to speak, "You walk out that door if you want, and if you do, it's over, all of it."

She stopped and looked at the five men and realized they were all waiting on her. "What the hell is all this about? You haven't told me a fucking thing." She walked back to the chair and sat down.

The man who had spoken to her first looked at her and said, "Listen to what I am about to tell you and pay attention. Your little stunt with the press left everyone asking if you were going to divorce the president. That isn't going to happen. He is our guy, and you are causing problems. What you are going to do is be a good wife and smile and say you are going to stand by him and all is forgiven."

The First Lady almost snarled at him. "The stupid bastard got caught with his dick in the mouth of an intern, and you want me to act like it's nothing! I've put up with all of his bullshit and him screwing anything wearing a skirt. I don't give a shit about any of that. The one thing I can't forgive is him making me look stupid."

The second man fixed her with a stare that silenced her. "You decide just exactly what you want, go along with what we need you to do, and you will be rewarded. Try to play the wife scorned and find out how fast the documents that implicate you in the land deal in Arkansas comes to light. The special prosecutor will love finding all of that. I don't think prison would treat you too well."

She looked into his eyes and the expression on his face told her all she needed to know. "What exactly is in this for me?"

"There is a list of choices you can have." Motioning to the head of the Democratic party, he continued, "He will tell you which seats are available and you can choose. Play ball and do what you are told and that will be only the beginning. The choice is yours."

The first lady of the United States looked around the room and realized she could get what she wanted out of this. Maybe the miserable prick had done her a favor. Senator Clinton had a nice ring to it, and it was only the first step in her plans.

# JUSTIN A. BAILEY

The Holbrook Residence
Election Night
November 7, 2000

    Reginald Holbrook was watching the election results come in. It had been an interesting evening; the presidential race was still undecided. The networks had called Florida for Bush. Less than an hour later, it went back to undecided and too close to call. Another network had called it for Gore then back to undecided. It didn't really matter, either way they were in control. Reggie took another sip of his scotch and then rubbed his left arm; it was giving him trouble again. The New York Senate race had played out exactly as they had planned. Daniel Patrick Moynihan had announced he would not seek another term almost two years before. The seat had been promised to the first lady in exchange for her cooperation. The only difficult part was getting Giuliani out of the race.
    The mayor of New York had announced his intention to run two years before. His mayoral term would be up at the end of 2001, and he could not run again. He was immensely popular for what he had done for the city and he had played that into national prominence. He had help of course; however, he really didn't know about that or how it was done.
    Reggie moved his arm again and felt the familiar tightness in his chest. Damn. Getting old was a bitch. His seventy-eighth birthday was in another month or so, and it was hard to believe. It seemed like only yesterday he had been selected chairman; hard to believe that was thirty years ago. They were so close to their goal of not only complete control, but the final destruction of the government of the United States was less than twenty years away. He desperately wanted to be around to see all of the years, no centuries of work bear fruit. That had cost him twenty years before. This election proved it. The people were becoming more divided with every year that passed. He smiled inwardly; if they could only see how really ignorant they were. They paid more attention to football and television than the running of their country. He doubted most of them could tell you a damn thing about what was really going on in the world. He thought of everything they had done.

Control of the monetary system, inflating the cost of everything, creating an energy crisis they had made billions—no, trillions—on that alone. They controlled the hard assets and got everyone to invest in worthless paper assets.

The illegal immigration had diluted the makeup of the nation, and they had actively worked hard to keep all the minorities in their place and the animosity toward each other alive. That allowed them to make blocks of minorities, targeting the message to them and leading them in how they wanted them to vote. They had controlled education, teaching what they wanted the public to know, destroying their respect for freedom. Creating a dependence on the government, some of them would figure it out, and they would be the first to go. What was so special was they would bring it on themselves. They would cry out for more and more government to provide benefits and keep them safe, and they would willingly give away their freedom for security and safety. If they only knew, it wouldn't be much longer.

Reggie turned his attention back to the television and watched as more races were called. It didn't really matter who won most of them, they had candidates running against each other now. *It is only a matter of time*, he thought. The massive spending, the uncontrollable debt and deficits, it was all coming together; they could provoke a crisis when they needed, so they could deploy the troops overseas, especially those that wouldn't kill their fellow Americans to keep order. It would all crash when they decided and do it so quickly none would be prepared but them.

Just as they planned, the Senate race in New York had gone to the first lady. Reggie really loved that one. She wasn't even from New York. *Hell*, he thought, *the Clintons hadn't ever owned a house before buying the one in New York so they could claim residency*. Then winning the New York Supreme Court case, keeping her on the ballot, The real gem was getting the mayor out of the race with the threat of a scandal and then using the excuse of prostate cancer to withdraw. If he hadn't, they would have destroyed him and he knew it. It was all so easy; Reggie tossed back the last of his scotch and turned the television off. He didn't really give a damn about the presidential race. Either way they would win.

He left his study and walked down the corridor through the great room and headed toward the master suite. He was tired; he never liked to stay up this late anymore. Reaching his bedroom, he stepped into the master bath to relieve himself before going to bed; he washed his hands and went back in the bedroom. Throwing the covers back and slipping the dressing gown off his shoulders, he tossed it on the ottoman and went to bed. Turning out the light, he drifted off to sleep. Sometime during the night his heart just simply stopped, and he would never wake up. His wife would find him in the morning; they hadn't slept in the same room for the last ten years.

Another chairman would have to be selected. The Committee was getting older by the day. This one would be number twenty-two. The nation had almost twice the number of presidents as the Committee had chairman; they didn't know it yet, but this one would be the last.

The Committee
New York, New York
January 23, 2001

The last of the members of the Committee had entered the conference room on the 101st floor of tower one. The meeting had been called earlier than normal due to the passing of the chairman. They had to select a new chairman and another member, the business of the Committee would continue as it had for over two hundred years. At least that's what they believed; they had made mistakes they were soon to discover.

The chair at the head of the table was empty; the other members were almost reluctant to begin. Finally, Coral took the floor. "Gentlemen, we must begin this meeting for the first time in thirty years with the need to select a chairman. Some of us in this room have never been part of that process. We will pick a chairman from those of us in this room. A simple majority is all that is required. After that, we must select a new member, which requires a unanimous agreement. I will ask each of you to write your choice for chairman and pass them to me."

After several long moments, the members of the committee each began to write their choice on the legal pads in front of them, folded the sheets of paper, and passed them to Coral. He began to unfold them and sort them; there were four stacks in front him. One stack had four; two had two each and the last had one had a single piece of paper. Coral looked at the assembled members and announced "We have four votes for Malachite, two each for Gold and Coral, and one for Onyx. I make a motion we remove the member with one vote and vote again. Are there any objections?"

There were none, and they proceeded to vote again. Once again Coral read the results. "We have four votes for Malachite, three for Coral, and two for Gold. If there are no objections we will proceed as we did previously and vote again." There were no objections.

The votes were counted again and Coral announced, "We now have five votes for Malachite and four for Coral."

With the announcement, Malachite slowly stood and made his way to the empty chair at the head of the table and sat down. "Thank you, gentlemen, for your vote of confidence. The next order of business is the selection of a new member. Most of us in here have participated in this before. A unanimous vote is required. I will pass around the list of potential members, and we can either take nominations or proceed to the vote. The floor is open for a motion."

Malachite was a very experienced chairman of the board and conducted the meeting as he would with any other of the many boards he sat on. There was a motion from Gold to take nominations and surprising him it was seconded by Onyx.

The rest of the Committee quickly agreed, and the list of potential members was circulated. The nominations were taken and the vote proceeded. After several rounds of voting, they finally selected Grayson Carmichael. The Committee then moved on to the rest of their business as they had before. Benjamin Templeton now known as Diamond would shortly find out just how much power he really had.

As with every one of the chairmen since John D. Rockefeller had held the position, a plan had been put in place to inform the successor after the death of any chairman just how much more there was to know. There were events on the horizon they had put in place that would rock the committee to their very core. As careful as they had been, the past had left a trail that someone was slowly following.

Congressman Cain's office
Washington DC
September 11, 2001

Ben Cain was in early; there was legislation he was reviewing that would be voted on. As he did with everything, he was painstakingly reading the details. He was the first one in the office, which constantly surprised his staff. He had gotten in early around 7:00 a.m. He had a lot of reading to do and found he was more productive when he was left alone, morning was the best. He took another sip of his coffee and rolled his neck and rubbed his eyes he had been at it almost two hours. He glanced at his watch, 8:45. He had to be in conference at 10. He would have to wrap it up in the next twenty minutes.

Shortly after he had turned his attention back to the papers on his desk, his door was unceremoniously opened by Craig Bennett, his chief of staff who never said a word just rushed in and turned the television on. "You need to see this."

The news anchor was speaking and the footage was showing an airplane crashing into the World Trade Center Tower One, flames erupting from the opposite side of the building. Ben barely heard the words the anchor was speaking, "Right now, all we know is what appears to be a plane of some sort has apparently crashed into Tower One of the World Trade Center complex in lower Manhattan. The footage you are seeing was taken by a film crew on-site doing a documentary. We will have live coverage as soon as we can get the feed from the crew on the ground. This appears to be some sort of accident. We do not have any further details at this time. We are trying to find out from the authorities if they have any information on exactly what type of aircraft this was and where it was from. I am just being informed the live feed is now in place. Let's see if we can get that." The screen changed and a live shot of the Twin Towers came into view. Thick black smoke was curling from the charred opening in the building, and flames were visible. The news anchor continued to talk and the scene changed again to the film crew on the ground looking up at the stricken tower. Sirens sounded in the background and the reporter on the scene began to talk with the news anchor.

# THE COMMITTEE

The congressman's entire staff began to gather in his small office and watched the television mesmerized. The excited voice of the reporter on the ground went up as the camera caught another plane flying low and headed directly for Tower Two. They watched as it impacted the building lower than the one that had hit tower one. The fireball erupted from the building, and the screams of the crowd on the ground were plainly heard.

The excited reporter tried to maintain his composure. "Oh my god, another plane has just struck the second tower. This can't be an accident. Something has to be terribly wrong."

The entire office staff was too stunned to speak; they all stood transfixed watching the horrible images on the television. The outer door of his office burst open, and a Capitol police officer shouted in the door, "Everyone out now. The building is being evacuated. Move. Get going now!"

It was a long moment before anyone could respond; the officer grabbed the arm of the closest staff member to him and shook her arm and pushed her toward the door to the hall. "I said get moving now. Get out of the building." There was a rush to the door into the crowded hallway of the congressional office building as the police were evacuating the entire building. Congressman Cain found himself caught in the mad rush headed to the exit of the building. None of them yet knew what had happened beyond the two planes hitting the twin towers in New York.

Ben Cain found himself being hustled away by a member of the Capitol police force and led to a police vehicle and rushed from the area. It all happened so fast he never realized he was only one of a few that were given such an escort from the panicked crowd.

McAllister Halstead
Corporate Headquarters
Oklahoma City, Oklahoma
September 11, 2001

August Braden was watching the news reports like everyone else in the nation. He was in his office at the corporate headquarters of

McAllister Halstead. The difference was he knew who was responsible for this. At least he knew who had provided the money that made it possible for the terrorists to destroy much more than just the buildings. The only thing on any news networks was everything that had happened—the damage at the Pentagon, the fire still raging. People he knew, no friends of his, had died there. They had been brothers in arms. Both of the twin towers in New York had collapsed, and all of lower Manhattan was in utter chaos and nearly devastated.

The news anchor was talking about the passengers revolting on flight 93 causing the terrorist's to fly it into the ground. He knew that it had really been shot down by an air force fighter pilot and the White House had been the target. They had even protected the President that was why the trip to the school in Florida had been scheduled. He hung his head in shame. How had it all come to this?

He had run everyone who had tried to come into his office out. He didn't want to talk to or face anyone. He was afraid the guilt would show on his face. The bastards on the Committee had allowed this to happen. All they knew was that an attack was planned and what the targets were. After the 1993 bombing of the towers, they had threatened to cut off the money if the terrorists didn't give them a target list. They had a little more than two months warning. Instead of trying to stop it, they had moved all of the employees from floor 102 and all the computers and the information they contained to Los Angeles. It was all done under the guise of starting a West Coast division of Atlas. They had sacrificed all of the 100th floor employees who actually had no idea they were nothing more than window dressing. He was pissed at himself for not having the balls to do something about it. More innocent Americans had died than at Pearl Harbor. At least there it was a military target and most of the dead had been in the military. They had engineered that one as well. At least he hadn't been responsible for that. It had happened before his time on the Committee. This was different.

What bothered him the most was the casualties were just numbers to the rest of them. He reminded himself again he was the only one who had been in the military and actually watched men die. He was going to have to do something; he just didn't know what he could do. The secure phone ringing broke his train of thought. He gave it an annoyed look and debated if he should answer. He knew he didn't have a choice. He picked it up and spoke only one word, "Yes."

Gold was on the other end. "What in the hell are we going to do about this?"

"I don't think there is a damn thing we are going to do about what has already happened. The real question is, what can we do to stop anything else from happening?" Onyx wondered if Gold was actually developing a set of balls; he hadn't been able to himself.

"We can't allow this to go on."

"No, we can't. I don't think I can live with myself if something like this happens again. The only option we have is to convince the rest of them we can use what has happened to further the rest of the agenda, and there is no need to allow another attack." Onyx turned to stare out the window.

There was silence before Gold's response, "Is that the best we can do?"

"It's a start. We will have to give it some more thought and convince them it's their idea."

"My god, have we come so far in our lust for power we are destroying our own nation as well as its citizens?"

"In the beginning, I was naive enough to think it was about making the United States the leader of the world. It appears the rest of them are happy to destroy it to control the world." Onyx paused before finishing his thought, "No amount of power is enough."

"You realize we're on our own with this?"

"It's been that way for the last twenty years. We are going to have to be very careful. The problem is this whole thing almost runs itself. Our security is also our keepers."

"I know. I keep telling myself if we don't do something there isn't anyone who can." The stress in Gold's voice betrayed him.

"We better do something before it all gets completely out of control."

Gold paused and couldn't stop himself from replying, "I'm afraid it already is and has been for some time."

There was nothing else either of them could say. What they didn't know was the trail was slowly and quietly leading to them.

# JUSTIN A. BAILEY

Office of the Governor
Boston, Massachusetts
January 5, 2003

Governor Cain walked into the meeting room of the State Capitol; his staff was already assembled. To the surprise of those in the room, he was carrying a white board and a small easel. He stopped at the head of the table and set up the easel and put the white board in place. Reaching into his jacket pocket, he produced a set of markers and eraser. He still had said nothing as he began to write one word at the top of the board in large capital letters.

GOALS. He turned to his staff and said, "The first thing we are going to do is start by putting our goals here. Then we are going to list under each one how we are going to try to accomplish those. We all need to bear in mind that I am a Republican governor and both the legislature, and let's face it, the majority of voters in this state are members of or at least identify with the Democratic party. All of us live here. I do not want party politics and squabbles to come between us preventing what we need to do to make this state work better for all of us." Borrowing a line from his father, he looked around one by one at each of his staff members then said, "How do we make our arguments without being argumentative?"

The meeting ended thirty-five minutes later. Ben Cain had learned from his father not to let meetings like this drag on. Say what needed to be said and get to work. He had impressed that on his staff. They had work to do and would need the support of the people to get it done. Ben Cain was learning the art of politics and being a chief executive of a state.

Governor Cain was sitting at his desk when the phone buzzed; he looked up from the document he was reading and picked up the phone. "Yes, Melissa?"

Mellissa had worked for Ben Cain since his days in the State house. One more thing he had learned from his father: find a good executive assistant, pay them well, and take care of them. She guarded his time carefully. "Governor, Benjamin Templeton is on the phone for you."

"Put the call through. I'll talk to him of course, and thank you, Melissa."

The phone buzzed again and Ben picked it up. "Hello, Mr. Templeton. How are you doing, sir?"

There was a chuckle from the other end. "Ben, you are a governor now. You can call me by my first name."

"Sir, there are some things I am very old-fashioned about. I will always think of you as Mr. Templeton. I do not want to make my mother mad either. She drilled it into my head to treat everyone with respect."

Templeton laughed on the other end. "Congratulations on the election, Governor. I must say I am very proud of you. Who would have thought twenty years ago when you came to work for us you would be the governor of the state, and I would be calling you to offer congratulations."

"Thank you, sir. I must say it doesn't seem all that long ago that I was just out of college and looking for a job. Who would have thought this is where I would be."

Templeton smiled inwardly at that. "Well, Ben, I really just wanted to call and tell you personally just how pleased and proud of you I really am. Also I'm sure I can speak for James Bradley as well as all of us at Wellington. You will always be family to us."

"Thank you, sir, and if I can ever be of service, please let me know."

"I can't think of a thing at the moment. This really was just a social call. We can get together and talk about old times later. Also, let me wish you well in your new job and tell you again how proud of you I really am and also wish your family well for me."

"I'll do that, sir. It was good to talk to you and pass along my best as well."

"Take care, Ben. I expect great things from you." Diamond hung up the phone. He was pleased; things were progressing well. The strategy was coming together, and Ben Cain would be right in the mix. It just wouldn't be quite how the Committee had planned.

JUSTIN A. BAILEY

FBI Field Office
Richmond, Virginia
May 28, 2004

    The computer screen in front of Dan Oliver was coming to life, and he was waiting to log on. This would be the last time. He had put his papers in two months before, and Harlan J. Starks, the pompous asshole, couldn't get him out fast enough. Dan smiled inwardly at the thought. *He might be getting me out of his office,* Dan thought, *but he can't get me out of not only his computer system but those of the Justice Department, the Department of Defense, several others, and now the CIA.* That was when he decided he could now retire when "The Mole" had sent the codes for that one out. He now had to distance himself from the very government he had served for over thirty years. He didn't want to still be working where they could find him, and he was afraid they were close. His house was up for sale, and he had announced he was going to travel the world as he had always wanted.

    He was more afraid for Pam; he had shut down her curiosity a couple of years before and made damn sure she didn't know what he was up to. She was married now and was expecting her first child and that he was not willing to risk.

    He had a plan in place; if he really needed to disappear, he could. What he didn't like about it was what it would do to Pam and Becky. He couldn't tell either of them; it was for their own protection. The computer came to life, and he finished logging on. There were things he had to clean out he didn't want anyone to see. He slipped another CD into the drive, typed in the access code, and hit enter when the prompt came on. If you didn't know when and what to enter, all you would get was the music. This one would clean out everything and the computer would crash after a certain number of startups and the hard drive would fry. No matter how good you were there wouldn't be any retrieving anything on it. He wasn't taking any chances.

    The CD ejected, and he dropped it into the box of stuff he was removing from his desk. The program had been hidden in the background of a Garth Brooks CD. He had help from Mossad, the Israeli intelligence agency. Even they didn't know what he was working on; if anything happened to him, they would. They had written the programs he was using. Before his wife had died, he had worked on a terrorism task force for the FBI and had spent a year in Israel. He had maintained contact with and become friends with several of their agents. His safe house was in Tel Aviv and was under Mossad protection. He knew there was going to come a time when he might need it. The problem might be getting there.

Dan finished putting the last of the items from his desk into the box and shut down the computer. He was going to have a drink with a couple of his friends from the office and then he was no longer a government employee. He stood up, picked up the box, and headed out of the office for the last time. Now his real work was going to begin.

The Templeton Residence
Milford, Pennsylvania
June 12, 2006


The sun was setting, and it was a brilliant display as it cast its light on the tranquil waters of the Delaware River. Benjamin Templeton had bought the land almost forty years before after his selection to the Committee. It sat between Milford and Matamoros in eastern Pennsylvania. It was remote and isolated and thus very private. He had built his estate overlooking the Delaware River. He spent as much time here as he could. Now that he was retired from his day-to-day running of his financial empire, he spent most of his time here. Not many people knew who owned the land, and he liked it that way. This was his refuge, and he had spent a great deal of money on its security and had spared no expense on its comfort as well.

Money was of no concern. The Committee and each of its members controlled vast financial and business enterprises that were each worth billions of dollars. They had learned how to funnel money out of the government through defense contractors starting at the beginning of World War II and had refined it since then throughout the Federal and even some state governments. It was all part of their strategy. They really didn't care how much they spent. While they were all highly successful bankers and businessmen and didn't waste money, they controlled such vast sums they didn't think of it the way the average American did.

They controlled everything that was really of value. Land, mineral resources, water rights, and what they didn't own outright they controlled the corporations that did. What they really considered to be one of the final pieces to their plan of control was the mortgage and banking the average American depended on. The American dream of home ownership. Get them to buy homes at vastly inflated prices, carry a mortgage, and pay three times the price. Even if they managed to pay it off, the interest went to the banks they controlled. When it all crashed and the banks repossessed the homes, they got the land and everything they had paid. Some of them were smart enough to plan for their retirement; those that weren't could be convinced to get a reverse mortgage. In the end, they got worthless money, and their land went back to the bank.

Benjamin Templeton had been instrumental in developing and implementing that part of the Committee's plans. He was enjoying the sunset and the spectacular view out of the floor to ceiling windows of his private study. The secure phone ringing broke the silence of his quiet reverie. It took him several long moments to stand from his leather recliner. He was in his mideighties, and while still in the best of health, he wasn't as nimble as before. He walked to his desk and picked up the phone. All of the members answered the same way; it aided in the voice recognition software of the system.

"Yes" was the one word answer.

The head of security was on the other end. "We may have a potential problem."

Diamond was immediately concerned, "What type of problem?"

"There appears to be someone looking into the financial records of some of the candidates."

"How is that possible?" Diamond's concern showed in his voice.

For a long moment, there was silence on the other end. "One of the computer security experts found something in one of the computers. He's trying to run down where it came from."

"What exactly does 'something' mean?"

The head of security took a deep breath before he answered. "I'm not really a computer geek, but the way he put it is, it is some kind of background program that gives someone access to whatever system it has been introduced to."

"Are you telling me someone has been looking into our computers?"

"From what I understand, it doesn't work quite that way. It sends out information. I don't think someone can just access the system if that's what you mean."

"How in the hell did this get onto one of our computers and which ones?" Diamond's throat tightened; they were too close for something like this.

"We're working on that. As you know, essentially every computer that has access to the government network we can look into. That also means they are in a sense linked to ours. The expert doesn't think anything has been sent out. What he's worried about is how this got into our system and where it came from and how long it has had to work. He found it in the system in one of the offices that we set up in one of the defense contractors."

Diamond had a sudden fear of where it had been found. "Which one?"

"It came through McAllister Hallstead. The expert said it didn't originate there. He's working on that. It may take some time."

"Can we shut it down?"

"Whoever wrote this knew what they were doing. There is no type of program that will find it. Every single computer will have to be looked at. He thinks he can write a program that can track the specific lines of code. Remember I told you this is not my area of expertise. I'm trying to explain this as best I can."

"Any ideas at all who is behind this?" Diamond began to feel sweat break out.

"Not yet. Remember whoever wrote this is good. The expert thinks it originated within the government system somewhere. If the person who wrote the code is within one of our agencies, we can find them pretty quickly. If it came from somewhere else, we may not be able to track it right away."

"Find out. Make this the highest priority. I don't care what it takes. Any asset you need is available. Get to the bottom of this as soon as you can."

"It may take some time. All we have is what we found in the computer system. He is going to try some things to find the source of the program. That may not tell us who is behind getting it into the computer that started this."

"Find out." Diamond slammed the phone down. They were too close to let this happen now.

On the other end of the secure phone, Atlas's head of security heard the phone click; he hung up his phone and took another deep breath. He hadn't told him how long this had been in their system and how much he was afraid it had sent out; the truth was, they didn't really know.

The Oliver Apartment
Richmond, Virginia
July 4, 2006

The computer screen in front of Dan Oliver changed as he entered the secure program that gave him access to The Mole. Slowly but surely, he was making progress unraveling the source of all the money spent on the political campaigns. The more he found, the more astonished he was. What was publicly disclosed by the candidates was hardly a drop in the bucket of what was really spent. He had a long way to go. Since he had retired from the FBI, he had been digging into all this nonstop.

The way the secure program worked he could look for specific things through a back door the software put in every computer system it was introduced into. It was slow and tedious but as secure as it could be made; he knew nothing was perfect. The older the program got, the less secure it was. It was almost impossible to update without more help from his asset, as he thought of the Israeli intelligence agency. He was reluctant to ask for help. He had a direction now. Everything led back to the defense contractors. Not all of them but three of the largest. What he had found was staggering, Billions of dollars had been funneled off going back further than he could look. What he was working on now was trying to find how it had made its way to the political campaigns that spent it. The disparity in spending was staggering.

Suddenly, Dan sat bolt upright in his chair, the alarm built into the program was suddenly on his screen; he had been warned about that. He yanked out the cable that connected the computer to the internet. He knew it was too late; they had found him. This is what he had feared for the last three years. Now he was going to have to disappear. He stood up, opened the desk drawer, pushed a button, grabbed the bag by the door, and just walked out of the apartment. He didn't know how long it would be before they got here.

Three hours later, Dan was watching as the two black vans stopped in front of the building where he had his apartment, two more were in back. Four well-dressed men got out of each van and not a word was said they just dispersed and covered the entire building. The vans quickly drove away; if you weren't watching, in less than a minute you wouldn't know they were there. It was all very professional. One of them walked across the street and slid into the back of a car that was parked there. It had been there over two hours. He knew they would be fast. What they didn't know was he had planned for this.

The team entered the apartment; Dan had left the door open for them. He hadn't set any type of traps for them. What he had done was set a security system in place to get their pictures. He was going to try and find out just exactly where they were sent from. This had government agency all over it.

The team leader exited the car across the street and walked to the building and into the apartment. He took a long look around and found his second in command. "What did you find?"

"Whoever this was, he is a professional. Look at the computer." He pointed to one of the bedrooms.

The team leader walked into what was normally a second bedroom that had been set up for an office and took a look around. The room was mostly intact, but the desk and the computer on it was a pile of rubble. He knelt down and looked at the remnants of the computer. "There was a charge inside the computer. He was prepared. Go through everything. He's good, but he left something. Find it."

The team leader left the apartment, walked back across the street, got in the passenger side of the car, it pulled away and left.

Several buildings away, Dan Oliver was watching everything that was going on. The cameras that were hidden throughout the apartment would be found but not before they had recorded the images of the entire team and sent it out. He had leased this office before the apartment and now he would have to leave that too. He had kept this totally separate from his apartment, but he knew they would find this as well. It was only a matter of time. He had made his preparations for this certainty, and now he would have to disappear. But not before he left them a message.

The Templeton Residence
Milford, Pennsylvania
July 6, 2006

The secure phone ringing caused Diamond to excuse himself from the dinner party he was hosting. Very few people were invited to his estate on the Delaware River. Those who were, generally had some connection to his business; he held social functions in one of his other residences in either Boston or New York. "If you gentlemen will excuse me, I have a call I must take."

Reaching the door to his private study, he closed the door and answered the secure phone. "Yes."

"We have a lead on the identity of the security breach." The security chief had been under constant pressure to find who was responsible for the program in their computer system.

"What have you found out?"

"We set a trap for the next time he tried to access the system at McAllister Halstead. It led us to an apartment in Richmond, Virginia. This guy is a professional. There wasn't much there. We lifted prints from the apartment and ran them through the FBI. They belong to a retired FBI agent named Daniel Oliver. He retired in 2004 as the ASAC of the Richmond field office. So far, we haven't been able to find him."

"What do you mean you haven't been able to find him?" Diamond's voice rose in anger.

"I told you this guy is a professional. He was prepared to leave in a hurry. There isn't anything left of his computer. He had that rigged to explode. We won't get anything from that." He was prepared for the next question.

"How in the hell did he know you were coming?" Diamond managed to contain his temper.

"The geek tells me he had some kind of alarm in the computer program. The moment we traced it back to him, he knew. He was probably out of there within five minutes."

"How much does this retired FBI agent know?" Diamond realized he was clenching the phone tighter and forced himself to relax his grip.

The head of security paused before he spoke, "We don't know yet. We can't get anything from his computer, and we are going to have to go to the NSA to see what we can find on his Internet records. We have to do that carefully. That program is highly classified, and we only have limited ways we can access that. It will take a few days to get our source there to run the search from the inside."

Templeton was furious. "What the hell do you mean limited access? That program is only in existence because we want it to be. We should have access to anything we want!"

"We do have access to whatever we want. We just can't pick up the phone and say get me everything I want. It doesn't work that way. Remember, we also don't want to bring attention to us either. It all has to be done very quietly. We have to keep our security intact."

"Well, that seems to have been a challenge, doesn't it? I don't care what you have to do. Find this guy and shut him down." Diamond slammed the phone down in anger. All the resources they had, all the money they spent, and they couldn't find one goddamned retired FBI agent. He walked slowly to the bar in his study and poured himself a drink. His hand was shaking; he took a sip and forced himself to take a deep breath. They were too close to let this happen now. Diamond had learned to compartmentalize things over his career, he finished the drink, forced it from his mind, and returned to his guests. Had he known how deeply they were penetrated, he wouldn't have been able to force it from his mind.

North Beach Marina
Miami, Florida
July 15, 2006

The ocean was starting to get choppy, Dan Oliver was glad he was about to the marina. He was tired; it had been a long haul from Virginia Beach. He was ready to tie up the *Quiet Time* before the weather got any worse. As soon as he had left his apartment when he realized they had found him, Dan had gone to his office. It was rented under another name, and he made sure he never used a computer there for anything online. He had worked carefully on his escape plan and wasn't going to risk the office being found at the same time as his apartment. They would find it because of the cameras hidden in the apartment. The images had been sent out minutes after they had entered his apartment. The computer they had been sent to he had hidden in the building, but not his office; it had been set up exclusively for that purpose. Fifteen minutes after the images were taken, the connection was ripped out. He had left the computer for them to find.

He had been as careful as he could; he never drove the car under his name anywhere near the office. He told no one about the office. He had rented it through an out-of-town realtor under one of the several identities he had set up, and the rent was paid through them. He had paid them once a year in advance. They thought he was a salesman for an overseas company. The car he had used to drive from Richmond to Virginia Beach was registered to another of his identities; it would never be found. He had kept the *Quiet Time* in a marina in Virginia Beach and never used it. It was set up as charter rental with two others, and the leasing company was always told to have at least one in port for his use a week at a time. They were further instructed to have them fully provisioned and ready to go. They were all paid through an offshore account linked to the Middle East. The leasing agent thought it was a wealthy Saudi prince. An e-mail was sent later telling him the prince had taken the *Quiet Time*, and he was free to keep renting the other two. The rentals had almost paid for the whole thing.

Dan had taken a page from those he was chasing and had set up accounts funneling off money from the government through the very same Federal agencies they were using. He had taken a chance with that but was betting it wouldn't be looked at. As far as the government knew, it was payments to another defense supplier. The money was sent overseas and broken up among several accounts. All the years he put in chasing people who had done this had taught him to be an expert. He had never used any of it for personal gain. In the end, he hoped he would be able to tell them where it all went; he had kept track of every dime. He had lived on his retirement and investments. He had sold the house in Richmond. That had been painful. It was his last connection with his life before his wife had died and the daughter he had to raise by himself.

When he had rented the apartment, he had never wanted his daughter Pam or Becky, the lady he had been seeing, to even know he had it. He kept another that he actually lived in. What he was going to have to do to protect them would be painful for both of them.

Dan eased the *Quiet Time* into the slip at the marina. Like everything else, he had instructed the charter company to lease slips all along the east coast for use in the charters. They had used them regularly; no one paid any attention to the *Quiet Time*, it had frequented the marina before. He tied it up with the help of one of the marina employees. He had it fueled and provisioned all at the expense of the charter company; they would pay it and bill the Saudi prince accordingly. He was going to disappear.

Dan left the boat and walked down the street toward the Starbucks outside the entrance to the marina. He was going to need help. He walked into the Starbucks and walked up to the counter.

"May I help you?" The young man behind the counter smiled at Dan.

"I would like a large black coffee please." Dan was surprised at the young man's response.

Almost a snicker, as he said, "A grande, sir?"

"Sure, that will be fine." Dan was almost surprised at the cost; he didn't frequent Starbucks, but they had Wi-Fi, and he needed to get a message out. He paid for it, stuffed a dollar in the tip jar, took the coffee, and sat down at a table in the corner. He took out the small notebook computer he had put in his bag that he had left his apartment with. He had set it up, made sure it would work, kept it ready, and never used it. He had saved it for when he needed it.

Dan turned it on, entered his password, and connected to the Internet. He picked a service and used a bank card to pay for it. The account was one he had under another alias; he was taking no chances. He logged onto an e-mail that was also paid through the same account as the card and wrote an e-mail and sent it out. Dan knew about the National Security agency and the facility they had to monitor just about everything over the Internet. The e-mail contained nothing that would raise any suspicion. The recipient would know how to extract from it what Dan wanted him to know. As soon as it was sent, he logged off, closed the notebook, and left. He wouldn't be in Miami more than forty-eight hours.

Consulate of Israel
Atlanta, Georgia
July 16, 2006

Jonah Kauffman parked his car in the small parking lot behind the consulate building. He made sure to lock it and carefully looked around as he walked across the parking lot into the building. He went through his normal routine as he took a cup of coffee into his office and sat down at his desk. He went through what he thought of as the overnights, things that had happened while he was out of the office and required action on his part or was simply information. When he finished those, he logged on to his computer and then logged in to his e-mail. He suddenly sat upright at the sight of one of the e-mails and who had sent it. He opened it and read through it very carefully. He printed it out and immediately deleted it. He stood up, left his office, and headed toward the basement.

He walked toward the secure door with the keypad next to it, paused and entered a code, waited and entered another code. Thirty seconds later, the door opened, and he walked into the secure communication facility.

Joseph Sharron looked up from his desk when Jonah walked in and asked, "What brings you down here?"

Jonah handed him the printout and said, "I need this decoded as soon as you can."

He took the paper from him, looked at it, and turned to his computer and brought it to life. When the program he wanted came up, he began to type very rapidly. Several long moments later, the printer spit out a sheet of paper. He took it, read it, and then handed it to Jonah. "I guess you are going to be out of the office for a couple of days from the look of that."

"I wondered how long it was going to be before that came in. A friend of mine needs help, and I have been expecting it for the last three years."

"Anything I can do? That is a priority request." Joseph looked up into the eyes of his friend; they had been through a lot together over the years.

"Not yet. I don't even know what he was working on. All I know is this was as quiet as we could keep it. He was solo, and we set this up if he needed help."

"I don't have to tell you to be careful, do I?" His concern was evident in his voice.

"I plan on being careful. You are the only one who knows other than me. I will contact you when I know something."

Dan Oliver had called for help; Jonah owed him. He would do whatever he could to help, even if it cost him.

## JUSTIN A. BAILEY

Bowman Center
Richmond, Virginia
July 17, 2006

They had traced the security cameras installed in Dan Oliver's apartment to this building. Now they knew exactly which office was his. It had taken them longer than it should have; at least that's what the security chief had told the team. This bastard was good. Edgar had been doing this type of work a long time, and this was the first time he had run into anybody this good. They had no idea where he was.

Edgar slipped the small pick into the lock of the office and quietly opened the door. They already knew there was no alarm; even if there was, it didn't matter. He stepped inside the office and took a look around; his partner was still checking the rest of the building. It was obvious the office wasn't really a working office, at least to a professional. There was dust on the telephone and in some other places; there wouldn't be if the office was regularly used. The computer was not even hooked up to the Internet, and it was an old desktop. The copier didn't have paper in the tray.

Edgar continued his search. There was nothing to find. Wherever the computer was that the security system was connected to, it wasn't in this office. It had to be elsewhere in the building; they would find it.

Two hours later, they finally located it right out in the open. It was a laptop set up in a mechanical room with the building's air conditioning system; it was in a control panel for the building automation system. It even had an Ethernet cable hooked up to the automation system and a control program installed on it. The building didn't have an automation system. To the casual observer, they would have never noticed anything unusual. They just unplugged it and took it with them. They turned it over to the tech guys. It was obvious he had intended them to find it.

The computer was password protected. Enough to stop the better than average but simple to the professionals; it hadn't taken them long to get through it. He had pictures of every member of the team that had been in the apartment. It had all been downloaded to a zip drive, and he had taken it with him. He left the pictures for them to find.

He had even left them a message, a word document outlining enough of what he had and telling them if anything happened to anyone he cared about, it would be released on the Internet. He even told them which defense contractors they were funneling the money through and let them know he had more much more. He had made it clear it was between them. Two of the members of the team that had families found their pictures on the computer. They had reached an agreement. He wanted the professionals to settle it.

The Safe House
Tel Aviv, Israel
July 21, 2006

Dan Oliver had a cup of coffee in his hand and was sitting at the table in the small kitchen of his safe house. Jonah Kauffman was seated across from him. He had arranged for the Gulfstream that had flown both of them to Israel. He had set up an Angel flight to bring a small Palestinian child from the west bank to Miami for treatment of a rare disorder. The press had eaten it up. They didn't pay any attention to the plane leaving the airport; they were too interested in the story of the child. Both he and Dan Oliver had gotten on as part of the ground crew servicing the plane.

Jonah had made friends with Dan while he had been in Israel for the FBI on the anti-terrorism task force. Dan had saved his life when the car they were in had been ambushed by the terrorists they were tracking. He had shot the one that had Jonah in his sights before he could shoot him and the other one that was trying to hit them with an RPG. That would have killed all of them. Jonah owed him.

"What in the hell have you gotten yourself into? You wouldn't tell me three years ago." Jonah had to wait to ask until they were here.

"I don't want to tell you. I haven't got all of it yet." Dan finished the last of his coffee.

"You're going to have to tell me something. I can't be of much help otherwise."

Dan took a long look straight into his friend's eyes. He was right; he was going to need help. "Jonah, seven years ago, my daughter came home from college and brought me the original of a letter James Madison had written to his dead friend Thomas Jefferson."

"You are talking about the James Madison that was president of your country almost two hundred years ago?" There was a look of disbelief and skepticism on his face.

"That's the one. In it he made a reference to a committee they had set up and asked God's forgiveness for what they had done."

Jonah interrupted him. "If you don't mind me asking, what in the hell does this have to do with what you've gotten yourself into?"

"Maybe you need to read the letter before I explain anymore." Dan stood up.

"Wait a minute, are you telling me it's here?"

Dan smiled at his friend. "It was the only place I could think to keep it and a whole lot more. I have been in the FBI a long time. There were a lot of cases I was taken off over the years. There wasn't any good reason to stop looking into them. I was the expert on financial manipulations and hiding money. Most of the cases I was taken off had to do with politicians and government agencies. What they had in common was they were all then made to go away. This may explain the origins. Let me show you." Dan left to retrieve the letter.

Dan went to the basement of the safe house; there was a room in the back that was locked with a heavy steel door. Retrieving a set of keys, he opened the door and went in. It was set up much like an office. In one corner was another door that looked like a small closet. Opening that, Dan stepped in and closed the door behind him; there were two file cabinets against the back wall. He opened the lower drawer of the one on the right and moved it out of the cabinet. Setting it aside, he took a pocket knife from his pocket and carefully pried up the bottom panel. Below it was a floor safe. He worked the combination, removed a folder designed to protect the contents, and put everything back in place. He wasn't going to even tell Jonah this was here. If anyone ever got in, he was hoping they would stop at the file cabinets.

Dan left the small office in the basement, went back upstairs, and handed the file folder to Jonah. "Read this and then maybe you will understand what set me on this search." He sat down across from him at the small table.

Jonah took the file folder from Dan and began to read the letter James Madison had penned to his deceased friend Thomas Jefferson a hundred and seventy four years before.

My dearest Thomas,

As I write these lines to you, I realize you will never read them. Many years have gone by since you have passed, and I became the last to carry on. You are the only one who will understand the burdens we carried so long. The chairmanship passed to me when you were taken from this world, and I have tried to live by the principles with which we founded this nation. I fear as time passes those to whom we entrusted positions on the committee will no longer abide by the guiding principles of faith the founders sought to live by.

    I know you and I shared the same self doubts if we were right to form the committee. Our purposes noble and our intentions honorable, we did not trust our citizens to make the right decisions of leadership this nation has needed. We chose to implement our will by choosing who those leaders would be. Those of us who fought to bring this nation forth may have understood our concern for those Americans who were never willing to fight for their principles of faith, freedom, and liberty. Yet these have been our guiding light. I fear it will not always be so to those who follow. We have given them the power to decide the fate of this nation. As the years passed and we lost the original members of the Committee, General Washington, Samuel Patterson, Jonathan who sacrificed so much, all the others, to Alexander who was struck down by the madman Burr. I am the last, and the power has passed to those that we chose. I pray we have chosen wisely, and I fear we have not. The course they choose will determine the fate and freedoms we cherished and sacrificed to provide yet may be the cause of their demise. I will answer for my sins of this world when I meet our creator. It may not be far in the future for me now. They have set me aside and treat me with respect, yet I fear they seek power never intended. May God forgive us for what we have sown, and I pray what we feared shall not come to pass. I am powerless to stop them. History will tell what our decisions have wrought. May God forgive us and bless this nation and protect it from the committee with which we so inadvertently burdened it.

*James*

Jonah read the letter again twice more. He looked up into the face of his friend. "My god what have you gotten yourself into?" He handed the letter back to Dan.

"This is what started it all. I had often thought there were things going on in our government that just didn't add up. Politicians, huh, most aren't really that bright, not only getting elected but reelected, massive amounts of money in their campaign. That's only the tip of the iceberg. All the political action committees or PACS as we call them, spending millions to endorse or destroy those running for office. Every time I was investigating the trail of money the last thirty years, I was stopped. That's not all I have. I kept copies of everything I worked on. There have been billions funneled out of our government going back further than I can look."

Dan got up, went to the coffee pot, and poured another cup for himself and another for Jonah. He sat back down and continued, "I decided the way to find out was to start with what I already had. Remember I was looking into this already. Before, I was trying to nail the politicians, who I thought were dirty. When Pam came home with the letter, I realized they weren't the ones behind it. I started tracing the source of the money; all of it has come out of the government through defense contractors primarily. Not all of it went to the campaigns. I haven't found it all."

Jonah stared at the letter in Dan's hand yellowed with age. He said what came to mind, "I think both he and his deceased friend Thomas would approve of you nailing the bastards behind this."

The Sutton Home
Richmond, Virginia
July 22, 2006

Rebecca Dalton pulled her car into the driveway of the house belonging to Dan Oliver's daughter, Pam, and her husband. Pam had been married for almost five years, and her son was almost two now. Becky knew more about what Dan was looking into than she had ever let on. She also knew Pam had found something that set Dan on this quest he was on. Dan had tried to keep both of them out of whatever he was working on. Now he had disappeared.

Becky got out of her car and walked to the door and pushed the button for the doorbell. Several long moments later, Pam opened the door. "Come on in, Becky. I guess you haven't heard anything either, have you?"

Becky walked into the living room. "Not yet. It's too soon to start worrying. Pam, he's good at what he does, one of the best. He'll be okay."

"I wish I could believe that. I'm afraid of what he was doing." Pam and Becky walked into the kitchen of the house. "I know it's still a little early, but I'm going to have a drink. You want one too?"

"Yeah, I could use one. Where is the little one?" Becky took the offered wine glass from Pam.

"Jeff took him over to his grandparent's. I haven't gotten much sleep lately. I haven't told Jeff anything. Not that I could tell him much." Pam took the bottle of wine from the refrigerator and opened it. She filled both of their glasses.

"Pam, do you know what your dad was working on?" Becky took a drink of her wine.

Pam set her wine glass on the table; she put her hands to her face and tried not to cry. She took a long moment to compose herself before she could speak. "I have an idea. He wouldn't tell me. Made me promise him I wouldn't ask or get involved. He said it was for my own safety. God, Becky, what are we going to do if something has happened to him?" Pam couldn't control the tears anymore.

Becky set her glass down and embraced Pam. She was about to cry herself. "Pam, I probably shouldn't say anything, but I know more about what he was doing than he knew. He was very careful. I don't think anything has happened yet." Becky hesitated before going on; she didn't want to give Pam too much hope. "A couple of days ago, the office was visited by another one of the government agencies. I'm not going to say which one. They were questioning everyone who worked with Dan. It was obvious they were still looking for him. Nothing official has come through. They wouldn't say why they wanted to talk to him. When I asked, they just said they knew he had retired, and it was about some old cases he had worked on and they wanted to talk to him. If they had found him, they wouldn't have been at the office."

Pam desperately hoped Becky was right. "God I hope you're right. It's my fault he's doing this."

"What do you mean it's your fault?" Becky held Pam by the shoulders and looked her in the eye.

Pam took a deep breath; she hadn't told anyone what she knew. "I found a letter in the library my senior year at Virginia. It was written by James Madison to Thomas Jefferson. Something about it didn't sit right with me, and I stole it and brought it home to Dad. Since then, he has been like someone obsessed. When I asked about it later, he stopped me and made me promise never to mention it to anyone and never ever ask him what he was doing. He sold the house and that was hard for him. I think he was afraid of what was going to happen."

Dan had told Becky very little of what he had been doing. She still had more questions than answers. "Pam, I'll let you know if I find out anymore. Until then, try not to worry."

Across the street and a couple of houses down, Edgar was sitting in the front seat of a car watching the house. He had been ordered to watch everyone that came or went. Sooner or later he thought, one of them will lead us to him.

JFK International Airport
New York, New York
August 1, 2006


The British Airways flight from London landed, and the plane taxied to the gate. Dan Oliver was returning to the United States. Further back in the aircraft were two agents Jonah Kauffman had insisted on sending with Dan. He wasn't flying under his own name; it wouldn't matter. Dan knew they would know he had come into the country. There was facial recognition software built into the security system the government could use to pick him out of the returning passengers. Dan knew there were a number of ways they would find him, that was what they wanted. He couldn't continue digging into this mess as long as they were looking for him. The hard part might actually be surviving being found. The plan he and Jonah had decided on was to let them find him and make the attempt they knew was coming. If it was handled properly, they would believe they had been successful. It was risky; it was also the only way to protect those that Dan cared about. Once they thought he was dead, maybe Pam and Becky would be left alone.

The flight attendant was giving the instructions to remain seated until the plane came to a complete stop. Everyone had heard the speech so many times they didn't pay any attention. The plane came to a stop, and the ground crew was hooking up the auxiliary power and the luggage cart was pulling alongside. It always annoyed Dan that everyone stood up in the aisle. It always took time to get your carry-on out of the overhead and get off the plane. Everyone getting in the way of those ahead only made it take longer. Dan had flown coach this trip and was just in back of the wings; it was going to take a few minutes to get off the plane.

It was finally his turn to make his way out of the aircraft, and Dan slowly and carefully walked up the jet way toward the terminal and immigration. He had to retrieve his luggage; it would have been odd if an international passenger didn't check a bag. They would have picked up on that faster. He had allowed the two agents traveling to get ahead of him. He was waiting on the carousel to start so he could get his luggage and continue to immigration; the two agents were already there, one on each end of the carousel looking just like the rest of the tired passengers.

The luggage started coming off and dropping onto the carousel, and it began to rotate. He was careful when he picked his bag up to make sure he was in between the two agents. One already had his luggage and was already headed to immigration. The other would wait and follow. Dan retrieved the suitcase and was patiently walking toward the immigration lines. His senses were on high alert; if they had found him as he got on the plane in London that would be a problem. It was finally his turn before the immigration officer; Dan smiled as he handed his passport over.

The officer took it, glanced at it, stamped it with all of the other stamps, and looked at Dan and said, "Welcome back to the United States, Mr. Wheeler."

"Thanks. I'm glad to be back" was all Dan said as he took his passport and left, another carefully set up identity with a long history of international travel, but not so careful they wouldn't find him. That was what he wanted after all.

He finally had dealt with all of the customs and immigration paperwork and the time it had taken to get through the airport. There was a car waiting for him; the driver was holding a sign that said "Wheeler." Dan walked up and said, "I hope you haven't been here too long. The headwind was slowing us down."

All he said in return was "The job pays the same if I'm waiting or driving." He opened the door for Dan and took his luggage and put it into the trunk.

Dan almost thought the exchange was silly, but it told each of them the other was genuine. The driver got in behind the wheel, and they left the airport. The two agents that had accompanied Dan were in another car back in traffic; they all knew where they were going.

In the airport, a TSA supervisor picked up the phone on his desk and dialed the number to the Department of Homeland Security. The phone was answered on the first ring. "This is Agent Owens with the TSA. We got a hit on the recognition system. Yes, sir, the name on the passport was a Daniel Wheeler." He proceeded to give the rest of the information they had. The hunt was back on. The question was who the prey was.

The Department of Homeland Security
Washington DC
August 1, 2006


Howard Lehman hung up the phone. He grabbed his jacket and left his office and walked down the corridor toward the elevators. He wasn't sure why but the instructions had come from the top. They were looking for a former FBI agent named Daniel Oliver. The phone call he had just gotten from the TSA supervisor at JFK airport confirmed the facial recognition program had picked him out coming through immigration on a British Airways flight from London. It was a "locate but do not detain," and he had been the one the call would come to. He had followed the rest of the instructions. He now had to go upstairs and tell the director himself. The instructions had been specific; once he was informed, he had to go to the director and personally give him what they had. That was highly irregular. He wondered just who this former FBI agent was that demanded this level of attention. Maybe, he thought, it would be better if he didn't know.

Howard left the elevator and walked to the double doors of the director's office; he walked in and told the receptionist who he was and to his surprise was escorted straight into his office.

The director stood, walked around his desk, and offered his hand. "Thanks for coming up, Howard. Tell me what you have."

Howard was stunned; he had never met the director personally and now he was being treated like they were buddies. "Well, sir, we got a hit on the recognition system at JFK this afternoon. He came in on a British Airways flight at 2:20 this afternoon. The flight originated in London. We are checking to see if we can find where he was before he boarded the flight in London. The passport he used was under the name of Daniel Wheeler. It has been used before but not in the last six months."

The director stopped him with a question. "Have you implemented the locate portion, or is this all you have?"

"We had two agents at the airport. They were instructed to follow him as soon as we got the hit. I haven't heard back from them yet. It's only been a little over an hour since he got in, I—"

The director stopped him again. "Good job on that, Howard. As soon as the agents let you know where he is, let me know and put as many agents on this as you have to." His tone changed noticeably. "And, Howard, don't let him get away. We really need to talk to this guy."

Howard left the director's office. He had gotten the message loud and clear. His ass was on the line if they lost him. This guy must either be really important or seriously pissed somebody off. Probably both, Howard wondered if he would ever know.

# THE COMMITTEE

The Intercontinental Hotel
New York, New York
August 1. 2006

    The four-man team exited the van parked in the loading dock of the hotel. The van had the logo of a telecom company on its side. The four had on jackets that had the logo on the front. Each of them was carrying what would pass for a small satchel or a tool bag. They had already been cleared through security; the hotel management had been told it was a matter of national security. They were not going to interfere. As soon as they entered the service elevator, they took off the jackets and exchanged them with ones in the bags they were carrying. They looked like any other guests of the hotel.
    The elevator stopped on the tenth floor; the team exited one floor below the target's room. They dispersed and entered the stairwells and went up one floor. The elevators were going to be out of service for the next ten minutes; it should be enough time. They exited the stairwells and converged again outside of room 1120. They looked around to make sure the hall way was empty; two members of the team faced outward and covered the other two as they prepared to enter the room. The one on the right side of the door produced the key card and slid it into the lock; as soon as he got the green lights, he opened the door and the other agent rolled around the door frame with his gun drawn and was quickly followed by the other agent through the door. The last two team members entered the room and closed the door behind them. The room was empty. There was a suitcase opened and sitting on the bed, beside it was a laptop. The four agents holstered their weapons. As the team leader began to look into the suitcase, the door flew open and a flash bang grenade was tossed in. Four men entered the room and quickly disabled the four agents that were in the room; it was all over in seconds.
    Fifteen minutes later, the two agents that had remained in the van exited the elevator on the eleventh floor. They hadn't been able to contact the team, and they hadn't returned to the van. They were concerned; it shouldn't have taken this long. The door to 1120 was closed but not latched. They glanced at each other, drew their weapons, and

one stood on each side of the door. They nodded to each other, and the one on the left pushed open the door and the other rushed in gun drawn quickly followed by the second agent.

If they weren't professionals, they might have laughed at the sight of the three members of their team on the floor. They had tape over their mouths; their wrists were taped together and each one was naked from the waist down. Their ankles were also taped together and their government ID was lying on their chests. The fourth member was nowhere to be found.

They checked out the room to make sure it was empty before freeing the hands and feet of the three on the floor. Their trousers and underwear had been dumped in the floor of the shower, and the shower was left on. They cut the tape from their feet and ankles, and as each one got up, they took the tape from their mouths.

"What in the hell happened, and where is Paul?" One of the two who had cut the tape loose asked when they had freed all of them.

"Whoever they are, they obviously were expecting us. This was a setup. As soon as we got in the room, there was an open suitcase and laptop on the bed. Paul started looking into it and a flash bang was thrown into the room. Two seconds later, they were in the room and put all of us down. These guys were pros. If they wanted us dead, we would be. Where in the hell are my pants?"

Jason, one of the two fully clothed, almost couldn't stop himself from laughing when he said, "Go look in the shower." He didn't tell them he was grateful he had stayed in the van.

Eric walked into the bathroom and turned the shower off. He reached down and picked his pants up from the tub and swore under his breath as he wrung the water out of them. The other two came in and got their pants from the shower, wrung them out, and put them on. Their shoes were nowhere to be found. They found their socks in the toilet. They left them there.

Jason looked at the three members of the team wearing wet trousers and no shoes. "You still haven't told me where Paul is."

"It's pretty obvious they took him. They were out of here two minutes after they had us on the floor."

Jason simply said, "You guys stay here. I'll go call this in and see if I can find you some clothes."

Several blocks away the laundry van was turning into the bay door of a warehouse on the waterfront, four men in the back, a linen cart that contained three pairs of shoes, the weapons they had taken from them, and a drugged Paul.

They had been in the two rooms across the hall and had checked in three days before. Only two of them had registered. The other two had come in earlier in the day and come up to the rooms. They had set it up with a reservationist at the hotel several days before; flashing a government badge had the desired effect. As soon as the team entered the room, they had tossed in the flash bang and disabled the four agents. They had taken their shoes and put their pants in the shower to take them out of any chase. They had taken the fourth member of the team to find out just exactly who was after Dan Oliver. He had never been at the hotel. It was now clear to both sides they were dealing with professionals. That was the way they wanted it.

The warehouse
New York waterfront
New York, New York
Later that same day

Paul slowly shook the cobwebs from his head. He tried to raise his hands to his face and slowly realized he couldn't. He looked down and realized his arms were taped to the arms of a chair. He also realized he was naked and that his ankles were also taped to the chair. A light suddenly came on just in front of him, and he screwed his eyes shut, his head hurt.

The voice asked him, "Who are you?"

Paul opted not to respond. His head was jerked backward, and he felt a knife against his throat. "You can choose whether you live or die. Now would you care to tell us exactly who you are?"

"Paul Raymond, Department of Homeland Security." The knife was removed from his throat. His leather government ID folder was dropped in his lap.

"That's what that told us. Now would you care to tell us why you were in the room at the hotel?"

Paul didn't say anything. The knife appeared in front of his face, and he jerked his head backward. The hand holding the knife was encased in latex surgical gloves, and Paul watched as it slowly dropped in front of him and stopped two inches below his navel. The tip of the knife dropped and was slid under his penis.

"It's your choice, Paul, which way this goes. We are going to find out what you have to tell us or the information will be extracted piece by bloody piece. Starting with this."

Paul felt the knife slowly lift up, and he felt the tip rotate under his penis until he felt it resting on the razor sharp edge. He took a deep breath and almost screamed, "Okay, okay, I'll tell you whatever you want to know!"

"Now that you have decided cooperation is in your best interests, tell us why you were in the hotel."

"We were sent there to pick up the guy in room 1120." The knife was removed from under his penis, and Paul then felt the tip rest behind his left ear.

"Who was the guy in room 1120, Paul?"

"I don't know we were given his picture and told to pick him up."

"You are going to have to do better than that." Paul felt the knife nick his ear and warm blood started to run down the side of his face.

"Jesus Christ I swear to God I don't know all we were told was to pick up the guy in 1120, and we were given his picture!" The sweat started running down his face and started mixing with the light flow of blood from his ear.

"Let's assume for a moment that is all you know. Where were you supposed to take him after you picked him up?"

Paul took another deep breath; the knife was placed behind his right ear. "That's the strange part. We were told after we got him we would be met and to turn him over to whoever met us."

The knife was moved from his right ear, and Paul watched as it once again was lowered two inches below his navel. "Paul, that doesn't sound right to me. You have to know more than that. Would you care to try again?"

"I swear to god that's all I know. We were told this was a matter of national security, and we were the only ones available to pick this guy up, and he was to be turned over to another team. We weren't told who that was. Just that it was important, and he was considered armed and dangerous but they wanted him alive."

"Who exactly told you this, Paul?" The knife was slowly moving downward again.

"Howard Lehman is the one who sent us out. He said it came from the director. That's all I know."

The knife was removed from in front of Paul. "You better be telling me the truth, Paul. I will find you and next time you will tell me everything, or you will be taking the family jewels home in a box."

Paul felt the sting of a syringe, and his world went dark.

Dan Oliver had heard the entire exchange; the two Israeli agents cut the tape from Paul's wrist and put him in the laundry cart, put that back in the truck, and left the truck in the loading dock of the warehouse. There was no evidence left that they had ever been there.

The Lehman Home
Arlington, Virginia
August 2, 2006

Howard Lehman backed his car out of his garage and hit the button on his remote to close the door. It was still dark outside, and he was headed into work early. He put the car in drive and started down the street. The fiasco with the team the day before had put him in a bad mood. It had been made clear to him he had to find the former FBI agent. He knew he wasn't the only one working on it. Every agency was trying to locate him. Unfortunately for him, he was the only one who had the assets that were watching JFK. Whoever this guy was, he had managed to have enough assets to put his team down. It had taken them several hours to find the missing agent. If he had wanted the team dead, they would be. They had finally found Paul in the back of a stolen laundry truck naked and taped up in a laundry cart in the back. They had gone to a lot of trouble to make sure he survived. The doors of the van had been left open and wet towels had been put on top of him. August in New York was hot enough to have killed him if he had been in the van too long. An anonymous call had come in to the local police precinct directing them to the vacant warehouse where the laundry van was parked at the loading dock in back of the building. They had left all of the weapons, the shoes they had taken from the rest of the agents, and even Paul's government ID.

Howard was still trying to figure out what this guy was up to; none of it made sense. He was a retired FBI agent, and they were acting like he was a wanted terrorist. It had all been kept very quiet. Howard was obviously distracted; the blue lights of a police cruiser came on behind him. He glanced down at the speedometer and realized he was exceeding the speed limit. Shit, he didn't need this now; he pulled to the side of the road and rolled down his window. The spotlight of the cruiser hit his side-view mirror, blinding him.

The officer approached the car and asked, "Can I see your license and registration please?"

"Sure, Officer." Howard reached into his back pocket and pulled out his billfold and handed his license to the officer. He reached in the pocket of his jacket to pull out his government badge, and the next thing he knew there was a revolver stuck in the side window.

"Remove your hand slowly and place it on the steering wheel." The officer was holding the revolver rock steady with both hands. The passenger side door opened and another officer was holding a gun on him.

Howard was rattled; this had never happened to him before. "Calm down. All I was doing was reaching for my government ID. It's in my jacket pocket. I'm with Homeland Security."

"Keep your hands where I can see them and step out of the car now." The driver's door opened, and the gun never moved from being trained on Howard.

Howard slid out of the car, keeping his hands straight out in front of him. Before he knew what happened, he was on the ground and both hands were behind his back, and he felt the handcuffs click on his wrists. He was jerked upright and hustled to the police cruiser and shoved in the back. "There must be some kind of mistake. I'm with Homeland Security."

# THE COMMITTEE

There was no response from the officer. Suddenly Howard was really frightened. The second officer got in the back with him, and the first officer got in, put the car in gear, and pulled away. Howard's car was pulling out in front of them. The next thing he knew a rag was shoved in his mouth and a bag was pulled over his head, and he was shoved into the floorboard and he felt a plastic tie going around his ankles. Howard realized whoever was behind this was a professional; he only hoped they didn't want him dead either.

The cruiser stopped, and Howard heard the doors open and then he felt a pair of hands pulling him out of the back of the cruiser. He was picked up and carried to the back of some kind of van and shoved to the floor again. He heard the door close, and he felt the van move. He was listening for anything to tell him where he was; the next thing he knew something was covering his ears and he couldn't hear a thing. The only thing that kept Howard from really losing it was the knowledge they hadn't killed Paul or any of the others; they could have.

Howard lost all sense of time. He wasn't sure how long they had traveled and then the van stopped again. He felt the hands on him again, and he was lifted over someone's shoulder and carried; he wasn't sure where he was. He was dropped onto some kind of hard concrete floor, and he felt whatever they put on his head to cover his ears pulled off. He felt the strap around his ankles being cut then his shoes were taken off, and he felt his pants being taken off as well. The strap went back around his ankles. Someone grabbed his arms, and he felt the handcuffs taken off his wrists. His arms were held out to his sides, he felt someone unbutton his jacket, take his tie, and then his shirt off. His arms were then pulled behind him and cuffed again. The bag was pulled from his head, and there was a light shining directly into his face. The rag was pulled from his mouth, he felt a blindfold slip over his head and then he was shoved none too gently into a chair. He was alone.

Howard wasn't sure how long he was left alone. He felt a hand on his shoulder. "Howard, we need to have a talk, and you are going to tell us what we want to know. I really don't care if you survive or not the choice is yours. Are we clear on that?"

Howard didn't trust himself to speak. "I understand" was all he managed to say.

"Good. Do you know who you were looking for at the hotel today?"

Howard didn't say anything. He felt something slip over his head and tighten around his neck. "That is a noose, Howard, and I don't give a good god damn if you die. Are we clear on that?" Howard heard some kind of motor start and felt the noose lift up in back. He had to stand up to keep it from picking him up. "The noose is attached to an electric winch, Howard, just so you know."

"All right I'll tell you whatever you want to know." Howard screamed at whoever was in the room with him. "For god's sake stop!"

The noise stopped then started again, and he felt the noose loosen, and he managed to sit down. Howard had wet himself.

"Well, Howard, I know you're not a field agent, but that is really embarrassing. Now tell me who you were looking for today at the hotel and the answer better be right or that's the last question I ask. Understand?"

"We were looking for some retired FBI agent named Oliver, Daniel Oliver."

"Well, we seem to be getting somewhere that was the correct answer. Why are you looking for this guy, Howard?"

"I don't know. All we were told is it was national security, and he was considered armed and dangerous."

"Who are you reporting to?"

Howard took a deep breath. "The director of Homeland Security was who I was told to personally deliver the message to when we found him."

"Okay, Howard, now this is really important. If you had managed to get him at the hotel, what had you been told to do with him?"

Howard paused before he answered. He heard the motor start and the noose tighten again. "I was told to turn him over to a special team." The motor stopped; the pressure was still there.

"Go on, Howard, tell me the rest."

"This is black ops. It doesn't get any quieter than this. If I tell you, they'll kill me."

"I will kill you if you don't, Howard. Your choice." The motor started again.

"All right I'll tell you." The motor stopped again. "There is a special team. They are all former Delta force or Seals I don't know who they are or who they work for. These guys would kill you for fun. Every one of them was sent packing for some kind of reason. They should all be in prison for what they have done. They work so deep nobody even knows who they work for. I don't even think the director knows. All he told me was not to fuck with them. The only reason we were to pick up this guy is they couldn't get here fast enough, and they didn't want him to get away. We were told to turn him over and forget it happened. I swear that's all I know."

The motor started again, and Howard felt the pressure release from his neck. He slumped in the chair. The blindfold was taken from his eyes, and he was looking into the face of Dan Oliver. "Well, Howard, you are going to deliver a message for me. You tell the director if anything happens to the people I care about there will be a release of documents that will make Watergate look like a day at the circus. The bastard should know who to tell. This is between me and whoever they are, my family and those close to me are all I have. They don't know what this is about or where to find me. You tell him they can come after me. I have it all set up if anything happens to Pam or her family or Rebekah or her family. It all comes out. You got all that, Howard?"

All Howard could do was nod in the affirmative. He felt a prick in the back of his neck and the world went dark.

The Templeton residence
Milford, Pennsylvania
August 4, 2006


Benjamin Templeton was pacing back and forth in his study. The floor-to-ceiling windows behind him and the Delaware River beyond weren't even registering on his thoughts. They were still trying to find the former FBI agent. The secure phone ringing broke into his thoughts, and he quickly answered it, "Yes."

"The supervisor from Homeland Security was found early this morning. He is alive and unharmed." His chief of security got right to the point.

"What happened?"

"His car was found in the rest area off the interstate across the state line in Maryland. A state trooper found it early this morning. He thought it was odd that the windows were down, and it was parked right up by the building. When he looked in the car, he found him naked and lying in the back floorboard. His hands and feet were taped and all his clothes, ID, and everything else including his weapon were locked in the trunk. They found his car keys on the floor under him."

"What else?" Diamond forced himself to loosen his grip on the phone.

There was hesitation before the reply. "He was still unconscious. He had been drugged, and he was taken to the hospital and checked out. As soon as he was fully conscious, he told them to call Homeland Security, and they shut off the local investigation. He refused to talk to anyone but the director. As soon as they could, they got him out of the hospital, and he was taken to see the director. He told him he had been given a message and to tell no one but the director."

"Go on. Let's have the rest." Diamond felt his hand tighten on the phone; he was powerless to stop it.

"He told him this was between him and whoever they are. Those he cared about didn't know anything about it or where he was and if anything happened to quote 'Pam or her family or Rebekah or her family there would be a document release that would make Watergate look like a day at the circus.' I believe him."

"How much does he have?" Diamond almost couldn't breathe.

"There is no way to be certain. He is sending us a message to leave the family alone and come after him. What we found on the laptop in Virginia wasn't much, but it is enough to let us know he has more. We did some checking into his background. This guy was one of the best at what he did. He spent almost thirty years in the FBI tracking down money laundering and banking fraud. He spent some time on the antiterrorist team tracking down their source of funding. He was shut down more than once."

"How in the hell has he managed to do what he has? He has to have help."

"I told you this guy is one of the best. You don't get put on the antiterrorist team unless you are highly skilled and trained in the arts of self-defense. There are a number of places you can hire the type of help he needs. What we do know is it's not a government agency. We control those. I think this guy is solo."

"Why hasn't he gone public with what he has? Something is stopping him." Diamond began to run the possibilities in his mind.

"My guess is he doesn't know everything, at least not yet. Anyway, who could he release it to and survive? He knows we'll find him. I think that's what he is really telling us. Come after him and leave his family alone. If we get him, I think it all stays buried."

"How can you be so sure? That may be one hell of a risk."

"He has gone to a lot of trouble to send us a message. It would have been far easier for him to kill the team sent to get him. Instead, he leaves them alive, and we find them. He takes one of them and the only thing he knew was who sent them out. He could have killed him. Instead he calls the police, and he is found alive. Then he grabs their boss at Homeland Security to find out who told him to make the grab. When he finds out it's the director, he tells him this is between me and whoever they are and the bastard will know who to tell. If he knew who was behind it, he wouldn't have had to go to all this trouble. I think he didn't kill any of them for two reasons. One, he sees what he is doing as a noble cause. Two, and this may be the most important, dead bodies where he would have left them create unwanted attention, for both him and us. Even the Homeland Security guys are pros. Not at the level we are, but they are embarrassed and know they are lucky to be alive. This isn't something they will want to talk about. The last reason is, if all he knows about is money being funneled off, or if that's all he can prove, that's just somebody being greedy. A few congressional hearings, an investigation, and pretty soon, it will all be forgotten."

"Find him and get rid of him. We can't let this get out and leave his family alone. He made it clear that's what he wants. You had better be right." Diamond hung up the phone.

None of them knew that was exactly what Dan Oliver wanted. Now he had them playing his game.

Hartsfield Jackson Airport
Atlanta, Georgia
September 1, 2006

Dan Oliver was walking down the A concourse away from the gate. He had flown in from Charlotte, North Carolina. He and Jonah had discussed the options. They needed him to be found but didn't want them to have much time from when he got on the plane in Charlotte to when he landed in Atlanta. He had actually bought several tickets under false identities checked in with one on a flight to New York and then flown to Atlanta under another. Several of Jonah's agents had been involved. One had checked in with the Atlanta flight while he had checked in to New York under another identity. They each had IDs that matched the other except the pictures were different. They then simply boarded the other's flight. They had decided on Atlanta for several reasons. The airport was extremely busy. They had flown in when the terminals would be crowded. Dan needed them to find him, but he was going to make it as difficult as possible. Their hope was they would pick him up with the facial recognition software in Charlotte and think he was going to New York. He would be on the Atlanta flight, which would get in before the New York flight. When he left the airport here, they would probably realize he had not gone into New York. This airport was big enough and busy enough to be sure they would pick up his trail and the identity he was now using. Not before he got out of the airport. Jonah was based out of the Israeli consulate of the Southeast in Atlanta; he considered this his home field. They would need every advantage they could get.

Dan hadn't bothered to check in luggage. He took the escalator from the A concourse down to the transportation area where you could take the train or the moving sidewalk or just walk from any of the concourses to the terminal. He was close to the terminal, and they had decided he would walk to the terminal; he looked like any other businessman with his briefcase. Two of Jonah's agents were already here and would make sure nothing happened before he got out of the airport. Dan took the escalator back up from the transportation to the north terminal and walked past the baggage claim area and out to the end of the terminal. When he exited the terminal, he was in the ground transportation area where you could get a taxi or wait on one of the small shuttle buses that would take you to their respective car rental agencies. He walked over to the Enterprise shuttle and got on. The driver was about ready to leave, and there were several other people on the shuttle with him. This was exactly how they wanted it.

The shuttle pulled out of the line and merged into the traffic and left the airport. Dan Oliver looked around at the other people on the shuttle with him. There were two other businessmen and a family with two kids; he smiled at the kids and prayed he wouldn't get any of them hurt. He didn't think the bastards looking for him would care as long as they got him. He wondered how many other innocent victims there were. He looked out the window and watched the traffic. It was fairly light, and the van turned into the Enterprise lot. The rental was all set up; the car was rented under the same name he had flown in on, and Jonah had taken care of the other requirements. Dan waited his turn and approached the counter. He was grateful the family with their two kids had already left. He didn't know just how fast they were going to find him; he would be prepared as soon as he left here.

He smiled at the pretty leasing agent behind the counter and handed her his driver's license. "Hello, I have a reservation for Donald Wallace." He looked at her name tag and noticed her name was Joelle; she reminded him of Pam.

"Hello, Mr. Wallace, I hope you had a good trip. Yes, sir, we have you all taken care of. I hope a Ford Taurus is okay. All I need you to do is sign the form and initial where I have the *x*'s and here is the insurance form. If you will sign that as well, I will have Javier bring the car up and do the inspection. Enjoy your visit to Atlanta."

"Thank you, Joelle. Have a nice day." Dan waited just inside the door until he saw the dark blue Taurus pulled out front. It was still the middle of the day, and the sun was still beating down. Dan walked outside and went over to the blue Taurus.

Javier walked up to him, and they began the walk around. Javier began to point at the car and said, "Our mutual friend said you would need some things. There is a briefcase in the floorboard. There is a GPS in the glove box. It will tell us where you are all the time. There is a cell phone in the console. The numbers are programmed in." Javier opened the trunk and picked up Dan's carry-on and put it in the trunk. "There are some heavier things in here. Hopefully you won't need those. I don't have to tell you to be careful with that stuff. When you leave here, turn right and head to the interstate. The backup will follow you. They are in a red Mercedes. Now sign this and be careful. Jonah wants you alive." Javier extended the clipboard for Dan's signature then tore off the carbon and handed it to Dan.

"Thanks, Javier. I plan on being careful. We have a lot of work to do." Dan Oliver got in the car and reached for the briefcase. There was a silenced .40 caliber Glock with two extra magazines. The note said there was a round in the chamber. With it was a skeleton holster for the small of his back. There was a smaller .9mm Glock with two extra magazines and an ankle holster. The last item was a knife in a scabbard that could be strapped just above the wrist. He closed the briefcase and exited the lot. He kept the case unlocked and on the seat beside him. Hopefully, he wouldn't need any of this on the trip to the hotel. Dan started the car, put it in gear, and exited the lot. The hunt was on.

Department of Homeland Security
Washington DC
September 1, 2006

The director of Homeland Security hung up the phone. He had been waiting on the call he had just taken. The facial recognition software had picked up the rouge former FBI agent. Whoever this guy had made mad, the director was glad he wasn't in his place. There was an all-out effort to find him. Every agency was looking for him. This time they had better not miss; none of the regular field teams were going after him. He picked up the secure phone waited on it to be answered, and when it was, he simply said, "We located the target coming out of the Atlanta airport. He came through Charlotte this afternoon." He paused and listened to the response and then said, "Yes, I know I told you he was going to New York. He apparently is still availing himself of help. He checked in on a flight to New York under the name of Nathaniel Benson. He showed up on another flight in Atlanta before the New York flight landed. He flew under the name of Donald Wallace." There was another Pause. "Whoever boarded the New York flight checked in to the Atlanta flight. They apparently took each other's flight and must have had separate IDs. We have people going through all of the security camera footage to see if we can find out who his help is."

The director listened and then responded again, "We have an alert on any credit card transactions that match that name or any of the others he has used. This guy is good. He may not use those names. We are going to find this guy. It's just a matter of time." There was a much longer pause this time. "Yes, sir, I understand."

There was a click and silence on the other end. The director hung up the phone and took his handkerchief out and wiped the sweat from his brow. Everyone was under enormous pressure to find him. He had made them all look bad the last time they had found him. He hadn't been talked to like that in a long time. Worst of all, he wasn't even sure who he had been talking to. All he knew was this came from the top. His cooperation hadn't been asked.

The security chief hung up the secure phone and set back in his chair. Atlanta, there had to be a reason why; he didn't think this guy was just going to walk out with a sign saying "whack me." He was as much a professional as any member of his team was, and he was smart. They were not going to take any chances. He had a six-man team ready to go. They would be in Atlanta before the sun set. They not only wanted him dead, they wanted it done quietly. If it didn't work out that way, as long as he was dead, he would take the result. He had a feeling there was more to what Dan Oliver wanted. He had read his jacket. He reached over and picked up the file and read it again. He had missed something. He would find it. That's why he was the head of security for the Committee. He had as much riding on this as they did.

# JUSTIN A. BAILEY

Sheraton Suites Galleria
Atlanta, Georgia
September 1, 2006

    Dan Oliver parked the rented Ford Taurus on the top level of the parking deck of the Sheraton hotel. Before exiting the car, he looked around carefully; there wasn't anyone else around. He opened the briefcase Javier had left in the car, carefully removed the Glock pistol, and leaned his shoulders back on the seat and slid forward enough to slip the skeleton holster in the small of his back. Looking around again, he took the smaller pistol and strapped it to his right ankle and slid the cuff of his trousers over to make sure it wasn't visible. Retrieving the knife, he dropped that into his jacket pocket inside of his coat. He would have to wait to put it in the proper spot on his arm. The cell phone from the console went into his side pocket. Making sure he wasn't attracting any attention, he glanced in the mirrors and opened the driver's side door and got out. He opened the trunk and removed his carry-on and the other suitcase left in the trunk by Javier.

    He was as prepared as possible under the circumstances. He picked up the carry-on and slung the strap over his left shoulder and picked up the suitcase in his left hand. That left his right hand empty if need be. He walked with a purpose toward the elevator and pressed the button. He stood to one side then turned slightly so that both the approach and the hopefully empty elevator would be in his field of vision. The door slid open, it was empty. He stepped inside and pressed the button for the lobby. Several long moments later the door slid opened, and Dan carefully glanced around before moving toward the reservations desk.

    "Hello. May I help you, sir?" the gentleman behind the desk asked.

    "Yes My name is Donald Wallace. I should have a reservation." Dan carefully looked around and saw his two cover agents in the lobby. One was sitting in a chair reading a newspaper and the other was standing inside the main entrance off to the side of the door in an animated conversation with his cell phone.

"Yes, sir. Mr. Wallace, we have you in 220." He slid the form across the counter toward Dan who completed the form and slid it with his credit card across the counter. "Thank you, Mr. Wallace. My name is Thomas, and please let me know if I can help you in any way." He handed Dan a room key card and then his credit card and then tore the copy and handed it to Dan. "Enjoy your stay with us and have a nice evening."

"Thank you, Thomas, and have a great day." Dan turned from the counter and retrieved his luggage and went back to the elevator. He took that to the second floor and did a quick walk around and found the stairwells and the location of his room. He paid careful attention to the layout and where the location of any electrical rooms and other maid's areas and service areas were. After his reconnaissance, he then went to his room and slid the card in the door and stood aside as he opened the door. The room was empty. He went into the room and wondered just how long it would take for them to find him. He knew it wouldn't take long.

The two cover agents exited the lobby and one at a time went to the second floor. They were in rooms on either side of 220. They were as prepared as they could be. One had checked in before Dan and the other shortly after. The game was on.

The Israeli Consulate
Atlanta, Georgia
That same day

Jonah Kauffman was worried; he had done everything he could. He found himself pacing in his office. The cover agents were in place, and the rest of the team was prepared. The problem was this was off the books, and he had to use what he considered outside contractors for the team. All he could do was use only the two agents. It was not politically acceptable to stage an operation against Israel's strongest ally. He was the only one who knew what this operation was about. He owed Dan. In this business, you had very few friends; this one he was determined not to lose. They knew it would not be hard for the trail Dan was leaving to be picked up. That was what they wanted, but it couldn't be too obvious. The real problem as Jonah saw it was they would want it quiet. His mind was in overdrive. There was something he had missed; he just had to figure out what it was. All at once, Jonah stopped pacing; the realization hit him. They would have access to the file on Dan Oliver. Whoever these people were, they had access and control at the highest level of the United States government. If they put it all together and looked at his time on the antiterrorist team, it wouldn't take long to figure out who else had been on it and find out Jonah was stationed in Atlanta. He had made a mistake. Now he had to figure out how to turn it to their advantage. Jonah grabbed his jacket and left the consulate. He was going to improvise; the problem was would he have enough time?

Jonah ran out of the consulate and to his car. He jumped in, started it, and backed out of his parking space and peeled out of the parking lot. One advantage of diplomatic tags, he thought, was he wouldn't be stopped. He grabbed his cell phone and hit the speed dial for the one Javier had given Dan Oliver.

Dan Oliver was sitting in the bar of the Sheraton when the phone in his pocket buzzed. He reached in, pulled the phone out, and answered. "Hello?"

"Get out of the hotel now. Leave the car, go into the mall, I'll call the others to cover and pick a spot. I'll call back." Jonah hung up the phone and messaged the other two to pick up Dan and get him out. He breathed a sigh of relief as the acknowledgement from both came across the screen. He needed a busy place, crowded where he could cover him, blend in, and most important he hoped they wouldn't risk making an attempt in too much of a crowd. He sent another text and made the turn from Spring Street toward the nearby interstate. He merged into the ever increasing flow of traffic and prayed.

Dan Oliver motioned the bartender and mimed for the check. The bartender nodded his acknowledgement. One of the two of the Israeli agents walked by the bar never said a word to Dan and accidentally dropped a napkin right beside Dan. He continued walking by and headed toward the men's room. Dan stood up when the bartender brought his tab, signed it, and dropped his wallet when he slid a tip to the bartender. He retrieved it and the napkin the agent had dropped, casually stretched, read what was on it and left the bar.

Two minutes later, Dan exited the hotel. He was walking toward the nearby Cumberland Mall. Both agents would cover and mix in with the crowd. Dan carefully made his way across the parking lot headed into the mall and walked around window shopping trying to stay mixed with the crowd.

Dan was careful and aware of his surroundings; he had some time to kill before he was to meet Jonah. He glanced at his watch and tried to judge the timing. He walked as slowly as he could into the food court casually looking at the various restaurants and types of vendors as if he was trying to decide. He acted as if he finally made a decision, ordered Chinese, and took it to one of the tables in the middle of the food court. Jonah showed up fifteen minutes later, went to one of the vendors, ordered, and walked up to the table where Dan was seated by himself. He motioned toward all the other full tables and asked, "Mind if I sit here and share a table?"

"Help yourself. There aren't a lot of empty seats," Dan replied as Jonah set his tray down and sat across the table from Dan.

"I may have screwed up picking here. I realized they will have access to your file, and it won't take them long to figure out who is helping you." Jonah looked into the smiling face of his friend.

"Then let's turn it to our advantage. It's still our home field." It didn't take the two long to finish their conversation, and Dan stood and left the table while Jonah finished the meal he didn't really want.

The dark Chevy Suburban pulled into the parking deck of the Sheraton and cruised through the parking deck until they spotted the Taurus rented to Donald Wallace on the upper level. They proceeded right back around and parked half a level down and faced the center where they could keep an eye on the Taurus. The passenger side door opened and one of the two men inside got out and casually walked toward the Taurus carrying a briefcase. As he passed behind it, he stumbled and dropped the briefcase, and it sprung open as it hit the concrete floor of the parking deck. He swore loud enough for anyone around to hear and knelt down to pick up the contents of the spilled case. He reached inside, took a small device, flipped a switch, stuck it under the car, and felt the magnet adhere to the frame. He then continued picking up the contents of the case, closed it, stood up, and walked away.

On the top floor of the hotel in one of the rooms overlooking the parking deck the curtains slid back in place as the pair of binoculars was pulled away from the window. The agent in the room picked up his cell phone, opened it, and sent a text. He then put the phone back in his pocket, put the binoculars back to his eyes, and trained them out the window back to the top level of the parking deck.

Sheraton Suites Galleria
Atlanta, Georgia
That same night

The dark blue van stopped in the deserted parking lot of the mall behind the Sheraton Hotel. The door opened, and three men quietly and quickly exited the van, and it pulled away and parked in a quiet corner of the empty lot. The fourth member exited the van and made his way toward the hotel. The four men separated, and each quietly went a different way into the hotel. The first of them went to a side door off the main lobby and walked toward the elevator. He pushed the button, waited, and when the doors opened, pushed the button for the second floor. One went in the main entrance and walked with a purpose toward the corridor where the stairwell was. He walked to the end of the corridor and opened the door for the third member of the team. The two then quickly went to the stairwell and walked up to the second floor and waited on the landing just inside the door. The fourth member of the team also entered through the main entrance and went to the elevator and took it took it to the second floor.

The elevator opened, and he exited the elevator and walked down the corridor toward room 220. The first member of the team who had taken the elevator was already in the corridor on the opposite side of the floor from room 220. He then walked down the corridor, caught up with the other member of the team, and met him just outside Dan's room. They stepped on opposite sides of the door. One nodded they both pulled their weapons from their pockets. One took a small device, slipped it into the card key lock, and pushed the door open. The one on the right rolled into the room quickly followed by the other.

The room was empty. Nothing but the small suitcase Javier had left in the trunk of the Taurus was on the bed. The first stated the obvious, "He's not here."

The camera concealed in the suitcase told Jonah's agent in the room down the hall they were in Dan's room. As soon as they moved close enough to the bed, he pressed a button and a small explosion no louder than a small ball hitting a wall went off in the suitcase. The plastic canister inside exploded and a chemical instantly released, dropping the two before they could take two steps toward the door. They passed out on the floor.

One of the two members of the team that were on the landing glanced at his watch and watched the minute hand roll around to 11:32, as the second hand hit 12, he pushed open the stairwell door and both exited the landing and walked down the corridor. Just before they got to room 220, the door of room 218 next to it opened and a young woman staggered from the door. She was obviously drunk and was only partly clothed; she had her dress over her left hand and was clad in only her undergarments and had her shoes in her right hand. No sooner had she stepped into the corridor when a second woman with her dress unbuttoned and her shoes in her hand stumbled out of the door into the corridor. She called out to the first woman. "Stop. Wait, you left the money." She held out a wad of cash toward the first woman.

The first woman stopped, turned back toward the other, and stumbled right into one of the two men who had stopped and waited for her to pass. In a reflex action, he caught her as she fell into him. A muffled pop erupted from her left hand under the dress, and the silenced slug hit him under the chin and penetrated his brain. He was dead before he hit the floor. The second of the two was reaching for his pistol under his coat when another muffled pop from the silenced pistol the second woman was holding struck him under his left eye.

The door to 218 opened, two of Jonah's agents stepped out, grabbed the two dead men, and dragged them into the room. A man wearing the uniform of a hotel maintenance staff member exited the room, pushing a cart, stopped, and began to clean up the brain matter from the wall across the hallway.

The two women stepped into room 220 where the two members of the team were still down on the floor. The woman clad only in her undergarments pulled an ice pick from her shoe and quickly inserted it into the ear canal and shoved it deep into the brain of one and then the other of the two men on the floor. Two minutes later, the door opened and two laundry carts were pushed into the room by the men of Jonah's team who had pulled the two dead agents from the hallway.

They handed each of the two women maid's uniforms and shoes. While the two changed, they picked up the two bodies, piled them on top of the other two bodies already in the carts, and covered them with sheets. The two women dressed as housekeepers each took a linen cart and, chatting in Spanish, took the service elevator to the loading dock where the laundry van was waiting. No one paid them any attention. They pushed the carts into the van; the driver closed the door, chatted with them for a moment, got in the van, and headed into the night. The two women still chatting walked toward the lot where the employees parked, got in a beat up Toyota Corolla, and left the lot. On the second floor with the hallway now cleaned up, the man in the maintenance uniform pushed his cart to the service elevator and disappeared.

Jonah had booked the entire second floor and had arranged for all of the staff working that floor to be part of his team. With the Convention center across the street hosting a medical conference, it wasn't unusual to have an entire floor booked. The hotel staff never knew anything happened on the second floor. That left the two in the Suburban to deal with. The hard part would be convincing them they had succeeded in taking out their target.

Fort Bragg
North Carolina
September 1, 2006


Ron Cole dropped the file on Dan Oliver on his desk. He rubbed his eyes and rolled his neck; he had been at this for hours. There was something there; he just had to find it. He stood up walked over to the small kitchen in the headquarters building the security team used at Fort Bragg. They had been here for the last twenty years. All of the members of his teams were former special forces, navy seals, or delta force. Every single one of them had been involved in some sort of incident that had seen them quietly retired or they were about to be eliminated. The type of work they had done would not allow for a public court martial. Any other member of the military that had done what they had would have been imprisoned for life. His intervention had prevented them from being eliminated by the government they had served and done things for. The politicians, the public, and even the commanders who had ordered it didn't want to think what they had done much less admit they were responsible for ordering them to do it. They would prefer they just disappeared. They had been happy to allow them to hide here.

He picked up the coffee mug, reached for the pot in the coffee maker, refilled the cup, and set the pot back in the machine. He left the kitchen, walked toward the door, and headed out to walk around the part of the base he was on. Darkness was beginning to settle in and push the daylight away. He had learned there were times you had to stop thinking about what you had been trying to solve and let your mind clear; the answers would usually find you when you quit looking for them. He had been head of security for the Committee for the last fifteen years. He would figure it out. That's what they paid him for.

He turned and walked down the gravel road that led to this quiet corner of the Fort Bragg reservation. This part of the base was restricted to everyone but his people. The majority of the military didn't even know it was here. Those who did wouldn't talk about it. He took a sip of his coffee and let his mind wander; sooner or later, he would figure it out.

Less than an hour later, he realized what he had overlooked. He stopped walking turned around and began running back to his headquarters. He opened the door, went right to his office, picked up the file he had left on his desk, and turned to the page with the summary of Dan Oliver's assignments. There it was: the antiterrorist task force. He turned to his computer and began the arduous task of finding out the other members Dan Oliver had worked with. He ran them down one by one; four hours later, he had the connection to Atlanta. He reached for his encrypted cell phone and called the leader of the team he had sent to eliminate the troublesome former FBI agent. Jonah Kauffman, the bastard would pay. Right after they dealt with Dan Oliver.

Sheraton Suites Galleria
Atlanta, Georgia
September 1, 2006

The cell phone chimed that he had a text message. The team member was still sitting in the front of the Suburban parked half a level below the Ford Taurus that was rented to one Donald Wallace. The other member of the team was still in the passenger seat and glanced over as the driver and head of the team read the text. "That must be important. The boss usually doesn't distract us when we're on a mission."

The team leader finished reading the text, put the phone away, and replied to his partner. "It is. We now know why they chose here and who is helping him. We are up against real professionals. Our target is being helped by the Mossad. His contact is Jonah Kauffman. He works out of the Israeli consulate here in Atlanta. The boss is sending another team to back us up. After we deal with the target, we have another job." His focus changed as the target walked out of the elevator and got in the Taurus. "Try to contact the rest of the team. Our target is getting in his car. They should have rolled him up by now. Something happened."

His partner pulled out his cell phone and began to send a text. The driver started the engine and waited until the Taurus made the turn from the uppermost level of the parking deck and began to head down past them. The driver waited until he was down almost a full level below them backed out and began heading down to follow wherever the Taurus went.

Dan Oliver glanced in the rearview mirror and took careful note of the Suburban. They were prepared to handle being followed. If everything worked as they planned, it would all be over tonight. He didn't want to think what would happen if it didn't.

# THE COMMITTEE

Dan reached the exit of the parking deck, turned right, and headed into the night. The Suburban turned behind him, and he was hoping they were going to depend on the tracking device they had put under the car. That was critical if the plan was to work. He made the left at the traffic light onto Cumberland Parkway that would take him to the interstate and the planned ending of his life as Dan Oliver.

In the Suburban behind him, the tracking device was being watched on the screen that looked like an ordinary GPS device. The second member of the team was still unsuccessfully trying to contact one of the four members of the team that had gone in to the hotel to try and roll up the target. They had been told to try and take him alive if they could, eliminate him if they couldn't. The boss wanted to know how much information he had put together. "I can't get a response from any of the team. We have to presume they got them, and we are on our own."

"I thought as much when he came out of the hotel. Let's not forget he's a pro and so are those helping him. They wouldn't leave him out here without backup." They enjoyed winning against those that were almost equals. The loss of the rest of the team didn't matter to them; the mission was all that did. They would take stock of their losses later.

Five minutes later, the GPS tracking device stopped sending the signal back to the Suburban. "Damn it we lost the signal. Close up and get a visual. We can't lose him." The driver pushed the accelerator down and changed lanes. Just out of his sight ahead of him, Dan Oliver in the blue Ford Taurus flipped the switch on the jamming device that blocked the signal from tracking device that was under the car. In the lanes behind him, the tractor trailers were blocking the view of the following Suburban in case they had gotten close enough for a visual. Directly in front of Dan's Taurus was another identical blue ford Taurus with matching license plates. Timing was everything. the exit was coming up. Dan accelerated off the exit followed by a large box truck screening him from view. The two tractor trailers dropped back and moved into the right lanes, one behind the other. As soon as he hit the exit ramp, Dan Turned right and drove into the residential area, made a right turn, parked the Taurus in the driveway of a house, got into the pickup truck parked there, and drove off into the night.

The two team members in the Suburban caught sight of the Blue Ford Taurus as they entered the outskirts of the city of Atlanta. "Close up and let's get a visual. We have to be sure." The team leader wasn't taking any chances. The driver changed lanes again to get around the traffic in front of him. Just as they were closing in, a motorcycle flew around them, weaving in and out of traffic. Less than a half a mile in front of him, the Taurus was in the right lane, and the motorcycle cut him off dodging the car in the lane next to him. The Taurus swerved to the right, and the brake lights flashed on. The car next to the Taurus the motorcycle had just missed braked hard, and the back end spun around and veered into the Taurus just as it began to straighten up in the right lane.

The impact was just enough to cause the Taurus to lose traction and spin out; the car that hit the Taurus somehow managed to straighten up. The tractor trailer following the Taurus couldn't stop as smoke began billowing from the tires and the trailer began to come around to the right as the driver tried to steer to the left. The impact caught the Taurus on the passenger side and pushed it toward the concrete abutment on the side of the interstate. Fifty yards later, the tractor came to a screeching stop with the Taurus halfway under the trailer.

The driver in the Suburban swore as he steered to the left to try and miss the swerving vehicles in front of him that were trying to avoid the twisted metal the trailer was becoming. They managed to pass the entanglement as it screeched to a stop. They never saw the driver of the Taurus get out and run toward the cab of the tractor trailer whose driver was getting out. As he reached the truck driver, no one saw him press the button on a small device in his hand. Seconds later, the gasoline began to spread and pool around the mangled Taurus. Almost instantly, the gasoline began to burn and moments later the fumes of the gasoline exploded and both the tractor trailer and the Taurus were fully engulfed as the flames spread.

Less than five minutes later, the sirens could be heard, and the first of the police cruisers arrived. Within fifteen minutes, the firemen had almost put out the wreckage. Shortly thereafter the Atlanta police officer was beginning to take statements of the witnesses. None of the witnesses interviewed had seen the driver get out of the Taurus; they all swore they saw the two men get out of the cab of the tractor trailer and try to get the driver out of the car. They both told the police officer they had tried to get the driver out but couldn't because it began to burn and then exploded. He then questioned the two good Samaritans in the Suburban that had stopped to try and help. It would take longer than they could stay on the scene for the victim to be removed from the remnants of the incinerated Taurus.

"Officer, we just happened to see the accident and stopped to see if we could help. We never saw what happened." The team leader told the Atlanta police officer who was working the scene. As much as they hated being brought to the attention of the authorities, they had to be sure their target was in the car. This all seemed just a little too weird.

The police officer handed back the ID of the team leader and said, "Okay, I have your information. I appreciate what you guys tried do. The poor guy in that car wasn't getting out. If we have any more questions, we will call you. You can go on about your way." They walked back toward the Suburban, got in, and left. They would follow up just to be sure; they had ways of getting any information from the medical examiner they wanted. This one was too important to take chances.

Fulton Business Park
Great Southwest parkway
Atlanta, Georgia
September 3, 2006


Homicide detective Denarius Blaire pulled his beat-up, unmarked car around the back of the vacant warehouse in the almost deserted part of the industrial park. He was part of "The Hat Squad" as the homicide detectives were known because of the brimmed hats each of them wore. It was their trademark, and it signified they were the elite homicide detectives. He knew he wasn't going to like this one. He parked the car and lifted up the crime scene tape and walked up to the crime scene investigator taking pictures of the interior of a dark blue van. "What have we got, Billy?"

William Haskell had been working as a crime scene technician for the best part of the last ten years. He hated being called Billy, and all the detectives knew it. He knew if he objected it would only get worse; he just ignored it. He had resorted to using the nicknames the detectives had stuck each other with. It was easier. "Hey, Dino, we have four victims. This one should be a real challenge. I don't think this is your run-of-the-mill drug deal gone wrong. Four well-dressed white guys, two obvious gunshot wounds, two don't have a mark on them. Dump job. The van was found by two of our finest residents." He nodded toward two scruffy black men sitting on the edge of the unused loading dock under the watchful eye of a uniformed officer. "They found the van and admitted breaking in." He pointed to the broken passenger side window and the piece of pipe they had used on it lying on the ground. "Said it had been here since yesterday, and they had been watching it. Figured it was stolen or something and they decided to break in and see if there was anything worth taking. I think it scared hell out of them to find this mess." He pointed to the four bodies in the back of the van.

"I see you have been playing detective again, Billy. Figured that out all by yourself, have you?" He enjoyed taking shots at the crime scene guys, especially this one. He was the brightest of the bunch and had been invaluable helping them sort through all the evidence. Their job was hard enough, and they had learned to make it as light as they could.

"I wouldn't dream of taking your glory. I was smart enough to listen while they told that to the uniform."

Dino laughed as he pulled on a pair of latex gloves and stepped into the back of the van. There were sheets that had been wrapped around the bodies. Two were bloodstained where they had been around the wounds caused by the gunshots. He looked at the pattern on the sheets. To his trained eye, he could tell this wasn't where they had been killed. The bodies were dumped on top of each other, two in between the front and second row seats and the other two in the back. He took a good look around the van. The darkened windows were impossible to see in from the outside. There was a small suitcase lying in the back. He reached over and opened it. Not sure what he was going to find inside, the contents surprised him. A low whistle escaped his lips. "Holy shit what have we got here?" The case contained a pair of silenced weapons and a set of handcuffs. There was also a pillow case, a roll of duct tape, and long zip ties. It contained another small black case, and Dino carefully lifted it out of the suitcase to take a look. He was no longer surprised when the open case contained syringes and a vial containing some kind of drug. He couldn't read the label. It had been wiped with some sort of solvent that caused the ink to smear. He couldn't stop the thought that entered his mind; the hit men got hit. This one was going to cause him a lot of sleepless nights. And in the end, he knew it would probably go in the cold case files. Whoever had whacked these guys were pros. He doubted they would ever find where they had been killed.

Dino carefully got out of the van and looked at Billy. "Take a lot of pictures and make damn sure we get fingerprints. Maybe we'll get lucky after we eliminate those two prints. I won't be surprised if nothing shows up. Whoever did this was a pro. Three to one there won't be anything useful." Dino would run down whatever he had. The tag on the van would at least tell them who it was registered to. How much more they could get probably wouldn't be worth the trouble. Dino walked back toward his car to the sound of Billy taking more pictures. They would call him with whatever else they turned up.

Atlanta Homicide Division
Atlanta, Georgia
September 5, 2006

Denarius Blaire looked up from his desk to see his captain walking out of his office toward him. He had that look; whatever it is has to do with the dump job in the van. Somehow he just knew. They hadn't turned up anything, and they had run the tag on the van, which had been a dead end. It was registered to a rental agency that didn't exist. The fingerprints on the four "vics," as he thought of them, had been run through the FBI. They hadn't got anything back on that yet. Even the weapons in the suitcase had been professionally sanitized. The serial numbers were long gone. Dino doubted they had ever been there; this had government written all over it. He wondered what agency had lost four of their agents and which side they belonged to.

Dino looked up into the face of his captain who just looked at him and motioned toward his office and said, "Now." He didn't look happy. Dino stood up and followed him in and shut the door behind him. There were two gentlemen in suits sitting in front of the captain's desk. "Detective Blaire, these two gentlemen are from the FBI. They have come here to take over the investigation of the four homicide victims that were found in the van. Turn over everything we have so far. The medical examiner has already turned over the remains to the team of agents that showed up there this morning. They will accompany you while you put everything together. Thank you, Detective."

Dino knew better than to say anything; he just got up and left, followed by both of the FBI agents who so far hadn't said a word to him. He knew it wasn't the fact they were losing the investigation. Both he and the captain knew this would remain unsolved. Every single time the FBI or for that matter any other of the various government agencies they dealt with got involved it was the air of superiority that pissed them off. They had all the money, the best of everything, and we get treated like a redheaded stepchild. Then they wondered why they piss us off. At least I get one off my plate that I can't solve. Dino sat down at his desk and took as long as he could while the two agents stood and watched. At least I can make them wait. He took a long fifteen minutes to put everything he had together. He then handed the folder to one of the two agents who still had said nothing. They just nodded and left. Let the pricks have it. Dino had plenty of others to work on.

Thirty minutes after Dino had gotten rid of the FBI agents, he stood up from his desk, grabbed his fedora, set it at the correct angle on his head, and left the office. He was still bothered by the four men in the van. He went to the parking lot, got in his beat-up unmarked, and went to see the medical examiner.

He parked his car in front of the building, walked in, and turned down the corridor to the lab. He opened the door and caught the eye of the technician he wanted to talk to and waited for him to finish what he was doing. Terry Ward had worked in the ME's office a long time and knew all of the homicide detectives; he was not surprised Dino had shown up. He stood up, just pointed to the door, and nodded as both he and Dino left the lab and went outside before either of them said a word.

"I guess you got a visit too huh? The Fibies marched in, handed us paperwork, loaded those four up, and hardly said anything. They even waited while we gave them even the originals of everything we had. Fingerprint cards, blood tests, everything."

"Yeah, it happened pretty much the same for me. Something isn't kosher here. They never are that quiet. They like to tell us how superior they are. Whoever these guys were, they want to keep what happened quiet."

Terry took a good look around before telling Dino what else had happened. "That isn't all of it. A couple of days ago, we had a fatality brought in from a traffic accident on the interstate. A car got run over by a tractor trailer, the car caught fire, and the gasoline exploded and burnt up the car and trailer. The driver didn't get out, was practically cremated on scene. They took that one too. I have no idea how the two are connected. We had found out the ID on that one through the car rental agency." Terry took out a pack of cigarettes, shook one out, put the pack away, and lit up.

Dino shook his head deep in thought. "You need to give that up, Terry. Those things will kill you. I wouldn't want you to end up on one of your own slabs." Neither one said anything for a couple of minutes. Terry was the first one to break the silence.

"Dino, what I didn't tell them was I highly suspected the car crash and the fire didn't kill that guy."

Dino looked at Terry, "Go on."

Terry shook his head before saying anymore. "What I didn't tell anybody, not even the ME was that I think that body was in our office before. I started doing the tests, and I had printed out a blood tox screen, and I remembered seeing the exact same results before. Guy dropped dead of a heart attack, and I did just the basics. He was on some special blend of medicines for seizures. You don't get two results like that, exactly the same. I set that aside and didn't give it to them. You are the only one who knows. That guy wasn't driving that car; he was dead before, and he damn sure wasn't who he was ID as. They pissed me off when they came in the way they did. Let them figure that one out."

Dino looked at Terry and whistled as he shook his head. "I think the best thing we can do is keep this between us. Get rid of that test result and forget you ever ran it. Things like that have a way of getting people hurt. If they never figure out we know that guy isn't who they think he is, too bad for them." Dino didn't like the way the Feds had stolen the case. He was now more positive than ever there was more to this than he wanted to know, and it wasn't worth getting involved. He meant what he had just told Terry. Knowing things like that could get you killed. There had been five bodies to prove it.

The Israeli Consulate of the Southeast
Atlanta, Georgia
September 8, 2006

Jonah Kauffman was worried. Their plan to have Dan Oliver die a fiery death on the interstate had worked. That had really been the easy part, as hard and expensive as it had been. Money wasn't the issue; Dan had provided plenty of that. What had him worried was all the work they had done beforehand, replacing all of the records in the database relating to Dan Oliver. There were no fingerprints on the body to worry about, that was why the fire had been so important. They knew they already had those. They had even covered themselves with the medical records in the doctor's office of Dan's family doctor. Making them believe he was really dead was important. They had done everything they could. It probably wouldn't take long to find out if it had worked. Dan was actually going to Israel for enough cosmetic surgery to change his appearance. It may not be enough if they knew he was still alive. The stakes they were playing for were more than just high.

Jonah really believed the very survival of not just the United States but of Israel was at stake. If the government of the United States was compromised, he didn't think they would care about Israel. They had always had to fight for their very existence. Jonah turned from the window he was staring out of and decided to go home. He had done everything that could be done; the rest was out of his hands.

# THE COMMITTEE

Jonah exited the consulate building and walked to his car; he unlocked it, put his briefcase in, and climbed in. He exited the parking lot and headed home. He lived in a quiet neighborhood several miles from the consulate, and it didn't take long for him to drive there. Jonah had a lot on his mind and wasn't as diligent as he normally was; he never noticed car parked across the street from his home.

He put his car in park, opened the door, got out, and reached back in for his briefcase. Standing up and shutting the car door, he turned toward the door of his home. The car across the street accelerated and the passenger window rolled down, and three shots broke the late afternoon silence. The impact of the bullets caused Jonah to turn and fall on his back as the car sped away down the street.

Hearing the shots and then the tires of the car screeching as it turned the corner and sped away, Jonah's neighbor across the street looked out his front window and saw Jonah lying in his driveway. "Oh god no!" he screamed, grabbing his cell phone, dialing 911 as he rushed outside across the street to where Jonah was down on the driveway. Jonah was still alive as they loaded him into the ambulance and rushed him to the hospital. The Committee would brook no interference in their plans.

The office of the Governor
Boston, Massachusetts
July 14, 2009

Governor Cain leaned back in his chair and rubbed his eyes. It was the end of another long day. As governor, he had a lot to handle. He had managed to guide his state through the financial crisis that had caused not only a severe economic downturn but the need to bailout many of the nation's financial institutions. They had come out a lot better than most, thanks to his experience in the financial markets. There had been plenty of warning; both he and his father had talked many times about their fears of the crazy manipulations they had seen in the markets. The knock on his door brought him out of his thoughts and back to the present.

His office door opened, Melissa his assistant, who considered herself his gatekeeper, stepped into his office and closed the door. "Governor, Steele Davis is here to see you. I know it's late and I—"

Ben Cain held up his hand to stop her. "It's okay, Melissa. Go ahead and send him in. He knows I'll take the time to see him."

"I'll send him in. Try not to let him keep you too long. I know how late you normally work. You do have a family and even you need a break." Melissa turned and left to escort Steele Davis in to see her boss. She didn't care much for him; he never cared about people, just winning at politics.

Steele Davis walked in the door of Governor Cain's office and extended his hand and smiled. He really liked Ben. Sometimes he thought he was just too nice a guy for this business of politics. They had managed everything around him well, and he didn't realize how much work had been put into keeping him viable for what they had in mind for him. Steele extended his hand as the governor stood and walked around his desk. "Thanks for taking time to see me, Governor. I know how busy you are."

"Steele, good to see you. I hope the family is doing well?" The two men shook hands.

"They are fine. Thanks for asking. How about Marilyn and Edwin?"

"Both are doing well. Thanks." Ben motioned toward the chair. "Have a seat while I get us something to drink." Ben walked toward the small bar set in the side of his office. He picked up a bottle of Famous Grouse and two glasses and handed one to Steele.

That was one of the things Steele liked about Ben Cain; he was never one to be waited on hand and foot by the staff. Most of the politicians he dealt with were arrogant and self-serving; Ben was as genuine as they came.

Ben poured the drinks and set the bottle down on his desk as he walked around it to sit down. "Tell me, Steele. What brings you around this time? I can't run for reelection, and I know you have already settled on who is going to run for this job next."

"Ben, I'm hurt. You always seem to think I want something when I come to see you. Can't I just stop by to see an old friend?"

Ben laughed. It was always the same thing. "I know you too well and for too long. You never stop by for a social visit. You plan those too far in advance around all of your real work. What's on your mind, Steele? It really has been a long day, and I have a long day scheduled tomorrow."

Steele Davis set his glass down on the edge of Ben's desk; he took a long moment as he looked Ben in the eye. "Ben, you never were one for banter. Okay have it your way. The Republicans got trounced in the last election, Ben. Bush wasn't popular when he left office, and let's face it, McCain wasn't going to win. The decision was made that we need a good viable candidate for president to run against an incumbent Democrat in 2012. The names mentioned so far in my opinion don't have a chance. The party has decided you are our only chance to defeat Obama. We need you, Ben."

There it was, the moment Ben had thought about for a long time. The atmosphere in the room had changed considerably. This was the moment Ben Cain had been groomed for since he had stepped into the political arena. "Steele, I have to admit I have thought about it. That's as far as its gone thinking about it. With everything going on right now, it may be better to wait until 2016. I think a Republican will have a very hard time beating an incumbent, especially this one."

"Ben, you will be out of this office by then, and I think when you look at what being a sitting governor does for you, trust me you can't wait till 2016. You would have to win a Senate seat, and in this state, that is almost impossible. You need the national exposure, and if you are going to do this, you need to start now. That election is only a little over three years away, and the sooner we get your name out there the better. We don't know how well the current president will do over the next three years, and this reminds me of 1980 all over again. We have to be ready."

The Committee had learned the lessons of the past well. They were not taking any chances. Their plans would not be interrupted by anything as simple as an unexpected result of an election anymore. The path Ben Cain was on had been set in motion.

The Safe House
Tel Aviv, Israel
November 8, 2010

    Dan Oliver stood up and stretched; he pushed his laptop back on the desk where he had been sitting. A lot had happened over the last four years; he hadn't risked going back to the United States. The surgery he had was enough to alter his facial appearance, but they couldn't do anything about his fingerprints, and with the advances in biometrics, he was afraid they would still be able to pick him out. Making yourself dead was one thing, staying out of the sights of whoever this group was, was something else entirely. He was still not convinced they had stopped looking for him. They had even tried to take out Jonah Kauffman; they would have succeeded had it not been for his neighbor, a doctor, who had heard the shots and called 911 and managed to stop the bleeding until the paramedics got there. Jonah had been brought back to Israel after that, and they still couldn't tell even the Israeli intelligence agency Mossad what they were working on.
    They had made a lot of progress; the depth of the control they had over the government was downright frightening. The one thing Dan had been able to do was to track more of where the money was going. They had control of most of the major defense contractors and were funneling money out of almost every government agency. It went even beyond that. There were even some state governments that had money funneled out. Dan had spent years following the money and charted where it all had gone. They had made one major mistake, and Dan had found it. Atlas International, each and every one of the companies had in one way or another, funneled money to Atlas. When you looked at the money, some things couldn't be hidden. Dan was just the first one to look.
    The major breakthrough had been a matter of public record. It had taken Dan a lot of hours to put it all together. It turned out to be as simple as looking at the board of directors or presidents and CEOs of each and every one of the corporations they were using; he began to find a pattern of the names. Each in turn had led him to Atlas

International. The board of directors of Atlas International was made up of ten men. Each one of them sat on various boards of directors or was CEOs of all of the companies that were involved in funneling out money. Atlas was the only one they all had in common. The funny part was how clever they thought they were. Atlas had no direct dealings with the government, and it was privately held. Once he had figured that out, he could tell who was behind it all. He could even tell who some of the previous men behind it were. Once he started looking into the finances of Atlas, it was plain to see; the sales they actually did were only a small part of the money that went through it.

Dan walked out onto the small balcony that was concealed behind the courtyard walls of his safe house. What he had just discovered about Atlas really frightened him. They were the only major tenant of the World Trade Center towers who had vacated part of their leased space prior to 9/11. They had relocated part of their operation to Los Angeles less than two months before the terrorist had flown the planes into the twin towers. That couldn't be coincidence. That meant they knew. Some of the business Atlas did was legitimate. Dan was speculating they would have moved all of their vital functions as it related to funneling the money out of the towers before the terrorist attack. Following that logic, it stood to reason the bastards behind all of this had knowledge of what the terrorists had planned. Not only were they willing to let all of the innocent people in the towers die, they killed some of their own to cover it up. It would have looked funny if only Atlas had moved out prior to the attacks.

Once he knew what to look for, it was obvious. Atlas had not only survived the attack better than just about every other business there, they had thrived. That led Dan on another train of thought, how did they know what Al-Qaeda had planned? Were they in on it? Were they funneling them money? If they were, there was a motivation behind it. Dan had a lot more digging to do. He was now more convinced than ever of how dangerous and utterly ruthless they were. He still didn't know how he was going to stop them. Somehow he had to. He was going to have to risk it and find a way.

The Committee
Rockefeller Center
New York, New York
May 10, 2011

    Benjamin Templeton was seated in the back of the limousine on the way to the meeting of the board of Atlas International. They had shifted back to Rockefeller Center after the destruction of the Twin Towers on 9/11. The Committee had moved the critical functions of Atlas to Los Angeles, but none of the members really wanted to travel to LA, and they had deemed it important to rebuild Atlas's presence in New York. Traveling was harder on him now as he was well into his eighties and so were most of the others. They had lost a couple of members and had selected the new ones in the same way they always had. Their business would continue no matter what happened. Diamond was desperately hoping he would still be around to see their success. They were getting closer with every day that passed.

    His thoughts were interrupted by the stopping of the limo. They had arrived. The door was opened for him by the security that was a constant anytime he was outside of his estate. At least there they weren't so ever-present. It took him a few long moments to exit the limo and make his way into the elevator that would take him from the parking garage into the building and up to the boardroom where the Committee now met.

    Diamond was the last to enter and the others were taking their seats and the security left the room. In here, it was only for the ears of the ten members of the Committee. "Gentlemen, we have a number of things to discuss. I would like to begin with my concern for the growing popularity of the Tea Party movement. We cannot allow that to continue. We have worked too long and hard to train the American people to accept the politicians we give them. We have to develop a way of shutting them down. The floor is open."

    Jade took the opportunity to start. "This is a grassroots movement. I think it will be short-lived. They have had success in one election. I don't think they will be able to carry over their success into the next election."

# THE COMMITTEE

Coral was the next to offer his opinion. "You may be right. However, I don't think we can afford to take the chance. I think a better solution would be to see they have trouble organizing and raising money. They can never match us, but the damage they could do if they just win a couple of key seats is unacceptable. Let's find a way to shut off as much of their money as we can."

Obsidian raised his hand and was given the floor. "One thing we have in our favor, gentlemen, is we still control all of the federal agencies. Take a moment and think of which agency is capable of stopping them from organizing and raising money."

Onyx exchanged glances with Gold and raised his hand and was given the floor. "Gentlemen, I think we are at a very critical point in our planning. Let's not be reckless. I think this Tea Party thing will be short-lived. We have always said we have never had a set timetable. We must use extreme caution. One election will not make a difference. I think the best strategy is to wait. We can always adjust as we have in the past."

Gold motioned for the floor. "I agree with both Jade and Onyx. The one thing we do not need to do is panic. A lot will be determined after the next election cycle. Gentlemen, we rushed things once before and that cost us dearly. Let's not do that again."

Granite decided to enter the debate and was given the floor. "We had almost total control of the government, and we let that get away by pushing our agendas too fast. We let the Tea Party gain traction, and we have to shut them down." He turned to Obsidian and asked, "What exactly do you have in mind?"

Obsidian smiled and said, "The one agency that is perfect to shut them down is the IRS. All of the PACs want tax exempt status. All we have to do is hold up their approval and make it as hard as possible to organize. If anything ever comes out, it looks like corrupt politicians. A few hearings and the whole thing goes away."

Diamond held up his hand to stop the debate. "We will explore that option. I am concerned for the next election. If we really do have voter rebellion, then we better have our options ready. There are a number of candidates on the Republican side for the president that we do not control. We cannot allow one of them to stumble into the nomination. Let's take a look at what our options are on that side."

Malachite was the first. "The one that concerns me the most is Herman Cain. He is not one of ours, and he is dangerous. He is gaining a following and since he is a minority, as is the current president, it will make it difficult to use the race game to defeat him if he did get the nomination. I think we have to get him out of the race. Also we cannot have two men named Cain in the race."

Obsidian was next, "I agree with Malachite on that. My other concern is the former speaker of the House. He has always been a wild card. I don't think he can wage a strong campaign. The governor of Texas is also a concern. I think our best option is the governor of Massachusetts. He has never been controversial, and he is articulate. If the electorate decides they don't like the current president, then he is a very attractive option."

Ebony motioned to Diamond and was given the floor. "I agree with Obsidian. As we have done in the past, there are things we can do. We control the majority of the money the candidates will get. The pizza man, Herman Cain, scares me the most. I think we need to create a scandal around him. There has to be something in his past. Even if it's not real, the allegations will be enough to derail him. The former speaker will implode. If the governor of Texas doesn't do or say something stupid, we can do the same thing to him."

Diamond stopped the debate, "We have other options as well to influence which of the candidates will get the nomination. Let's finish with the rest of our business, and we will implement it as we have in the past."

The business of the committee continued as it had—decisions made, strategies implemented, and careers made or destroyed.

# THE COMMITTEE

McAllister Halstead
Corporate Headquarters
Oklahoma City, Oklahoma
November, 4 2012

August Braden was lost in his own thoughts. The television was droning on in the background; it was election night. He was hardly paying any attention to who the winners and losers were. He was one of the few who knew it didn't really matter. He and Gold had done whatever they could to slow down the rapid decline of the nation they loved. They had been as careful as they could. So far they had gotten away with it. He put down the drink he was holding and switched the television off. He couldn't stand any more of it. He often wondered if he just held a press conference and told what he knew. Nice thought. He would be dead before the microphone was turned on.

The door to his outer office opened, and the sound surprised him. The office building had already closed for the day, only the security and janitorial staff were in the building. His office was off limits, and the private security he had never needed to come up here. That was one reason he spent as much time here as he could.

August turned and realized he had left the door to the inner office open. That was why he had heard the door. Suddenly his stomach knotted; if the Committee had figured out how he really felt, he was in trouble. He heard nothing from the outer office. The realization hit him he was unprepared if they meant to eliminate him. He turned toward the door and decided what the hell, if this was it, so be it. He stepped through the door into the outer office. It was empty. "Damn, am I getting paranoid?" Turning to go back into his office, he walked through the door and stopped in his tracks. There was a man sitting in his chair behind his desk.

"Close the door. We need to have a talk." The gun in his hand was rock steady.

August closed the door and resigned himself to his fate. The bullet never came. Dan Oliver looked at August Braden and said, "I have gone to a great deal of trouble to get in here where we can talk. Your security doesn't know I'm here. The alarm and phone are disconnected. If you try and run, I will kill you."

For some reason he never could understand, August Braden was relieved. "What exactly is it we need to talk about?"

Dan Oliver sensed this was a decent man. "I want you to tell me all about Atlas International." There it was.

August looked him in the eye. "What do you want to know, and would you mind telling me who in the hell you are?"

"I think it would be best if you don't know who I am. Let's just say I have been tracking all ten of you for better than ten years. As far as what I want, you are going to tell me just exactly what the game is. I know about all the money that's been funneled out of the government further back than I care to look. I know how it has all been used to control the outcome of elections. I know how you have destroyed careers. I know how the country is slowly being led down a path I don't care to see it go. I know this has gone on damn near since the founding of this nation. The founding fathers who started this never intended for you corrupt bastards to destroy the freedoms they wanted to protect. You are going to tell me." The gun in Dan Oliver's hand never wavered.

August Braden breathed a sigh of relief. Maybe his prayers had been answered. "This has all gone way beyond what I thought it was going to be. I was selected a long time ago. In the beginning, for me it was all about making this nation the strongest on earth." August sat down in the chair across the desk from Dan Oliver.

"You are right. This has gone on from the founding of this nation. I need to tell you the whole thing so you will understand." August was lost in thought before he continued, "Somewhere along the way, it wasn't enough to control the government. The rest of them want to control the world. No wait; there is one other who feels the way I do. For the last twenty years, we have done what we can to slow them down. It hasn't been enough."

Dan interrupted him, "Are you telling me you aren't part of this?"

August laughed. "Oh no, I am guilty. As I said, when I was first recruited, I was naive enough to believe what we were doing was for the betterment of this nation. I didn't realize, until later on, what the real agenda was. Let me tell you this, I am the only one who has been in the military. That is one of the myriad of reasons I feel the way I do. I have seen and done things none of the rest of them have. They have manipulated and controlled everything. There is too much to explain. I will try to simplify it as much as I can."

Dan Oliver shook his head; this wasn't what he had expected. "Let me save you some time. I know far more than you think. I know about all the money and where it all goes. How it's been used to control elections and destroy political opposition. I know how it started and how it strayed from what the founding fathers intended. It might surprise you just how much I know. What I want to know is what the plan really is. Only then can I figure out how to stop it."

August shook his head. "I have prayed I could find a way to stop them. Our security is our keepers. This thing has almost taken on a life of its own."

"Tell me what they are planning." Neither one of them knew for sure they could trust each other. Dan decided to take a chance. He lowered the gun he had been holding rock steady.

"Let me tell you what the end game is. It scares the living hell out of me." August Braden paused and looked into a future only he could see. He never realized or cared Dan Oliver was no longer holding the gun on him. "Sometime even before I was selected a decision was made. I really don't know exactly when. They don't tell you everything until later. These men have become totally corrupted by their own power." August looked Dan Oliver in the eye and continued.

"They decided the United States was in the way of what they wanted to achieve. They want control of everything. A lot of things have been done to achieve the collapse of the government. The national debt was run up to the extreme to where there is no hope of repaying it. Deficit spending taken to new levels, billions of dollars are being printed every month. Millions of Americans on one form of government assistance or another, welfare, social security, disability, snap, food stamps, section eight housing. You pick the program, almost half the population is on them. The whole healthcare program, nothing but a way to control the population. That's just the tip of the iceberg. Our foreign policy is designed more to provoke a crisis than to keep peace in the world. We know which troops will be loyal and fire on Americans.

The rest will be deployed overseas. When the collapse hits, they'll be abandoned. The Occupy Wall Street Movement was nothing but a test to see if the civil unrest could be put in motion when it's wanted. The divisive politics all designed to divide Americans. It makes them easier to manipulate." Dan Oliver sat in stunned silence.

August Braden stopped, shook his head, and looked to the floor. He raised his head, made eye contact with Dan, and continued. "The Committee even began to fund the terrorists. That led to creating fear in the people. Convince them to give up their freedoms for security. The Patriot Act, NSA Surveillance programs, billions of dollars spent building facilities to keep track of everything every American does. They want to know who will be loyal and who they have to worry about. FEMA building camps to house those who will be considered malcontents, all done under the guise of disaster preparedness."

August Braden stopped; even he had never said all of it. Now that he had started he had to say the rest; he couldn't stop now, and it all came spilling out. "The key to the whole collapse is the dollar. The US Dollar is the world's reserve currency. At one time everyone needed dollars for foreign trade. That gave the United States the ability to print virtually unlimited amounts of money. We made credit easy, get everything mortgaged. We control all of the hard assets, land, minerals, water, and all the financial institutions. We have made trillions manipulating all of it. Create an energy crisis. We knew what was coming. It was easy to profit and then funnel the profits into controlling all the real assets and leave everyone else holding worthless paper."

The picture he was painting frightened even him. He began again, "When the dollar is yanked as the world's reserve currency, money will be worthless overnight. Imagine the chaos when all the government welfare and benefits can't be paid. Corporations won't be able to buy fuel, goods will stop moving, what happens when people can't go to the store and buy food? Complete and total chaos. There will be no police or National Guard to restore order. The looting and rioting will start. Those who have planned ahead will be forced to kill to survive. Massive depopulation, what's left of the government bureaucrats will protect themselves and then they can go to the United Nations and ask for international peacekeepers to restore order. The vehicles, supplies, and weapons have already been stockpiled. Foreign governments bought off. Those that are left will embrace anyone who can feed and protect them. They will be willing to completely give up freedom and submit. And the Committee is planning it all."

August Braden stopped and hung his head; he had said all of it. Dan Oliver sat in stunned silence. He couldn't comprehend what he had just heard, it was far worse than what he had even imagined. The worst part was they were capable of doing all of it, human nature at its worst.

Dan stood up. He walked to the door of the office. Turning to look back at August Braden, he saw a man who was dealing with his private demons. "I don't know how, but I am not going to let that happen. I was prepared to kill all of you one by one. Then I realized while you were talking it wouldn't stop this. I can't get to all of them fast enough. This is so inconceivable the public will never believe it. This has already cost me more than I care to think about. Somehow I don't think you will tell them I was ever here. Deep down, I think you are a decent man. Don't make me regret my decision not to kill you." And then he was gone.

The Cain Campaign
Boston, Massachusetts
November 4, 2012


The race had been called. The country had elected a new president. Ben Cain hung up the phone; he had just received a call congratulating him from the current president he had just defeated in the election. He had been waiting for the call. Protocol demanded his opponent concede before he made the appearance, thanking his supporters and claiming victory. It was just before midnight in Boston.

Ben Cain could hear the cheers from the crowd celebrating their win in the election. In just a few minutes, he was going to have to give a victory speech. First, he wanted a few minutes alone and then with his family. His mind began to wander. It had been a long road. College, then Valerie leaving, that had all been a long time ago; Ben had never completely gotten over her. Then meeting Marilyn that summer in

Washington as an intern in Senator Moynihan's office, from there his job at Wellington Capitol. He would never have believed Benjamin Templeton asking him to run for the state legislature would have led to this. He thought about everything else, going to Congress, two terms as governor, that second term was when Ben began to realize he had a chance to be president. The campaign had been grueling. In the end, Ben had been the last man standing after the primaries. He had thought early on he might not win. The businessman Herman Cain had won the poll in Florida and that had worried him. The nation was tired of politics as usual. Out of nowhere the scandal had erupted, and he had dropped out. Ben never knew it had all been manufactured and a decision had been made that he would be the Committee's candidate to ensure their control of the presidency.

Ben's reminisces were interrupted by the door opening and his father, Edwin, stepped into the suite where Ben was standing staring out the window. He turned and walked to his father, neither said a word. The embrace between the two said it all. The embrace ended, and Ben met his father's eyes. Edwin looked at his son and said, "I'm proud of you, Ben. Let me be the first to tell you what a good president I think you will be."

Ben didn't trust his voice for a long moment. "I learned most of what I know from you. I'm proud of you too, Dad. Let's go see the rest of the family before I have to go down and thank everyone. I just spoke with the president, and he was very gracious. It really hasn't sunk in yet that I will be president of the United States."

The two turned to the door where the rest of the family was waiting, and as they passed through, the two Secret Service agents were waiting to escort the president elect to the crowded ballroom where he would give his victory speech.

In his home in Milford, Pennsylvania, Benjamin Templeton watched the television as his candidate stepped up to the podium. Diamond smiled, either way the election had gone, the Committee was still in control.

# THE COMMITTEE

Palm Breeze Condominiums
Naples, Florida
November 4, 2012

The television was turned to NBC; election coverage was all that was on every channel. Brian Williams was speaking, "Florida has just been called for the Republican Ben Cain. That is enough to push him over the magic number of 269. It is now projected Bennett Arthur Cain will be the forty-fifth president of the United States. This has been a very historic night; this election has been so close and too close to call almost all night long. For the first time since 1992, an incumbent president has lost in his bid for reelection. Once again Florida played a key role for the winner; if you are just tuning in, we are calling Florida for Governor Ben Cain from Massachusetts. It looks like he will win with at least 272 electoral votes. The popular vote is so close we still do not know how that will go. As you know, it is the electoral votes that determine the winner. Once again, Florida has been called for Governor Cain."

Valerie Jackson walked over to the television and turned it off. She then went to the sliding glass door and stepped out onto the balcony. In another life, she had been Valerie Hollis. That was a long time ago. She had wondered then what they had in mind for Ben. She had followed his career and had watched the Republican convention when he had accepted the nomination. Somehow she knew Ben had never forgotten her. She had never gotten over Ben.

Her thoughts wandered back to that day in October of 1981. She had left work and taken the bus like she normally did. After getting off the bus and walking the last few blocks, she had been approached by the man just outside of the diner. He told her he needed to talk to her about Ben. Taking her in the diner and buying her dinner, he had told her just exactly what she was going to do. She knew she didn't have a choice. She had never seen or talked to Ben after she had broken up with him. They had watched her for all of the last thirty years. Every so often, one of them would approach her. The last time had been less than a week ago while she was in the grocery store. They had taken care of her. She had been given enough money to buy the condo, and she had been given a job at one of the local resorts. All in all, it had been a pretty good life. She had never wanted for anything. She understood as long as she never told anyone who she really was and never even mentioned Ben Cain to anyone the retirement account that had been set up for her would last her the rest of her life. It was also understood if she broke the rules she wouldn't have to worry about breaking them again.

Valerie stood on the balcony and felt the breeze on her face. She had never married; over the years, she had dated and had relationships that lasted for some time, but there was never anyone she had wanted to grow old with. It wouldn't have been fair to any of them knowing they would always be watching her. None of them would have been the love of her life. No matter she would never see him again; she would never get over Ben. Valerie turned and went back inside; the tears were already starting. It would not be the first time, and she knew it wouldn't be the last time she ever cried for what never was.

Island Marina
Naples Florida
July 13, 2013


The *Quiet Time* was tied along the slip, the weather was perfect, and the boat gently moved up and down with the passing of another boat headed out of the harbor. Dan Oliver was sitting on deck holding a can of beer that was growing warmer by the minute. He had a lot on his mind and didn't really care about drinking the beer, but it served to give him the appearance he was looking for. He had been busy finding everything he could about the new president. He still hadn't completely figured out how he was going to derail the Committee. He was beginning to think of them in that term since his late night meeting with August Braden. That was how he referred to what they had set up and so had James Madison in the letter he had written that had started Dan on his quest. It seemed to fit.

A lot of things troubled him. He wasn't sure just how honest Braden had been with him, at least not at first. He had detected no sign that they were looking for him again. He had done more than just disable the phone in Braden's office. He had left a small listening device and had stayed and waited and listened to see if he had made any calls or sounded the alarm. If he had, there was nothing to prove it; every time he checked, the device was still active. That by itself didn't mean anything. Somehow he knew Braden was a good man caught up in something he couldn't control.

It had been seven years since he had disappeared, and as far as everyone was concerned, Dan Oliver had died a fiery death on the interstate. The painful part was Rebecca and Pam; for their own protection, they couldn't know he was alive. He had spent most of that time digging into everything he could find to figure out just exactly who was behind it. Once he had found Atlas International, that had revealed them. Even now he was amazed at how really brilliant people could make such an obvious mistake. All of them were highly successful, wealthy, and extremely intelligent. It was never enough.

Dan shifted in the deck chair he was sitting in and set the now warm can of beer in the holder on the arm of the chair. He had pulled into Naples yesterday evening and would be gone in a couple of days. By then he hoped he would know more about the next president. He had spent a great deal of time looking into his background. That only told you so much; he needed to talk to someone who knew him personally. He was still trying to find a way to bring down the Committee. That required someone with enough power to make it happen. The major problem was who had the power to make it happen. That limited his options considerably.

Dan had given this a great deal of thought. He stood up and stretched his legs; the sun was beginning to set and what he had to do here in Naples was best done in darkness. He made his way down the deck and went into the cabin. He was going to pay another visit. Dan had decided the best option was to find out if this president was as committed to the Committee's agenda as he believed some of the past ones had appeared to be. He knew enough about the money trail to know both campaigns had been financed by the Committee. That had gone back for almost the last thirty years. He hadn't looked much before that; there wasn't a lot of reason to.

When he had looked into the background of this president, he had found something very interesting. He had found a former girlfriend from high school and college. That wasn't the interesting part. While he was tracing the money, he had found a small trail and had decided to follow it. A transfer of a couple of hundred thousand dollars, small by the numbers he was finding, had found its way into the account of one Valerie Jackson. She hadn't existed before 1981. Continued digging had turned up the name of Valerie Hollis. She hadn't existed after 1981. Somehow they had gotten her away from Bennett Arthur Cain. Why, that was the question. He was going to find out.

Palm Breeze Condominiums
Naples, Florida
Later that same night

In another news cast, the anchor was telling the viewers about the trip the president was on to Europe and the G8 Summit. The footage they were showing was of the president speaking to the British prime minister. Valerie couldn't watch anymore; she stood up, walked to the television, and turned it off. She went into the kitchen and opened the cabinet, took down the bottle of aspirin, took two, closed the bottle, and put it back. Moving to the refrigerator, she took a bottle of water opened it, popped the aspirin in her mouth, and took a swig of water. Walking to her bedroom and finishing the last of the water, she was going to go to bed. She was tired and had a headache; it had been a tiring day.

Valerie flipped the light switch and stopped dead in her tracks. They had never come into her home before. Sitting on her bed, Dan Oliver smiled and said, "Hello, Valerie. I just need to talk with you."

Valerie was so frightened she couldn't move. The man made no move and said, "Valerie, I am not going to hurt you, and I am not one of those who have been keeping track of you all these years."

Stammering, all Valerie could manage to say was "Who are you?"

Dan made eye contact with Valerie. "My name is Dan, and the same people who have been responsible for you being here have tried and think they have killed me. I will not hurt you."

Valerie began to breathe again. "What do you want?"

"I just want to talk to you, Valerie. I need information that you can help me with."

"What information could I possibly have?"

"What I have uncovered has frightened me. This has gone on longer than you can imagine. I need you to tell me about the president. What kind of man is he?"

Valerie was still in shock. "Wait, what makes you think I could possibly know anything that could help you?"

Dan smiled again. "Valerie, I know you were his girlfriend, and then you were made to disappear. There is a reason why. It might help me figure out how I am going to deal with them."

Valerie had begun to regain her composure. "I need to sit down." Valerie turned and went back into the living room and almost slid down into the couch. Dan followed her into the living room and sat down in the chair across the room from her. Valerie shook her head. "How could you possibly know that?"

"Valerie, I was in the FBI for thirty years. I retired and tried to disappear. Something was discovered that put me on the trail—" Dan paused. "I don't want to tell you anything that might get you killed. These people play for keeps."

Valerie laughed. "You think I haven't figured that out? Why do you think I left all those years ago? Do you think I had any choice? If I tell you, they will kill me anyway."

"Valerie, this goes way beyond whatever you think. I am trying to figure out how to stop what they have planned. There is only one way. The president of the United States is the only one with enough power. The problem is they put him in that office. I have to know…Is Bennett Cain the kind of man who would willingly be a part of something like this?"

If there was one thing Valerie had never had any doubt of, it was that Ben was truly a good man. In the last thirty years, she had never met anyone as honest as Ben. She knew he would never have willingly been a part of anything like this man was suggesting. Valerie was lost in the past for a long moment. "I have never, ever believed that Ben could have known what happened. I don't know what you found out, but Ben would never be willing to go along with anything like you are suggesting."

For the first time since he had started looking into this, Dan Oliver had a prayer of hope he could stop them. He saw in Valerie's eyes the pain even after thirty years. "Tell me what happened."

For some reason, Valerie needed to tell this man what had happened. There had never been anyone she could tell. She sensed he was much like Ben, a truly good man.

Dan Oliver had listened to the story Valerie had told him. He hadn't said anything while it all came spilling out. The pain in her eyes and the tears she couldn't hold back. Dan was more determined than ever to find a way to bring them down.

Dan Oliver left Valerie's condo the same way he had come in. The one thing he couldn't take a chance of was being seen leaving. He had found a way through the attic of the building and exited through the vacant condo on the end of the building. As quietly as he could, he went around the corner of the building and checked around front. There was a car sitting across the street from the building that hadn't been there earlier. The hair on the back of his neck stood up.

Dan slipped the pick in the back door of Valerie's condo and slipped inside. He stepped through the kitchen and moved toward the living room, his silenced automatic extended in front of him. Valerie was struggling with the man who had his hands around her neck. He never saw Dan as he double-tapped the trigger, and two muted spits erupted from the silencer and hit him in the head. He was dead before he hit the floor.

Valerie was still struggling to breathe, and the fear on her face said it all. "He was trying to kill me."

Dan looked at Valerie. "You can't stay here. I will deal with this. Go put some clothes and what you need in a bag. Be as fast as you can. We don't have long."

Valerie turned and went into her bedroom never saying a word. Dan followed her and grabbed the covers on the bed, threw them back, and pulled the top sheet off; he turned and went back in the living room. He went through the dead man's pockets, removed his wallet, car keys, and searched him. He removed the weapon from his pocket and the holster and backup from around his ankle. The knife that was strapped to his wrist also went into Dan's jacket pocket. He couldn't afford to leave anything. His cell phone went in the other pocket. He wrapped the body in the sheet, picked it up, and moved it to the garage. He went outside making sure there wasn't anyone watching. Getting in the car, he backed it up to the garage and popped the trunk release. He went inside, opened the garage door, picked up the sheet-wrapped body, put it in the trunk, and closed it. Closing the door, he went back in and cleaned up the blood and brain matter from the floor and wall. Dan was grateful the floor was hardwood.

Valerie watched Dan as he finished cleaning up. She was standing just outside the bedroom door with a small suitcase on the floor beside her; she had changed clothes and had her purse over her shoulder. Dan looked at her and said, "We have to go now."

They turned off the lights, locked the condo, got in the car with the body in the trunk, and left. For a long time neither of them said a word. Valerie was the first to break the silence. "He came in right after you left. He wanted to know who had been in the house with me. He didn't believe me when I said I had been alone. I don't think he saw you come in or leave. He told me he had been watching and knew I wasn't alone." Valerie couldn't control the shaking that suddenly overtook her. "My god if you hadn't come back…"

Dan looked over at her. "I told you they have tried to kill me. I'm not in the mood to let these bastards get away with what they are trying to do. I knew they were watching you. I had hoped to get in and out without them knowing. You can't go back."

Valerie had regained her composure. "What am I going to do now? They gave me a job, bought me the condo, and made sure I had enough to live on. If I went anywhere, they watched me. I never could save enough to leave. They promised me a retirement account that would be set up the same way, enough to live on not enough to leave," Valerie said what she was thinking. "If they find me, they will kill me."

Dan stopped the car; he handed Valerie another set of keys. "I'm not going to let that happen. You are going to have to drive my car." He pointed to the jeep Cherokee they had stopped beside. Just follow me where I get rid of this car. We have to hurry. They will be looking for you before long. We will be out of here before then with a little luck." Valerie took the keys, never said a word, and got out of the car. They were in the parking lot of the shopping center several blocks from her condo. She got in the jeep, started it, and followed Dan as he left the parking lot.

They drove about twenty minutes when Dan stopped the car. Valerie was right behind him. He pressed the button to roll the windows down, opened the driver's door, got out, closed the door, and left the car running. Reaching through the window, he dropped the gear shift into drive and the car began to inch forward. The car was on a slight incline; it began to pick up speed as Dan walked back to the jeep, got in the driver's seat as Valerie slid over to the passenger side. He watched as the car started to go over the embankment and dropped into the river below. As he turned the jeep back the way they came, he reached in his pocket, took out the cell phone he had taken, and threw it out the window as far as he could into the river below the bridge. Valerie sat in silence wondering how she had ever gotten into this mess. She looked over at Dan and it hit her full force; her life was in his hands.

Fort Bragg
North Carolina
July 14, 2013


The secure phone ringing woke Ron up. He picked it up and answered with the requisite "Yes."

His team leader from Florida was on the line. "We have a situation. The overnight operator on the detail watching the woman never reported in this morning."

Ron sat upright, swung his feet over the side of the bed, and put them on the floor; he was wide awake. "Tell me the rest."

"We increased the surveillance when you ordered it. There were times she was never watched. For the last year, it was full time. Overnight there was only one man on the detail. He went on at eleven.

They were on four-hour shifts. His replacement showed up at three. He never found the other operator. He went in the condo. She wasn't there. It looked like there had been a hurried departure. He did a thorough search. Only a few personal items, her purse, and some clothes are all that are gone. Her car is in the garage. The tracking device is intact. The bed was unmade and a sheet was missing. He thinks something happened. There had been some cleaning in the living room done. He found a trace of blood between the cracks of the hardwood floor. We have run a track on his phone. It went out just before one this morning. We have not been able to locate him or the woman."

Ron thought for a moment before replying. "I'll send a team down to go through the condo. Don't let anyone else in. Keep it quiet. I have a bad feeling about this. Keep looking for him and the car. Check back with me in four hours." He hung up the phone and looked at the clock beside his bed. It wasn't quite five in the morning. He got up went in the small kitchen, put the coffee pot on, and went to take a shower. He would wait for a couple of hours before sending the team down. There were times you did not want to draw any attention to what you were doing. He also knew nothing that was done at this point was going to change the outcome. She was gone and an agent was dead. What he had to figure out was who had done it and where she was. The answers were there; his job was to find them.

He was just stepping out of the shower when the answer hit him. He had never been completely satisfied that the FBI agent had really died in Atlanta. They had checked everything, even the dental records; it had all matched. Then it hit him. They had discovered Dan Oliver was on the trail through the computer program that was discovered. Whoever had written the program was top notch. If he had gotten by with that for as long as Ron had suspected, it wouldn't have been hard for him to alter dental records and even his other medical records in the computer systems, even the files of the FBI and his doctors. He was still out there; he couldn't have gotten far from Florida in the limited time he had. Ron was going to find him. He would kill him himself and then her and there would be no loose ends this time.

Aboard the *Quiet Time*
The Gulf of Mexico
July 14, 2013

Valerie had never been on board a boat anything like this. She looked around the cabin Dan had told her to use. It was tastefully decorated yet not overdone. There was a lot of woodwork, and the few pieces of furniture were comfortable and appeared sturdy. For some reason she had slept well. After everything that had happened, she hadn't expected that. She finished dressing and went up on deck; Dan was sitting in a chair up on top of the cabin. She climbed the small ladder up to where he was. "Who is steering, if you don't mind me asking?" She looked at the unattended wheel.

Dan laughed and took a sip from the coffee mug he was holding. He pointed to the thermos and said, "Help yourself. Would you believe me if I said no one? This thing is fully automated. I had it set up that way when I bought it. Everything is state of the art. There is a radar system tied in to the computer that runs the auto pilot. I can steer it myself, of course, but even I need sleep. It does bother me to sleep while being underway, but sometimes there is no choice."

Valerie looked around the boat. "Are you telling me you could sleep last night?"

Dan looked her in the eye. She was not what he had imagined. She hadn't screamed when she first saw him sitting on her bed. She had kept it together even when he had put the bullets in the brain of the guy trying to strangle her. Everything he had told her to do she had and never questioned him. This was one tough lady. "I couldn't risk it last night. It would have looked funny if we had pulled out at three in the morning. I had to get the jeep back where I got it and then wait until first light to leave the marina. I don't think they had more than one person watching you, but I couldn't take the risk. If they had followed us to the marina, it would have been dicey. I don't think they know where we are."

Valerie had poured a cup of coffee and put the thermos back. Her face turned deadly serious. "What now? Somehow I don't think they are going to stop looking. I really don't even know who is behind this or why. I have often wondered why they didn't just kill me a long time ago. All I really know is they didn't want me around Ben."

Dan thought for a long moment before he answered her. "Valerie, it doesn't really matter now how much I tell you. We are both a risk to them now. The reason they left you alive, this is just an educated guess, killing people is messy and it draws unwanted attention. The other reason is control. Even now, how would the president react if he was shown a picture of you and there was a knife at your throat? Then he was told if he didn't do what he was told, you would be killed. I told you these people play for keeps. As for what happens to you now, I get you out. You can't go back. At least not until this is over, depending how it ends, maybe not even then." For the first time since he had started hunting them down, Dan voiced to someone else his fear he might not be able to stop them. "Let me tell you all of it."

He told her everything; when he was done, Dan felt a sense of relief that at last someone other than Jonah and him knew, the one thing he left out was Jonah Kauffman and the Israeli help he had. That was too sensitive for anyone to know.

Valerie had listened to everything Dan told her. When he finished, she asked him the one question he didn't know how to answer. "You came to find me to ask about Ben, what kind of man he is. You said he was the only one with enough power to stop this. The one thing you haven't told me is how you plan to get to him."

Dan smiled at her and answered with total honesty. "I don't have any idea how in the hell I can get access to him. I don't think walking up to the White House and knocking on the door and saying, 'Can I speak to the president?' is going to work. There has to be someone who has access to him. The problem is this all sounds so crazy they'll think I am some kind of lunatic or a conspiracy theorist."

Valerie provided him with the answer he had been searching for. "There is someone who will have access that will never be questioned. I think you will have a much easier time getting to his father than you will the president."

For a long time, Dan never said anything; it was so simple. He was the one person who could get to the president. His mind kicked into high gear. The former governor of New Jersey was now in his eighties. "I have to admit, I hadn't thought about him. That is assuming of course he isn't in on this."

Valerie smiled at Dan. "You don't know either of them. While I had my differences with his father, I first thought he was behind trying to get rid of me. I realized he would never have done anything this drastic. Then I had a lot of time to think about it. I realized he really loves his son. While he never thought I was good enough—no, that isn't right—he knew we came from different worlds." Valerie paused lost in the past. "I talked to him once about it. Ben never knew. I never told him. His father was more concerned that Ben would get hurt. I think he knew I loved Ben. He asked me to be careful. He then told me he would accept whatever Ben wanted. From then on, we understood we both loved Ben. His father tried to help me after Ben went to college. I wouldn't let him. Then when they approached me and I had to leave, I asked them if his father was behind it. I will never forget the way he grabbed my arm when I tried to leave. I knew then he would have killed me if I didn't do what they wanted. Ben and his father are a lot alike. They are both good men with a strong belief in right and wrong. Neither of them would ever do anything like what you have told me."

Dan had listened to everything Valerie had told him without interrupting her. He knew her pain was still there after all this time. Maybe there was a way out of this mess after all.

The White House
January 21, 2013
3:30 AM

Gene Everett had just stepped out the door of the Oval Office. He nodded to the Secret Service agent standing watch outside and said as calmly as he could, "Agent Owens, give him a moment then look in on him, see if he needs anything. He needs to get some rest. You know the drill. Till they learn the job, we have to guide them."

"Yes sir, Mr. Everett. I know what you mean. They usually learn quickly."

Gene patted the agent on the shoulder and said, "I appreciate it. Thanks. I'm going to take my own advice and get some rest. All the new details start in the morning. It's going to be a long day." He walked down the hallway as calmly as he could. He still had no idea why he had been made to have that conversation with the new president. When he had been called into the director's office earlier in the day, he looked at his watch and realized it was really yesterday; there was another man sitting in the office. The director had told him, "This gentleman," he had used those exact words, "has a job for you to do. I want you to do exactly what he asks, no discussion of this is desired and you will start your new assignment tomorrow." He had then walked out of his own office and left Gene alone with the man sitting there who so far hadn't said a single word. When the director of the Secret Service told him what he wanted and no discussion was desired, Gene had no choice.

Gene recalled the entire conversation with the nameless man."Supervisor Everett, I have a job for you to do." He then handed Gene a sheet of paper outlining just exactly what he was to say to the new president. "You will be told when to go in to the Oval Office. The agent outside will be instructed to let no one else in until you are done."

Gene read the sheet of paper; he had been shocked. "You really don't expect me to tell this to the president. You can't be serious. What is this, some kind of a test?"

The man never stood up; he just reached in his pocket, pulled out an envelope, and handed it to Gene. When he opened it, there were pictures of Gene, naked, with two Latin American women who were also naked. On the table beside the bed was a packet of what Gene knew was cocaine. The white powder was obvious. Gene remembered having to clean it up the next morning; he had apparently spilled some during the sexual Olympics that night.

"Gene, I don't think it would go well for your career if those pictures of how the agents of the advance team the Secret Service sent ahead of a presidential visit spent their time was ever made public, do you?"

Gene looked up from the pictures he was holding into the face of the man. He continued, "There is a reason why you are being told to do this. I am not at liberty to tell you what that is. The director knows about this. As he told you, no discussion is desired."

He had then told Gene. "Finish reading that. Make sure you understand exactly what it says then give it back to me."

Gene had read it, made sure he understood it, and then handed it back to the man. The man had then stood up and said, "You can keep the pictures. I have others. Wait here for the director." He then turned and walked out the door. The director had then come back in.

"Supervisor Everett, I have no doubt you will do exactly as you were instructed. As I told you before, no discussion of this is desired. You can return to your assignment. Thanks for your time."

Gene had then left the office. He had just finished the discussion with the new president. He had no idea what it had all been about. The cell phone in his pocket rang. He reached in his pocket, pulled it out, looked at the number on the screen, and decided he had better answer it even though he had no idea who it was. "Everett."

"Gene, I was just calling to inquire how the meeting with the new president went. I trust you did everything I asked." Gene recognized the voice from earlier in the day.

"Yes, I did" was all Gene had replied; he wasn't expecting the reply.

"Good, now forget that any of this ever happened." The click told him the caller had hung up. He had no idea what any of this had been about. He decided the best thing he could do was exactly what he had been told. He would forget any of it had ever happened.

Ron Cole pressed the end button of the secure cell phone. He smiled and shook his head. He would listen to the recording again, just to be sure Supervisor Everett had done exactly what he had been told.

Ben Cain was still stunned at the conversation he had just had with the man who had just left the office. The glass of Famous Grouse was still setting on the desk untouched. It took him a moment to realize he was now president of the United States, and he was sitting in the chair behind the resolute desk in the Oval Office. He reached down and picked up the letter on what was now his desk. It was addressed to "45." It took Ben a long moment to realize he was now the forty-fifth president of the United States. Just then the door opened and the agent who had been outside stepped in and asked, "Everything okay, Mr. President? Is there anything I can do for you?"

The president looked up at the agent and slipped the letter in his jacket pocket and said, "No, everything is fine. I'm just about to head upstairs to bed. It's been a very long day."

The agent smiled and replied, "The first day on the job usually is. Have a good night, Mr. President."

President Cain stood up and walked out of the Oval Office, his head was still spinning from the conversation he just had with…thinking about it, he didn't even know who in the hell the man was. He had realized how everything had been planned for him. The letter in his pocket felt as if it weighed ten pounds. He was tired and now this. He stepped on the elevator that would take him to the residence upstairs. Ben had learned to be decisive in his political career. For the first time, he had no idea what in the hell he was going to do. He knew he was going to have to do something. He began to regain his composure. He made the first decision on how he was going to deal with this. He was going to go to bed, he was tired, and he never thought well when he was this tired. He would read the letter in the morning. Then he would try and figure out what in the hell all of this was about and how he was going to stop it.

The White House
The Oval Office
January 21, 2013
9:00 AM


President Cain walked down the same corridor toward the Oval Office that he had less than six hours before; there was a different Secret Service agent standing just outside the door. Ben looked over at him, "Good morning. How are you doing today?"

The agent was surprised. Most of them were arrogant and treated them like they were nonexistent, and he never let his surprise show. He replied, "Good morning, Mr. President. Fine. Thank you."

Ben stepped through the door the agent opened for him and stepped into what was now his office. They had told him the night before he could sleep in until 8:30. He knew from here on out it would be different. He sat down behind the desk. He was still tired from the night before. The letter was in his pocket still unopened; he felt the weight of it. He looked down on his desk; the schedule his chief of staff had prepared was there. Melissa, his assistant, who had been with him for longer than he cared to think, came in the door. She smiled at him as she carried in a cup of coffee and set it on his desk. "They told me there is a staff to take care of this for you. I told them I have brought you coffee every morning for almost the last twenty years and the first cup you were going to be served was by me."

Ben smiled at her and said, "Thank you, Melissa. What would I do without you?"

"Probably very well, Mr. President. I like the sound of that. Mr. President, that sounds better every time I say it. Now down to business. You have about fifteen minutes before your first meeting. The chief of staff will be in with the director of the Secret Service. You have the schedule for the rest of the day on your desk." She looked at her watch. "You have about ten minutes. Enjoy your coffee. You have a busy day." Melissa left him alone in the office.

Ben took a sip of his coffee and felt the weight of the letter in his pocket. The previous night seemed like a dream, maybe it had been and he then reached in his pocket and pulled out the letter. He looked at it, "45" prominently on the front. Ben took a deep breath and opened the envelope and slid out the letter. As he unfolded the sheet of paper, a series of photographs fell out on the desk; Ben reached down and picked them up. He was not prepared to see himself naked with a woman, also naked, on top of him. He quickly looked through the rest. More of the same, the last one showed a black lace thong sitting on the bed beside them. He put all of the photographs in the envelope. He closed his eyes for a long moment. The conversation with the unknown man replayed in his head. They had set him up. Ben remembered little of the night it happened; it seemed like a dream at the time. The one thing he remembered the next morning was finding the black lace thong on the floor and throwing it away. Now he knew why. He reached down and opened the letter.

# THE COMMITTEE

**THE WHITE HOUSE**
**WASHINGTON**
1600 Pennsylvania Avenue,
Washington DC

*President of the United States*

Congratulations, Mr. President, on running a successful campaign. By now I am confident that you have been contacted and have learned things are not always what you expect. Those that have put all of us in this office expect certain things. As I have been and you now are entrusted with this knowledge, you will understand it cannot be shared with anyone. You will soon find out who will be contacting you with the instructions you are required to carry out.

I can assure you my reaction to the letter my predecessor left for me was probably much like yours. This job, as you will find out, is not what everyone believes, you are now part of that knowledge. This information must never be shared with anyone.

Once again, Mr. President, I congratulate you on a well-run campaign. Things will progress quickly, and you will soon learn how to deal with all of it. I have faith you will execute the duties this office requires of you as well as can be expected. Trust me when I share with you to be prepared for other surprises. May God bless you as you struggle with this knowledge, as all of our predecessors surely must have as well. I will pray for you and this nation.

I will leave you with one final piece of advice: everything you say in this office and almost everywhere else you will be is known to those whom we owe our presence in this office. I am sure you understand why I am sharing this with you.

*The President of the United States*
*44*

Ben Cain was beyond being stunned. He folded the letter and put it with the photographs back in the envelope and slid it back in his pocket. He now had absolutely no idea how he was going to deal with the information he now had. He believed he was past the point of being shocked. He was not prepared for what was about to happen.

The door to his office opened and his chief of staff walked in. "Good morning, Mr. President."

Ben was suddenly brought back to the reality of his present situation. He was the president of the United States, and he had to act like one. He smiled at his chief of staff. He had been with Ben Cain since his days as a congressman. "Good morning, Craig. I hope you got more rest than I did."

"Probably not, Mr. President. We have a busy day. The first thing on the agenda is a quick meeting with the director of the Secret Service. Now that you have been sworn in, some of the agents of the protection details are going to change. He is going to introduce you to the new head of your protection detail as well as those of your wife and son. This shouldn't take long. Then we can move on to the rest of the schedule." The knock on the door stopped any further conversation. "There they are now." Craig walked over to the door and opened it and shook hands with all four of the men that walked in.

Ben Cain looked up and was incapable of standing for a long moment. He looked past his chief of staff and the director of the Secret Service, the third man following him in the office was the same one that was in this chair, in this office, when Ben walked in at a little after three this morning for the first time. He never remembered shaking hands with the director or being introduced to the other two. He never paid any attention to their names. The next thing Ben remembered was the director saying, "Mr. President, this is Supervisor Gene Everett. He is the head of protection for your son."

Supervisor Everett extended his hand toward the president who had just finished shaking hands with the director and the other two supervisory agents. He was trying as best he could to maintain his composure; he had no idea how the president had kept his. As they shook hands, their eyes met, "I am pleased to meet you, Mr. President."

The president continued a very firm handshake and looked Supervisor Everett straight in the eye. "You look very familiar to me. Are you sure we haven't met before?"

"I don't believe so, Mr. President. You have probably seen me on one of the details before."

"That's probably true. When we have a chance, I would very much like to have a talk with you about my son and his security."

"I'd like that, Mr. President." The message was clear. This president was tough as nails.

Craig Bennett stepped in and said, "Thank you, gentlemen, for coming in. I'm sure you will get to know each other." He ushered them out the door shut it and turned back to the president. For a moment, Craig stopped and looked; the president had a strange look on his face and seemed lost in thought. "Ben, are you okay?"

He looked at Craig and seemed to come back to the present. "Yes, I am, just a moment of reality of where we are and what we have to do." He smiled at his chief of staff.

Craig had no idea what his remark meant, somehow he knew there was something to it.

Aboard the *Quiet Time*
The Cayman Islands
July 25, 2013

Dan Oliver steered the *Quiet Time* away from the Harbor toward the open ocean. He had spent a couple of days taking on fuel and resupplying the *Quiet Time*. Everything was being billed to the Saudi prince; at least the rental agency thought that was who had been paying the bills. He had continued to maintain the three yachts and had sent them instructions where he wanted the *Quiet Time* for the prince's use. He had set Valerie up in a home he had purchased as a safe house, and courtesy of Jonah, there was plenty of security. Valerie was finally safe, and he hoped they wouldn't find her. He had owned the house for almost five years and had leased it out several times. The idea was to make it appear as normal as they could make it. He had used it as his base of operations several times as well.

He could no longer go back to the house; he wouldn't risk her being found. He knew they had the complete resources of all the intelligence agencies the government had to offer. The more he found, the more frightened he became. As he cleared the harbor, the increase in the swells told him he was almost clear of the breakwater. He was heading back to the United States. There was unfinished business to take care of. He was going to find a way to get to the president's father. That was going to be difficult. He highly suspected they were watching him as well. The one problem in getting Valerie out was that they now knew he was back on the trail. He never underestimated what they were capable of. He was willing to bet by now they knew he hadn't died in Atlanta. That had bought him enough time to uncover who was behind it. His clandestine meeting with August Braden had given him more reason to worry. When he had first told him what they were planning, he couldn't believe it. The more he thought about it, the more he realized they were capable of doing what Braden had told him. He had never found any evidence Braden had ever told anyone he was ever there.

Dan realized he had no choice, trying to disappear and living his life to its natural conclusion without having stopped them? He couldn't live with himself. The problem was he wasn't so sure he could stop them. The fact they knew he was still out here was going to make it that much more difficult. He missed Pam and Becky. He had never seen one of his grandchildren. Dan tried to fight back the tears; every once in a while what he was missing got to him. He didn't want his grandchildren to live in the world they were planning. That might cost him his life. He changed course of the *Quiet Time*. He was headed back, and he knew one way or another a resolution to this was going to happen. He could only pray it was going to go the way he wanted.

The Cain Home
Forrest Hills, New Jersey
August 30, 2013

Dan Oliver had driven by for the fourth time. He was doing his reconnaissance; this was a very upscale area, and the Cain home was one of the larger estates. For the better part of the last week, Dan had been studying the neighborhood and the surrounding area. He was trying to find a way to get to Edwin Cain without the security knowing about it. As far as he could tell, the Secret Service was not protecting the president's father; there was security. Some he was sure Edwin Cain didn't know about. His regular security was good, but they were obvious. They weren't the problem; Dan had spent a lot of time trying to find out just exactly who he was up against. What he had found hadn't surprised him; they were all former special forces or navy seals, the best of the best.

He had found that out when they had first shown up at the apartment in Richmond. He had taken the pictures his security system had sent out and found out who some of them were. That was one reason why he had to disappear and convince them he was dead. He knew he would never win against them in a head-to-head fight. He was badly outnumbered. He was going to have to outsmart them and that was going to be difficult.

He had found the weak part of the security; he could get in. Trying to convince Edwin Cain of what was going on without him raising the alarm and then getting out was the challenge. The plan was coming together; much as they had done with Valerie, they set routines. They were not expecting him, neither was Edwin Cain.

The car was parked down the street from the Cain's residence. Dan had guessed they didn't want to be so obvious to Edwin. The agent in the car regularly got out and walked past the Cain's home; the last time he had, Dan walked by and subtly sprayed the door handle. He had just as quickly kept walking and timed it so the agent never knew he had been there. Dan was watching as he opened the door and got back in the car. Fifteen minutes later, the compound he had sprayed on the door handle had been absorbed into his bloodstream, and he just went to sleep. He would be out long enough.

Dan had managed to cross the lawn without being seen and slip the pick in the basement door. The alarm hadn't been set. Edwin was still up. He had watched enough to know his routine. The risk was his wife; if luck was with him, she would be in bed. Dan had studied the house and quickly disabled the phone line and then the alarm. As quietly as he could, he slipped up the steps and angled the small mirror so he could see around the corner. The hallway was empty. Edwin's study was just off the main living room of the house. If he was true to his routine, he would come in the study before he went to bed. He managed to get inside without being seen. He stood against the wall beside the door and waited.

Edwin Cain was worried about his son. Even if he was president of the United States, he was still his son. Something had changed since he was sworn in. Ed didn't know what; he didn't think it was just the stress of the office. Ben was constantly on his mind, his mind occupied with worries about his son. Edwin walked back down the hallway, opened the door of his study, allowing it to close behind him, and sat down at his desk. He reached up to turn the desk lamp on and then reacted to the sight of the man leaning against the wall.

Dan Oliver said, "Hello, Ed. I need to talk with you about your son."

Ed's heart skipped a beat; he had been so distracted that he hadn't seen him when he walked in. He made no move; he just stood there. Ed's heart began to beat again. He began to breathe. "What the hell."

"I'm sorry to have gotten in like this. I couldn't just walk up and knock on the door."

"If all we are going to do is talk, why don't you have a seat?" *While I try to figure out how to deal with this man*, Edwin thought to himself.

Dan Oliver slowly breathed a sigh of relief. He was amazed at how calm the former governor was. He slowly stepped forward and sat down across the desk from the former governor and the father of the president who was now in his eighties. He kept his hands where Edwin could see them. "My name is Dan Oliver, I spent thirty years in the FBI. I have uncovered something…" Dan paused, not knowing how to continue.

Ed looked him straight in the eye. "Go on, there has to be more. You didn't break in here to stop now." Ed began to relax. He didn't know why; there was something in the way this man acted. His sixth sense was telling him this was an honorable man.

"No, I didn't. I just don't know where to begin. I have spent my career trying to do what I have always believed is right. There were too many investigations of corrupt politicians and money funneled out of the government, at least that's all I thought it was. Every time I was stopped. The investigations taken away. It couldn't have been coincidence. Then fourteen long years ago my daughter came home from college with a letter, written by James Madison. She found it in the library in some documents at the University of Virginia. My daughter is a very intelligent woman."

"Wait a minute. Let me stop for a moment. What does a letter written by James Madison, and I am assuming we are talking about the patriot and president. What does James Madison have to do with corrupt politicians and money funneled out of the government?"

"The letter is what made it all come together for me. The letter was written to his deceased friend Thomas Jefferson. He knew he was dead. I don't think he was as senile as is thought. He said, 'You are the only one who will understand,' and then he described a Committee they had set up." Dan paused, unsure how to go on. "He mentioned some names of the founders as he called them. George Washington among them. The purpose of the Committee was to select the leaders of this nation. He stated they didn't trust their own citizens to pick the type of leaders who would protect the freedoms they had sacrificed for. Then he asked God's forgiveness for what they had done and these words stay with me, 'Yet I fear they seek power never intended.' They were selecting the president of the United States. What I have uncovered scares the hell out of me."

Edwin was lost in thought for a long moment. It was as if a light had been turned on. The change in Ben. "My god, you're trying to tell me this Committee still exists."

Dan was unable to speak for a long moment. "It's far worse than that. They have controlled campaigns with millions of dollars, set up political action committees. They own the government of the United States." He looked down, took a deep breath, made eye contact with Edwin again, and continued, "They have designs far beyond that, and they are perfectly happy to destroy the United States to accomplish it."

Edwin was shaken to his core. It explained so much. His mind flashed back to when he was governor; all the things that seemed so improbable and unstoppable. "Are you trying to tell me you think Ben is part of this?"

Their eyes met. "I pray to God he isn't. If he is, there isn't a prayer of stopping them."

For several long moments, neither of them said anything. Then Edwin broke the silence. "There's more, let's have the rest."

Dan took a deep breath. "When was the last time you spoke to Valerie Hollis?"

Now it was Edwin's turn to take a deep breath. "My god, what does Valerie have to do with this? It's been thirty years. What the hell…"

"I found a small sum of money, at least by the amount they usually deal with. It was used to buy a condo in Naples, Florida. The owner is Valerie Jackson. She is really Valerie Hollis. I decided the only person with enough power to stop this is the president. It seemed to me so many of his predecessors were complicit. I needed to know what kind of man he really is. I tracked her down to ask. She told me what happened. They forced her to leave thirty years ago and then they tried to kill her after I found her."

Edwin was stunned. He knew something had changed; Ben was not acting like the son he knew. And then he got mad. "We are not going to let these bastards get away with this. You're right. The president is the only one with enough power to stop them, and I'm the one with enough access to get to him. Let me tell you what we are going to do." Edwin then told him just exactly what the plan was.

The agent sitting in the car outside Edwin Cain's home woke up; he looked at his watch. He had been asleep almost two hours. He picked up his cell phone; he hadn't missed any calls. He shook his head to clear it. He had never fallen asleep like that before. He got out, walked around, and checked out the area. Nothing. He made the decision to keep to himself he had fallen asleep. The chief of security was not forgiving; he vowed to himself that it would never happen again. He never knew Dan Oliver had walked by less than twenty minutes before, sprayed the neutralizer on the door handle, and then drifted into the night.

# THE COMMITTEE

The White House
Washington DC
November 28, 2013

The president was sitting at the head of the table. He looked slowly around and took in his family and close friends that were around this table enjoying Thanksgiving dinner. He tried to smile and act as if he were enjoying being with them. Normally he would be. The knowledge he now had wouldn't allow it. No matter the problems he had to deal with, and God knew there were enough of them, he never could get out of his mind of how they controlled him. It turned out it was the national security advisor with whom he met every single day that had told him what the Committee expected of him. What was never said was that his family was under their control and so was he. He smiled and said all the right things. He knew it was written on his face. Everyone thought it was the stress that came with the job; there was plenty of that. His wife, Marilyn, smiled at him; he smiled back. He found nothing that led him to believe she knew. The words that had been said never left his thoughts. "Even your wife was approved by the Committee." He had finally come to terms with that. Maybe she didn't know, but she had been put in his path and selected for him along with everything else.

Dinner was finished and they were reminiscing; his father caught his eye and motioned him over. "Son, let's you and I go take a walk around the grounds. I have always wanted to do that. The roses may not be in bloom, but I have often wanted to walk though them."

"Whatever you like, Dad." The two men left and slipped their jackets on. November in Washington could get cold. They were escorted by the usual crowd of Secret Service agents.

They walked outside and for a long few moments nothing was said; they continued around the grounds. Edwin moved closer to his son and slipped his arm around him. Ben never felt the letter his father slipped in the pocket of the overcoat, Edwin then said as quietly as he could, "I put a letter in your pocket. Read it when you are alone. Show it to no one and do what I have asked."

Ben tried not to react. His throat caught. For a long moment he couldn't speak. He said the first thing he could. "Okay. I love you, Dad." For some reason, he needed to tell his father that.

Edwin stopped and embraced his son. "You may be the president of the United States, but you are my son, and I love you too." The embrace ended, and they resumed their walk.

Ben Cain was back in the White House after the walk with his father. He had taken the letter from his overcoat pocket and slipped it in his back pocket. It had stayed there for the rest of the time with his family and everything else he had done. It might have been Thanksgiving Day, but the job of being president never ended. Ben finally managed to head upstairs to the residence at the end of another long day; he had waited until Marilyn had gone to bed. He was finally alone. He took the envelope from his pocket. His father had written "Happy Thanksgiving Ben" across the front. Ben opened it. It was a Thanksgiving card. When Ben opened it, a sheet of paper had been folded and slipped inside. He unfolded it and began to read.

# THE COMMITTEE

Ben,

I know what you are dealing with as president. I am not talking about the job and the stress that comes with it. I have recently come into knowledge of the situation you find yourself in. I am not at liberty at this point to tell you exactly what I know. Ben, trust me when I tell you I will deal with this. I want you to follow the instructions I have listed. First, talk to no one and tell no one of this letter. After you have read it, destroy it. Do exactly as I ask.

Take a piece of White House stationary and hand write a letter. Address it specifically to General Clayton Billingsley. He is commandant of the Marine Corps. He is a friend of Rodger Crawford, who, if you remember, retired from the Marine Corps and was my head of the New Jersey state police. Instruct him to carry out the request Rodger is going to discuss with him. Also advise him that Rodger is acting at your specific request and to discuss this with no one, no written records, e-mails, or government communication of any kind is to be used. It is also forbidden for him to use the chain of command, and the orders he receives from Rodger are to be acted upon as if they come from you. Also tell him the operation is considered of the highest priority and the security of the nation is at stake and no discussion is desired. I trust you will know how to write what needs to be said. Then sign it as president and commander in chief.

Ben, this is extremely important for you to do this exactly as I ask. After this is over, I pray with the grace of God we will be able to discuss how I came to be in possession of the information which led me to understand the situation you have found yourself in. Ben, know that I will do everything in my power to extract this nation from the direst circumstances it has faced since it's founding.

Do not write the letter until you can schedule a visit with me at home. It may be best to wait until Christmas. Also consider bringing the blank stationary and envelope here. We cannot risk it being discovered. Ben, please pray for this nation and what we must undertake. Know I am praying for you.

With all of my love,<br>Your father

Ben couldn't stop the tears that were flowing. His father had somehow found out. His prayers had been answered. He read the letter again and then once more; he committed the names to memory. After he was sure he understood exactly what his father wanted him to do, Ben walked over to the fireplace, ripped the letter his father had written into small pieces, and set it in the grate. He took the log lighter from the mantle and lit the paper. He stood and watched as it burned until the last of the embers had turned to ashes.

Ritz Carlton Resort
The Cayman Islands
January 3, 2014

Rodger Crawford sat back in the first class seat on the American Airlines flight. He hadn't planned on taking this trip; he wasn't here to take a vacation, but that was how it had to appear. He had even brought his golf clubs. He felt the aircraft bank; it brought him back to the present, his mind had been on the meeting he had with Edwin Cain less than a week ago. He had been invited to spend Christmas with the former governor and his family. He was not expecting the president to be there. He was even more surprised to have been asked to step into Edwin's study and then the president told the Secret Service agent his presence was not required. He had tried to object. The president had stood with his nose two inches from his and told him he had known Rodger his whole life and he by God was going to have a drink with him and his father, and if he needed him, he would let him know.

They had then gone in Edwin's study and had that drink. Edwin had reached down in his desk drawer and turned something on. It turned out it was a device to stop any eavesdropping. Even through the windows. Rodger was then surprised to see the president reach in his pocket and pull out blank White House stationary and begin to write a letter. Edwin had then told him what he needed him to do. That was why he was on this plane taking a trip that he hadn't planned.

He felt the thump as the pilot lowered the landing gear and a few moments later the bump as they touched down. The plane taxied to just outside the terminal, he watched as the stairway was pushed up to the door and the door opened. He left the plane and mingled with the flow of passengers to the terminal and passed through immigration. Thirty minutes later, he was on his way to the Ritz Carlton Resort where he would be staying. He was told by the driver that had been waiting for him that he was going to have a meeting to explain the rest of it to him. When he had asked who was meeting him, the response had been a laugh and "Don't worry. They'll find you."

When he had checked in, everything had been taken care of then he had been shown to a suite and had his entire luggage including his golf clubs taken to his room. Fifteen minutes later, the phone in the room had rung, and he was told his tee time had been scheduled. He was playing golf in the morning.

The next morning, Rodger woke up and took a long moment to realize where he was. Yesterday had seemed like a dream. He rolled out of the bed and slowly walked into the bathroom of his suite. He had been retired just short of twelve years. He had lost his wife five years ago and had not handled it well. He had a very hard time watching her lose the battle with Alzheimer's. He was not yet seventy, and he had never imagined living his retirement years without his Millie.

Edwin Cain had been one of the best friends he could have ever asked for and probably hadn't deserved. After Millie had died, Rodger had crawled into a bottle and tried to ease the pain. As he reached in to turn the shower on, Rodger recalled what Edwin had done. Rodger had woken up in a jail cell after getting stopped for a DUI. When he was taken in to be booked, the desk sergeant had realized who he was and knew how embarrassing it would be for the former head of the state police to be arrested and charged for DUI. The fortunate thing for all concerned was that there was no accident and he was by himself, and it hadn't become public knowledge. He had taken him to an isolation cell and kept him out of sight and called in some favors. The next morning he was put in the back of a state police cruiser and driven to Edwin's home. He stayed for a week and then Edwin had taken him to a private facility in Florida.

He owed Edwin more than he could ever repay. As he stepped into the shower and let the water run over him, Rodger knew that whatever he was asked to do for him he would. He finished his shower, grabbed the towel, and dried off. Fifteen minutes later there was a knock on his door and one of the bellmen came in, grabbed his clubs, and took him down to the lobby where another man escorted him to the pro shop at the Blue Tip Golf Club. His clubs were loaded onto a cart and he was pointed to the pro shop.

As he approached the counter, Rodger was greeted by name, "You must be Mr. Crawford. If you would just sign for the cart, you can go out to the practice green where I believe the gentleman you are paired with is. Enjoy your round."

"Thanks for all your courtesy." Rodger was amazed at just how much he was being taken care of. He was in for more than amazement.

He stepped out of the clubhouse and walked over to the putting green where a tall middle-aged man wearing shorts and a golf shirt with the logo of the Blue Tip Golf Club was stroking putts across the green. They were the only two there. Rodger walked over to introduce himself and waited while the man finished his putting stroke. The ball slowed and missed the cup by no more than six inches and stopped a foot past. The man then looked up and stuck out his hand "You must be Rodger. Edwin said good things about you." They shook hands and Rodger felt the almost crushing grip.

"Rodger Crawford and you are?"

"You can call me Dan." Dan Oliver quickly sized Rodger up and knew they had a lot in common. Edwin had told him about Rodger's wife and his bout with the bottle. Dan knew if it hadn't been for Pam, he might have done the same thing. Taking care of his daughter had spared him the same fate. "You may as well take a few putts. The greens are really fast. I'm ready whenever you are."

Rodger took a few putts and never rolled anything in; his mind really wasn't on the practice. "We may as well get started. I don't think any more practice will help." He walked over to the cart, dropped the putter in his bag, and sat down in the cart. Dan released the brake, turned the cart, and headed toward the first tee.

Rodger teed off first and to his surprise hit one right down the middle. Dan still hadn't said anything; he walked to the tee box, teed up the ball, and outdrove Rodger by twenty yards. "Nice shot, Dan."

# THE COMMITTEE

"Thanks" was all he got in reply as they both got in the cart. When they had driven about halfway to Rodger's ball, Dan finally broke his silence. "I understand you are friends with Clayton Billingsley?"

Rodger waited to gather his thoughts before he replied. All he really knew was that the president had written a letter, sealed it in an envelope, handed it to him, and thanked him. Edwin had then told him to not let it out of his sight. "Do not open it, and I hope you have a fine time in the Caymans."

"Clayton and I served together in the Corps. I did my twenty, got out, and went into law enforcement. He stayed in and did rather well."

"That's not quite accurate. Clayton served under you and was your junior when you were a battalion commander. It is true he stayed in and did rather well. I also understand you and he have remained close through the years."

Rodger looked Dan in the eye as he stopped the cart by Rodger's ball. "You obviously know a great deal."

"Your shot. I outdrove you."

Rodger reached for a club, walked up, hit the ball without really thinking about it, and got in the cart. Dan drove up to his ball, took a club from his bag, and quickly stroked the ball toward the green. He got back in the cart and took up the conversation right where it had left off. "You were given a letter by the president. What he wants you to do with it is deliver it to Clayton for him when you get back."

"If you don't mind me asking, couldn't the president deliver it himself? Clayton is the commandant of the Marine Corps. In a manner of speaking, he works for the president."

They had reached the green. Dan parked the cart on the path, reached for his putter, and walked to the green. "That was a nice shot. You're on in two and I'm out." He walked over to the flag, pulled it out of the cup, and dropped it away from the hole and proceeded to line up his putt.

Rodger's head was still spinning with everything, and he watched as Dan took a practice stroke and then went ahead and took the putt. The ball went past the hole by no more than six inches. He tapped it in and waited while Rodger lined up his putt and then knocked it four feet past. He dropped in the next one then pulled the ball out of the hole and waited while Dan put the flag back in. They both teed off before the conversation resumed.

"I understand you held a rather high security clearance before you retired. You should understand there are certain things that need to be done that can't go through normal channels and chains of command. This has to be kept quieter than anything, and I mean anything ever has been before. What I am about to share with you will get all of us killed if any of it leaks. This is how the president is going to deal with this. The letter you were given instructs General Billingsley on what the president wants done. It's important you can look at him and tell him how you got it, directly from the president. There can be no communication between them directly."

They continued playing, and Rodger's mind was not on playing golf. "What exactly is this about?"

"Rodger, the entire government of the United States has been compromised. Even the office of the president is compromised."

Rodger couldn't take in what he was being told. "When you say compromised, are you trying to tell me the president isn't in control?"

"In a manner of speaking, no, he isn't. Rodger, it's time you found out just exactly what is going on. There is a group of men who have worked tirelessly for a long time to gain control of the government. We are going to stop them, you are going to meet General Billingsley give him that letter and the other information I am going to give you. He is going to conduct an operation at the orders of the president."

They had played all nine holes, Rodger still wasn't aware of playing most of them. "How much are you going to tell me?"

They walked slowly off the green toward the cart. "As little as I can. Enough to get you killed if they find out. There will be a car to take you on a tour of the island tomorrow. We will finish our conversation then, and you'll get the information for General Billingsley. By the way, nice round. You shot a forty-five."

Rodger got out of the cart then turned to say something to Dan; he was gone. He never saw him leave; he just seemed to disappear. Rodger shook his head and walked toward the clubhouse. This was getting stranger by the moment. If he hadn't met with Edwin Cain and his son who was the president of the United States, who then handed him a sealed letter that he had personally seen him write, Rodger would never believe this was really happening to him.

The Ritz Carlton Resort
The Cayman Islands
January 4, 2014

Rodger had just stepped into the lobby and walked toward the front entrance when the bell captain intercepted him and said, "Your driver is waiting for you. I hope you have a nice tour of the island, and please let me know of anything you require."

"Thank you. I can't think of a thing at the moment." He had then escorted Rodger to the car that was waiting for him and opened the rear door. Rodger got in.

The car pulled away from the hotel and his driver still had yet to say anything. Rodger just waited. Ten minutes later, the driver finally broke the silence. "I am going to show you a few of the sights. It would look funny if we don't actually tour the island. One of the things we are going to do is go to the Tortuga Rum Factory and take the tour. When the guide asks if you dropped your wallet, look for it and acknowledge that you have. Then follow the security guard who will escort you. Then do what he tells you." They stopped several times, and Rodger got to see the sights and never remembered any of them. An hour or so later, they pulled into the Tortuga Rum Factory, and the driver asked Rodger to give him his wallet. "Give me your wallet. Don't worry, you'll get it back." Rodger handed it to him and then they got out of the car and went in.

They walked into a reception area where there was a small group of tourists milling about waiting for the tour to start. The tour guide looked at her watch and began the welcome. "Thank all of you for visiting with us today. We will begin the tour shortly. First let me remind you this is a working factory so please use caution." Rodger never paid attention to the rest of the speech and the tour began. When they got to the bottling area, a security guard walked up to the tour guide said something, and they both approached Rodger. "Excuse me, sir, you didn't happen to have dropped your wallet by chance, did you?"

Rodger felt around and checked his pockets. "Oh, I must have. I can't seem to find it."

"One has been turned in to security, and the guard thought he recognized you from the picture on your ID. If you would go with him to security, they will return it to you."

"Thank you. I don't know what I would do if someone hadn't found it." Rodger followed the security guard to a small office. When he walked in, the guard never followed just shut the door behind him. Rodger was stunned when he walked in. he could have been looking at his double.

"We only have a couple of minutes. We need to change jackets. The rest of the outfit will pass." He then handed his jacket to Rodger who took his off and handed it to him. The man was dressed identically to Rodger. He then handed him his wallet. "Wait here while I rejoin the tour." He left Rodger alone in the office. A couple of minutes later, the door opened and another security guard came in, handed Rodger a hat, and said, "Follow me."

They left the office, and he led Rodger to a box truck with the Tortuga Rum logo clearly displayed on the side. "Get in" was all he said.

Rodger stepped up into the cab and settled into the passenger seat. The driver never said a word, just started the truck, and pulled out of the loading dock and onto the street. Ten minutes later, he stopped at a warehouse where a large roll-up door was raised, and they pulled inside. The driver still never said anything to him. Rodger's door was opened, and a man motioned for him to get out. He was led though the building to where a car was sitting by another smaller garage door. The man opened the back door of the car, and Rodger got in. He looked at the driver in surprise. The man he had played golf with the day before was behind the wheel.

"Hello, Rodger." He started the car as the door was opened, and he pulled out into the traffic. Nothing else was said for the rest of the ride. Rodger just sat back and waited. Twenty or so minutes later, they drove into a small private marina where a security guard walked out of the small guard shack, looked at the driver, and raised the barrier to let them pass. The car was parked in a parking lot right across from the dock where a variety of yachts were moored. "Let's go" was all he said to Rodger.

Rodger followed him to the very end of the dock where a yacht named the *Quiet Time* was tied up. He stepped aboard as Dan went up to top of the cabin and started the engines. Roger could smell the diesel exhaust as Dan went down and loosened the lines. Apparently, they were going to sea.

Thirty minutes later, Dan pulled the throttles back to idle as they entered a small inlet, Rodger felt the boat come to a stop. He had never been on anything larger than a small fishing boat and never anything like this. He was fascinated with watching Dan set the anchor and shut the engines down.

Dan motioned for Rodger to follow him as he went below to the main cabin. He walked over to the refrigerator and pulled out a couple of bottles of water. He tossed one to Rodger and said, "Have a seat."

Rodger sat down across the table from Dan. "Rodger, I'm sorry to have put you through all this just so we can talk. I need to tell you everything I can. We don't have much time. I can't take the risk on being followed."

Rodger shook his head and said, "I'm still trying to figure out why the president or his father just didn't tell me what they wanted me to do."

"Let me explain as best I can. Fourteen years ago my daughter came home from college with a letter written by President Madison sometime in the later years of his life. I was in the FBI for thirty years. I was the expert at tracking down money and was stopped more times than I can count when there was no good reason to shut me down. My notes, files, everything was taken, then I was told that I was no longer on the case. It happened every time I was investigating government corruption involving defense contractors overbilling or corrupt politicians funneling money out of their campaigns. I started keeping separate files they didn't know I had."

Rodger held up his hand to stop him. "Slow down. You just said your daughter found a letter written by President Madison. What in the hell does that have to do with government corruption and the government and the president being compromised?"

Dan stood up and said, "Let me show you a transcript of the letter. That's what put some things in perspective for me." Dan went to one of the cabins and returned with a file folder a few minutes later. He opened it, took out a sheet of paper, and handed it to Rodger.

# THE COMMITTEE

My dearest Thomas,

As I write these lines to you, I realize you will never read them. Many years have gone by since you have passed, and I became the last to carry on. You are the only one who will understand the burdens we carried so long. The chairmanship passed to me when you were taken from this world, and I have tried to live by the principles with which we founded this nation. I fear as time passes those to whom we entrusted positions on the committee will no longer abide by the guiding principles of faith the founders sought to live by.

I know you and I shared the same self-doubts if we were right to form the committee. Our purposes noble and our intentions honorable, we did not trust our citizens to make the right decisions of leadership this nation has needed. We chose to implement our will by choosing who those leaders would be. Those of us who fought to bring this nation forth may have understood our concern for those Americans who were never willing to fight for their principles of faith, freedom, and liberty. Yet these have been our guiding light. I fear it will not always be so to those who follow. We have given them the power to decide the fate of this nation. As the years passed and we lost the original members of the Committee, General Washington, Samuel Patterson, Jonathan who sacrificed so much, all the others, to Alexander who was struck down by the madman Burr. I am the last, and the power has passed to those that we chose. I pray we have chosen wisely, and I fear we have not. The course they choose will determine the fate and freedoms we cherished and sacrificed to provide yet may be the cause of their demise. I will answer for my sins of this world when I meet our creator. It may not be far in the future for me now. They have set me aside and treat me with respect, yet I fear they seek power never intended. May God forgive us for what we have sown, and I pray what we feared shall not come to pass. I am powerless to stop them. History will tell what our decisions have wrought. May God forgive us and bless this nation and protect it from the committee with which we so inadvertently burdened it.

James

Rodger read the words James Madison had penned so long ago. He read it again, stunned at what he was finally beginning to understand. He looked up into the face of Dan Oliver. "This Committee they started still exits and is controlling the government of the United States?"

Dan smiled at Rodger. "I have the original of that letter. That brought it all together for me. At that point I knew they were out there. I have spent the last fourteen years tracking them down. I know who all of them are. They have tried to kill me several times. I finally convinced them I had died, that meant I have had to disappear. Unfortunately, they now know I am alive. Some things I am not going to share with you. I will tell you my original plan was to kill them one by one. I then figured out I couldn't do it fast enough to stop them, and they would know I was coming after them. The only person with enough power to do it is the president. I had to find out if this one could be trusted. It seemed to me so many of his predecessors were in on it. I started digging into the president's past. Everything I found out told me he was a good man. That told me somehow they were controlling him. I couldn't just walk up to the White House and ask to speak with him. That left me trying to figure out how to get to him. That's when I realized his father was the only way. Edwin was the one who figured out the only way to bring them down. The problem is they know everything that happens, even in the Oval Office. That's why the president had to write the letter for you to give General Billingsley. They control virtually every government agency, even most of the Pentagon. I checked out General Billingsley and found out he's not very popular among the rest of the joint chiefs. I know he isn't part of this."

Rodger handed the letter back to Dan. "Now I understand why the president can't just call Clayton in for a meeting and tell him what he wants done. Anything he does they know."

Dan smiled at him. "Rodger, I think you are finally beginning to understand. I don't have time to go into everything, and there is a whole lot more. They all have to be rolled up at once. That is going to take a lot of assets I just don't have. Tracking them down is one thing, taking them down is something else. I also know they have their own resources that are looking for me and do other things for them. I haven't yet figured out where they are. I do know who some of them are. Let's just say they are the very best at what they do. I have been extremely lucky so far."

"What you want me to do is contact Clayton, give him the letter the president wrote, and let him take them down."

Dan handed Rodger a flash drive. "Give him this. It has everything on it and will explain it to him. The president's letter gives him the authorization. Tell him to buy a new computer. Do not hook it up to the Internet and do not put anything else on it or use it for anything else. If the information on that gets into the wrong hands, the consequences will be disastrous. No e-mails, no telephone conversations, nothing written. They will know if he does. Now you know why it is so important you can tell him you got that letter directly from the hand of the president."

Rodger met the eyes of Dan Oliver; they said far more about what he had been through than Dan would ever tell him.

Fort Bragg
North Carolina
January 5, 2014

He moved the mouse until the cursor was over the area just off the coast of Naples, Florida. He clicked the mouse and the image began to grow larger. Ron Cole was sill hunting for Valerie, and he highly suspected Dan Oliver. He had never believed the former FBI agent had died in Atlanta. He had never stopped hunting for him; the trail had gone cold after Atlanta. Until July of last year, Valerie had disappeared, and he had lost an agent. That was unacceptable. He had been trying to find them since then. He was reviewing the satellite imagery. Somehow he had gotten her out of Naples; her car was still there. He had checked everything he could; it had taken months to run everything down. They hadn't left by any method of public transportation. He hadn't expected they would. The problem was he didn't have direct access to the satellites; he could get access to anything he wanted to look at. It just wasn't real time. He had already reviewed everything on the land around the condo. That was how he had found where they had pushed the car in the river. He had found where the jeep had been left. What he couldn't find was how he had gotten out. Last week he realized the one thing he hadn't looked for, a boat.

The image began to grow larger; there it was another yacht he had to check out. He had been at this every spare minute he had. Over the last six months, that wasn't much; that's why it was taking him so long. This was personal; he was going to find them. The image he was looking at was the morning after they had disappeared. He had checked everything that was in the area. There were two people on the deck of the yacht, a man and a woman; he zoomed in closer. There wasn't much doubt it was her. The resolution wasn't good enough to print out, but it was good enough to tell. Now he knew how he had gotten not only her but himself out. Now all he had to do was find out where they had gone, he moved the cursor again. He began to zoom as much as he could on the stern of the yacht. He enhanced the resolution as much as he could; there it was, the *Quiet Time*. Now all he had to do was find out where it had been and where it was now. It would take some time, but not as much time as it had taken to find him. He was going to find them both; they were too close now to let them interfere. What he was trying to figure out was why he had tracked Valerie down. There was only one reason and that was the president. How could she help him with that? They had the president contained just as they had all of them. His job was to figure it out and he would, just like he always had. He had business first; he would kill both of them. After that, it wouldn't matter.

The Pentagon
Washington DC
January 10, 2014

The phone on his desk ringing broke General Billingsley's train of thought. He picked it up and answered. He was not much on formality; only a few friends had this number. "Hello."

"Got any more new war stories? I not only have heard all of them, I was with you for most of them."

# THE COMMITTEE

"Rodger, what in the hell are you up to?" He recognized his old friend's voice. "The last I heard you were retired and spending all of your time fishing and playing golf."

"Yeah, and I am bored out of my mind. I was in town and thought you might buy me lunch."

Clayton laughed. He knew about Rodger's problem with the bottle after he had lost his wife. He had been one of his only friends left; all the others had run away for fear of it damaging their careers. Clayton didn't care; he knew this was the last stop for him. He had been one of the few who had tried to help. "What the hell, why not. It's Friday and I'm not going to finish this anyway." He looked at his watch; it was four thirty. "Lunch. Rodger, you realize its four thirty?"

"I can tell time Clayton. I figured you would be too busy today. I thought maybe tomorrow?"

"Tell you what, how about meeting me tonight for dinner? The wife is out of town, and I really don't want to fend for myself tonight. Seven work for you?"

"Yeah, and I'll tell you what. I will even pick you up. I assume you will be working until then."

"Unfortunately. I'll tell them downstairs, and they will pass you in, no farther than the lobby. I will meet you there."

"See you then. Since you're paying, you can choose where." The phone clicked. Rodger had hung up.

Clayton laughed again. *Just like him to give me orders and then hang up so I can't argue.* He turned his attention back to the papers on his desk.

Two and a half hours later, Clayton heard the phone buzz again, it was his assistant calling to tell him a Colonel Crawford was in the lobby waiting for him. He chuckled to himself; it really was true. "Once a marine, always a marine." Even when you retired, they always used your rank. Clayton stood up, put all the paperwork in the desk, and locked it. He took his tunic from the back of his chair, slipped it on, and buttoned it. He picked up his headgear; he still thought of it that way, tucked it in the crook of his arm and left his office to meet Rodger in the lobby.

Rodger was waiting for him in the lobby, talking to one of the young marines standing just inside the doors. Clayton shook his head; even now Rodger still had an air about him that the troops respected. He walked over to him and waited while they finished their conversation and surprising him not at all as soon as they stepped outside, put on their headgear the young Marine Saluted them and Rodger returned it.

"I don't think you're supposed to do that, Rodger. You're not in the corps anymore."

"Kiss my ass, Clayton. Maybe you've heard once a Marine always a Marine."

Clayton couldn't stop himself from laughing. "You are probably the only one with enough balls to tell me that. How in the hell are you, Rodger?" The handshake turned into a quick embrace that just as quickly ended. "Come on, let's get out of here. I have had enough bullshit today."

They left the Pentagon and walked toward the visitor's parking lot. Rodger led him toward his car, unlocked the doors with his clicker, they got in and left.

"Tell me where we can get a good steak. A nice and expensive steak since you're buying."

"You really are going to make me buy, aren't you?"

Now it was Rodgers turn to laugh. "Hell yes. I'm retired, remember?"

"In that case, how about Ruth's Chris? You can get a good steak, and I get a healthy dinner check."

"Okay, that works, but first we need to talk where we can't be heard, and this car is secure." Rodger's voice changed, and Clayton picked up on it.

"This isn't just a social call then." Clayton was as serious as Rodger had been.

"I wish it were, Clayton. There is a briefcase on the seat beside me. Here is the key, open it." He reached in his jacket pocket and produced a key and handed it to him.

Clayton took the key and began to wonder what the hell was going on. He opened the briefcase.

"Clayton, inside you will find an envelope with a letter inside on White House stationary. I received that directly from the hand of the president. I was sitting in his father's study and watched him write it. Just so you know how important this is."

Clayton took the letter from the briefcase; he was now surprised and intrigued. He had no idea what was going on. "Rodger, if you don't mind me asking, why in the hell are you delivering a letter from the president?"

"That's exactly what I asked when I was told to deliver it. Clayton, I don't know what the letter says. I do know what it's about. I was invited to Edwin's for Christmas. We went into his study for a drink. The Secret Service agent was going to go in with us. The president walked up to him, stood two inches from his face, and in a voice that would have done a DI proud, told him he had known me all of his life and he was going in the study with his father and me and have a drink. 'You are not invited, and if I need you, I'll let you know'. When we went into the study, Edwin turned on a device that prevented any type of electronic surveillance. The president then sat down at his father's desk and pulled the stationary from his pocket and wrote the letter that is now in your hands. It has not been out of my possession since then."

Clayton took the envelope that bore the White House address and the seal of the president and opened it. He took out two sheets of White House stationary; he began to read the top letter.

**THE WHITE HOUSE**
**WASHINGTON**
1600 Pennsylvania Avenue,
Washington DC

General Billingsley,

You will be receiving additional information from Colonel Crawford with whom I know you are friends. As you know, he worked for my father as well. There is to be no direct communication between you and I. Any information is to go through Rodger. Use of any government communication of any type or any phone or e-mail of any type is expressly forbidden. All orders you issue in regard to this are to be verbal only and no written orders or communication is permitted. I cannot stress how important this is. The office of the president has been compromised along with virtually all of the government. There is a group of men behind this, and it is my intention to prevent them from destroying this great nation and gaining control of the government of the United States.

I know you have many questions, the additional information you will be receiving from Colonel Crawford will explain in much more detail than I can. I am ordering you to conduct an operation to take into custody those responsible for this. This is to be done as quickly and as discreetly as possible. You are authorized to use any assets at your disposal. It is expressly forbidden to divulge any information or knowledge of what you have been ordered to do to any member of the command structure of the United States

## THE COMMITTEE

THE WHITE HOUSE
WASHINGTON
1600 Pennsylvania Avenue,
Washington DC

military. I urge you to keep the rank of those you order to conduct this operation to be captain or lower. Do not tell them under any circumstances why this is being done. If any of this is leaked, the consequences will be disastrous. The very existence of this nation is at stake. I have included another letter giving you authority to issue orders to any member of the United States military and that you are conducting an operation directly under my authority.

General, I am placing a great deal of faith and trust in you. I know that we share a love of this great nation, and the task you have been given is of the utmost importance and may be the only thing that is the salvation of this nation. No discussion of this is desired. May God bless you in this endeavor. I will pray for you.

*Bennett Arthur Cain*
*President of the United States*

General Clayton Billingsley, commandant of the United States Marine Corps, read the letter from the president of the United States. He read it twice more to make sure he understood; he then folded the letter and slid it back in the envelope. He looked over at Rodger. "What in the hell is this about, and how in the hell did you get involved in this?"

Rodger pulled the car to the curb and stopped. "General, let me tell you I was as stunned as you are. There is a zip drive in the briefcase; it has the rest of the information on it. Do not put it in any government computer or any computer that is connected to the Internet. I was told to tell you to buy a new computer and use it for nothing but this. Thinking about it, I wouldn't take it to the office. For that matter, I'm not sure I would keep it at home either."

"You still haven't answered my question, how did you get involved with this?"

Rodger looked his friend in the eye. "I will tell you this. I met the guy that tracked them down. That's where I got the zip drive from. He is a former FBI agent, spent thirty years there. It took him fourteen years to track them down. I can't begin to tell you how many times they tried to kill him. He even staged his own death. The way he put it to me was he was going to kill them one by one and realized it wouldn't stop them. He then told me the only person with the power to roll them all up at once was the president. He's right. The problem is he knew the president was compromised. They know everything. He couldn't just walk up to the White House and say I need to talk to the president. He got to the president's father. That's how I got involved. Obviously they know everything that goes on in the White House. Hell, they know damn near everything. If they figure out what were up to, needless to say, they will come after us."

Clayton Billingsley, commandant of the United States Marine Corps, folded the letter, put it back in the envelope, and slid it in his pocket. He took the flash drive from the briefcase and slid that in his pocket. He was a marine. He had his orders, and he was going to carry them out. He looked over at Roger. "Let's go get that steak." He didn't say what he was thinking; every condemned man gets a last meal.

# THE COMMITTEE

Walmart
Alexandria, Virginia
January 12, 2014

    Clayton Billingsley was strolling down the electronics aisle looking at laptops; he understood why he had been told to buy a new computer and use it for nothing but this. He was one of the few who really understood just how much the government surveillance could find out. Every e-mail, web search, text message, phone call, virtually anything you did electronically could be monitored. He was going to have to disable and remove the wireless modem before he even turned on the computer. He selected the laptop he wanted, got the clerk to get it out for him, and paid him for it in the electronics department. The clerk taped the receipt to the box with tape bearing the Walmart logo, handed it to him, and said, "Just so they know that you paid for it, sir. Thank you for shopping at Walmart." He set it in the shopping cart and went into the sporting goods department. He had some other purchases to make. He also wanted to make sure the computer wasn't the only thing he left the store with. He didn't want anyone to know what he was up to.

    He left the store and pushed the cart to his wife's car, unloaded his purchases in the trunk, closed it, then pushed the cart to the return with the others. Walking back to his wife's car, he hit the clicker, unlocked the doors and got in. He then left the parking lot; Clayton had a lot on his mind. He wasn't popular with the other members of the joint chiefs; after his meeting with Rodger, he began to gain an understanding of why. There were things that happened that he never understood why the rest of them weren't as pissed off about as he was.

    Clayton had debated where he was going to go with his new computer and the flash drive. He needed a place that was first secure. It also had to be close to his home, most importantly, he needed a reason to go there that wouldn't draw any suspicion. The answer had hit him yesterday. Larry Fitzgerald, a close friend of his that had been forced to take a medical retirement after the first Gulf War. He had been a major under Clayton's command. In the first few days after they had crossed into Iraq, the Humvee he had been in hit a landmine. It flipped over and both the driver and the gunner were killed. Larry had survived, but he had lost both legs below the knees and had severe burns. He and Clayton had been friends long before that and Larry's wife had left him just before the deployment to Iraq. His parents were dead, and Larry had nothing to come home to. He had been in Bethesda for months; when he was finally released, Clayton had taken him in. He had struggled with all the issues you would expect someone to have who had lost both legs, his career, and almost his life.

He had finally worked his way through them and decided his life wasn't over. He was now the CEO of a private security firm. They specialized in discrete security for those that needed it and didn't want it to be obvious. One of the things Larry did was to hire a lot of former special operators and marines. He was one of the few people Clayton trusted. They had long conversations over the years and both of them felt something was going on within the government. Too many things he had seen during his career hadn't seemed quite right. Larry was the one person he had confided in that agreed with him. More importantly, because of what he did, Larry kept his home as secure as any private residence could be. He provided security to a lot of people the terrorists and just about every other group of bad guys would like to see dead. Larry was on their list as well. He was known to visit here occasionally; it wouldn't draw any suspicion, which was important.

Thirty minutes later, Clayton pulled up to the gate of the estate Larry owned. There were double gates with a speaker at the first set. Clayton knew the rest of the security wasn't visible, the second set of gates were twenty-five yards ahead around a curve in the drive way and there was a ten-foot-high wrought iron fence along both sides of the drive. Unless you knew they were there and that there was a security team on duty, you would never see them. He pressed the button on the speaker and waited for the voice to come over. Two seconds later, the voice answered. He told the voice he was General Clayton Billingsley. He was on the list. He drove through when the gate slid open and stopped at the second set. The guard at the second set of gates approached the car and recognized Clayton. "Good afternoon, General. It's good to see you. The boss is expecting you. I'll let them know you're here." He stepped back from the car and spoke into a

# THE COMMITTEE

handheld radio and the second gate opened. Clayton drove through and then proceeded the last hundred yards to the circular drive in front of the tasteful yet really modest home of his friend.

Clayton opened the car door, got out, and went around to the trunk. Opening it, he removed the box with the laptop and shut the trunk. Before he could get to the front door, it was opened and one of Larry's security team was waiting for him just outside the front door. "Good afternoon, General."

"How are you doing, Tony? It's good to see you."

"Doing fine, sir. The major is in the study. I'll escort you there, sir."

"I know the way, Tony. Thanks." Clayton was not surprised with the military ranks they used. All of them had been in the service, and it was second nature for them. Tony escorted him to the study where retired USMC Major Larry Fitzgerald was sitting in his recliner with a large cigar clenched in his teeth and a bottle of Jack Daniels sitting on the table beside him.

"Pardon me if I don't get up, Clayton. I left my legs off for a while." He pointed to his prosthetic legs on the floor beside him. "What do I owe the honor? I haven't seen you in a while."

"I just happened to be out doing some shopping and was close. I thought I would drop by and see how you were doing."

Larry laughed. "Bullshit, General, if you don't mind me saying so. Walmart, really?" He pointed to the computer box with the Walmart logo on the tape holding the receipt to the box. "If I can be so bold as to ask, what in the hell do you need a computer from Walmart for? Is the marines budget that bad?"

Clayton was deadly serious when he replied. "Larry, are we secure?"

All the levity was just as suddenly gone from Larry's voice as well. "Yes, but give me a minute to double check." He reached in the pocket of the vest he was wearing and pulled out a small device similar to an iPhone, just slightly larger. He tapped the button on the side, entered a password, and slid his finger across the screen. A few more finger strokes on the screen, he tapped the button again and put the device back in his pocket. "All right, Clayton. I even turned on the device to prevent our conversation from being picked up by any electronic surveillance. This stuff is even better than what the NSA uses. Nobody else has it. You know I don't trust the bastards."

Clayton reached in his pocket and pulled out the envelope with the letter from the president. He handed it to Larry and never said a word. Larry took the letter, raised his eyebrows when he saw the seal of the president, and began to read the letter. He read it again and then a third time. He folded it up, put it back in the envelope, and handed it back to Clayton. "So we have been right all along."

For a long moment neither of them said anything. Larry was the first to break the silence. "You're going to need my help. You can't do this by yourself."

"Yeah, I know. The problem is if I can't pull this off, a lot of people are going to get killed. I don't like to think what's going to go wrong."

"Okay, what we have suspected for a long time is true. Now tell me the rest."

"Larry, do you remember Rodger Crawford?"

"Yeah, I know you and he are friends. He did his twenty and got out. That was before Reagan was elected and fixed a lot of the mess. A lot of good guys got passed over for promotion and decided to hang it up. I was a very junior and brand-new lieutenant."

"He came to see me Friday. We had dinner. I thought that's all it was going to be. Let's just say I was surprised as hell when we got in his car and he told me we had to talk and it was secure. He pulled out that letter and told me how he got it directly from the hand of the president. He was invited to the president's father over Christmas."

"Wait a minute. The president's father was the governor of New Jersey, I'd forgotten that."

"That's right, Rodger was head of the state police for him. Let me tell you what little I know. Somehow some retired FBI guy figured all this out. He got to the president's father. When he invited Rodger for Christmas, the president and his father took him into his study to have a drink. The president sat down, wrote that letter and handed it to Rodger. Rodger told me he got that directly from the president, it was never out of his possession. Somehow Rodger met the guy, the FBI guy, who figured this out. He gave him a flash drive that spells out the whole thing. I haven't looked at it yet." He reached in his pocket and pulled it out. "Rodger then told me to buy a new computer, don't use it for anything else, and don't hook it up to the Internet."

"Well now at least I know why you went to Walmart. Whoever this guy is, he's right. Anything and I mean anything you do on the Internet, or even if you are hooked up, if they want to look in your computer they can. Every text message, every phone call, every e-mail, and I mean anything electronic can be accessed. Hell, I'm not telling you anything you don't know. You are on the joint chiefs after all."

"That's why I believe all this. We have both suspected for a long time there was something going on. I just wouldn't have believed it could go that far. I haven't even looked at the stuff on this yet." Clayton held up the flash drive.

"Well, fire up your new computer. Wait, before you do, take out the modem then we can disable any Wi-Fi. Then we can take a look at that and figure out how we are going to deal with this."

"Larry, I don't want to drag you into this. I have my orders from the president."

Larry held up his hand to stop him. "I may have been medically retired from the corp, but I took the same oath you did to protect this nation against all enemies both foreign and domestic. Besides, maybe you've heard. Once a marine, always a marine. Now open the damned box and let's get started."

The Fitzgerald Home
Alexandria, Virginia
January 12, 2014

Clayton Billingsley plugged in the new laptop from Walmart. As it booted up, his mind began to think about just how he was going to comply with his orders. It was the first time in his career he had absolutely no idea how he was going to do what he had been ordered. He finished setting up the computer and slid the flash drive in. The icon came up and he hit enter. The file opened. Larry, who had put his legs on, as he called it, was sitting beside him. The first thing that came up was an outline menu of what was on the drive. They quickly read through it. "This guy did his homework. Look at this. He's got it broken down into categories. Let's look at the money from the defense contractors."

Thirty minutes later after they had read through the documents in the section of defense contractors, Clayton couldn't believe what he had read. Billions of dollars funneled off from virtually every major contractor the defense department dealt with. Larry was the first to comment. "This goes back to World War II. Jesus, just how much have they funneled off?"

Clayton was silently furious; he saw just how much money had been funneled off, they had only looked at selected files. "How many of our marines, not to mention the other branches men, died because they didn't get what they should have?"

Larry was just as amazed and just as mad. "Get out of that and let's look at something else. I may be tempted to kill these guys myself."

Clayton went back and looked at the menu; he moved the cursor down and saw a document titled the Madison letter. He clicked on it. The letter James Madison had written a hundred and eighty years ago appeared on the screen. There was a copy of the original and then a transcript. Under it was a notation of where and when it had been found in the archives of the University of Virginia. It was followed by a single line that said, "This is what set me on the search." They both read the letter. They both were stunned.

"My god, this goes back even further than you can imagine." Larry looked at Clayton.

"Yeah, it does, but read that line, 'I fear they seek power never intended.' He knew then, and he said he was powerless to stop it. I have to agree with him. When he said they never trusted the American people, no, on second thought, I realize that makes me as bad as the bastards we have to stop."

"Clayton, go back. Look at the menu again, I think we have seen enough to know what they are doing. Go to the list of those responsible. He certainly called it the way it is. The more of this I see, the more I'm beginning to like this guy, whoever he is."

Clayton clicked on the file. There was a list of names, one in particular jumped out at him. There it was number three on the list

# THE COMMITTEE

August Braden, chairman of the board of McAllister Halstead, one of the largest defense contractors in the nation. They looked at each other; the evidence was irrefutable and there was no doubt. "Jesus, just look at the names on this list. Talk about the fortune 500."

They continued looking at everything in the file. "Clayton, pull up the file with the pictures of the teams of agents."

"Here it is. These look like they were taken by some sort of security camera. The enhancement is good. That must be one hell of a security system."

"Go back one image. Enlarge it. Jesus, I've seen that guy." Larry reached in his pocket, pulled out his device, then went through the sequence to activate it. "Let me get Tony in here. He may know." He tapped a message on the screen.

Tony walked in the door. "You sent for me, boss?"

"Tony, take a look at the picture on the screen. I've seen that guy somewhere. I can't remember where. Maybe you know."

Tony walked around behind them and looked at the screen. "Master Sergeant Al Stanton, Delta Force. He was thrown out after Kosovo. If what he was doing hadn't been black ops, he would have been up for a general court. Sometimes guys like him never made it back from black ops. The rest of the team would take care of it in the field. If you remember, we interviewed him. I did his background, and we never went any further. Somebody must have intervened on his behalf or he probably would have been made to disappear. What else do you want to know?"

"Tony, how in the hell do you remember all that?" Larry smiled and shook his head in amazement.

"It's what you pay me for, boss. Besides, I remember this guy. I checked him out. We don't hire the ones like that."

"Thanks, Tony." Tony left the two alone. "Tony has a photographic memory. He never forgets that type of stuff. That's why I need him. Clayton, if we are up against this type of operator, this could get real ugly real fast."

Clayton closed the file and pulled the flash drive from the computer and shut it down. "We have one hell of a lot of work to do."

Clayton handed the flash drive to Larry. "I need you to keep this and the computer. I can't risk taking it to the office, and if I leave it at home, it won't be in my possession. You have to keep it here. It's the only place it will be safe."

Larry took the flash drive. "I'll start training some teams and doing the recon on the locations. There are some other assets we're going to need."

"Yeah, I know. Larry, you can't do this yourself. I believe I was the one ordered to do this."

"I don't think I said I was going to do this by myself. What I am going to do is help you. If you are too obvious doing this, what you're going to do is blow this up. Clayton, you were my superior officer, if you remember what I did plans and training, let me do it. What I'm going to do is what I said, recon on the locations and figure out how we take all of them at once. Then I'm going to start training the team leaders. What you're going to do is decide that marine recon force and seal teams need training in hostage rescue and urban assault. Start a rotating training schedule. Get them trained up and then decide they need a training exercise. By the time you get that done, I'll know where all these bastards are."

"You do know what getting involved in this could cost?"

"Have you given any thought to what this is going to cost if we don't? Clayton, they have been working to destroy this nation. I don't know what it might cost both of us. I know what it will cost every American if we don't take them down. Leave the files here. I'll start working on it. Clayton, you are one hell of a combat commander. I know because I served under you. I know you are going to take these bastards down because I'm going to help you do it."

"Yeah, I have thought about it. I was ordered to take them down. You don't have to do this, Larry."

"The hell I don't. These bastards have been responsible for the death of more than one of my friends. You read the same stuff in that file I did, and we haven't even been through all of it. Besides I can't leave you alone on an operation like this. You have a tendency to get in trouble without me. Clayton, this type of stuff is what I do. Part of protecting some of the people I'm responsible for is taking out those that are the threats. I can do things outside of the military you can't. You have the rest of the assets this is going to take."

Clayton Billingsley began to think for the first time since being handed the letter from the president they might just be able to pull this off.

The Pentagon
Washington DC
January 16, 2014

"General, if you don't mind me asking, why do you want to implement this type of training schedule? Force Recon is pretty well trained up."

"Colonel, I am one of those that believe they are never trained enough. I have a feeling that we are going to be involved in more of this type of thing. The terrorists we are dealing with are smart. How many hostages are they holding? Besides, we are moving into a new type of threat. We are going to have to find them where they are, and it's going to have to be done quietly. Look at the fall out after the raid that got Bin Laden and then there are the drone strikes. Foreign governments don't like them. I think we are going to be moving into a new era of fighting terrorism. I want to be prepared."

"I can't argue with your logic, General. You always have been ahead of the curve. I'll get to work on it. This will probably take six months to get the training regimen written and another couple of months to get the deployment schedule done."

General Billingsley held up his hand to stop his aide. "Colonel, I don't think you understand. I want this implemented now, not six months from now. What I want to do is replace the upcoming training that is already scheduled and paid for. I want the rotation schedule in my hand by the first of next week. Force Recon is not currently deployed. I want these guys trained up. There is a big difference between the mountains of Afghanistan and taking terrorists down covertly in the locations they feel safe. I am also going to recommend that the seal teams start implementing this as well. If the navy goes along, I want to be in the position of saying we are already set up and running with this. That way we control it. The navy will want in, if it doesn't cost them, they'll happily take advantage of using money the marines are spending."

Colonel Thornburg smiled at his boss; he was a master at this sort of stuff. "General, as usual you are right. All we have to do is modify the existing training from what is scheduled to this new type of urban training you want. When you offer it to the navy, the seal teams will want in."

"That's the idea, Ray. Now you understand what I want. I want them on board with this, not fighting against it."

"I'll get on this right away. I'll have the training set up and the schedule of deployments changed."

"Thanks, Ray. Keep me in the loop. I have some other ideas I'm going to start working on. Let's get busy." General Clayton Billingsley turned his attention back to the work on his desk; his aide, Colonel Thornburg. knew the general well enough to know he was being dismissed. The general never wasted any time when he wanted something done. He got up and left the general's office.

General Clayton Billingsley looked up as the door closed behind Colonel Thornburg. His stomach was in knots. He took his glasses off and rubbed his eyes. He then closed his eyes and said a prayer he could get by with what he had to do.

Fort Bragg
North Carolina
February 8, 2014

The image on the computer screen was still too small to positively identify. He moved the cursor over it, clicked on it, and began to zoom in. The marina began to come into sharper focus and the details began to emerge. There it was, the *Quiet Time*. He had been hunting for the location of the yacht since he had identified it months before. His patience was being rewarded. He now knew where the elusive former FBI agent was operating out of; there would be an advance team on the ground in twenty-four hours.

# THE COMMITTEE

Ron Cole reached for his secure cell phone; he scrolled through the contacts. The names weren't real. He knew what they meant. He found the one he was looking for. He touched the contact, selected text message from the menu, typed out what he wanted him to know, and hit send. Three minutes later, his phone beeped telling him he had a response to his text. He didn't even bother to read it. He knew it was just an acknowledgement of his orders to the team. They would be preparing to leave even before he read the message. In twenty-four hours he would know what else they needed and maybe with a little luck they could eliminate the threat this was becoming. He was running out of time; if he couldn't eliminate this threat, soon he was going to have to inform the Chairman. The timetable while not set in stone was scheduled to crash the economy and with it the government of the United States. The countdown had already begun.

The Templeton Residence
Milford, Pennsylvania
February 9, 2014

The massive gates of the estate were wrought iron flanked by large brick columns. On either side a ten-foot-high wrought iron fence stretched for over a hundred yards and then disappeared as it turned into the woods. Just after it entered the woods the fence changed to chain link with rolled razor wire on the top. Tony slowed the car he was driving just enough to be able to pay close attention to the details. The reconnaissance of the ten members of the Committee was well underway. Tony never ever trusted anything on a job like this until he had seen it for himself.

There were things the average person driving by would never see. Discretely placed on the top of the fence were laser transmitters and sensors, which put an invisible beam when broken, by say the presence of a hand of someone trying to climb the fence, which would announce their presence. Tony knew his teams were good at what they did. Larry only hired the absolute best, and Tony was the best of them. He had a photographic memory. He was doing his own scouting, that way when he read the reports and talked to the team leaders who had been assigned the various targets he could talk to them from a point of actually seeing it for himself. The Force Recon and the navy seal teams were being trained in urban assault. General Billingsley had set it up as part of the continuing war on terror. The raid that netted Osama Bin Laden had taught them a few things. He had convinced them the war on terror was going to be fought by taking the targets in an urban setting as well as the mountains of Afghanistan. They were no more than sixty days from taking all ten of their targets at once. It all had to happen not only simultaneously but without anyone in the command structure of the military knowing what they were doing. That was why the teams were being trained and Larry was having his security specialists doing the recon work and setting up the final training of the teams. If they were found out, it was game over and the consequences would be devastating.

Tony rounded the curve and maintained his speed; he would find a place to pull off the road and hide the car. The sun would be setting soon and what he had to do was best done in darkness. He found the dirt road that led down to the river that was seldom used in the summer and almost never this time of year. He was grateful there was no snow, which would have made tracks. He pulled the car off the side and hid it from view of anyone going down the highway past the dirt road.

Tony had found a small hill that overlooked the estate; he was just below the top in a small depression where he had a good view of the chain link fence that went right down to the river and the grounds beyond. He put his binoculars to his eyes and scanned the entire fence line. He made notes in the small notebook he carried. He never trusted his memory. He paid close attention to the routines of the security patrols; they were bored. It was the dogs that would be the hardest to overcome. They were free to roam about the estate and their handlers were on foot patrol. The entire estate was ringed with the motion sensors.

Tony put his binoculars away and silently slipped down the hill. He still had to find the weak spot in the security. He would, it was there; it always was. A little more than two hours later, Tony found what he was looking for. The river was the key. This stretch of the Delaware was seldom used, and the security had been designed to protect the occupants of the estate from an intruder coming from the land side. Entry by the river was the key. Tony walked back to his car, got in, and drove off, the plan forming in his head. He knew the other residences and offices of the ten targets were being kept under surveillance by other members of Larry's security firm that were just as capable as he was. Their job was to find the weakness of each one and plan the entrance and assault to take the ten members of the Committee alive and most importantly quietly. The problem was they were up against some of their own. The best of the best, all trained the same way, in the same military, had never squared off. The advantage, Tony thought to himself, is we know we are coming, they don't. He silently wondered if it would be enough.

The Marina
The Cayman Islands
February 10, 2014

Former Master Sergeant Albert Stanton sat back in the front seat of the rental car. He was sitting across the street from the marina where the yacht they were looking for had been docked. He had been watching since late the previous night. He raised the binoculars to his eyes and rolled the knob until the stern lettering came into focus. There it was, the *Quiet Time*. They now knew how the retired FBI agent had gotten away from them, not only from Virginia when they first found him, but had also then gotten the woman out of Florida.

He lowered the binoculars and started the car, dropped it into gear, and pulled away from the side of the road. He turned around and headed back toward the airport. The rest of the team would be coming this afternoon, and he had arrangements to make. The weapons they would need had to be picked up and vehicles rented. This was all being done quicker than they liked. Sometimes he thought you just had to get it done; this was one of those times.

Dan Oliver had been watching the car and had seen the man with the binoculars watching him. He turned and went back aboard the *Quiet Time*. He had known he couldn't keep from being found. He now had to put his plan into place. He picked up his cell phone and sent a quick text message. Jonah would know what to do. The Mossad agent had been retired after he had been shot in Atlanta. The one thing Dan had enough of was money. They had hired some of the best special operators in the business for their security. Dan smiled to himself; it was probably the only time former Spetznaz, Israeli, and American special forces were all on the same team. What he hoped his opposition didn't know was that Valerie was in Israel. One of his other yachts was moored next to the *Quiet Time* with four of his special operators aboard. They had been expecting them for some time; the night might prove quite interesting.

The yacht was still moored at the marina; a light was burning in the main cabin. Al Stanton made his way down the deserted dock. He was wearing shorts and a flowered shirt and was walking unsteadily. He smelled like he had consumed a fair quantity of spirits. There were four of his men in the water. They would slip aboard the yacht and try to secure it and kill whoever was on board. The time was too close to take any chances.

The four men in the water silently approached the yacht. They were on board in seconds and stealthily covered one another as they entered the cabin. After a quick and quiet search, they found it was empty. On the dock, Al Stanton waited until he was sure the yacht had been secured and began walking down the dock toward the *Quiet Time*. He walked across the gangplank and entered the cabin. The team had searched every square inch and had found it empty. Something wasn't right; he turned and the realization hit him. he motioned for the others to get off the yacht. They moved onto the deck as quickly and quietly as they could. It was all over in seconds. One by one the five were cut down by the muted spits of the silenced weapons.

The bodies were pulled inside the cabin of the *Quiet Time* and the lines were quickly cast loose, and the yacht quietly left the harbor. The bodies would be weighted and thrown overboard once they were out far enough into the open sea. The *Quiet Time* would never be found. The Committee had lost another of their teams. Dan Oliver stepped onto the deck of the *Easy Life* and watched as the *Quiet Time* eased away from the dock. He knew everything was drawing to an end. One way or another it had to end. He had lived with this for fifteen years. He turned and went back into the cabin.

The Fitzgerald Home
Alexandria, Virginia
May 11, 2014

"Tell me, Clayton, how many teams have you got ready to go?" Larry put his cigar in the ashtray on the end table beside his recliner.

"Right now the first few companies of Force Recon are rotating out. We have scheduled advance training for them after a short review of the completed training. We can field ten complete teams. We sent companies from several of the different stations one at a time. We are continuing the rotation through the end of the year, and the seals have decided they want in. They get the next rotation. Ten teams are enough to take them down."

"Let's not forget about Atlas International. That has to happen at the same time. How are you going to get the teams in place?"

"What I have in mind is the advance training. What we have in the training schedule is a mock operation for each team at the end. Part of that is individual infiltration of the teams to assemble at the time of the operation. Each member of the team is told to prepare his own infiltration route and then contact the team leaders for assembly before the assault. We are allowing a week for that. Each team leader is going to be ordered to report for the details of their training targets. They assemble the teams for a briefing and give them contact information. The idea is to give them a chance to do recon on a target they have never seen. Then plan and carry out the assault. What I am going to do is intercept each team leader after the briefing and bring them in on what is really happening. That's where your guys come in."

"From that point on, the team leader will not be left alone, and we brief him on the individual targets. The rest of the teams still think it is a training run. My guys have done the recon on each of the actual targets. They have planned the assaults and will go over all of it with the team leaders. That will give them a chance to revise the plan." Larry picked up his cigar and relit it. That bought him some time to tell Clayton what else had to be done.

"Larry, I selected the first teams to be trained carefully. I don't think we have to worry about their loyalty. I know all of them. These guys are going to be pissed when they find out what is really going on. We owe them the truth. What we can't take a chance on is any of this getting out. The rest of the team will not be brought in until they assemble. I have set it up so the training targets are within the same general area as the real targets. What we have done is set up teams to defend the training target and set up helicopter extractions from them. They don't know it yet but that's how we get the targets out."

"Have you told the teams defending the training targets anything?"

"Not yet. I want only the team leaders involved. After we take each of the targets, we have a place to keep them. That's the real purpose of the training targets. The problem then is going to be finding out just how deeply the Secret Service has been penetrated. We have to think about the president. He has to be protected. I have no idea how we are going to pull that off."

Larry smiled. "Clayton, I think that would be a good time for the president to present some medals to the troops at say Bethesda Naval Hospital. I'm sure you can slip in enough of our guys to protect him in that environment."

"I'll try and get that in the works. It's always good PR to have the press there. They love a good film op. I have a hard time believing the Secret Service could be in on this kind of thing."

"Clayton, we can't take the chance. If they are compromised, it could be game over. We don't know just how much control they really have, and we will have a very limited window to find out. After we take them down, we then have to run down the entire organization. That will take time, and the one problem we have is we don't know where the security force they run is based out of. There has to be headquarters somewhere."

"Larry, that brings us back to Atlas International. We have to take that at the same time. We have to do it without giving them a chance to destroy anything. If they manage to destroy everything, we may never find out how deeply the government is penetrated. We need to know as soon as we can."

"I had Tony do all the recon on the ten targets and Atlas as well. They work regular hours and only have a night security force. They are all retired special forces. That's going to make it dicey. I have a team training for that. We go the same night the rest of the teams take the targets."

"For right now, we have done everything we can. It will be another two weeks before we go. That gives us a little time. We better use it well."

Camp Lejeune
Jacksonville, North Carolina
May 15, 2014

Marine Captain Victor Owens and his men had just finished the revised urban assault training. He had to admit it had been intensive and effective. Now he had just finished giving his men the orders for the final part of the training regimen. He had mixed emotions about the last part of this training schedule. Every single member of his ten-man team had been given a certain amount of cash, told to change into regular street clothes, then make their way to Scranton, Pennsylvania. Their target was a small estate on the outskirts of town. They had to rendezvous and plan an assault. They had to do their recon, plan and carry out an assault, capture the target, then get him out alive. The target was going to be protected by a team of navy seals who were waiting on them. The whole idea was for one side to win based on the outcome. If the seal team stopped them, they won. If they got past them and got the target out, they won. The winners got a ten-day leave.

First they had to get there; part of the training was to get past the local police who were given their pictures. If any of the team got caught, they had to repeat the whole thing. He had never been part of anything like this before. Some chair warmer had gotten a wild hair up his ass and this was the result.

They had to be in place and ready to go by Wednesday of next week. They then had three days in which to plan and carry out the assault. It was the strangest training they had ever come up with, and for some reason, his team was as excited about it as he had ever seen them get, at least about training.

He had been ordered to report to the colonel before going off base. The clock was starting as soon as he had done that; the team had been released already. He had to pick up his orders and then he was off.

Vic stepped inside the building they were using and walked up to the marine sitting at the desk. The sergeant stood up and snapped to attention. "I'm Captain Owens here to see the colonel."

"Yes, sir, right this way." The sergeant led him to the door of the small office, knocked, and then opened the door. "Captain Owens is here, sir." He motioned him through the door and stood aside as he stepped through the door and then closed it behind him.

Captain Owens approached the desk and came to attention. He was surprised to see the commandant of the United States marine corps swivel the chair around and say to him, "At ease, Captain, have a seat." He was even more surprised to see him in BDU's and that he was armed. He couldn't stop himself from looking at the 45 strapped to his side.

General Clayton Billingsley smiled at him and said, "I said at ease Captain, take a seat."

All he could do was say, "Yes sir," then sit down in the chair across from the desk.

"Captain, the training your team just completed was my idea. I want you to hear from me what this is really all about. " He reached in his pocket, pulled out an envelope, and extended it toward Captain Owens. "Read this and then we need to have a talk.

Vic took the envelope and was stunned to see the seal of the White House on the outside in the corner. He met the commandant's eyes and saw that he was deadly serious. He opened the envelope and pulled out the single sheet of White House stationary. He unfolded it, dropped his eyes to the page, and began to read the letter.

# THE COMMITTEE

**THE WHITE HOUSE**
**WASHINGTON**
1600 Pennsylvania Avenue,
Washington DC

*To all military personnel,*

*General Clayton Billingsley is conducting a classified operation at my direct orders. Any orders he issues verbally are to be taken as if they were coming directly from the president of the United States. No discussion of these orders is desired. This may not be discussed with anyone unless authorized by General Billingsley.*

*All military officers are required to provide any assistance, personnel, and material requested by General Billingsley. At my direct orders, only officers in the grades up to and including captain are eligible to carry out the assigned mission. At my direct orders, no discussion in any manner to any member of the chains of command is permitted unless specifically ordered by General Billingsley.*

*I cannot stress the importance of the mission that I have ordered General Billingsley to undertake. The very existence of our nation is at stake. I have the utmost trust and faith in the members of the finest military in the world to successfully complete the tasks each of you have been ordered to undertake. May God bless each and every single member of the military and know that my utmost faith and trust is placed in those of you chosen to complete this mission. Know that I am praying for each and every one of you.*

*Bennett Arthur Cain*
*President of the United States*

Captain Owens read the letter twice, raised his eyes, and met those of the general. The general extended his hand, and Captain Owens refolded the letter put it back in the envelope and handed it back. "Thank you, Captain. I hate to have to take that back, but I'm not quite done with it."

Captain Owens sat in stunned silence; his eyes met those of General Billingsley. In his sixteen-year career in the United States marine corps, this was the first time he had not only personally met the commandant, he had then been handed a letter written on White House stationary by the president of the United States.

"I understand what you must be thinking, Captain. Please feel free to speak whatever is on your mind."

"Yes, sir. General, what in the hell is this about?"

"Captain, there are some things I am not at liberty to tell you right now. I will tell you the training your team just completed was set up to carry out the mission you will be assigned. The real target of your mission is not the estate on the outskirts of Scranton. That's cover for what you will really be doing. This will be a real extraction against former special operators. The target has already been under surveillance, a lot of the initial planning has been done. You are going to be briefed by another former special operator that will give you the rest of the details. I'm sorry I can't tell you more, Captain. I will give you this."

General Billingsley reached in his pocket and pulled out another envelope and handed it to Captain Owens. "This will tell you where you are to meet the gentleman who will fully brief you on your target and the rest of the details. I will remind you again, Captain, of the letter from the president. No discussion of these orders with anyone is permitted. If anyone asks you what you are doing, you are to tell them of the training mission. I will tell you this, the president was not exaggerating when he said the very existence of our nation is at stake. You will be told the rest when time permits. There just isn't time right now." General Billingsley stood up and offered his hand to Captain Owens.

Captain Owens Stood up and extended his hand to the general. The two men shook hands and then Captain Owens was again surprised by General Billingsley. The general snapped to attention and saluted. Captain Owens in a reflex action snapped to attention and returned the salute. He was surprised for several reasons. The salute was usually offered by the junior officer to the senior and marines did not salute indoors. "Good luck, Captain, may God bless you and your men."

The Templeton residence
Milford, Pennsylvania
May 22, 2014

Darkness, the best friend of any special operator, had fallen. Tony focused the night vision binoculars on the estate below him. Captain Owens was lying on the ground beside him peering through his own night vision binoculars. For the last two days, they had been here watching and waiting; Tony had done all of the initial scouting, everything had been top notch. They had planned the assault that was getting ready to take place. Everyone was in place; they were going tonight. The timetable could not be altered. Tony had told him this was not the only operation going. There were ten others, and they all had to be done simultaneously.

Captain Owens looked at his watch; the luminescent hands showed it was 0327 hours. Three minutes until it started. Timing was everything, the shift change of the security had happened at 2300 hours. This was the time the let down would usually happen. They had gotten in their routines. The problem was these guys were as good as his team. He had a slight numerical advantage; they usually had four on the grounds on patrol all the time. There were two more in the house. That wasn't the real problem. The real problem was the dogs. Two of them, they had the run of the grounds. Whoever had set this up was good.

Tony had provided the solution for the dogs; two of his men were armed with silenced rifles that fired tranquilizing darts. That would take some time to work, and they had to be isolated from the guards. They would alert the four men outside on patrol if it was noisy. Each of the four was being targeted by a sniper. This was a "take no prisoners" assault, except of course for the occupant of the house that was the object of this mission. Tony had told him none of the security force could be allowed to escape or survive.

He looked down at his watch again; it was time. He motioned to Tony who silently nodded and then just seemed to disappear. If he hadn't known where he was going, he wouldn't have ever known he had been beside him seconds ago. Captain Owens moved into position, the signal came the dogs had been put down. He moved silently toward the fence. Thirty seconds later, the device had been put in place on top to deflect the beams without interrupting them, and he was over the fence dropping into the grounds of the estate. Tony was already ahead of him, and he was covering him. One of the security appeared as if by magic in front of him; as he dropped down to fire, he heard a muffled spit and the first one was down. Damn Tony was fast.

Two more of his men were securing the other side, the report of gunfire erupted, breaking the silence of the night. All bets were off as they sprinted toward the main house. Tony got there first and a burst from his weapon dropped one more. Vic felt the air around him almost vibrate as the slugs whipped past him. He dropped, rolled, and brought his weapon up and trained it on the figure and pulled the trigger. He wasn't fast enough; the figure disappeared around the corner of the column at the edge of the patio. He had to get into the house.

Benjamin Templeton was jarred into consciousness by the sound of automatic gunfire. Before he could even get out of bed, the bedroom door was thrown open, and his security team leader was inside the bedroom grabbing him and unceremoniously pulling him out of the bed. The next thing Diamond knew he was being hustled down the corridor toward the door to the basement.

The door was thrown open, and he was shoved into the door and practically pulled down the steps. He heard glass breaking and a small explosion somewhere in the main part of the house above him. He was still trying to get his bearings while he was still being dragged by his left arm toward the door at the far end of the basement. The next thing he knew there was a bright flash and a loud explosion almost in front of him. Diamond was thrown to the ground, and he heard the sound of gunfire directly in front of him, and he felt something fall almost on top of him. The breath was knocked out of him, and as he tried to move, his body just wouldn't respond.

Corporal Terrence Reed placed the small shaped charge on the door and ducked around the corner away from the door. Three seconds later, he was rewarded by a small thump and the door flew open on its hinges. The other two members of the assault team were already preparing to roll around the corner and cover him. One of them tossed in the flash bang, and they followed it in. The ripping sound of gunfire echoed back toward them. Thirty seconds later another burst and then two more shots. Corporal Reed burst through the door, one of his men was down, blood covering the side of his face, and the other had just dropped whoever had shot him. On the floor in front of him Diamond was trying to get up; the weight of his dead security team leader was pinning him to the ground.

Corporal Reed reached down, rolled the dead man off him, and then jerked Diamond to his feet. Terrified, Benjamin Templeton looked into the camouflaged face paint of Corporal Terrence Reed and felt his knees buckle and his world went dark.

It was all over. Seventeen minutes was all it had taken. Captain Owens was securing the estate and taking stock of his losses, two killed and three wounded including him. He had taken a bullet through the sleeve of his BDUs. Fortunately, it hadn't done any serious damage. He was pissed. Two of his men had been killed and two more seriously hurt. They had dropped all six of the security detail. Two of them were still alive. The sound of a chopper broke through his thoughts. He stepped around the back of the estate toward the river where a chopper pad had been built. The bird sitting on it had been disabled early on. That way the target had no way of getting out on it. The medic was trying to get his attention.

"Captain, the medevac chopper just landed. We gotta get out of here, sir."

"Get them loaded up. We have to stay and secure the estate."

"Sir, you've been hit. I want you on that chopper, sir." The medical sergeant was pulling Vic toward the chopper.

"I'm all right, Sergeant. Get them out of here."

The sergeant grabbed Captain Owens arm and pulled his knife out and proceeded to cut through the material of his BDU jacket. "Let me take a look, Captain. I have to make a decision. Those two are hurt bad, and we gotta get them out of here, sir."

Captain Victor Owens jerked his arm away from the sergeant and replied, "I told you I'm okay, Sergeant. Get them out of here. Get moving. You can dress this when they're on their way."

The sergeant took a quick glance at his arm and decided he wasn't going to bleed to death and made a decision. "Yes, sir." He trotted off toward the chopper.

AT&T Center
Los Angeles, California
May 22, 2014

The building was quiet, only the security and the night shift of several of the building's tenants were working. Several of the floors were vacant or under renovation. Atlas International occupied three of the buildings floors; somehow they had managed to get the top three of the buildings thirty-two floors. The problem, retired captain Greg Everett thought, was they hadn't been able to get enough intelligence. They knew the floors Atlas occupied. That wasn't the problem; the problem was they didn't know exactly which of the three floors had the computers they were trying to capture before they had a chance to destroy the data they contained. The one thing that they had was the plans for the building. Any type of renovation and construction required a set of plans to be filed and approved by the city building department. Those had been obtained and carefully studied.

Greg knew it didn't tell the whole story. He had been tasked with doing the recon with Tony on the building and putting together the plan they were getting ready to put into action. There was a night shift of technicians that worked for Atlas. There was also private security that was not part of the building's normal security. They were all former special operators. This was going to be a tough nut to crack.

The team was in place; they were going in less than ten minutes. It had to be done perfectly or they would lose the data in the computers. The key to the operation was the building's mechanical system. There were air handlers on each floor that provided the air conditioning. They had a common outside fresh air system. They had tied into the building's automation system and were going to shut down all of the air handlers except for the top three floors. The chemical was going to be introduced into the intake opening on the roof. Hopefully it would disable anyone that inhaled it. The problem was the computer rooms had their own air conditioning systems. If by chance any of the staff were in there, they might not be disabled. They had contemplated disrupting the power to the building, another problem; the computers had a backup uninterrupted power supply that was in each of the computer rooms. Even in a total power loss, they would still be powered. Greg was willing to bet they had a way of destroying the data at the touch of a button or a keystroke.

He even knew what type of security system they had. Entire areas, especially the entrances to the floors, were covered by cameras. There was a security office on the thirtieth floor they all fed into. They had hacked the feed and recorded ten minutes of the previous night's footage. They were going to play it back and feed it to the monitors the guard was watching. The problems with that were obvious. If there was something on the screen he was watching that wasn't on the previous night's footage, they were screwed.

No time to worry about that now. The retired FBI guy was part of this team. Greg didn't like working with people he hadn't had that much time to train with. He also was a little long in the tooth; while he wasn't going to hold that against him, he had to admit he had kept up with them every step of the way, he was concerned. There were just too many potential problems. What really worried him was the unknowns; they had been unable to get eyes on the floors. There was no way to infiltrate anyone into the operation. They had to go anyway.

Greg looked at his watch. It was go time. He motioned to his team computer tech. A couple of keystrokes and the air handlers shut down. Another couple and the chemical was released. Four minutes later, the feed to the monitors was replaced with the tape and the team began the entry.

Dan Oliver followed the two former navy seals as they broached the door to the thirty-first floor, the other three assigned to this floor were coming in through the stairwell doors. The same was happening on the other two floors. The security guard was passed out on the floor. They rushed past covering each other as they went. The door to the computer room was just down the corridor. The two seals led the way, and the first one rolled around the corner and then the second, Dan was covering their back. The computer room door had a security card reader that locked the door. Dan inserted the card into the slot; the card was attached to a small handheld device that activated the release, two seconds later and the door beeped. Dan opened the door and the two Seals rolled into the room one after the other. There was a brief burst of gun fire then two muffled spits then two more.

Dan looked up; it was over. The technician had been dropped by the seals as he was reaching for the computer keyboard on the desk just inside the room. There was a security guard splayed out on the floor, a spreading pool of blood around him, the Uzi he had been carrying had been kicked away by one of the two Seals.

Retired Captain Greg Everett walked up to Dan Oliver. "We have secured all three floors. We have two wounded neither seriously. Four of the security and two of the technicians are down, the rest were put down by the gas. Our computer expert will be here in a few minutes. The local police have been called in. I don't think it would be a good idea for you to be here when they get here."

Bethesda Naval Hospital
Bethesda, Maryland
May 23, 2014

The motorcade pulled up and stopped. The doors to the black Suburban opened and the Secret Service agents stepped out and formed a protective corridor. The door of the center Suburban was opened and another agent slid out and scanned the area and then the president of the United States emerged. The entourage quickly moved into the main entrance of the hospital where the hospital commander was waiting with his senior staff.

# THE COMMITTEE

"Good Morning, Mr. President. We are honored to have you with us." Brigadier General Clark extended his hand toward the president.

"General, I'm pleased to be here, and I am the one honored to be here. The sacrifice that our men and women in uniform have made truly humbles me."

"Mr. President, let me introduce you to my staff and then we can make the rounds of visiting the troops."

With the introductions and handshakes all around that protocol dictated completed, the group proceeded into the heart of the hospital.

The entourage moved down the corridor toward the patient rooms. They reached one of the rooms and stopped. "Mr. President, right this way." General Clark opened the door and was immediately followed by the leading Secret Service agent. The president stepped into the room and was introduced to the patient in the bed by General Clark. "Mr. President, this is Lieutenant Russell Lynch. He was wounded in Afghanistan."

The President extended his hand toward the wounded marine. "Lieutenant, I am honored to meet you." The president's eyes were drawn to the young marine and he couldn't help but notice the missing left leg below the knee.

"Mr. President, the honor is mine, sir."

"I believe we have something for you." The president extended his hand and a medal box was handed to him. He opened it and took out a Bronze Star. The citation was read by another marine officer as the president pinned the medal on the young marine's bathrobe. Another medal case was handed to the president, which contained the Purple Heart. The president took that and pinned it beside the Bronze Star. "I cannot express how grateful I am for what you have done. "

"I am proud to serve my country, sir. I have done nothing more than what every other marine does every single day." The marine was looking directly into the eyes of President Cain.

General Clark stepped in. "Thank you, Mr. President. Right this way, sir."

The president turned and looked at General Clark. "I'm not quite finished talking with this fine marine general. I'll let you know when

I'm done." The president then turned his attention back and resumed his conversation with the lieutenant.

Several minutes later the president extended his hand, shook hands with the young marine and then turned his attention back to General Clark. "Thank you, General. I intend on talking to each and every one of our wounded heroes. I will take whatever time we need."

The group left the room, and the same scene was repeated in other rooms with other wounded heroes and the president was true to his word. He spent far more time than the schedule allotted.

The group moved from the patient rooms and the president turned to General Clark. "General, I think I would like to meet some more of our men and women that serve this nation. How about we go to physical therapy? I think it might encourage some of them to know just exactly how much their service and sacrifice means to me personally."

"Yes, sir, Mr. President. Right this way." General Clark led the entourage toward the elevator.

The Secret Service agents were not happy with the change in the plans. They were in for a major surprise.

Two of the Secret Service agents had gone ahead and were trying to clear the area before the group got there. The group exited the elevator and walked down the corridor to the surprised looks of the staff and the patients that were in the corridor. General Clark again led the way to one of the physical therapy rooms. He held open the door for the president and once again two of the agents entered the room first. The president walked in and headed right for one of the wounded warriors in the room. The doors closed behind them; none of the Secret Service agents were prepared for what happened next. The room was filled with patients undergoing various types of therapy. The president was engaged in conversation with the wounded warrior. Within seconds, each one of the agents found themselves surrounded by the wounded warriors. There were twelve of them in the room; the next thing they knew, each of them was being taken down by one of the wounded. Each one of the wounded was either delta force or navy seals, and they had prepared for what was going to happen. None of them were wounded; surprise was on their side. The president was standing alone in the middle of the room and put a stop to the whole thing by shouting, "Enough. I ordered everything that has happened. Each of you stop right now." He found himself the center of attention. "General Clark, this whole operation was ordered by me. I want every member of the Secret Service to be detained in this room. The Special Forces that have been ordered to do this are now charged with my security. Until this is over, no one, and I mean no one leaves this facility. General, I said lock it down now."

"Mr. President, what in the hell is going on?" General Clark was stunned.

"I issued you an order, General. I want this facility locked down, and I want all of the Secret Service agents in this facility detained. I will explain all of this when that is done. Move now, General." The tone of the president's voice left no doubt who was in command.

General Clark picked up the telephone mounted on the wall, "Security, this is General Clark. The president has ordered the facility locked down. I will explain all of this in a few minutes." He hung up the phone and almost glared at the president of the United States. "Now, sir, with respect would you mind telling me what is going on."

"General, let's you and I step into your office. I will then tell you what all of this is about." The president turned to the door surrounded by four very large and armed navy seals that previously were thought to be patients.

The door to General Clark's office was opened by one of the seals, and the president was ushered in followed by General Clark. General Clayton Billingsley, commandant of the United States marine corps was waiting there for them. He stood when the president entered. "Mr. President, the operation you have ordered me to undertake is completed, sir."

"Thank you, General. Now if you would be so kind as to tell General Clark why all of this was necessary and why I ordered you to do this. It would save me having to do it. I have some other things I have to take care of." The president reached down and picked up the phone.

## JUSTIN A. BAILEY

The White House
May 30, 2014

    The dark blue Suburban entered the parking garage in the building several blocks away from the White House. It then proceeded through the underground tunnel to the secure parking area. The Suburban stopped, the doors opened, the Secret Service agents got out, scanned the area, and then opened the rear door. Dan Oliver stepped out and was escorted to the elevator that would take him to the White House.

    The Secret Service agent standing just outside the door to the Oval Office opened it, and Dan Oliver stepped through the door. The others were already inside. Seated around the room were the president; the president's father, Edwin Cain; General Clayton Billingsley, USMC; Larry Fitzgerald, USMC retired; Rodger Crawford, USMC retired; Supervisory Agent Gene Everett, United States Secret Service; August Braden, chairman of the board of McAllister Halstead; George Britain, newly appointed director of the Secret Service; and Craig Bennett, the president's chief of staff.

    Those seated in the room stood up as Dan Oliver, Special Agent FBI, retired, entered the room. Handshakes were exchanged and everyone exchanged greetings.

    The president began, "Now that Director Oliver is here, we can get started."

    Dan Oliver looked at the president with a surprised expression. "Excuse me, Mr. President, did I hear you correctly?"

    "Yes, Director Oliver, I believe you did. The FBI is in need of a new director, I think under the circumstances the Senate will confirm you. Your name has already been sent over since the previous director has resigned as of a week ago. Let's get this started. We have a lot of work to do. General Billingsley, would you brief us on the status right now?"

    "Yes, Mr. President. The operation to take all ten of the members of the Committee was as you know successful. We had six of our Force Recon marines killed, another twelve were wounded and fortunately they will recover. The nine in custody right now are being held at a special facility where they are currently being interviewed. The tenth,

# THE COMMITTEE

Mr. Braden, is currently here with us and provided significant intelligence to us even before we conducted the operation. The headquarters of Atlas International was also successfully taken and the computers were recovered intact. I have a team there going over the information they contain. That will take several months. Under its new leadership, the FBI will be instrumental in going through all the financial data and interviewing all of the congressmen and senators that have been uncovered in this. We really won't know just how deeply this goes for some time."

The president then turned to newly appointed Director Britain of the Secret Service. "Director Britain, where do we stand with the Secret Service?"

"Mr. President, Supervisory Agent Everett provided us with significant insight into how they managed to control certain people. As you know, he was the one tasked with informing you that you were being controlled. They set him up much as they did you. Very few people were really in the know. A lot of it was done by blackmail, coercion, and outright bribery. If someone had a weakness, they would find it and exploit it. Very few agents of the Secret Service were actually being controlled. Under the circumstances, I am recommending Agent Everett to stay on the job."

The president turned to his chief of staff. "Craig, you met with my Cabinet shortly after all this happened. Where are we with them?"

"Mr. President, the secretary of state has tendered her resignation. I am recommending it be accepted. She has agreed to wait for a suitable amount of time since we cannot afford to have too many resignations all at once. The same situation with both the secretary of defense and the treasury secretary. We are still looking into the situation with the others."

The president shook his head and then looked at August Braden. "Mr. Braden, I am going to ask you to fill us in on what you believe the intentions of the Committee were."

August Braden met the eyes of the others in the room one by one and began to speak. "I believe, no, I know their intention was to collapse the economy of the United States. They, let me include myself in this, as I told Director Oliver long before, money was funneled out of virtually every government agency and many state governments. That funded everything. The national debt was run to astronomical levels. The manipulations are too numerous to list. This whole thing goes back to the very founding of this nation. Somewhere along the way it became about power and control. This was all started to protect the very freedoms the founding fathers sacrificed for." He paused to gather his thoughts. "Everything was done to control and manipulate the American people into giving up their freedoms and surrendering them in the name of safety and security. They even began to fund the terrorists. That way, things like the Patriot act could be enacted. The NSA is spying on every phone call, e-mail, text message, virtually every type of communication, all in the name of the war on terror. The real reason was control. More and more government benefits to an ever growing percentage of the population. Make them more and more dependent, that way they vote for the politicians that they think will give them more and more. The foreign policy designed to provoke a war. That gave them more and more money, deploy the military and then yank the dollar as the world's reserve currency. Watch it all fall overnight. Think of the consequences. Rioting, chaos in the street, massive unemployment, no military or police to put it down, ultimately massive depopulation, set it all in motion and then step in to save the day. They paid foreign dictators to be their police force when they needed them. The government would have completely collapsed. Then implement whatever government they wanted." August Braden hung his head in shame to think he had ever been a party to it.

The silence hung heavily in the room. The president's father was the first to break the silence. "The good news is they didn't get away with it. Now we have to figure out what we are going to do to fix all of this. I hope all of you realize, if any of this becomes public, the chaos he was talking about will be real and immediate. I am going to suggest that this has to be dealt with quietly. Soon we will know just exactly what they had on all the congressmen. Sorry, let me be politically correct, members of Congress."

Several of the group chuckled; the president was the first to voice what he had in mind. "Dad, are you trying to say we use the information the Committee had, blackmail them to get them to vote the way we want?"

Dan Oliver spoke up. "Mr. President, as much as it pains me to say this, he has a point. If the American people find out how they have been manipulated, there will be a rebellion. We have to undo everything that has been done. If we arrest every member of the government that was involved, it will destroy the nation. Let's face the truth. Most of them had no idea what was really going on. They didn't even break any laws. The sad truth is most of them really aren't all that bright."

The silence in the room was lengthy. Larry Fitzgerald was the one to offer the solution. "Mr. President, if I may?"

"Go ahead, Mr. Fitzgerald, you've earned the right to speak your mind." Every eye in the room was on him.

"We can't afford to let this get out. If it does, what little trust the American people have left in the government is gone. As bad as all this is, we are still in better shape than most nations of the world. We find out just exactly how deeply everything was penetrated. We force those out that were involved. As for the elected members of Congress and the Senate, we use whatever we have to. We get them to cooperate to fix this mess. Get the budget under control for one thing. We also make it clear to them things have changed and their reelection is not an option. Mr. President, respectfully, sir, you can't be involved in this. Neither can anyone that is in any way holding a government position. I have ways of convincing them to go along. When we get them out of the government, one by one, we shut it down and never let anything like this happen again."

The president made eye contact with each and every one of them. "Director Oliver, I think you should have the final say. This almost cost you your life."

Dan Oliver paused, looked the president in the eye, and then began, "I want to remind everyone in this room why this whole thing was started. The founding fathers of this nation, patriots every single one, wanted to preserve the freedoms they fought and died for. Let me quote James Madison from his letter that set me on this search. 'I pray that we have chosen wisely, and I fear we have not. They seek power never intended.' I, for one, do not want to ever let anything happen like that again. This was started for all the right reasons and look where it ended up. Having said that, we have to fix this. We don't have a hell of a lot of choice. We all have to be in agreement that we shut it down as soon as we can."

The Sutton Home
Richmond, Virginia
May 23, 2014

    The three dark blue Suburbans turned the corner and slowed down. The address they were looking for was just ahead. They pulled along the curb and stopped. The doors on two opened and four large and well-dressed men got out and scanned the street. One of them moved to the door of the center Suburban and opened it. Dan Oliver stepped out, the four agents formed around him, and the group began to walk toward the front door of the home.
    The front door of the house flew open, Pam Sutton ran out the door followed by her husband and their two children. Dan Oliver rushed toward his daughter. Pam practically jumped into his arms; she couldn't stop the tears that were streaming down her face. "Oh, Dad." She was unable to say anything else. She was sobbing uncontrollably. They were soon surrounded by her husband and their children.
    A blue Honda Accord turned the corner screeching to a stop; the door flew open, Rebecca Dalton got out not even bothering to close the door and ran right into the middle of the group. The four agents turned and faced outward, trying to be as inconspicuous as possible, none willing to admit they had lumps in their throats.

ABC News
New York, New York
November 4, 2016

    Brian Williams sat down behind the broadcast desk, straightened his tie, and picked up the stack of papers in front of him. Looking into the camera, he waited for the signal to tell him he was on.

"Good evening and welcome once again to ABC news election night coverage. This has been a historic night. I don't think I have ever seen anything quite like this." He turned to the panel seated beside him and asked, "Donna, would you care to comment on what the results so far tell us?"

"Well, Brian, I would say this is probably the first time I can remember we have had so many incumbents that either didn't run for reelection or were so easily defeated. Both the House and the Senate will certainly look different. The Tea Party has certainly made their presence felt."

Brian Williams then turned to the man seated beside her. "George, would you care to give us your take on all this?"

"I certainly agree with Donna. Not only has the Tea Party played a major role, it seems to me the American people have spoken. I think they are tired of politics as usual. Another thing that is different this year is there just doesn't seem to be such division. The American people have made it clear they want the partisan politics to stop."

Brian Williams turned again to face the camera. "Let's take a look at the map. We are now projecting Florida will go to the president. That will push him over the top. Bennett Arthur Cain has been reelected. Everything seems to be falling in line for the president. I haven't seen such a margin in the popular vote since Ronald Reagan was reelected in 1984. We are once again projecting Florida for the president Bennett Arthur Cain has been reelected."

Brussels, Belgium
January 20, 2017

The secure phone ringing penetrated the conscious thoughts of Rene Bergeron. He looked at the display on the base that told him who was calling. He picked up the handset and simply replied, "Yes."

"Rene, it's Georgic. Are you watching the television? If not, turn it on. BBC is showing something I think you might find quite interesting."

"I am watching already, Georgic. Tell me where we stand."

"Patience, my friend. These things take time. We are all agreed there is no timetable. The Americans went too fast and made too many mistakes. That has set us back considerably. Much as the Americans rebuilt us after World War II, we must now rebuild them. We have made much progress. All of the selections have been made. The new sources of funding will be ready in just a few weeks."

"What about the security, how much have we been able to reclaim?" Rene turned from the window he had been staring out and faced the television again.

"They haven't found nearly as much as they think they have. The head of security has set up a new base of operation. They never found him or even all of his operators. They never got all of the computer records. Many of the accounts are still intact. We know all of the ones in the pipeline, so we will begin the selection process when they meet for the first time."

"Georgic, have you talked to our friends in the east?"

"Yes, they are providing much of the funding. The Americans cannot fix their debt problem. Patience, Rene, things are in motion. Corrections are being made."

Rene picked up the remote and turned the volume up on the television. "I want to watch this. I will call you later." Rene put the secure phone back in its base and watched the scene unfolding on the television.

In the capitol of the United States, the president was standing before the chief justice and placed his right hand on the Bible the chief justice was holding. "I, Bennett Arthur Cain, do solemnly swear that I will faithfully execute the office of President of the United States and will to the best of my ability, preserve, protect, and defend the Constitution of the United States. So help me God."

The chief justice offered his hand. "Congratulations, Mr. President."

# ABOUT THE AUTHOR

Justin A. Bailey is an avid reader and history buff. He grew up in rural southern Ohio the youngest of eight children. Working for almost thirty years as a heating and air conditioning service tech with a love of antique automobiles and all things mechanical. He has now turned his active imagination to writing. The Committee is his first work of fiction. Justin has been married to his high school sweetheart for thirty years, together they have a daughter who is now in college. He resides in Woodstock, Ga.

CPSIA information can be obtained at www.ICGtesting.com
Printed in the USA
LVOW10s1402280415

436397LV00001B/1/P

9 781634 172813